Mick Herron's first Jackson Lamb thriller, *Slow Horses*, was shortlisted for the CWA Ian Fleming Steel Dagger and picked as one of the best twenty spy novels of all time by the *Daily Telegraph*. The second, *Dead Lions*, won the CWA Goldsboro Gold Dagger. The third, *Real Tigers*, was shortlisted for the Theakston Old Peculier Crime Novel of the Year and both the CWA Goldsboro Gold Dagger and the CWA Ian Fleming Steel Dagger. The fourth, *Spook Street*, has been shortlisted for both the Gold and Steel Daggers. Mick Herron was born in Newcastle upon Tyne, and now lives in Oxford.

Praise for Mick Herron's Jackson Lamb thrillers

'Mick Herron is shaping up to be the great spy novelist of our age'

Daily Telegraph *****

'Close to the class of Graham Greene'

Daily Mail

'Surely among the finest British spy fiction of the past 20 years . . . a narrative of breath-taking ingenuity. Brilliant'

Metro

'The new king of the spy thriller'

Mail on Sunday

'The new spy master'

Evening Standard

DEAD LIONS

MICK HERRON

JOHN MURRAY

First published in Great Britain in 2013 by Soho Press, Inc.

First published in 2015 by John Murray (Publishers)
An Hachette UK Company

This edition first published in 2017

013

© Mick Herron 2013

A CIP catalogue record for this title is available from the British Library

ISBN 978-1-47367-419-6
Ebook ISBN 978-1-47362-194-7

Typeset in Bembo by Palimpsest Book Production Limited,
Falkirk, Stirlingshire

Printed and bound by Clays Ltd, Elcograf S.p.A.

John Murray policy is to use papers that are natural, renewable and recyclable
products and made from wood grown in sustainable forests. The logging and
manufacturing processes are expected to conform to the environmental regulations
of the country of origin.

John Murray (Publishers)
Carmelite House
50 Victoria Embankment
London EC4Y 0DZ

www.johnmurray.co.uk

For MSJ

I

A FUSE HAD BLOWN in Swindon, so the south-west network ground to a halt. In Paddington the monitors wiped departure times, flagging everything 'Delayed', and stalled trains clogged the platforms; on the concourse luckless travellers clustered round suitcases, while seasoned commuters repaired to the pub, or rang home with cast-iron alibis before hooking up with their lovers back in the city. And thirty-six minutes outside London, a Worcester-bound HST crawled to a halt on a bare stretch of track with a view of the Thames. Lights from houseboats pooled on the river's surface, illuminating a pair of canoes which whipped out of sight even as Dickie Bow registered them: two frail crafts built for speed, furrowing the water on a chilly March evening.

All about, passengers were muttering, checking watches, making calls. Pulling himself into character, Dickie Bow made an exasperated *tch!* But he wore no watch, and had no calls to make. He didn't know where he was headed, and didn't have a ticket.

Three seats away the hood fiddled with his briefcase.

The intercom fizzed.

'This is your train manager speaking. I'm sorry to have to inform you we can't go any further due to trackside equipment failure outside Swindon. We're currently—'

A crackle of static and the voice died, though could faintly be heard continuing to broadcast in neighbouring carriages. Then it returned:

'—reverse into Reading, where replacement buses will—'

This was met with a communal groan of disgust, and not a little swearing, but most impressively to Dickie Bow, immediate readiness. The message hadn't ended before coats were being pulled on and laptops folded; bags snapped shut and seats vacated. The train shunted, and then the river was flowing in the wrong direction, and Reading station was appearing once more.

There was chaos as passengers disgorged onto crowded platforms, then realised they didn't know where to go. Nor did Dickie Bow, but all he cared about was the hood, who had immediately disappeared in a sea of bodies. Dickie, though, was too old a hand to panic. It was all coming back to him. He might never have left the Spooks' Zoo.

Except in those days he'd have found a patch of wall and smoked a cigarette. Not possible here, which didn't stop a nicotine pang twitching inside him, or a sudden wasp-sharp sting pricking his thigh, so real he gasped. He gripped the spot, his hand brushing first the corner of an oblivious briefcase, then an umbrella's slick damp nastiness. Deadly weapons, he thought. Your nine-to-fivers carry deadly weapons.

He was crowded onwards, like it or not, and suddenly everything was okay, because he'd secured visible contact once more: the hood, a hat shielding his bald head, his case tucked under an arm, stood near the escalator to the passenger bridge. So, corralled by weary travellers, Dickie shuffled past and up the moving stairs, at the top of which he sidled into a corner. The main exit from the station was across this bridge. He assumed that was the route everyone would take, once instructions about buses were issued.

He closed his eyes. Today was not ordinary. Usually by this time, just after six thirty, all sharp edges would have been smoothed away: he'd have been up since twelve, after five hours' stormy shut-eye. Black coffee and a fag in his room. A shower if needed. Then the Star, where a Guinness and whisky chaser would either set him right or serve him notice that solids were best avoided. His hardcore days were over. Back then, he'd had his unreliable moments: drunk, he'd mistaken nuns for whores and policemen for friends; sober, he'd made eye contact with ex-wives, no recognition on his side, and only relief on theirs. Bad times.

But even then, he'd never had a gold-standard Moscow hood shimmy past without clocking him for what he was.

Dickie became aware of action: an announcement about buses had been made, and everyone was trying to cross the bridge. He hung by the monitor long enough for the hood to pass, then allowed himself to be carried forward, three warm bodies behind. He shouldn't be this close, but there was no accounting for the choreography of crowds.

And this crowd was not happy. Having squeezed through the ticket barriers on the other side, it hassled the station staff, who placated, argued, and pointed at the exits. Outside was wet and dark, and there were no buses. The crowd swelled across the forecourt. Crushed in its embrace, Dickie Bow kept both eyes on the hood, who stood placidly, waiting.

An interrupted journey, thought Dickie. You played the odds in this line of work – he had forgotten he was no longer in this line of work – and the hood would have finished processing them before getting off the train; he would go with the flow, make no fuss; continue on his way by whatever means presented. Where this might be, Dickie had no idea. The train had been Worcester-bound, but made plenty of stops before then. The hood could be getting off anywhere. All Dickie knew was, he'd be getting off there too.

And now there were buses, three of them, pulling round the corner. The crowd tensed, pressed forward, and the hood sailed through the mass like an icebreaker carving an Arctic field, while Dickie slipped through spaces in his wake. Someone was calling instructions, but didn't have the voice for it. Long before he'd finished, he was drowned out by the muttering of people who couldn't hear.

3

But the hood knew what was what. The hood was heading for the third bus, so Dickie sidled through chaos in his wake, and boarded it too. Nobody asked for a ticket. Dickie simply trotted on and headed for the rear, which boasted a view of the hood, two seats ahead. Settling back, Dickie allowed his eyes to close. In every operation came a lull. When it did, you shut your eyes and took inventory. He was miles from home, with about sixteen quid on him. He needed a drink, and wouldn't get one in a hurry. But on the upside, he was here, it was now, and he hadn't known how much he'd missed this: living life, instead of easing through it on the wet stuff.

Which was what he'd been doing when he'd spotted the hood. Right there in the Star. A civilian's jaw would have hit the table: What the *hell*? A pro, even a long-defunct pro, checked the clock, drained his Guinness, folded the *Post* and left. Loitered by the bookies two doors down, remembering the last time he'd seen that face, and in whose company. The hood was a bit player. The hood had held the bottle, poured its contents directly into Dickie's clamped-wide mouth; strictly a non-speaking role. It wasn't the hood who sent electric shivers down Dickie's spine . . . Ten minutes later he emerged, and Dickie fell into step behind him: Dickie, who could follow a ferret through a wood let alone a leftover ghost. A blast from the past. An echo from the Spooks' Zoo.

(Berlin, if you insisted. The Spooks' Zoo was Berlin, back when the cages had just been unlocked, and frightened thugs were pouring from the woodwork like beetles from an upturned log. At least twice a day, some sweating, would-be asset was at the door claiming to have the crown jewels in a cardboard suitcase: defence details, missile capability, toxic secrets . . . And yet, for all the flurry of activity, the writing was on the newly dismantled Wall: everyone's past had been blown away, but so had Dickie Bow's future. *Thanks, old chap. Afraid there's not much call for your, ah, skills any more . . . What pension?* So naturally, he'd drifted back to London.)

The driver called something Dickie didn't catch. The door hissed shut and the horn was tapped twice; a farewell note to the lingering buses. Dickie rubbed his thigh where the edge of a briefcase or umbrella-tip had nipped him, and thought about luck, and the strange places it dragged you. Such as, from a Soho street into the Tube and out the other end; into Paddington, onto a train, then onto this bus. He still didn't know whether that luck was good or bad.

When the lights went out the bus briefly became a travelling shadow. Then passengers switched overhead bulbs on, and blue screens gleamed upwards from laptops, and fists wrapped round iPhones grew spectrally white. Dickie fiddled his own phone from his pocket, but he had no messages. There were never any messages. Scrolling through his contact list, he was struck by how short it was. Two seats in front, the hood had rolled his newspaper into a baton, wedged it between his knees, and hung his hat upon it. He might be asleep.

The bus left Reading behind. Through the window, dark countryside unfurled. Some distance off, an ascending sequence of red lights indicated the mast at Didcot, but the cooling towers were invisible.

In Dickie's hand, the mobile was a grenade. Rubbing his thumb on its numberpad, he registered the tiny nipple on the middle button that allowed you to orient your fingers in the dark. But nobody was hanging on Dickie's words. Dickie was a relic. The world had moved on, and what would his message be anyway? That he'd seen a face from the past, and was following it home? Who would have cared? The world had moved on. It had left him behind.

Rejection came softer these days. Dickie heard occasional whispers on the Soho songlines, and these days even the useless were given a chance. The Service, like everyone else, was hamstrung by rules and regulations: sack the useless, and they took you to tribunal for discriminating against useless people. So the Service bunged the useless into some godforsaken annexe and threw paperwork at them, an administrative harassment intended to make them hand in their cards. They called them the slow horses. The screw-ups. The losers. They called them the slow horses and they belonged to Jackson Lamb, whom Dickie had encountered, back in the Spooks' Zoo.

His mobile gave a blip, but there was no message; only a warning that it was running out of power.

Dickie knew how it felt. He had nothing to say. Attention wavered and refocused elsewhere. Laptops hummed and mobiles whispered, but Dickie had no voice. Had no movement, bar a feeble flexing of his fingers. The tiny nipple on the keypad's middle button scratched beneath his thumb: *scratch scratch*.

There was an important message to deliver, but Dickie did not know what it was, nor to whom it should be sent. For a few luminous moments he was aware of being part of a warm, humid community, breathing the same air, hearing the same tune. But the tune slipped out of earshot, and became beyond recall. Everything faded, save the scene through the window. The landscape continued unrolling one black fold after another, dotted with pinpricks of light, like sequins on a scarf. And then the lights blurred and dimmed and the darkness rolled over itself one final time, and then there was only the bus carrying its mortal cargo through the night, heading for Oxford, where it would deliver one soul fewer than it had gathered, back in the rain.

Part One

Black Swans

2

Now that the roadworks have finally gone, Aldersgate Street, in the London borough of Finsbury, is calmer; nowhere you'd choose to have a picnic, but no longer the vehicle-related crime scene it once resembled. The area's pulse has normalised, and while noise levels remain high, they're less pneumatic, and include the occasional snatch of street music: cars sing, taxis whistle, and locals stare in bafflement at the freely flowing traffic. Once it was wise to pack a lunch if you were heading down the street on a bus. Now you could while away half an hour trying to cross it.

It's a case, perhaps, of the urban jungle reclaiming its own, and any jungle boasts wildlife if you look hard enough. A fox was spotted one mid-morning, padding from White Lion Court into the Barbican Centre, and up among the complex's flower beds and water features can be found both birds and rats. Where the greenery bends over standing water, frogs hide. After dark, there are bats. So it would be no surprise if a cat dropped in front of our eyes from one of the Barbican towers and froze as it hit the bricks; looking all directions at once without moving its head, as cats can. It's a Siamese. Pale, short-haired, slant-eyed, slender and whispery; able, like all its kind, to slip through doors barely open and windows thought shut, and it's only frozen for a moment. Then it's off.

It moves like a rumour, this cat; over the pedestrian bridge, then down the stairs to the station and out onto the street. A lesser cat might have paused before crossing the tributary road, but not ours; trusting instincts, ears and speed, it's on the pavement opposite before a van driver finishes braking. And then it vanishes, or seems to. The driver peers angrily, but all he can see is a black door in a dusty recess between a newsagent's and a Chinese restaurant; its ancient black paintwork spattered with roadsplash, a single yellowing milk bottle on its step. And no sign of our cat.

Who has, of course, gone round the back. No one enters Slough House by the front door; instead, via a shabby alleyway, its inmates let themselves into a grubby yard with mildewed walls, and through a door that requires a sharp kick most mornings, when damp or cold or heat have warped it. But our cat's feet are too subtle to require violence and it's through that door in a blink, and up a dog-legged flight of stairs to a pair of offices.

Here on the first floor – ground level being assigned to other properties; to the New Empire Chinese, and whatever the newsagent's is called this year – is where Roderick Ho labours, in an office made jungly by electrical clutter: abandoned keyboards nest in corners, and brightly coloured wires billow like loops of intestine from backless monitors. Gunmetal bookshelves hold software manuals, lengths of cable, and shoeboxes almost certainly containing oddly shaped bits of metal, while next to Ho's desk wobbles a cardboard tower fashioned from the geek's traditional building block: the empty pizza box. A lot of stuff.

But when our cat pokes its head round the door, it'll find only Ho. The office is his alone, and Ho prefers this, for he mostly dislikes other people, though the fact that other people dislike him back has never occurred to him. And while Louisa Guy has been known to speculate that Ho occupies a place somewhere on the right of the autism spectrum, Min Harper has habitually responded that he's also way out there on the git index. It's no surprise, then, that had Ho noticed our cat's presence, his response would have been to toss a Coke can at it, and he'd have been disappointed to have missed. But another thing Roderick Ho hasn't grasped about himself is that he's a better shot when aiming at stationary targets. He rarely fails to drop a can into a wastebasket half the office away, but has been known to miss the point when it's closer than that.

Unscathed, then, our cat withdraws, to check out the adjoining office. And here are two unfamiliar faces, recently dispatched to Slough House: one white, one black; one female, one male; so new they don't have names yet, and both thrown by their visitor. Is the cat a regular – is the cat a fellow slow horse? Or is this a test? Troubled, they share a glance, and while they're bonding in momentary confusion our cat slips out and nips up the stairs to the next landing, and two more offices.

The first of which is occupied by Min Harper and Louisa Guy, and if Min Harper and Louisa Guy had been paying attention and noticed the cat, they'd have embarrassed seven bells out of it. Louisa would have gone onto her knees, gathered the cat in her arms and held it to her quite impressive breasts – and here we're wandering into Min's area of opinion: breasts that couldn't be called too small or too large, but breasts that are just right; while Min himself, if he could get his mind off Louisa's tits long enough, would have taken a rough manly grasp of the cat's scruff; would have tilted its head so they could share a glance, and each understand the other's feline qualities – not the furry, soft ones, but the night-time grace and the walking-in-darkness; the predatory undercurrent that hums beneath a cat's daytime activities.

Both Min and Louisa would have talked about finding milk, but neither would actually have done so, the point being to indicate that kindness and milk-delivery were within both their scopes. And our cat, quite rightly, would have relieved itself on the mat before leaving their office.

To enter River Cartwright's room. And while our cat would have crossed this threshold as unobtrusively as it had all the others, that wouldn't have been unobtrusive enough. River Cartwright, who is young, fair-haired, pale-skinned, with a small mole on his upper lip, would immediately have ceased what he was doing – paperwork or screenwork; something involving thought rather than action, which perhaps accounts for the air of frustration that taints the air in here – and held our cat's gaze until it broke contact, made uncomfortable by such frank assessment. Cartwright wouldn't have thought about providing milk; he'd be too busy mapping the cat's actions, working out how many doors it must have slipped through to make it this far; wondering what drew it into Slough House in the first place; what motives hid behind its eyes. Though even while he was thinking this our cat would have withdrawn and made its way up the last set of stairs, in search of a less-stringent reckoning.

And with this in mind, it would have found the first of the final pair of offices: a more welcoming area into which to strut, for this is where Catherine Standish works, and Catherine Standish knows what to do with a cat. Catherine Standish ignores cats. Cats are either adjuncts or substitutes, and Catherine Standish has no truck with either. Having a cat is one small step from having two cats, and to be a single woman within a syllable of fifty in possession of two cats is tantamount to declaring life over. Catherine Standish has had her share of scary moments but has survived each of them, and is not about to surrender now. So our cat can make itself as comfortable as it likes in here, but no matter how much affection it pretends to, how coyly it wraps its sleek length round Catherine's calves, there will be no treats forthcoming; no strips of sardine patted dry on a Kleenex and laid at its feet; no pot of cream decanted into a saucer. And since no cat worth the name can tolerate lack of worship, ours takes its leave and saunters next door . . .

. . . to Jackson Lamb's lair at last, where the ceiling slopes and a blind dims the window, and what light there is comes from a lamp placed on a pile of telephone directories. The air is heavy with a dog's olfactory daydream: takeaway food, illicit cigarettes, day-old farts and stale beer, but there will be no time to catalogue this because Jackson Lamb can move surprisingly swiftly for a man of his bulk, or he can when he feels like it, and trust this: when a fucking cat enters his room, he feels like it. Within a blink he'd have seized our cat by the throat; pulled up the blind, opened the window, and dropped it to the road below, where it would doubtless land on its feet, as both science and rumour confirm, but equally doubtless in front of a moving vehicle, this, as noted, being the new dispensation on Aldersgate Street. A muffled bump and a liquid screech of brakes might have carried upwards, but Lamb would have closed the window by then and be back in his chair, eyes closed; his sausagey fingers interlinked on his paunch.

It's a lucky escape for our cat, then, that it doesn't exist, for that would have been a brutal ending. And a lucky escape twice over, as it happens, for on this particular morning the nigh-on unthinkable has happened, and Jackson Lamb is not dozing at his desk, or prowling the kitchen area outside his office, scavenging his underlings' food; nor is he wafting up and down the staircase with that creepily silent tread he adopts at will. He's not banging on his floor, which is River Cartwright's ceiling, for the pleasure of timing how long it takes Cartwright to arrive, and he's not ignoring Catherine Standish while she delivers another pointless report he's forgotten commissioning. Simply put, he's not here.

And no one in Slough House has the faintest idea where he is.

Where Jackson Lamb was was Oxford, and he had a brand new theory, one to float in front of the suits at Regent's Park. Lamb's new theory was this: that instead of sending tadpole spooks on expensive torture-resistance courses at hideaways on the Welsh borders, they should pack them off to Oxford railway station to observe the staff in action. Because whatever training these guys underwent, it left every last one of them highly skilled in the art of not releasing information.

'You work here, right?'

13

'Sir?'

'Were you on shift last Tuesday evening?'

'The helpline number's on all the posters, sir. If you have a complaint—'

'I don't have a complaint,' Lamb said. 'I just want to know if you were on duty last Tuesday evening.'

'And why would you want to know that, sir?'

Lamb had been stonewalled three times so far. This fourth was a small man with sleeked-back hair and a grey moustache that twitched occasionally of its own accord. He looked like a weasel in a uniform. Lamb would have caught him by the back legs and cracked him like a whip, but there was a policeman within earshot.

'Let's assume it's important.'

He had ID, of course, under a workname, but didn't have to be a fisherman to know that you don't go lobbing rocks in the pool before you cast your line. If anyone rang the number on his card, bells and whistles would sound at Regent's Park. And Lamb didn't want the suits asking what he thought he was doing, because he wasn't sure what he thought he was doing, and there was no chance in hell he was going to share that information.

'Very important,' he added. He tapped his lapel. A wallet poked visibly from his inside pocket, and a twenty pound note peeped visibly from inside that.

'Ah.'

'I take it that's a yes.'

'You understand we have to be careful, sir. With people asking questions at major transport hubs.'

Good to know, thought Jackson Lamb, that if terrorists descended on this particular transport hub, they'd meet an impregnable line of defence. Unless they waved banknotes. 'Last Tuesday,' he said. 'There was some kind of meltdown.'

But his man was already shaking his head: 'Not our problem, sir. Everything was fine here.'

'Everything was fine except the trains weren't running.'

'The trains were running here, sir. There were problems elsewhere.'

'Right.' It had been a while since Lamb had endured a conversation this long without resorting to profanity. The slow horses would have been amazed, except the newbies, who'd have suspected a test. 'But wherever the problem, there were people being bused here from Reading. Because the trains weren't running.'

The weasel was knitting his eyebrows together, but had seen his way to the end of this line of questioning, and was picking up speed on the final stretch. 'That's right, sir. A replacement bus service.'

'Which came from where?'

'On that particular occasion, sir, I rather think they'd have come from Reading.'

Of course they bloody would. Jackson Lamb sighed, and reached for his cigarettes.

'You can't smoke in here, sir.'

Lamb tucked one behind his ear. 'When's the next Reading train?'

'Five minutes, sir.'

Grunting his thanks, Lamb turned for the barriers.

'Sir?'

He looked back.

Gaze fixed on Lamb's lapel, the weasel made a rustly sign with finger and thumb.

'What?'

'I thought you were going to . . .'

'Give you a tip?'

'Yes.'

'Okay. Here's a good one.' Lamb tapped his nose with a finger. 'If you've got a complaint, there's a helpline number on the posters.'

Then he wandered onto the platform, and waited for his train.

★

Back on Aldersgate Street, the two new horses in the first-floor office were sizing each other up. They'd arrived a month back, within the same fortnight; both exiled from Regent's Park, the Service's heart and moral high-ground. Slough House, which was not its real name – it didn't have a real name – was openly acknowledged to be a dumping ground: assignment here was generally temporary, because those assigned here usually quit before long. That was the point of sending them: to light a sign above their heads, reading EXIT. Slow horses, they were called. Slough House/slow horse. A wordplay based on a joke whose origins were almost forgotten.

These two – who have names now; their names are Marcus Longridge and Shirley Dander – had known each other by sight in their previous incarnations, but department culture kept a firm grip on Regent's Park, and Ops and Comms were different fish, and swam in different circles. So now, in the way of newbies everywhere, they were as suspicious of each other as of the more established residents. Still: the Service world was relatively small, and stories often circled it twice before smoke from the wreckage subsided. So Marcus Longridge (mid-forties, black, south-London born of Caribbean parents) knew what had propelled Shirley Dander from Regent's Park's Communications sector, and Dander, who was in her twenties and vaguely Mediterranean-looking (Scottish great-grandmother, nearby POW camp, Italian internee on day release) had heard rumours about Longridge's meltdown-related counselling sessions, but neither had spoken to the other of this, or indeed of much else yet. Their days had been filled with the minutiae of office co-living, and a slow-burn loss of hope.

It was Marcus who made the first move, and this was a single word: 'So.'

It was late morning. London weather was undergoing a schizoid attack: sudden shafts of sunlight, highlighting the grimy windowglass; sudden flurries of rain, failing to do much to clean it.

'So what?'

'So here we are.'

Shirley Dander was waiting for her computer to reboot. Again. It was running face-recognition software, comparing glimpses snatched from CCTV coverage at troop-withdrawal rallies with photofit images of suspected jihadists; that is, jihadists suspected of existing; jihadists who had code names and everything, but might have been rumoured into being by inept Intelligence work. While the program was two years out of date it wasn't as out of date as her PC, which resented the demands placed upon it, and had made this known three times so far this morning.

Without looking up, she said, 'Is this a chat-up?'

'I wouldn't dare.'

'Because that would not be wise.'

'I've heard.'

'Well then.'

For almost a minute that was that. Shirley could feel her watch ticking; could feel through the desk's surface the computer struggling to return to life. Two pairs of feet tracked downstairs. Harper and Guy. She wondered where they were off to.

'So given that it's not a chat-up, is it okay if we talk?'

'About what?'

'Anything.'

Now she gave him a hard stare.

Marcus Longridge shrugged. 'Like it or not, we're sharing. It wouldn't hurt if we said more than shut the door.'

'I've never told you to shut the door.'

'Or whatever.'

'Actually I prefer it open. Feels less like a prison cell.'

'That's good,' said Marcus. 'See, we've got a discussion going. Spent much time in prison?'

'I'm not in the mood, okay?'

He shrugged. 'Okay. But there's six and something hours of the working day left. And twenty years of the working life. We could spend it in silence if you'd rather, but one of us'll go mad and the other'll go crazy.' He bent back to his computer.

Downstairs, the back door slammed. Shirley's screen swam bluely into life, thought about it, and crashed again. Now conversation had been attempted, its absence screamed like a fire alarm. Her wristwatch pulsed. There was nothing she could do about it; the words had to be said.

'Speak for yourself.'

He said, 'About?'

'Twenty years of working life.'

'Right.'

'More like forty in my case.'

Marcus nodded. It didn't show on his face, but he felt triumph.

He knew a beginning when he heard one.

In Reading, Jackson Lamb had tracked down the station manager, for whose benefit he adopted a fussy, donnish air. It wasn't hard to believe Lamb an academic: shoulders dusted with dandruff; green V-neck stained by misjudged mouthfuls of takeaway; frayed shirtcuffs poking from overcoat sleeves. He was overweight, from sitting around in libraries probably, and his thinning dirty-blond hair was brushed back over his head. The stubble on his cheeks sang of laziness, not cool. He'd been said to resemble Timothy Spall, with worse teeth.

The station manager directed him to the company which supplied replacement buses, and ten minutes later Lamb was doing fussy academic again; this time with a bottom note of grief. 'My brother,' he said.

'Oh. Oh. I'm sorry to hear that.'

Lamb waved a forgiving hand.

'No, that's awful. I'm really sorry.'

'We hadn't spoken in years.'

'Well, that makes it worse, doesn't it?'

Lamb, who had no opinion, gave assent. 'It does. It does.' His eyes clouded as he recalled an imaginary infant episode in which two brothers enjoyed a moment of absolute fraternal loyalty, little knowing that the years to come would drive a wedge between them; that they would not speak during middle age; which would come to a halt for one of them on a bus in dark Oxfordshire, where he would succumb to . . .

'Heart attack, was it?'

Unable to speak, Lamb nodded.

The depot manager shook his head sadly. It was a bad business. And not much of an advert, a customer dying on a unit; though then again, it wasn't as if liability lay with the company. Apart from anything else, the corpse hadn't been in possession of a valid ticket.

'I wondered . . .'

'Yes?'

'Which bus was it? Is it here now?'

There were four coaches in the yard; another two in the sheds, and as it happened, the depot manager knew precisely which one had unintentionally doubled as a hearse, and it was parked not ten yards away.

'Only I'd like to sit in it a moment,' Lamb said. 'Where he sat. You know?'

'I'm not sure what . . .'

'It's not that I believe in a life force, precisely,' Lamb explained, a tremor in his voice. 'But I'm not positive I don't believe in it, do you see what I mean?'

'Of course. Of course.'

'And if I could just sit where he was sitting when he . . . passed, well . . .'

Unable to continue, he turned to gaze over the brick wall enclosing the yard, and beyond the office block opposite. A pair of Canada geese were making their way riverwards; their plaintive honking underlining Lamb's sadness.

Or that's how it seemed to the depot manager.

'There,' he said. 'It's that one over there.'

Abandoning his scanning of the skies, Lamb fixed him with wide and innocent gratitude.

Shirley Dander tapped a pencil uselessly against her reluctant monitor, then put it down. As it hit the desk, she made a plosive noise with her lips.

'. . . What?'

'What's "wouldn't dare" supposed to mean?' she said.

'I don't follow.'

'When I asked if you were chatting me up. You said you wouldn't dare.'

Marcus Longridge said, 'I heard the story.'

That figured, she thought. Everyone had heard the story.

Shirley Dander was five two; brown eyes, olive skin, and a full mouth she didn't smile with much. Broad in the shoulder and wide in the hip, she favoured black: black jeans, black tops, black trainers. Once, in her hearing, it had been suggested she had the sex appeal of a traffic bollard, a comment delivered by a notorious sexual incompetent. On the day she was assigned to Slough House she'd had a buzz cut she'd refreshed every week since.

That she had inspired obsession was beyond doubt: specifically, a fourth-desk Comms operative at Regent's Park, who had pursued her with a diligence which took no heed of the fact that she was in a relationship. He'd taken to leaving notes on her desk; to calling her lover's flat at all hours. Given his job, he had no trouble making these calls untraceable. Given hers, she had no trouble tracing them.

There were protocols in place, of course; a grievance procedure which involved detailing 'inappropriate behaviours' and evidencing 'disrespectful attitudes'; guidelines which carried little weight with staff who'd spent a minimum of eight weeks on assault training as part of their probation. After a night in which he'd called six times, he'd approached her in the canteen to ask how she'd slept, and Shirley had decked him with one clean punch.

She might have got away with this if she hadn't hauled him to his feet and decked him again with a second.

Issues, was the verdict from HR. It was clear that Shirley Dander had issues.

Marcus was talking through her thoughts: 'Everybody heard the story, man. Someone told me his feet left the floor.'

'Only the first time.'

'You were lucky not to get shitcanned.'

'You reckon?'

'Point taken. But mixing it on the hub? Guys have been sacked for less.'

'Guys maybe,' she said. 'Sacking a girl for flattening a creep who's harassing her, that's embarrassing. Especially if the "girl" in question wants to get legal about it.' The inverted commas round girl couldn't have been more audible if she'd said quote/unquote. 'Besides, I had an edge.'

'What sort of edge?'

She kicked back from her desk with both feet, and her chairlegs squealed on the floor. 'What are you after?'

'Nothing.'

'Because you sound pretty curious for someone just making conversation.'

'Well,' he told her, 'without curiosity, what kind of conversation have you got?'

She studied him. He wasn't bad looking, for his age; had what appeared to be a lazy left eyelid, but this gave him a watchful air, as if he were constantly sizing the world up. His hair was longer than hers, but not by much; he wore a neatly trimmed beard and moustache, and was careful how he dressed. Today this meant well-pressed jeans and a white collarless shirt under a grey jacket; his black and purple Nicole Farhi scarf hung on the coatstand. She'd noticed all this not because she cared but because everything was information. He didn't wear a wedding ring, but that meant nothing. Besides, everyone was divorced or unhappy.

'Okay,' she said. 'But if you're playing me, you're likely to find out first-hand just how hard I hit.'

He raised his hands in not entirely mock-surrender. 'Hey, I'm just trying to establish a working relationship. You know. Us being the newbies.'

'It's not like the others put up a united front. 'Cept maybe Harper and Guy.'

'They don't have to,' Marcus said. 'They've got resident status.' His fingers played a quick trill across his keyboard, then he pushed it away and shunted his chair sideways. 'What do you make of them?'

'As a group?'

'Or one by one. It doesn't have to be a seminar.'

'Where do we start?'

Marcus Longridge said, 'We start with Lamb.'

Perched on the back seat of a bus where a man had died, Jackson Lamb was looking out at a cracked concrete forecourt and a pair of wooden gates, beyond which lay Reading town centre. As a long-time Londoner, Lamb couldn't contemplate this without a shudder.

For the moment, though, he concentrated on doing what he was pretending to do, which was sit in quiet recall of the man he'd said was his brother, but who in reality had been Dickie Bow: too daft to be a workname, but too cute to be real. Dickie and Lamb had been in Berlin at the same time, but from this distance, Lamb had trouble recalling the other man's face. The image he kept coming up with was sleek and pointy, like a rat, but then that's what Dickie Bow had been, a street rat; adept at crawling through holes too small for him. That had been his key survival skill. It didn't appear to have helped him lately.

(A heart attack, the post-mortem had said. Not especially surprising in a man who drank as much, and smoked as much, and ate as much fried food as Dickie Bow. Uncomfortable

22

reading for Lamb, whose habits it might have been describing.)

Reaching out, he traced a finger over the back of the seat in front. Its surface was mostly smooth; the one burn mark obviously ancient; the faint tracery in a corner suggesting random scratching rather than an attempt to etch a dying message . . . It was years since Bow had been in the Service, and even then, he'd been one of that great army who'd never quite been inside the tent. You could always trust a street rat, the wisdom ran, because every time one of them took money from the other side, he'd be on your doorstep next morning, expecting you to match the offer.

There was no brotherhood code. If Dickie Bow had succumbed to a mattress fire, Lamb would have got through the five stages without batting an eye: denial, anger, bargaining, indifference, breakfast. But Bow had died on the back seat of a moving coach, without a ticket in his pocket. Booze, fags and fry-ups aside, the PM couldn't explain Bow's being in the sticks when he should have been working his shift at a Soho pornshop.

Standing, Lamb ran a hand along the overhead rack, and found nothing. Even if he had, it wouldn't have been anything left by Dickie Bow, not after six days. Then he sat again, and studied the rubber lining along the base of the window, looking for scratch marks – ridiculous perhaps, but Moscow rules meant assuming your mail was read. When you needed to leave a message, you left it by other means. Though in this instance, a thumbnail on a rubber lining wasn't one of them.

A hesitant, polite cough from the front of the coach.

'I, ah—'

Lamb looked up mournfully.

'I don't mean to rush you. But are you going to be much longer?'

'One minute,' Lamb said.

Actually, he needed less than that. Even while he was speaking he was sliding his hand down the back of the seat, forcing it between the two cushions, encountering a gobbet of ancient chewing gum hardened to a tumour on the fabric; a welter of biscuit crumbs; a paperclip; a coin too small to be worth pocketing; and the edge of something hard which squirted out of his reach, forcing him to delve deeper, the cuff of his overcoat riding up his arm as he pushed. And there it was again, a smooth plastic shell snuggling into his grip. Lamb scratched his wrist deep enough to draw blood as he pulled his treasure free, but didn't notice. All his attention was focused on his prize: an old, fat, bottom-of-the-line mobile phone.

'Lamb, well. Lamb's everything he's made out to be.'

'Which is?'

'Some kind of fat bastard.'

'Who goes way back.'

'A long-lived fat bastard. The worst kind. He sits upstairs and craps on the rest of us. It's like he gets pleasure out of running a department full of . . .'

'Losers.'

'You calling me a loser?'

'We're both here, aren't we?'

Work was forgotten. Marcus Longridge, having just called Shirley Dander a loser, gave her a bright smile. She paused, wondering what she was getting into. Trust nobody, she'd decided when she'd first set foot in this place. The buzz-cut was part of that. Trust nobody. And here she was on the verge of opening up to Marcus simply because he was the one she was sharing an office with: And what was he smiling at? Did he think he was being friendly? Take a deep breath, she told herself; but a mental one. Don't let him see.

This was the crux of Communications: find out all you can, but give nothing away.

She said, 'The jury's still out on that. What do you make of him, anyway?'

'Well, he's running his own department.'

'Some department. More like a charity shop.' She slapped a hand on her PC. 'This should be in a museum for a start. We're supposed to catch bad guys with this shit? We'd have a better chance standing on Oxford Street with a clipboard. Excuse me, sir, are you a terrorist?'

'Sir or Miss,' Marcus corrected her. Then said, 'We're not expected to catch anyone, we're supposed to get bored and go join a security firm. But the point is, whatever we're here for, Lamb's not being punished. Or if he is, he's enjoying it.'

'So what's your point?'

He said, 'That he knows where some bodies are buried. Probably buried a few himself.'

'Is that a metaphor?'

'I failed English. Metaphor's a closed book to me.'

'So you think he's handy?'

'Well, he's overweight and drinks and smokes and I doubt he takes much exercise that doesn't involve picking up a phone and calling out for a curry. But yeah, now you mention it, I think he's handy.'

'He might've been once,' Shirley said. 'But there's not much point in being handy if you're too slow to be any good at it.'

But Marcus disagreed. Being handy was a state of mind. Lamb could wear you down just standing in front of you, and you wouldn't know he was a threat until he was walking away, and you were wondering who'd turned the lights out. Just Marcus's opinion, of course. He'd been wrong before.

'I suppose,' he said, 'if we stick around long enough, we might find out.'

Coming back down the coach Lamb rubbed a finger in his eye, which made him look grieving, or at any rate like he had a sore eye. The depot manager seemed uncomfortable, ill at ease with a stranger's sorrow, or else he'd noticed Lamb with his arm down the back seat, and was wondering whether to address the topic.

To short-circuit any such attempt, Lamb said, 'The driver around?'

'What, who was driving when . . . ?'

When my brother kicked off, yes. But he just nodded, and wiped his eye again.

The driver didn't much want to talk to Lamb about his uncooperative passenger; the only good ones are the ones that walk away being the standard bus-driver take on the general public. But once the depot manager had made a final apology and shuffled back to his office, and Lamb had indicated for the second time that morning that he had a twenty pound note in his possession, the driver opened up.

'What can I say? I'm sorry for your loss.'

Though seemed happy enough about his own potential gain.

Lamb said, 'Was he talking to anyone, did you notice?'

'We're supposed to keep our eyes on the road, mostly.'

'Before you started.'

The driver said, 'What can I say?' again. 'It was a bleedin' circus, mate. Couple of thousand stranded, we was just getting them shifted. So no, I didn't notice, sorry. He was just another punter until . . .' Realising he was heading up a conversational cul-de-sac, he tailed off with 'you know.'

'Until you got to Oxford with a stiff on your back seat,' Lamb supplied helpfully.

'He must have gone peaceful,' the driver said. 'I pretty much kept to the limit.'

Lamb looked back at the coach. The company livery was red and blue, its lower half flecked with mud. Just an ordinary vehicle, that Dickie Bow had stepped on and never stepped off again.

'Was there anything unusual about that trip?' he asked.

The driver stared.

'Corpse aside.'

'Sorry, mate. It was just, you know. Pick 'em up at the station, drop 'em off at Oxford. Not like it was the first time.'

'And what happened when you got there? Oxford?'

26

'Most of them was off like the clappers. There was a train waiting to take 'em the rest of the way. They must've been an hour behind by then. And it was pissing down. So they wasn't hanging around.'

'But someone found the body.' The driver gave him an odd look, and Lamb surmised the reason. 'Richard,' he said. They'd been brothers, hadn't they? 'Dickie. Someone realised he was dead.'

'There was a huddle at the back of the bus, but he was already gone. One of them, a doctor, he stayed behind, but the rest left to catch their train.' He paused. 'He looked quite calm, like. Your brother.'

'It's how he would have wanted to go,' Lamb assured him. 'He liked buses. So you what, called an ambulance?'

'He was past help, but yeah. I was stuck there rest of the evening. No offence. Had to give a statement, but you'd know that, right? Being his brother.'

'That's right,' Lamb said. 'Being his brother. Anything else happen?'

'Business as normal, mate. Once he'd been, you know, taken away, and I'd tidied the bus and everything, I came back here.'

'Tidied the bus?'

'Not cleaning it or anything. Just check the seats for anything left behind, you know? Wallets and that.'

'And did you find anything?'

'Not that evening, mate. Well, just a hat.'

'A hat?'

'On the overhead rack. Near where your brother was.'

'What sort of hat?'

'Black one.'

'Black one what? Bowler? Fedora? What?'

He shrugged. 'Just a hat. With a brim, you know?'

'Where's it now?'

'Lost property, 'less it's been picked up. It was just a hat. People leave hats on buses all the time.'

Not when it's pissing down they don't, thought Lamb.

A moment's reflection told him this wasn't true. When it was raining, more people wore hats, so more people left them on buses. It stood to reason. A matter of statistics.

But the thing about statistics, Lamb reasoned, was statistics could take a flying hump at the moon.

'So where's your lost property?' He waved in the vague direction of the depot office. 'Over there?'

'Nah, mate. Back in Oxford, innit?'

Of bloody course it is, thought Lamb.

'So what about Ho?'

'Ho's a dweeb.'

'Newsflash. All webheads are dweebs.'

'Ho's dweebness goes deeper. You want to know the first thing he said to me?'

'What?'

'The very first thing, right? I mean, I haven't even got my coat off,' Marcus said. 'First morning here, thinking I've just been shipped to the spooks' equivalent of Devil's Island, and I'm wondering what happens next, and Ho picks up his coffee mug and shows it to me – it's got a picture of Clint Eastwood on it – and he says, "This is my mug, okay? And I don't like other people using my mug."'

Shirley said, 'Okay. That's bad.'

'It's way past anal. I bet his socks are tagged left and right.'

'What about Guy?'

'She's doing Harper.'

'Harper?'

'He's doing Guy.'

'I'm not saying you're wrong, but that hardly amounts to a character portrait.'

He shrugged. 'They've not been doing each other long, so right now, that's the only significant thing about them.'

Shirley said, 'That must have been them going out earlier. I wonder where they went?'

'We're still persona non grata at the Park then.'

Which was an odd thing for Min Harper to say, given that they were in a park, but Louisa Guy knew what he meant.

'Do you know,' she said, 'I'm not entirely sure that's the reason.'

The park they were in was St James's, and the park they weren't in was Regent's. They were heading for the palace end and a woman in a pink velvety tracksuit was approaching them along the footpath at about two miles an hour. At her ankles waddled a small hairy dog with a matching pink ribbon round its neck. They waited until she'd passed before continuing.

'Explain?'

So Louisa did. It was to do with Leonard Bradley. Until recently Bradley had been Chair of the Limitations Committee, which effectively controlled the Service purse strings. Every op planned by Ingrid Tearney, First Desk at Regent's Park, had to be cleared by Limitations if she didn't want budgeting issues, which was what running out of money was now called. Except Bradley – Sir Leonard, if the title hadn't been repossessed yet – had lately been caught with his fingers in the till: a Shropshire 'safe house', fully staffed for the recuperation of officers suffering Service-related stress, had turned out to be a beachfront property on the Maldives, though to be fair, it was fully staffed. And the result of Bradley's peccadilloes . . .

'How do you know all this?' Harper interrupted. 'I thought he'd just retired.'

'Ah, that's sweet. But you've got to keep an ear to the ground in this business.'

'Don't tell me. Catherine.'

She nodded.

'Girls' talk? Quick confab in the ladies'?'

He kept it light, but there was an edge. Something he was excluded from.

She said, 'Catherine's hardly likely to call a press conference. When I told her we'd been summoned, she told me this was going on. She called it an audit.'

'How does she know about it?'

Louisa said, 'She's got a connection. One of the Queens.'

The Queens of the Database were who you went to when you needed information, which made them useful friends, and even more useful connections.

'So what's this audit?'

. . . And the result of Bradley's peccadilloes was what was being termed an audit, but might more accurately be called an Inquisition. Limitations' new Chair, Roger Barrowby, was taking the opportunity to clean the stables: this involved in-depth interviews with all staff, covering their financial, operational, emotional, psychological, sexual and medical histories; just to make sure everything was squeaky clean. Nobody wanted further embarrassments.

'Bit of a cheek,' Min said. 'I mean, Bradley was the one stealing cookies. Any embarrassment should be the Committee's, not the Park's.'

'Welcome to the world, baby boy,' Louisa explained.

There was a bright side, though. 'I bet Taverner's going spare,' he mused.

But there wasn't time to explore what Taverner might be going, because here came James Webb, who'd summoned them to this al-fresco meeting.

Webb was a suit. He wasn't actually wearing a suit today – he wore fawn chinos and a dark-blue roll-neck under a black raincoat – but he wasn't fooling anyone: he was a suit, and if you cut him open he'd bleed in pinstripes. Today's outfit he probably thought was Tradecraft: what you wore for a leafy stroll. But the impression he gave was that he'd popped along to his man in Jermyn Street, explained he was going for a walk in the park, and wanted to dress accordingly. He was as much a man in casuals as the pink lady was a jogger.

Still, he was Regent's Park to their Slough House. Getting the call at all was a jawdropper. When he nodded they nodded back, and fell into step either side of him. 'Any trouble getting away?'

He might have been asking how traffic had been.

Louisa said, 'The back door jams. You have to kick it and lean on the handle at the same time. Once we were through that, it was a breeze.'

Webb said, 'I meant with Lamb.'

'Lamb wasn't around,' Min told him. 'Is he not supposed to know about this?'

'Oh, he'll find out eventually. It's no big deal anyway. I'm seconding you, that's all. Not for long. Three weeks or so.'

I'm seconding you. Like he was a big wheel. Over at the Park, when Ingrid Tearney was in DC, which was about half the time, Lady Di Taverner took the hot seat: she was one of several Second Desks, but top of most people's list whenever there were rumours of a palace coup. As for Spider Webb, his desk didn't have a number. He was basically HR, Min and Louisa had heard, and had this connection with River Cartwright neither of them knew the details of, beyond that they'd been through training together, and that Webb had screwed River over, which was how come River was a slow horse.

Maybe some of this leaked out from Min and Louisa's silence, because Webb said: 'So you'll be reporting to me.'

'On what sort of job?'

'Babysitting. Maybe a bit of vetting.'

'Vetting?' Vetting was mostly clerical, which was the slow horses' lot, but demanded resources Slough House didn't run to. And anyway, usually fell to Background, Regent's Park's skeleton-rattling department, with the Dogs – the internal security mob – providing back-up as and when.

But Webb affected to believe Min was unfamiliar with the term. 'Yes. Personal checks, identity confirmation, location cleansing. That sort of thing.'

'Oh, vetting,' said Min. 'Thought you said petting. I wondered if things were getting heavy.'

'It's not complicated,' Webb said, 'because if it was, I wouldn't be asking a smartarse to do it. But if you're not up to it, just say the word.' He came to a halt, and Min and Louisa each took an extra step before realising. They turned to face him. He said, 'And then you can piss off back to Slough House. And whatever important tasks you're busy with this week.'

Min's mouth began responding before his brain was in gear, but Louisa got in first. 'We've nothing much on,' she said. 'We'd be up for it.'

She shot Min a glance.

'Yeah,' he said. 'Sounds like a blast.'

'A blast?'

'Within our sphere of competence, he means,' Louisa said. 'We're just a little . . . nonplussed by your choice of venue.'

Webb looked around, as if only just noticing they were outside: water, trees, birds. Traffic, aware of the Palace, hummed politely beyond the railings. 'Yes,' he said. 'Well. Always nice to get out.'

'Especially when things are dodgy at home,' Min couldn't stop himself saying.

Louisa shook her head: I have to work with this?

But Webb pursed his lips. 'It's true the Park's a bit manic right now.'

Yeah. You're touching toes for the bean-counters, thought Min. That must make for fun moments round the watercooler.

Webb said, 'Every organisation needs the odd shake-up. We'll see how things stand once the dust settles.'

And in the same instant, both Min and Louisa realised Webb was intending to emerge from this shake-up behind a desk with a number on it.

'But meanwhile, it's mend and make-do. Background's busy, as you might imagine, running checks on the Park's own staff. Which is why we find ourselves forced to, ah . . .'

'Outsource?'

'If you like.'

'Tell us about this babysitting,' Louisa suggested.

'We're expecting visitors,' Webb said.

'What kind?'

'The Russian kind.'

'That's nice. Aren't they our friends now?'

Webb chuckled politely.

'What's the occasion?'

'Talks about talks.'

'Guns, oil or money?' Min asked.

'Cynicism's an overrated quality, don't you think?' Webb marched onwards, and they fell into step, flanking him. 'HMG rather feels the wind of change from the East. Nothing imminent, but you have to prepare for the future. Always an idea to extend a friendly hand to those who might one day be, ah, influential.'

'Oil, then,' Min said.

'So who's the visitor?' Louisa asked.

'Name of Pashkin.'

'Like the poet?'

'Very nearly like the poet, yes. Arkady Pashkin. A century ago, he'd have been a warlord. Twenty years ago, Mafia.' Webb paused. 'Well, twenty years ago he was Mafia, probably. But these days, he's mostly a billionaire.'

'And you want us to vet him?'

'Christ, no. The man owns an oil company. He could have whole bloody boneyards in his closet, HMG wouldn't care. But he'll be bringing staff, and there'll be high-level talks, and all of this needs to run smoothly. If it doesn't, well, the Park'll obviously need someone to blame.'

'And that would be us.'

'That would be you.' He gave a brief smile which might have indicated humour, but neither Min nor Louisa were convinced. 'Any problems with that?'

'Sounds like nothing we can't handle,' Min said.

'I'd hope not.' Webb came to a halt again. Min was starting to have flashbacks to walking his two boys when they were younger. Getting anywhere was a struggle: anything in their path that snagged their interest – a twig, a rubber band, a till receipt – resulted in a five-minute delay. 'So,' Webb went on, too casually. 'How's things over your manor, then?'

Our manor, Min wanted to parrot. Innit.

Louisa said, 'Same old same old.'

'And Cartwright?'

'No different.'

'I'm surprised he sticks it out. No offence. But he was always full of himself. He must hate it over there. Away from the action.'

There was barely disguised satisfaction in the pronouncement.

Min had decided he wasn't a fan of Spider Webb. He wasn't a particular fan of River Cartwright come to that, but there was a baseline these days that hadn't always been there, and it was simply stated: Cartwright was a slow horse, same as himself, same as Louisa. Once, that hadn't meant more than being tarred with the same brush. But now, if they didn't stick together exactly, they didn't piss on each other in front of others. Or not in front of Regent's Park suits, anyway.

He said, 'I'll pass on your regards. I know he has fond memories of your last meeting.'

At which River had clubbed Webb unconscious.

Louisa said, 'Does Lamb know you're, ah, seconding us?'

'He will soon. Is he likely to kick up a fuss?'

'Well,' Louisa said. 'If it annoys him, I'm sure he'll keep it to himself.'

'Yeah,' said Min. 'You know Lamb. Natural-born diplomat.'

★

'Oh Christ,' said Lamb. 'Not you again.'

Back at Oxford station, after another half-hour wait for a train, Lamb was looking for someone to tell him where the lost property office was, and the first face he saw was the weasel's: still twitchy, still officious, and definitely not happy to cast eyes on Jackson Lamb.

He made to walk straight past, but Lamb's cover as just another member of the public was wearing thin. He caught hold of a uniformed elbow. 'A word?'

The weasel looked down at Lamb's hand, up at Lamb's face, and then, slowly, deliberately, at the transport policeman a few yards away, showing a pretty blonde woman how to read a map.

Lamb released his grip. 'If it's of any interest,' he said, 'I still have that twenty pound note.' In the teeth of the expectations of a Reading bus driver, he might have added. 'So there's no reason we can't proceed in a friendly fashion.'

He smiled to illustrate 'friendly fashion', though the yellow-stained result might have passed for 'evil intent'.

It was more probably the mention of money than the amiable overture that worked. 'What is it this time?' the weasel asked.

'Lost property. Where is it?'

'That would be in the lost property office.'

'This is going splendidly,' Lamb said. 'And where's that?'

The weasel pursed his lips and looked pointedly at the spot where Lamb's wallet nestled in his inside pocket. It was clear that mere promises were no longer cutting ice.

Finishing his geography lesson, the policeman glanced across. Lamb nodded at him, and received a similar nod back. Then he asked the weasel: 'Worked here long?'

'Nineteen years,' the weasel said. His tone suggested this was something to be proud of.

'Well if you want to make it to nineteen years and a day, start playing nice. Because I've spent nineteen years and then some finding things out people don't want me to know, so a bit of publicly available information from a turd in a uniform really shouldn't be this hard to acquire. Don't you think?'

The weasel looked round for the policeman, who was now ambling towards a coffee booth.

'Oh, seriously,' Lamb said. 'Can he get here before I break your nose?'

Nothing in his physical appearance suggested Lamb could move quickly, but something about his presence suggested you'd be unwise to dismiss the possibility. He watched this calculation crawl across the weasel's face, and, while it was struggling to its conclusion, yawned ferociously. When lions yawn, it doesn't mean they're tired. It means they're waking up.

The weasel said, 'Platform two.'

'Lead the way,' Lamb said. 'I'm looking for a hat.'

In St James's Park, Webb had handed over a pink cardboard folder, its flap sealed with a sticky label, and taken his leave. Louisa and Min were now heading for the City, but were walking round the lake first, in case this turned out to be a short cut.

'If he'd said HMG once more, I'd have had to LOL,' Louisa said.

'Mmm. What? Oh, right. Good one.'

He sounded miles away.

'The wheel is turning,' she noted. 'But the hamster's dead.'

Min proved her point by grunting in reply.

She took his arm because they could always pretend this was cover. On a rock in the middle of the lake, a pelican stretched its wings. It was like watching a golf umbrella do aerobics.

She said, 'You've been eating your wheaties, haven't you?'

'Meaning what?'

'I thought you were gunna challenge him to a wrestling match.'

This earned a sheepish grin. 'Yeah. Well. He got on my tits.'

Louisa smiled, but kept it on the inside. Min had changed these past few months, and she was aware that she was the cause of it. On the other hand, she was equally aware that any woman would have done: Min was having sex again, and that would put a spring in anyone's step. Like her own, his life had gone down the pan a few years back: in Min's case, the pivotal moment had been leaving a classified disk on a Tube train. His marriage had been collateral damage. As for Louisa, she'd screwed up a tail job, an error which had put guns on the street. But a few months ago they'd stirred themselves out of their individual torpors enough to start an affair, at the same time Slough House had gone briefly live. Things had settled since, but optimism hadn't entirely died. They suspected Jackson Lamb now had serious dope on Diana Taverner; enough that, if she wasn't his sock puppet, she was at least in his debt.

And debt meant power.

Louisa said, 'Webb's the one River put on the floor, isn't he?'

'That's right.'

'I'm surprised he got up again.'

Min said, 'You think River's that tough?'

'Don't you?'

'Not especially.'

She barked a little laugh.

'What?'

'You. That shoulder roll you gave when you said that.' She gave an exaggerated imitation. 'Like, not as tough as me.'

'I did not.'

'Yes you did.' She gave the roll again. 'Like that. Like you were on *World's Strongest Man* or something.'

'I did not. And all I meant was, sure, River can probably handle himself. But he's hardly likely to dismantle Lady Di's lapdog, is he?'

'Depends what the lapdog did to him.'

They rounded the lake. Padding about on the grass, on feet too big for their legs, were two annoying birds neither could identify, while a short distance away a black swan glided. It looked cross.

'You okay with this?'

She shrugged. 'Babysitting. Hardly high excitement.'

'Gets us out of the office.'

'When it's not keeping us there. There'll be paperwork. Wonder what Lamb'll say.'

Min stopped so Louisa, her arm still through his, came to a halt too. Together they watched the swan patrol the choppy fringe of the lake, and jab without warning at something below the surface; its neck momentarily becoming a bar of black light beneath the water.

She said, 'Black swans. I was reading about them the other day.'

'What, they're on a takeaway menu? That's kind of sick.'

'Behave. It was in one of the Sundays. It's a phrase, black swan,' she said. 'Means a totally unexpected event with a big impact. But one that seems predictable afterwards, with the benefit of hindsight.'

'Mmm.'

They walked on. After a while, Louisa said, 'So what were you thinking back then? When you were so far away?'

He said, 'I was thinking last time we got dragged into a Regent's Park op, someone was looking to screw us over.'

The black swan dipped its neck once more, and buried its head in the water.

Shirley Dander lifted her take-out coffee cup, found it cold, and drank from it anyway. Then said, 'Standish?'

'The Lady Catherine . . .' Marcus made a swigging gesture with his right hand. 'She likes the bottle.'

That didn't sound right. Catherine Standish was wound pretty tight, and with her curiously old-fashioned way of dressing resembled Alice in Wonderland grown middle-aged and disappointed. But Marcus seemed sure:

'She's dry now. Years, probably. But if I know drunks, and I've known a few, she could have put me under the table in her day. You too. Sequentially.'

'You make her sound like a boxer.'

'Your really serious drunk approaches booze like it is a barfight. You know, only one of you's going to be left standing. And the drunk always thinks that'll be him. Her, in this case.'

'But now she's hung up her drinking shoes.'

'They all think they've done that too.'

'Cartwright? He crashed King's Cross.'

'I know. I saw the movie.'

Video footage of River Cartwright's disastrous assessment exercise, which had caused a rush-hour panic in one of London's major railway stations, was occasionally used for training purposes, to Cartwright's less than delight.

'His grandfather's some kind of legend. David Cartwright?'

'Before my time.'

'He's Cartwright's grandfather,' Marcus said. 'He's before all our times. But he was a spook back in the Dark Ages. Still alive, mind.'

'Just as well,' Shirley said. 'He'd be turning in his grave otherwise. Cartwright being a slow horse and all.'

Marcus Longridge pushed further back from his desk and stretched his arms wide. He could block doorways, Shirley thought. Probably had, back in Ops: he'd been on raids; had closed down an active terrorist cell a year or so back. That was the story, anyway, but there must have been another story too, or he wouldn't be here now.

He was staring at her. His eyes were blacker than his skin: a thought that reached her unprompted. 'What?'

'What was your edge?'

'My edge, huh?'

'That meant they couldn't sack you.'

'I know what you meant.' Somewhere overhead, a chair scraped on a floor; footsteps crossed to a window. 'I told them I was gay,' she said at last.

'Uh-huh?'

'And no way were they gunna fire a dyke for punching out some arsehole who felt her up in the canteen.'

'Is that why you cut your hair?'

'No,' she said. 'I cut my hair because I felt like it.'

'Are we on the same side?'

'I'm on nobody's side but my own.'

He nodded. 'Suit yourself.'

'I intend to.'

She turned back to her monitor, which had fallen asleep. When she shifted her mouse it grumpily revealed a screen frozen on a split-image of two faces so obviously not a match that the program must have been taking the piss.

'So are you actually gay? Or did you just tell them that?'

Shirley didn't reply.

On a bench at Oxford station sat Jackson Lamb; overcoat swamping him either side, undone shirt button allowing a hairy glimpse of stomach. He scratched this absently, then fumbled with the button before giving up and covering the mound instead with a black fedora, on which he then concentrated his gaze, as if it held the secret of the grail.

A black hat. Left on a bus. The bus Dickie Bow had died on.

Which didn't in itself mean much, but Jackson Lamb wondered.

It had been raining heavily when that bus reached Oxford, and first thing you'd do on stepping off a bus into the rain was put your hat on, if you had one. And if you didn't have one, first thing you'd do was go back for it. Unless you didn't want to draw attention to yourself; wanted to remain part of the crowd heading onto the platform, boarding a train, being carried away from the scene as quickly as possible . . .

He was being stared at, pointedly, by a woman who was far too attractive to be doing so out of amateur interest. Except, Lamb realised, it wasn't him she was staring at but the cigarette he now noticed he held between two fingers of his left hand, the one he was tapping the fedora with. His right was already rummaging for a lighter, a motion not dissimilar from scratching his balls. He gave her his best crooked smile, which involved flaring one nostril, and she responded by flaring both her own, and looking away. But he tucked the fag behind his ear anyway.

The rummaging hand gave up the search for a lighter, and found instead the mobile phone he'd collected from the bus.

It was an ancient thing, a Nokia, black-and-grey, with about as many functions as a bottle opener. You could no more take a photo with it than send an e-mail with a stapler. But when he pressed the button, the screen squeaked into life, and let him scroll down a contact list. Five numbers: Shop, Digs, and Star, which sounded like Bow's local, and two actual names; a Dave and a Lisa, both of which Lamb rang. Dave's mobile went straight to voicemail. Lisa's landline went nowhere; was a gateway to a humming void in which no telephone would ever be answered. He clicked onto Messages, and found only a note from Bow's service provider informing him he had 82p in his pay-as-you-go account. Lamb wondered what fraction of Bow's worldly goods 82p represented. Maybe he could send Lisa a cheque. He scrolled on to Sent Items. That was empty too.

But Dickie Bow had fished his mobile out shortly before dying, and had jammed it between the cushions of his seat, as if to make sure it would only be found by someone looking for it. By someone for whom he had a message.

An unsent message, as it turned out.

A train arrived, but Lamb remained on his bench. Not many people got off; not many got on. As it pulled away Lamb saw the attractive young woman glowering at him through a window and he farted quietly in response: a private victory, but satisfying. Then he examined the phone again. Drafts. There was a Drafts folder for text messages. He opened this, and the single-word entry of a single saved message stared back from the tiny screen.

Near his feet a pigeon scratched the ground in imitation of a bird that might make an effort. Lamb didn't notice. He was absorbed in that single word, keyed into the phone but never transmitted; locked forever in its black-and-grey box, alongside 82 pence-worth of unused communication. As if a dying word could be breathed into a bottle, and corked up, and released once the grim business of tidying away the corpse had been seen to: here on an Oxfordshire railway platform, with a late March sun struggling to make itself felt, and a fat pigeon tramping underfoot. One word.

'*Cicadas*,' Jackson Lamb said out loud. Then said it again. '*Cicadas*.'

And then he said, 'Fuck me.'

3

SHIRLEY DANDER AND Marcus Longridge had settled back into their tasks; the atmosphere only slightly altered by their conversation. In Slough House, sound seeped easily. If he were interested Roderick Ho might have rested his head against the wall separating his office from theirs, the better to hear them, but all he registered was the familiar buzz of other people establishing relationships – he was, anyway, busy updating his online status: adding a paragraph to Facebook describing his weekend at Chamonix; tweeting a link to his latest dancemix . . . Ho's name for these purposes was Roddy Hunt; his tunes were looted from obscure sites he subsequently torched; his photos were tweaked stills of a young Montgomery Clift. It still amazed Ho you could build a man from links and screenshots, launch him into the world like a paper boat, and he'd just keep sailing. All of the details that built up a person could be real. The only thing fake was the person . . . Constructing a mythical work pattern for his user ID had been the most brilliant thing Ho had accomplished this year. Anyone monitoring his computer-time would confirm his constant presence on the Service network, compiling an operations archive.

So Ho was uninterested in Shirley and Marcus's chattering, and the office above theirs was empty, because Harper and Guy weren't yet back. If they had been, it's likely that one would have knelt with an ear to the floor, and relayed each word to the other. And if River Cartwright had been in there, instead of in the room above Ho's, he might have done the same: it would have relieved the boredom. Which he should have been used to but it kept recurring, like a week-old insect bite that wouldn't quit. Though if that analogy were to ring true, River now thought, he'd have to be wearing boxing gloves too: unable to scratch; just rubbing away without effect.

Until a few months ago he had shared this room. Now it was his alone, though a second desk remained, equipped with a PC that was newer, faster and less battered than River's. He could have commandeered it, but Service PCs were user-specific, and he'd have had to log a request for IT to reassign it; a thirty-minute job that could take eight months. And while he could have short-circuited the process by asking Ho to do it, this would have involved asking Ho to do it, and he wasn't that desperate.

He drummed an off-beat rhythm with his fingers, and studied the ceiling. Exactly the kind of pointless noise that could draw a returning thump from Jackson Lamb, meaning both *shut up* and *come here*. The fact that there wasn't much to do didn't stop Lamb dreaming up tasks. Last week he'd sent River out collecting takeaway cartons: River had plucked them from bins, gutters, car roofs; had found a trove in a Barbican flowerbed, chewed by rats or foxes. Then Lamb had made him compare them with his own collection, the fruit of six months' afternoon snacking: he'd become convinced that Sam Yu, frontman of the New Empire next door, was giving him smaller cartons than everyone else, and was 'working up the evidence'. Borderline Lamb: he might have meant it, might have been taking the piss. Either way, River was the one up to his elbows in bins.

For a while, a few months back, it had looked like things were changing. After years of squatting upstairs, happily dumping on the poor saps below, Lamb had appeared to be taking an interest; at the very least, had enjoyed putting the screws on Lady Di Taverner at Regent's Park. But the mould was showing through again: Lamb had grown bored with excitement, preferring the comfortably unchanging days, so River was still here, and Slough House was still Slough House. And the work was the same gruntwork it had always been.

Today was a case in point. Today, he was a typist. Yesterday he'd been a scanner-operator; today the scanner wouldn't work, so today he was a typist, entering pre-digital death records onto a database. The deceased had all been six months old or younger, and had died while rationing was still enforced: prime targets for identity theft. Back then, you worked this by taking names from gravestones; a less innocent form of brass-rubbing. Birth certificates were then claimed lost and copies sought; after that, you simply traced the life the infant might have led, with all its attendant paperwork: National Insurance number, bank account, driving licence . . . All of the details that built up a person could be faked. The only thing real was the person. But anyone who'd actually done this would be collecting a pension by now. Any sleepers using the names River had found could have called themselves Rip van Winkle instead. So it was just makework for the slow horses, plugging gaps in a history book, nothing more. And where was Jackson Lamb?

Sitting here wouldn't answer that. Having risen without consciously deciding to, River went with the flow: out of his office, up the stairs. The top floor was always dark. Even when Lamb's door was open, his blinds were drawn, and Catherine's office, at the back of the building, sat in the shadow of a nearby office block. Catherine preferred lamps to overhead lighting – the only trait she shared with Lamb – and these didn't so much dispel the gloom as accentuate it, casting twin pools of yellow light between which murkiness swarmed. Her monitor gave a grey glow, and in its wash, as River entered her room, she seemed a figment from a fairy tale: a pale lady, hoarding wisdom.

River plonked himself on a chair next to a pile of vari-coloured folders. While the rest of the world pursued a digital agenda, Lamb insisted on hard copy. He'd once toyed with instigating an employee-of-the-month award, based solely on weight of output. If he'd had a pair of scales, and an attention span, River didn't doubt he'd have done so.

'Let me guess,' Catherine said. 'You've finished what you were doing, and want some more work.'

'Ho ho. What's he up to, Catherine?'

'He doesn't tell me.' She seemed amused that River thought he might. 'He does what he does. He doesn't ask my permission.'

'But you're closest to him.'

Her expression wavered not one inch.

'Geographically, I mean. You take his calls. You manage his diary.'

'His diary's empty, River. Mostly he stares at the ceiling and farts.'

'It's a captivating picture.'

'He smokes in there too. And it's a government office.'

'We could make a citizen's arrest.'

'We might want to practise on someone smaller.'

'I don't know how you stand it.'

'Oh, I offer it up.' Fear flashed in River's eyes. 'Joke? He'd drive a saint to suicide, anyway. Frankly, whatever he's up to, I'm just relieved he's somewhere else.'

'He's not at the Park,' River said. When Lamb was at the Park, he made sure everyone knew it. Probably hoping someone would break, and ask if they could come too. 'But something's up. He's been weird. Even for Lamb.'

Lamb's weirdness would pass for normality in other people. His phone had rung, and he'd answered it. He'd had Ho unfreeze his browser, which meant he'd been online. In fact, he'd given the impression of having a job to do.

'And he hasn't said a word,' River said.

'Not one.'

'So you've no idea what's lured him onto the streets.'

'Oh, I didn't say that,' Catherine said.

River studied her, an old-fashioned creature whose pale

colouring spoke of an indoor life. Her clothes covered her wrist to ankle. She wore hats, for god's sake. He guessed she was fiftyish, and until the business last year he hadn't paid her much attention; there was little in a wall-hugging woman her age to interest an uptight man of his. But when things had turned nasty she hadn't panicked. She'd even pointed a gun at Spider Webb – as had River. This shared experience made them fellow-members of a select club.

She was waiting for him to respond. He said, 'Tell?'

'Who's Lamb send for when he needs something?'

'Ho,' River said.

'Exactly. And you know how sound travels here.'

'You heard them talking?'

'No,' Catherine said. 'That's what was interesting.'

Interesting because Lamb was not in the habit of modulating his tones. 'So whatever it is, it's not for the likes of us.'

'But Roddy knows.'

It was also interesting that Catherine called Ho Roddy. Nobody else called Ho anything. He wasn't someone you engaged in casual chat, because if you didn't come with broadband, you weren't worth his attention.

On the other hand, he currently possessed information River would like to share.

'Well then,' he said. 'Let's go talk to Roddy, shall we?'

'Nice,' said Min.

'Best you can do?'

'Spectacular, then. Better?'

'Much.'

They were on the seventy-seventh floor of one of the City's newest buildings; a great glass needle that soared eighty storeys into London's skies. And it was some room they were in, a huge one, *yay* metres long and *woah* metres wide, with floor-to-ceiling views to north and west of the capital, and then the wide space beyond, where the capital gave up and the sky took over. She could spend days in here, Louisa thought; not eating, not drinking; just taking in as much of the view as she could, in every weather, and all types of light. 'Spectacular' didn't come close.

Even the lift had been a thrill: quieter, smoother and faster than any she'd known.

Min said, 'Cool, wasn't it?'

'The lift?'

'At Reception. The plastic cops.'

The security guys, who'd checked their Service ID with what Min had interpreted as awe and envy. Louisa thought it more the look state kids aimed at their public school counterparts: the age-old enmity of yobs vs toffs. A long-time yob herself, she savoured the irony.

She laid her palm against the glass. Then rested her forehead there. This brought a delicious feeling of safe vertigo; set a butterfly fluttering in her stomach, even while her brain enjoyed the view. Min stood by, hands in pockets.

'This the highest you've been?' she asked.

He gave her a slow look. '*Duh*, aeroplane?'

'Yeah, no. Highest building.'

'Empire State.'

'Been there, done that.'

'Twin Towers?'

She shook her head. 'They were already gone when I was there.'

'Me too,' he said.

They were quiet for a while, watching London operate way below, thinking similar thoughts: of a morning when people in a different city had stood at greater heights, enjoying similar views from different windows, not knowing they'd never put their feet on the ground again; that the threads of their future had been severed with box cutters.

Now Min pointed, and following his finger she saw a speck in the distance. An aeroplane: not one of the liners leaving

48

Heathrow, but a small, buzzy machine, ploughing its own furrow.

Min said, 'I wonder how close they get?'

'You think it's that important?' Louisa said. 'This mini-summit? Big enough for a . . . replay?'

She didn't have to specify what it would be a replay of.

After a while, Min said, 'No, I guess not.'

Or it wouldn't have been entrusted to them, Regent's Park audit or not.

'Got to do it properly, though.'

'Look at all the angles,' she agreed.

'Else we end up looking bad even when nothing bad happens.'

'You think this is a test of some kind?'

'Of what?'

'Us,' she said. 'Finding out if we're up to the job.'

'And if we pass it, we get back to Regent's Park?'

She shrugged. 'Whatever.'

This many people had made the return journey from Slough House to the Park: none. They both knew that. But like every slow horse before them, Min and Louisa hid secret hopes their story would be different.

At length she turned and surveyed the room. Still *yay* metres long and *woah* metres wide, it took up about half of the floor; the separate suite, also currently vacant, enjoying the views south and east. There was a shared lobby area where the smart lifts arrived; a third, the service lift, lay behind the stairwell, which was a vision of eternal descent. It passed floors and floors of high-end corporate offices, only some of which were yet occupied: the list in the folder Webb had provided included banks, investment companies, yacht salesmen, diamond merchants, a defence contractor. The tower's lower section was a hotel, its grand opening scheduled for the following month. She'd read it was fully booked through the next five years.

Spider Webb must have called in favours, or opened some classified folders, to secure the suite for his meeting, a few weeks hence. Any part of town, a space like this commanded respect. This high up, it demanded awe. Kitchen and bathrooms aside, it was a single room, designed for business; its centrepiece a beautiful mahogany oval table big enough for sixteen chairs, which, if it hadn't been larger than Louisa's entire flat, she'd have coveted. But like the view, the table belonged to the moneyed. This wasn't supposed to factor into her motivation, but still. Here they were, the pair of them, and they'd be ensuring the safety of some hotshot whose pocket change equalled twice their joint salaries.

Forget it, she thought. Not relevant. But couldn't help saying: 'Kind of flash for a discreet meeting.'

'Yeah, well,' Min said. 'Don't suppose they'll have anyone peeping through the windows.'

'How do they clean them, do you think?'

'Some kind of hoist? We'd better find out.'

That was just for starters. They'd need an itinerary; where the Russian was staying, and the route from there to here. Who was catering. Drivers. They'd need to study Webb's notes and do extra digging, because Webb was as trustworthy as a snake. And they'd need sweepers to check for bugs, and maybe a techie to provide interference, though she doubted parabolic eavesdropping was possible. The nearest high building was a dwarf by comparison.

Min touched her shoulder. 'We'll be fine. Jumped-up Russkie oligarch is all. Coming over here. Buying our football teams. It's babysitting, like Webb said.'

She knew. But Russkie oligarchs weren't the most popular breed on the planet, and there was always the possibility something would go wrong. And underneath that, a very faint glimmer of possibility that everything would go right.

It swam into her mind again that this could be a test. And alongside it swam a creepier notion: What if a successful outcome resulted in a single ticket home; a desk at Regent's Park for one of them but not the other? If it were hers, would she take it?

If it were Min's, would he? He might. She couldn't blame him. She might too.

All the same, she shrugged his hand off her shoulder.

'What's up?'

'Nothing. We're at work, that's all.'

Min said, 'Sure. Sorry,' but there was nothing snarky in his tone.

He wandered towards the doors, through which lay the lifts, the other suite, the stairwell. Louisa, in his wake, veered off into the kitchen. It was spotless, unused, gleaming, and fully equipped with a fridge that was restaurant-sized, but empty. Fixed to the wall was a friendly red fire extinguisher; next to it, behind a glass cover, a fire blanket and a small axe. She opened bare cupboards, closed them again. Returned to the big room and its windows, through which she could now see an air-ambulance, seemingly stationary over central London, though possibly swinging like a randy divorcee from the point of view of those it carried. And she thought again of the black swans, and the huge and improbable events they'd lent their name to. It was only afterwards you knew you'd encountered one. The helicopter was still hovering there when she went to find Min.

Ho didn't like having his space invaded. Especially not by River Cartwright, who was one of those who ignored the likes of Roderick Ho except when he needed something only the likes of Roderick Ho could provide. Technological competence, for instance. Competence was generally beyond Cartwright. For a while, Ho had used a CCTV still of the King's Cross chaos as a screensaver, until Louisa Guy suggested River might break his elbows if he found out.

But Catherine Standish was with him, and while Ho didn't precisely like Standish, he couldn't put his finger on a reason for disliking her. Since this put her in a select category, he decided to see what they wanted before telling them he was busy.

River made a space on the spare desk, and perched on its corner. Catherine pulled out a chair and sat. 'How are you today, Roddy?'

His eyes narrowed with suspicion. She'd called him that before. He said to River, 'Don't move my stuff.'

'I haven't moved anything.'

'My stuff on the desk there, you just rearranged it. I've got everything sorted. You put it out of order, I won't be able to find it.'

River opened his mouth to make a number of points, but Catherine caught his eye. He changed direction. 'Sorry.'

Catherine said, 'Roddy, we were wondering if you could do us a favour.'

'What sort of favour?'

'It involves your area of expertise.'

'If you want broadband,' Ho said, 'maybe you should just think about paying for it.'

'That would be like asking a plastic surgeon to do ingrown toenails,' Catherine said.

'Yeah,' said River. 'Or getting an architect to wash your windows.'

Ho regarded him suspiciously.

'Or a lion tamer to feed your cat,' River added.

The look Catherine flashed him indicated that he wasn't helping.

'The other day, in Lamb's office,' she began, but Ho wasn't having it.

'No way.'

'I hadn't finished.'

'You don't need to. You want to know what Lamb wanted, right?'

'Just a clue.'

'He'd kill me. And he could do it, too. He's killed people before.'

'That's what he wants you to think,' River said.

'You're saying he hasn't?'

'I'm saying he's not allowed to kill staff. Health and safety.'

'Yeah, right. But I'm not talking *killing* killing.' Ho turned back to Catherine. 'He'd kill me on a daily basis. You know what he's like.'

'He doesn't need to find out,' she said.

'He always finds out.'

River said, 'Roddy?'

'Don't call me that.'

'Whatever. A few months ago, we did a good thing. Yes?'

'Maybe,' Ho said, suspiciously. 'So what?'

'That was teamwork.'

'It was kind of teamwork,' Ho admitted.

'So—'

'The kind where I had all the ideas. You did a lot of running around, I remember.'

River bit back his first response. 'We all play to our strengths,' he said. 'My point is, for a while there, Slough House worked. Know what I mean? We played as a team, and it worked.'

'So now we do it again,' Ho said.

'That would be good, yes.'

'Only this time, instead of running around, you just sit there. While I do all the work again.' He turned to Catherine. 'And then Lamb finds out and kills me.'

River said, 'Okay, how about this. You don't tell us anything, but we find out anyway, and tell him you told us. Then he kills you.'

Catherine said, 'River—'

'No, seriously. Lamb never locks his computer, and we all know what his password is.'

Lamb's password was 'Password'.

Ho said, 'If you were gunna do that, you'd have done it. You wouldn't be bothering me.'

'No, well, it hadn't occurred to me till now.' He looked at Catherine. 'What's the opposite of teamwork?'

She said, 'It's not going to happen, Roddy. He's kidding.'

'It doesn't sound like he's kidding.'

'Well he is.' She looked at River. 'Isn't that right?'

He surrendered. 'Whatever.'

She said to Ho, 'You don't have to tell us anything you don't want to.'

As an interrogation technique, thought River, this lacked bite.

Ho chewed his lip and looked at his monitor. This was angled so River couldn't see it, but reflected in Ho's glasses he could make out a thin tracery of lines cobwebbing the screen, and green lights blinking on a black background. Ho could be navigating his way through an MoD firewall, or playing Battleships with himself, but either way, he seemed to be contemplating something else altogether at the moment.

'All right,' he said at last.

'There,' River said. 'That wasn't so hard, was it?'

'I wasn't talking to you. I'll tell her.'

'For fuck's sake, Ho, she'll tell me herself soon as—'

'And who's "she"?' Catherine asked. 'The cat's mother?'

The two men shared an unlikely moment of mystified brotherhood.

'Never mind,' she said. She pointed at River. 'Out. No arguments.'

There were arguments, and he made a few of them, but only in his head.

Back upstairs, he looked in on Harper and Guy's office, but they weren't back. 'Meeting,' Harper had said when River asked, which might have meant a meeting, or might have meant they were taking advantage of Lamb's absence to do whatever they did these days: a walk in the park, a movie, sex in Louisa's car. Park, though . . . They couldn't have gone to Regent's Park, could they? The thought stilled him, but only for a moment. It didn't sound likely.

In his own room, he spent five minutes reacquainting himself with the database of the dead and another ten staring out from behind the window's worn gilt lettering: *W. W. Henderson, Solicitor and Commissioner for Oaths*. There were three people at the bus stop opposite, and as River watched a bus arrived and took them all away. Immediately someone else arrived, and began waiting for the next bus. River wondered how she'd react if she knew she was being watched by a member of the Intelligence Service. Wondered, too, what she'd make of the notion that she almost certainly had a more exciting job than his.

He wandered back to his computer, where he entered a fictitious name and dates on the database, thought for a bit, then deleted them.

Catherine knocked and entered. 'You busy?' she said. 'This can wait.'

'Ha bloody ha.'

She sat. 'Lamb wanted a Service personnel file.'

'Ho doesn't have access to those.'

'Very funny. File was on an occasional from the eighties. A man called Dickie Bow.'

'You're kidding, right?'

'Real name Bough, but his parents were stupid enough to call him Richard. I take it you've never heard of him.'

River said, 'Give me a moment.'

He leaned back, mentally refocusing on an image of the O.B. – Old Bastard, an epithet bestowed by River's mother. He'd been largely raised by the O.B., whose long life had been dedicated to the Intelligence Service, and much of whose long retirement was spent doling out its highlights to his only grandson. River Cartwright was a spook because that's what his grandfather was. Not had been: was. Some professions you never gave up, long after they were over. David Cartwright was a Service legend, but the way he told it, the same held true for the lowliest bagman: you could change sides, sell your secrets, offer your memoirs to the highest bidder, but once a spook you were always a spook, and everything else was just cover. So the friendly old man trowelling his flowerbeds with a silly hat on remained the strategist who'd helped plot the Service's course through the Cold War, and River had grown up learning the details.

Which mattered. This, the O.B. had drummed into him before he was ten. Details mattered. River blinked once, then again, but came back with nothing: Dickie Bow? A ridiculous name, but not one River had heard before.

'Sorry,' he said. 'It means nothing.'

'He was found dead last week,' she said.

'In suspicious circumstances?'

'On a bus.'

He clasped his hands behind his head. 'The floor's yours.'

'Bow was on a train to Worcester, but it was cancelled at Reading because of signalling problems. The bus was taking passengers from there to Oxford, where the trains were okay. At Oxford everyone got off, except Bow. This was because he'd died en route.'

'Natural causes?'

'So the report says. And Bow's not been on the books for a while. So not what you'd call an obvious candidate for assassination, even if he'd ever done anything important.'

'Which you're sure he hadn't.'

'You know what personnel records are like. Secure stuff's redacted, and anything more sensitive than a routine drop-and-poke is secure. But Bow's file's an open book barring some drink-related incident near the end. He did a lot of toad work. Cash for info, mostly gossip. He worked in a nightclub, so he picked up a lot.'

'Which would have been used for blackmail purposes.'

'Of course.'

'So revenge isn't out of the question.'

'But it was all a long time ago. And like I say, natural causes.'

'So why's Lamb interested?' River mused.

'No idea. Maybe they worked together.' She paused. 'A note

says he was a talented streetwalker. That doesn't mean what it sounds like, does it?'

'Happily, no. It means he was good at shadowing people. Following them.'

'Well, then. Maybe Lamb just heard he'd died, and got sentimental.'

'Yes, but seriously.'

Catherine said, 'Bow didn't have a ticket for his journey. And he was supposed to be at work. I wonder where was he going?'

'I'd never heard of him until two minutes ago. I doubt my speculations are worth much.'

'Mine either. But it's got Lamb off his arse, so there must be something to it.' She fell silent. To River, her gaze seemed to turn inward, as if she were looking for something she'd left at the back of her mind. And he noticed for the first time that her hair wasn't entirely grey; that in the right light, might even look blonde. But her nose was long and pinched, and she wore hats, and it all added up to a kind of greyness, so that was how you saw her when she wasn't there, and after a while became the way you saw her even when she was. A sort of witchiness that might even be sexy in the right circumstances.

To break the spell, he spoke. 'Wonder what kind of something.'

'Assume the worst,' Catherine said.

'Maybe we should ask him.'

Catherine said, 'I'm not sure that's such a good idea.'

It wasn't such a good idea.

A few hours later, River heard Lamb whomping up the stairs like an out-of-breath bear. He waited a while, staring at his monitor without seeing it. 'Maybe we should ask him.' Simple enough while Lamb was elsewhere; a different proposition with him on the premises. But the alternative was to sit looking at reams of indigestible information, and besides, if River backed down, Catherine would think him chicken.

She was waiting on the landing, eyebrow raised. *Sure about this?*

Well, no.

Lamb's door was open. Catherine tapped, and they went in. Lamb was trying to turn his computer on: he still wore his coat and an unlit cigarette dangled from his mouth. He eyed them as if they were Mormons. 'What's this, an intervention?'

River said, 'We were wondering what's going on.'

Puzzled, Lamb stared at River, then plucked the cigarette from his lips and stared at that instead. Then returned it to his mouth and stared at River again. 'Eh?'

'We were—'

'Yeah, I got that. I was having a what-the-fuck moment.' He looked at Catherine. 'You're a drunk, so wondering what's happening's a daily experience. What's his excuse?'

'Dickie Bow,' Catherine said. Lamb's crack didn't visibly affect her, but she'd been in the business a while. She'd been Charles Partner's PA while Partner had run the Service; had filled that role until finding him dead in his bathtub, though her career had been interrupted by, yes, being a drunk. Along the way, she'd picked up clues about hiding emotions. 'He was in Berlin same time as you. And died last week on a bus outside Oxford. That's where you've been, isn't it? Tracing his journey.'

Lamb shook his head in disbelief. 'What happened? Someone come round and sew your balls back on? I told you not to answer the door to strangers.'

'We don't like being out of the loop.'

'You're always out of the loop. The loop's miles away. Nearest you'll get to being in the loop is when they make a documentary about it and show it on the History Channel. I thought you were aware of that. Oh god, here's another one.'

Marcus Longridge had appeared behind them, carrying a manila folder. 'I'm supposed to give this to—'

Lamb said, 'I've forgotten your name.'

'Longridge,' said Marcus.

'I don't want to know. I was making a point.' Lamb plucked a stained mug from the litter on his desk, and threw it at Catherine. River caught it before it reached her head. Lamb said, 'Well, I'm glad we've had this chat. Now fuck off. Cartwright, give that to Standish. Standish, fill it with tea. And you, I've forgotten your name again, go next door and get my lunch. Tell Sam I want my usual Tuesday.'

'It's Monday.'

'I know it's Monday. If I wanted my usual Monday, I wouldn't have to specify, would I?' He blinked. 'Still here?'

Catherine held his stare a little longer. It had become a matter between the two of them, River realised. He might as well not be here. And for a moment he thought Lamb might look away first, but it didn't happen; Catherine gave a shrug instead, one in which something seemed to leave her body, then turned away. She took the folder Longridge was holding, and went into her office. The other pair trooped downstairs.

So, that went well, he thought.

But before River had been at his desk twenty minutes came a godawful noise from upstairs; the kind you'd get if you tipped a monitor off a high-enough desk that the screen shattered when it hit the deck. It was followed by the scattering rattle of plastic-and-glass shards spreading across the available space. River wasn't the only one who jumped. And everyone in the building heard the oath that followed:

'Fucking hell!'

After that, Slough House went quiet for a while.

The film was grainy, jerky, black-and-white, and showed a train at a platform late in the evening. It was raining: the platform was roofed, but water trickled down from misaligned guttering. Seconds passed while nothing happened. Then came a sudden onrush, as if a gate had been opened offscreen releasing a swarm of anxious passengers. Their jerky motion was due to the film skipping frames. Movements gave it away: the sudden appearance of hands from pockets; umbrellas folding without warning. Mostly, the expressions on offer betrayed irritation, anxiety, the desire to be elsewhere. River, who was good at faces, recognised no one.

They were in Ho's office, because Ho had the best equipment. After Lamb had tipped his computer over while trying to insert a CD – a piece of slapstick River would have given a month's salary to have witnessed – he'd boiled in his room half an hour, then stalked downstairs as if this had been the plan all along. Catherine Standish followed a moment later. It might have been residual embarrassment which prevented Lamb from protesting when the other slow horses assembled in his wake, though River doubted it. Jackson Lamb couldn't have defined embarrassment without breaking into a sweat. And once he'd given Ho the CD, and it was up and running, it was clear he expected them all to watch. Questions would follow.

There was no sound; nothing to indicate where this was happening. When the platform cleared the train began to move, and there were no clues there, either: it simply jerked into motion and pulled out of view. What was left was an empty platform and a railway track, onto which heavy rain fell. After four or five seconds of this, which might have been fifteen or twenty in real time, the screen went black. The entire sequence had lasted no more than three minutes.

'And again,' Lamb said.

Ho tapped keys, and they watched it again.

This time, when it stopped, Lamb said, 'Well?'

Min Harper said, 'CCTV footage.'

'Brilliant. Anyone got anything intelligent to add?'

Marcus Longridge said, 'That's a west-bound train. They run out of Paddington into Wales and Somerset. The Cotswolds. Where was that, Oxford?'

'Yes. But I still can't remember your name.'

River said, 'I'll make him a badge. Meanwhile, what about the bald guy?'

'Which bald guy?'

'About a minute and a half in. Most of the others pile onto the train, but he walks up the platform, past the camera. Presumably he gets on board further up.'

'Why him?' Lamb asked.

'Because it's pouring. If everyone else is getting on the train within view of the camera, that suggests the rest of the platform's not covered. They're all trying to stay out of the rain. But he's not. And it's not like he's carrying an umbrella.'

'Or wearing a hat,' Lamb said.

'Like the one you brought in.'

Lamb paused a beat, then said, 'Like that, yes.'

'If that's Oxford,' Catherine said, 'then that's the crowd just got off the bus Dickie Bow died on. Right?'

Looking at Ho, Lamb said, 'You have been a busy bee. Anything else you've made public I should know about? My dental records? Bank account?'

Ho was still smarting from being reduced to entertainments officer. 'That'd be like asking a plastic surgeon to do your ingrown toenails.'

'I hope you don't think I'm insulting you,' Lamb said kindly. 'I—'

'Because when that happens you'll know all about it, you slanty-eyed twat.' He turned to the others. 'Okay,' he said. 'Cartwright wasn't wrong. And it's not often I get to say that. Our bald friend, let's call him Mr B, got on a train at Oxford last Tuesday evening. The train was headed for Worcester, but stopped several times along the way. Where'd Mr B get off?'

'Are we supposed to guess?' Min asked.

'Yes. Because I'm really interested in pointless speculation.'

River said, 'You got this footage from Oxford?'

'Well done.'

'Presumably other stations will have coverage too.'

'And aren't there cameras on trains these days?' Louisa put in.

Lamb clapped. 'This is fantastic,' he said. 'It's like having little elves to do my thinking for me. So, now you've established those facts, which would have taken an idiot half the time, let's move on to the more important business of me telling one of you to go check out such coverage and bring me an answer.'

'I can do that,' River said.

Lamb ignored him. 'Harper,' he said. 'This could be up your street. It doesn't involve carrying anything, so you don't need worry about losing it.'

Min glanced at Louisa.

'Whoah,' said Lamb. He looked at Ho. 'Did you see that?'

'See what?'

'Harper just shared a little glance with his girlfriend. I wonder what that means.' He leaned back in Ho's chair and steepled his fingers under his chin. 'You're going to tell me you can't.'

'We've been given an assignment,' Harper said.

'"We"?'

'Louisa and—'

'Call her Guy. It's not a disco.'

The thing to do here, they all decided independently, was not waste a whole lot of time asking why that might make it a disco.

'And also,' Lamb went on, '"Assignment"?'

Min said, 'We've been seconded. Webb said you'd know about it by now.'

'Webb? That would be the famous Spider? Isn't he in charge of counting paperclips?'

'He does other stuff too,' Louisa said.

'Like, ah, *second* my staff? For an "assignment"? Which is what, precisely? And please say you're not allowed to give me details.'

'Babysitting a visiting Russian.'

'I thought they had professionals for that sort of thing,' Lamb said. 'You know, people who know what they're doing. Except, don't tell me, this is Sir Len's legacy, right? What a circus. If we're that worried about him fiddling the books, why didn't we stop him years ago?'

'Because we didn't know he was doing it?' Catherine suggested.

'We're supposed to be the fucking Intelligence Service,' Lamb pointed out. 'Okay, you're seconded. I don't get a say in the matter, do I?' The wolfish grin which accompanied this carried a promise of happier days, when he would have a say in the matter, and would say it loud and clear. 'Which leaves me with this crew.'

'I'll do it,' River said again.

'For Christ's sake, this is MI5, not a kiddies' playground. Operational decisions don't turn on who says bagsies. I decide who goes.' Lamb counted them off from the right. 'Eenie meenie minie mo.' At mo, his finger rested on River. He moved it back to Shirley. 'Meenie. You're it.'

River said, 'I was mo!'

'And I don't base operational decisions on children's games. Remember?' He pressed eject, and the CD drawer slid open. He tossed the disc in Shirley's direction, and it sailed through the open door. 'Butterfingers. Pick that up and watch it again. Then go find Mr B.'

'Now?'

'No, on your own time. Of course now.' He looked round. 'I could have sworn the rest of you had jobs to do.'

Catherine arched her eyebrows at River, and left. The others followed, with visible relief, leaving only Ho and River.

Lamb said to Ho, 'I might have guessed Cartwright would want to continue the discussion. But it beats me why you're still here.'

'It's my office,' Ho explained.

Lamb waited.

Ho sighed, and left.

River said, 'You were always going to do that, weren't you?'

'Do what?'

'All that crap about putting the kettle on, fetching your lunch. It was a wind–up. You need us. Somebody has to do your leg-work.'

'Speaking of legs,' said Jackson Lamb, and raised his so they stuck out horizontally, then farted. 'I was always going to do that, too,' he pointed out. He put his feet back on the ground. 'Doesn't make it any less effective.'

Whatever you thought of Lamb's act, nobody ever accused his farts of lacking authenticity.

'Anyway,' he went on, unperturbed by his toxic gift. 'If it hadn't been for Standish, we wouldn't have gone all round the houses. *Don't like being out of the loop*, for Christ's sake. Can't blame it on the rag at her age. Unless pickling herself in booze all those years had a preservative effect. What do you think?'

'I think it's pretty strange you're so sure Bow was murdered when the post-mortem said his heart gave out.'

'That doesn't answer my question, but I'll let it pass. Here's another one.' Lamb folded his right leg over his left. 'If you wanted to poison someone without anyone finding out, what would you use?'

'I'm not really up on poisons.'

'Hallelujah. Something you're not an expert in.' Lamb had this magic trick: he could produce a cigarette out of almost nowhere; out of the briefest dip into the nearest pocket. In its opposite number he found a disposable lighter. River would have protested, but smoke could only improve the atmosphere. It was improbable Lamb was unaware of this. 'Longridge hasn't brought my lunch yet. I hope the sorry bastard's not forgotten.'

'So you do know his name.'

He regretted that as soon as he'd said it.

Lamb said, 'Jesus, Cartwright. Which of us does that embarrass more?' He took a deep drag on his cigarette, and the coal glowed orange, half an inch long. 'I'll be in late tomorrow,' he said. 'Stuff to do. You know how it is.' A thin cloud of tobacco smoke turned his eyes to slits. 'Don't break your neck down the stairs.'

'Up the stairs,' River said. 'Ho's office, remember?'

'Cartwright?'

River halted in the doorway.

'You don't want to know how Dickie Bow died?'

'You're seriously gunna tell me?'

'It's obvious, when you think about it,' Lamb said. 'Whoever killed him used an untraceable poison.'

4

UNTRACEABLE POISON, thought River Cartwright.
Jesus wept!

On the Tube, an attractive brunette sat next to him, her skirt
riding up as she did so. Almost immediately they fell into
conversation, and, getting off at the same stop, hesitated by the
escalator to exchange numbers. The rest followed like tumbling
dice: wine, pizza, bed, a holiday; first flat, first anniversary, first
child. Fifty years later, they looked back on a blessed existence.
Then they died. River rubbed an eye with a knuckle. The seat
opposite became free, and the woman moved into it, and took
the hand of the man next to her.

From London Bridge River went on to Tonbridge, which his
grandfather inhabited as if it were a territory annexed after a
lifetime's battle. The O.B. could wander to the shops; pick up
paper, milk and groceries; twinkle at butcher, baker, and post
office lady, and none of them would come within a mile of
guessing that hundreds of lives had passed through his hands; that
he'd made decisions and given orders that sometimes had altered
the course of events, and at other times – more crucially, he'd
have said – ensured that everything remained the same. He was
generally thought to have been something in the Ministry of
Transport. Good-naturedly, he took the blame for deficiencies in
the local bus service.

What enormous things must have happened, River sometimes
thought, to make sure that nothing ever changed.

After eating they sat in the study, with whisky. A fire blazed in the grate. Over the years, the old man's chair had moulded itself to hold him like a hammock; the second chair was getting the hang of River. As far as he knew, nobody else ever used it.

'You've something on your mind,' he was told.

'That's not the only reason I come to see you.'

This was dismissed for the irrelevance it was.

'It's Lamb.'

'Jackson Lamb. What about him?'

'I think he's lost his mind.'

The O.B. liked that, River could tell. Liked anything that offered the opportunity for psychological spelunking. And especially liked it when River bowled him a full toss: 'An insight based on your rigorous medical training.'

'He's turning paranoid.'

'If he's only just done that, he'd not have survived this long. But you're saying he's surpassed himself. How's this particular paranoia manifesting?'

'He seems to think there's a KGB wet squad at large.'

The O.B. said, 'Well, on the one hand, the KGB doesn't exist any more. And the Cold War's over. We won, if you're keeping score.'

'I know. I Googled it.'

'But on the other, Russia's president used to run the KGB, who are now the FSB by the way, and they may have changed the letterheads but they wear the same old boots. As for untraceable poisons, that's what the KGB's "Special Office" was all about. The poison factory. Back in the thirties a goon called Mairovsky, Mairanovsky, something like that, spent his whole career dreaming up untraceable poisons. Got so good at it they had to kill him.'

River looked down at his glass. He only ever drank whisky with his grandfather. Maybe that made it a ritual. 'You're saying it's possible.'

'I'm saying that any time Jackson Lamb's worried about an old-time Moscow-style op being run in our backyard, I'd pay attention. The name Litvinenko not ring bells?'

'Not for being untraceably poisoned.'

'Quite. Because that was a black flag operation. You think they couldn't have made it look an accident if they'd wanted?' This was a favourite O.B. trick; turning your argument against you. Another was not giving you a chance to regroup. 'Who's the victim?'

'Name of Bough. Richard Bough.'

'Good Lord. Dickie Bow was still alive?'

'You knew him.'

'Of him. Berlin hand.' Putting his drink down, the O.B. adopted his sage pose: elbows on the armrests, fingertips pressed together as if holding an invisible ball. 'How'd he die?' And when River had given him the details said, 'He was never what you'd call fast track,' as if the late Dickie Bow's sluggishness preordained him for death on a bus. 'Never first division.'

'Premier league,' River suggested.

His grandfather waved away such modern abominations. 'One of life's streetwalkers. And I think he had an interest in a night-club. Or worked in one. Anyway, he used to come up with titbits. Which minor official was stepping out on his wife or his boyfriend. You know the kind of thing.'

'And all of it was fed into the files.'

The O.B. said: 'That old saw about laws and sausages, about how you never want to see either being made? The same applies to intelligence work.' Dropping his invisible ball, he picked up his glass instead and swirled it thoughtfully, so the amber liquid washed round the tumbler's edge. 'And then he went AWOL. That was Dickie Bow's claim to fame. Went for a walk on the wild side, and had switchboards lit up from Berlin to bloody . . . Battersea. Sorry. Alliteration. Bad habit. Berlin to Whitehall, because he might have been small fry but the last thing anyone wanted right then was a British agent turning up on Red TV, claiming god knew what.'

'This was when?' River asked.

'September eighty-nine.'

'Ah.'

'Too bloody right, *ah*. Everyone in the game, all the Berlin hands anyway, knew damn well something was about to happen, and while nobody said it aloud for fear of jinx, everyone looked at the Wall while they thought it. And nobody, *nobody*, wanted anything that might throw history off course.' His swirling became agitated, and whisky sprayed from his glass. Setting it on the table next to him, the old man raised his hand to his mouth and licked the drops away.

'When you say *nobody* . . .'

'Well, I don't mean nobody, obviously. I mean nobody on our side.' He examined his hand, as if he'd forgotten what it was for, then let it drop to his lap. 'And it wouldn't have taken much. Dickie Bow might have been just the grit of sand on the tracks to throw the locomotive. So we were keen on recovering him, as you might imagine.'

'And evidently you did.'

'Oh, we found him all right. Or he turned up, rather. Waltzed back into town just as we were ready to slap black ribbons on every operation he'd ever had a sniff at. Well, I say waltzed. He could barely walk was the truth.'

'He'd been tortured?'

The O.B. snorted. 'He was blind drunk. Though the way he told it, not of his own volition. Held him down and poured the stuff down his throat, he said. Thought they meant to drown him, he said. Of course, why wouldn't they? Drown a man like Dickie Bow in booze, you're merely speeding things up.'

'And who were "they", in this scenario? The East Germans?'

'Oh, nothing so parochial. No, Dickie Bow's story was, he'd been snatched by actual hoods. The Moscow variety. And not your everyday foot soldier, either.'

He paused, milking the moment. River sometimes wondered how the old man stood it, doing his daily rounds – butcher, baker, post office lady – without succumbing to the temptation to perform for the whole sorry bunch of them. Because if there was one thing the O.B. liked these days, it was an audience.

'No,' said the old man. 'Dickie Bow claimed to have been kidnapped by Alexander Popov himself.'

A revelation which might have carried more impact if the name had meant anything to River.

Drive a saint to suicide, thought Catherine Standish.

Lord above!

I'm channelling my mother.

They were words she'd used earlier, about Jackson Lamb: that he'd drive a saint to suicide. Not a phrase she'd ever expected to hear herself say, but this was what happened: you turned into your mother, unless you turned into your father. That, anyway, was what happened if you let life smooth you down, plane away the edges that made you different.

Catherine had had edges once, but for years had lived a life whose borders were marked by furriness, and mornings when she wasn't sure what had happened the night before. Traces of sex and vomit were clues; bruises on arms and thighs. The sense of having been spat out. Her relationship with alcohol had been the most enduring of her life, but like any abusive partner it had shown its true colours in the end. So now Catherine's edges had been planed away, and alone in the kitchen of her north London flat she made a cup of peppermint tea, and thought about bald men.

There were no bald men in her life. There were no men in her life, or none that counted: there were male presences at work, and she'd grown fond of River Cartwright, but there were no actual *men* in her life, and that went double for Jackson Lamb. Nevertheless, she was thinking about bald men; about one in particular, giving a swift glance up at the camera before pacing into the driving rain of a railway platform, instead of boarding under shelter. And about the hat he wasn't wearing because he'd left it on a bus two minutes earlier.

And she was also thinking, because she often did, how easy it would be to slip out for a bottle of wine, and have one small drink to prove she didn't need one. One glass, and the rest down the sink. A Chablis. Nicely chilled. Or room temperature, if the off-licence didn't keep it fridged; and if they didn't have Chablis a Sauvignon Blanc would do, or a Chardonnay, or triple strength lager, or a two-litre bottle of cider.

Deep breath. *My name is Catherine, and I'm an alcoholic.* A copy of the Blue Book stood between a dictionary and a collected Sylvia Plath in the sitting room, and there was nothing to stop her settling down with it, peppermint tea at her elbow, until the wobble passed. The wobble: that was another one of her mother's. Code for a hot flush. A lot of codewords, her mother had used. Which was almost funny, given what Catherine did for a living.

So what would her mother make of her now, if she were alive? If she could see Slough House, its flaky paintwork, its flakier denizens . . . Catherine didn't need to ask, because the answer was blindingly clear: her mother would take one look at the worn-out furniture, the peeling walls, the dusty bulbs, the cobwebs that hung from the corners, and recognise it as somewhere her daughter belonged, somewhere safe from aspiration. It was better to build your life's ceiling low. Better not to put on *airs*.

Better, in the long run, not to think about what lay behind you.

So picking up her peppermint tea Catherine carried it into her sitting room, and for the many hundredth time didn't go out for a bottle. Nor did she browse the Blue Book – let alone Sylvia bloody Plath – but instead sat and thought about bald men, and their actions on rainy railway platforms. And she tried not to think about her mother, or about life's edges being planed away until you could see clear past them into whatever came next.

Because whatever came next, it was best to assume the worst.

★

From the seventy-seventh floor to this, thought Louisa Guy.

Holy crap!

A broadsheet's Beautiful Homes column had lately informed her that a little imagination and a small amount of cash could transform even the tiniest apartment into a compact, space-efficient dream-dwelling. Unfortunately, that 'small amount' was large enough that if she'd laid her hands on it, she'd have moved somewhere bigger instead.

As ever, damp washing was tonight's motif. A clothes horse, designed to be folded out of sight when not in use, was always in use, and anyway, there was nowhere to put it when it wasn't. So it leaned against a bookshelf, draped with underwear, her collection of which had undergone significant upgrading since Min Harper had entered her life. Elsewhere, blouses hung on wire hangers from anywhere they could be hooked, and a still-damp sweater reshaped itself on the table, its arms dangling heavily over the sides. And Louisa perched on a kitchen chair, laptop on her knees.

It was a fairly basic research technique, but Googling the day of Spider Webb's mini-summit was the first port of call. This revealed an International Symposium on Advanced Metallurgical Processes at the LSE, and a conference on Asiatic Studies at SOAS. Tickets went on sale for an ABBA reunion gig, and were expected to sell out inside two minutes, while central London would be more of a lunatics' day out than usual, because there was a Stop the City rally marching down Oxford Street: a quarter million demonstrators were expected. Traffic, Tube and normal life would doubtless come to a halt.

None of which had any obvious connection with the Russian visit. It was background, but background was important, and after the last time the slow horses had become embroiled in Regent's Park business, she wasn't relying on info supplied by Webb. But it was hard to concentrate. Louisa kept remembering that huge floor space in the Needle. She'd rarely been anywhere so roomy without being outside, a thought that inevitably dragged her home, a rented studio flat on the wrong side of the river.

And now two, sometimes three nights a week, Min was here too, and while this was still a good thing, it wasn't without its downside. Min wasn't messy, but he took up room. He liked to be clean and fresh when he came to her bed, which meant yielding precious inches of her bathroom shelf; he needed a clean shirt in the morning, so required wardrobe space too. DVDs had appeared, and books and CDs, which meant more physical objects in a space that was getting no larger. And then there was Min himself, of course. Who didn't lumber about, but didn't have to: the mere fact of his presence brought the walls nearer. It was nice to be close to him, but it would have been nicer to be close somewhere spacious enough to be further apart.

Elsewhere in the building a door slammed shut. The resulting draught whistled along the hallways and whispered under doors until, with a noise like snow sliding off a roof, a blouse fell from its hanger to the floor. Louisa studied it a moment or two, as if the situation might rectify itself without her intervention, and when this didn't happen she closed her eyes and willed herself elsewhere, and when she opened them again that hadn't happened either.

A draughty rented studio flat. With one extra terrible characteristic: that for all its faults, it was several steps up from Min's bedsit.

If they wanted to find somewhere nice together, they were going to need money.

Eleven thirty. Six and a half hours to go.

Frigging hell!

If he'd been asked to draw a picture of what he'd expected from private security work, Cal Fenton would have drawn it big. There'd have been manual combat training; utility belts, Kevlar vests, Tasers. And driving, too: rubber-shredding take-offs and sharp cornering. He'd have had one of those earpieces with a hands-free mic attached, a necessity in the adrenalin-rich world of the security consultant, where you never knew what the next second might bring. That was what Cal Fenton had had in mind. Danger. Excitement. A grim reliance on his own physical competence.

Instead, he had a uniform that was too small, because the last guy in the job had been a midget, plus a rubber torch with a fading battery. And instead of riding shotgun in an armoured limo, he had a nightly trudge up and down half a dozen corridors, calling in every hour on the hour; less to reassure management that the facility was still standing than to prove he was awake and earning his pay. Which was so slightly above minimum wage that if you split the difference, you'd have change from a quid. A job was a job, his mum never left off saying, but flush with the wisdom of nineteen years on the planet, Cal Fenton had found the flaw in this argument: sometimes a job was a pain in the arse. Especially when it was eleven thirty-one, and there were six hours twenty-nine minutes to go before you were out the door.

Speaking of which . . .

Cal was on ground level, pacing the facility's east-side corridor, and the door at its far end was open. Not hanging wide, but not firmly closed . . . Either someone had opened it since Cal's last circuit, or Cal hadn't closed it after his cigarette.

Cal and only Cal, because night shift was a one-man job.

Reaching the door, he pushed it gently. It opened with a creak. Outside was an empty car park bordered by a mesh fence, beyond which a potholed road disappeared into the shadow of the Westway. The building opposite used to be a pub, and maybe hoped to be a pub again one day, but for the time being was making do with being an eyesore. Posters for local DJs peeled from its boarded-up windows. After watching for a moment, Cal pulled the door shut. He stood in silence, aware of his heartbeat. But there'd been nobody outside, and there was nobody inside either, himself excepted. Eleven thirty-four. He stepped away from the door and checked the office.

Office. Facility. You could get away with words like that, if you weren't exposed to the reality.

Because the office was a glorified broom cupboard, and 'facility' an up-itself name for a warehouse: windowless brick on ground level, then wood for the second storey, like they'd run out of bricks halfway. It was newer than whatever had stood in the same place previously, but after that, you ran out of compliments. Like the once and future pub across the road, the whole place was basically counting out time until the area hit an upward swing, but that figured. DataLok was a cut-price operation, and what you got was less than what you saw. Especially if what you'd been looking at was the company catalogue.

Cal swung the torch in big, forgiving loops. There was nobody in the office. Least of all a guard dog, which a sign on the main gate warned patrolled the premises 24/7, but the sign came in at £4.99, which was a lot less than a 24-hour guard-dog presence cost.

And then he heard something along the north corridor. A scuffing noise, as if a heel had kicked against the tiles.

Cal's heart phoned in loud and clear. Lub-*dub* lub-*dub* lub-*dub*. Exactly as normal, only twice as loud and four times as fast.

Twenty-four minutes until his check-in call. Which he could make early, of course, on account of being totally spooked.

And here's how *that* conversation would go:

'I think I heard a noise.'

'You think you heard a noise.'

'Yeah, along the corridor. Like there might be someone there. But I haven't looked to see. Oh, and the door was open, but I might have left it open earlier when I nipped out for a smoke. Do you wanna send reinforcements?'

(With combat training, utility belts and Kevlar vests.)

But even a pain-in-the-arse job was better than none, and

Cal really didn't want to lose out on paid employment because a squirrel had wandered in. He weighed his torch in the palm of his hand. It felt solid enough, baton-like, and suitably reassured, he stepped out of the office and into the north corridor, at the end of which was the staircase.

The corridors were on the building's outer edges. The downstairs office was where the security shifts – himself and an edging-seventy ex-copper called Brian – kept their stuff; upstairs there was a techs' room, where incoming was processed. And the rest of the facility was a labyrinth of storage rooms: apart from the number pasted above each doorway, the bastards all looked the same. Sounded the same, too: a constant humming. This was the noise information made when it was waiting to be used.

That was what he'd heard one of the techies say once.

He was halfway along the corridor when the lights went out.

'Never heard of him.'

'Oh, poppycock!'

Which was unlike the old man. Put it down, River thought, to being on his third glass. He said, 'No, all these years you've been telling me spook stories, Alexander Popov's never rated a mention.'

That earned him a sharp look. 'I haven't been telling stories, River. I've been educating you. At least, that's always been my intention.'

Because if the O.B. ever learned he'd turned into an old gossip, it would destroy something deep inside him.

River said, 'That's what I meant. But Popov's never formed part of my education. I'm guessing he was Moscow Centre, yes? One of their secret wizards, pulling levers?'

'Pay no attention to the man behind the Curtain,' the O.B. quoted. 'That's quite good, actually. But no. What he was was a bogeyman. Smoke and a whisper, nothing more. If information

76

was hard currency, the best we had on Popov was an IOU. Nobody ever laid a finger on him, and that was because he didn't exist.'

'So how come,' River began, and stopped himself. *Asking questions is good.* An early lesson. *If you don't know something, ask. But before you ask, try to work it out for yourself.* He said, 'So the smoke and the whispers were deliberate. He was invented to have us chasing someone who wasn't there.'

The O.B. nodded approval. 'He was a fictional spymaster, running his own fictional network. It was meant to have us tying ourselves in knots. We did something similar in the war. Operation Mincemeat. And one of the lessons we learned from that was you can discover an awful lot from the details you're asked to believe. You know how the Service works, River. The boys and girls in Background prefer legends to the real thing. Truth walks a straight line. They like to peep round corners.'

River was used to ironing out the kinks in his grandfather's conversation. 'If the details you were being fed were fake, that didn't mean they couldn't tell you anything.'

'If Moscow Centre said "Look at this", the sensible thing was to look in the opposite direction,' the O.B. agreed. And then said, 'It was all a game, wasn't it?' in a tone suggesting he'd fallen upon a long-hidden secret. 'And they were still playing it when everything else they owned was up for grabs.'

The fire crackled, and the old man turned his attention to it. Watching him fondly, River thought what he often thought when they dwelt on such subjects: that he wished he'd been alive then. Had had a part to play. It was a wish that kept him at Slough House, jumping through hoops for Jackson Lamb. He said, 'There was a file, then. On Alexander Popov. Even if it was full of fairy tales. What was in it?'

The O.B. said, 'God, River, I haven't given it a thought in decades. Let me see.' He peered into the fire again, as if expecting images to emerge from the flames. 'It was patchwork. An old woman's quilt. But we had his birthplace. Or what we were led to believe was his birthplace . . . But let's not go round that bush again. The story was he came from one of the closed towns. You know about them?'

Vaguely.

'They were military research stations, served by civilian populations. His was in Georgia. Didn't have a name, just a number. ZT/53235, or something like that. Population of maybe thirty, thirty-three thousand. The crème were scientific staff, with a service industry propping them up, and military to keep them under control. Like most of these places it was founded in the post-war years, when the Soviet nuclear programme was in overdrive. That's what the town was about, you see. It was . . . not organic. It was purpose-built. A plutonium production plant.'

'ZT/53235?' said River, who liked to keep his memory sharp.

His grandfather looked at him. 'Or something like that.' He turned back into the fire. 'They all had names something like that.' Then he sat straighter, and got to his feet.

'Grandad?'

'It's just a—it's okay. Nothing.' Reaching into the log basket to the side of the fireplace, the old man pulled a long dry twig from the sheaf of kindling. 'Come on, now,' he muttered. 'Let's be getting you out of there.' He held the twig into the flames.

He'd seen a beetle, River realised. A woodlouse, scuttling blindly on the topmost log of the burning pyramid. Despite the heat, his grandfather's hand remained steady as he leaned forward, the end of the twig positioned so that the beetle's next circuit would bring it immediately into its path, whereupon the dying creature would presumably launch itself gratefully upwards, as if upon a rope dangled from a helicopter. What was beetle for *deus ex machina*? But the beetle had no words, Latin or otherwise, and avoided the offered escape route, making instead for the uppermost point of the log, where it balanced for a moment then burst into flames. River's grandfather made no comment. He simply dropped the twig into the fire, and settled back in his armchair.

River was going to say something, but turned the words into a throat-clearing noise instead.

The old man said, 'This was back in Charles's day, and he got quite exercised about it in the end. Talked about wasting time on fun and games when there was still a war on, if nobody had noticed.' The O.B.'s voice changed with these words, as he indulged in that harmless habit of imitating someone your listener had never met.

Charles Partner had been the Service's First Desk, once upon a time.

'And this was the man Dickie Bow claimed kidnapped him.'

'Yes. Though to be fair to Dickie, when he came up with his story, it hadn't been firmly established Popov didn't exist. He must have seemed like a good-enough alibi at the time for whatever Dickie was up to. Drinking and whoring, probably. When he realised his absence had sent balloons up, that was the story he invented. Kidnapped.'

'And did he say what Popov wanted? I mean, kidnapping a streetwalker . . .'

'He told everyone who'd listen, and quite a few who wouldn't, that he'd been tortured. Though as this took the form of being made forcibly drunk, he had difficulty summoning up sympathy. Speaking of which . . .'

But River shook his head. Any more, and he'd know about it in the morning. And he ought to be getting home soon.

To his surprise, his grandfather refilled his own glass. Then he said, 'That closed town. The one he was supposed to come from.'

River waited.

'It disappeared from the map in fifty-five. Or would have done, if it had been on a map.' He looked at his grandson. 'Closed towns didn't officially exist, so there wasn't a lot of admin involved. No photographs to airbrush, or encyclopedia pages to replace.'

'What happened?'

'Some kind of accident at the plutonium plant. There were a few survivors, we think. No official figures, of course, because officially it never happened.'

River said, 'Thirty thousand people?'

'Like I said. There were some survivors.'

'And they wanted you to believe Popov was one of them,' River said. His mind was conjuring a story from a comic book: an avenger arising from the flames. Except what was there to avenge, after an industrial accident?

'Perhaps they did,' his grandfather said. 'But they ran out of time. Our net filled up once the Wall came down. If he'd been flesh and blood, one of the bigger fish would have offered him up. We'd have had the whole biography, chapter and verse. But he remained scraps, like an unfinished scarecrow. Some reptile dropped his name in a debriefing session, but that was an admission of ignorance by then, because nobody believed in him any more.'

The O.B. turned from the fire as he finished. Light from the flames emphasised the creases in his face, turning him into an old tribal chief, and a pang ran through River as he realised there wouldn't be many more evenings like this one; that there ought to be something he could do to eke them out. But there was nothing, and never would be. Learning that was one thing. Living with it, another entirely.

Careful not to let those thoughts show, he said, 'Dropped his name how?'

'There was a codeword involved. I can't remember what it was.' The old man looked into his glass again. 'I sometimes wonder how much I've forgotten. But I don't suppose it matters now.'

Admissions of weakness were not on their usual agenda.

River put his glass down. 'It's getting late.'

'I hope you're not going to start humouring me.'

'Not without a bulletproof vest.'

'Be careful, River.'

That gave him pause. 'What makes you say that?'

His grandfather said, 'The streetlight at the end of the lane's gone. There's a dark stretch between there and the station.'

Which was true enough, it turned out. Though River didn't believe that was what had been uppermost in his grandfather's mind.

Cal Fenton was glad no one was around to hear him yelp like a girl in the dark:

'Jesus *Christ!*'

Though mostly he was worried there might in fact be someone around.

It wasn't a generator blow-out. The towers were humming; all that information safe and snug in electronic cocoons. The lights were on a different circuit, and it might just be a power cut, but even as Cal's mind reached for that possibility, his bowels were acknowledging that if there ever was a power cut, it wasn't going to happen two minutes after he'd noticed the door was open, or heard a scuffing noise.

Ahead of him, the corridor was empty of everything but shadows, which were larger and more fluid than usual. The stairs ascended into bigger blackness. Gazing into it Cal's breathing came faster, and his grip on the torch tightened. He couldn't guess how long he stood there: fifteen seconds, two minutes. However long it was, it came to an end when he hiccuped; an unexpected, belly-deep hiccup which surfaced as a squeak – the last thing Cal wanted was to face an intruder who'd just heard that. He turned. The corridor behind him was empty too. Heading along it, he broke into a jog as unintentional as his recent paralysis; this, then, was how Cal reacted in an emergency – he did whatever his body told him to do. Stand still. Wave a torch. Run.

Danger. Excitement. A grim reliance on his own physical competence . . .

Back in the office, he flipped the lightswitch, but nothing

happened. The telephone hung on the wall opposite. Swapping the torch from his right hand to his left he reached for it, and the receiver moulded to his grip with the exact smooth plastic shape of a baby's bottle. But the comfort only lasted a moment. In his ear, there was nothing; not even the distant-sea sound of a broken connection. He stood, torch pointing nowhere. The door, the possible noise, the lights; now the phone. Taken together, there was no chance he was still alone in the facility.

He replaced the receiver carefully. His coat hung on the back of the door, and his mobile was in its pocket. Except it wasn't.

First thing Cal did was check his pockets once more, a little more quickly, and the second was to do it again, more slowly. All the while, his mind was racing on different levels. In one gear, he was re-picturing his movements on getting to work; checking his mental negatives, in case they revealed where he'd left his phone. And in another, he was unfolding what he knew about the facility. Info-dump, the techies called it. Dumping, he'd learned, was what you did with a near-infinity of digital knowledge which nobody was going to want to consult again, barring remote circumstances involving lawyers. If not for that, the digital archives stored here would have long been erased – though *erased* wasn't the word he'd heard used; that had been *released*, and when he'd heard it, the image was of information being uncooped like a flock of pigeons, bursting into the air to the sound of applause . . .

The phone was nowhere. Someone had broken into the facility on Cal's watch; had fixed the lights, killed the phone, stolen his mobile. It was unlikely that having done this, they'd quietly left.

His torch beam wavered, as if this would be the next thing to go. Cal's throat was dry, and his heart pounding. He needed to step out of the office and patrol the corridors; head upstairs and check out that unlit labyrinth with all its stored knowledge, and he had to do this with a horrible chorus beating away in his brain:

That sometimes, information is worth killing for.

From the corridor where the shadows had gone to hide came the soft squeak of a rubber-soled shoe on lino.

And if information was worth killing for, thought Cal Fenton, someone generally had to die.

A quiet night in, thought Min Harper.

Bloody hell!

He poured a drink, and surveyed his estate.

That didn't take long.

Then he sat on his sofa, which was also his bed, though if dull technicality were to intrude neither were his; they came with the room. Which was L-shaped, the foot of the L being the kitchen area (a sink; a microwave atop a fridge; a kettle on a shelf), and the longest wall boasting two windows, the view from both being of the houses opposite. Since moving into a bedsit, Min had taken up smoking again; he didn't do it in public, but in the evening he'd hang out of a window and puff away. In one of those houses opposite a boy was often doing the same thing, and they'd give each other a wave. He looked about thirteen, the same as Min's eldest, and the thought of Lucas smoking gave Min a pang in his left lung, but he didn't feel anything about this kid doing it. He supposed if he'd still been living at home a sense of responsibility would have kicked in and he'd have had a word with the kid's parents. But then, if he'd been living at home he wouldn't have been hanging out of the window smoking, so the situation wouldn't have arisen. In the time it took him to think this he finished his drink, so he poured another then hung out of the window and smoked a cigarette. The night was cold, with a hint of rain later. The kid wasn't there.

When he was done, he returned to the sofa. It wasn't a particularly comfortable sofa, but the bed it unfolded into wasn't comfortable either, so at least it was consistent. And its lumpy narrowness was only one reason Min wasn't in the habit of bringing Louisa back here; others being the way cooking smells hung around all night, and the peeling floor in the bathroom down the hall, and the borderline psycho in the room below . . . Min should move; get his life back on a proper footing. It had been a couple of years since everything went down the pan, a process that had begun when he'd left a classified disk on the Tube, and woken next morning to find its contents being discussed on Radio 4. He'd been at Slough House within the month. His domestic life collapsed shortly afterwards. If his marriage had been strong to begin with, he sometimes lectured himself, it would have survived his professional humiliation, but the truth, he'd come to understand, held a tighter focus. If he himself had been strong, he would have ensured that his marriage survived. As it was, his marriage was definitely a thing of the past, what with Louisa being on the scene. He was pretty sure Clare wouldn't tolerate that particular development, and while he hadn't told her about it, he wasn't convinced she didn't know. Women were born spooks, and could smell betrayal before it happened.

His glass was empty again. Reaching to refill it, he had a sudden glimpse of a future in which this never changed; one in which he was always in this soul-destroying room, and never released from the career-ending Slough House. And he knew he couldn't let that happen. The failures of his past had been atoned for: everyone was allowed one mistake, surely? This olive branch from Regent's Park, in the shape of Spider Webb's summit; all he had to do was grab hold of it, and be pulled ashore. If this was a test, he intended to pass it. Nothing at face value, that had to be his mantra. He'd assume everything held a hidden meaning, and keep digging until he found what it was.

And trust nobody. That was the most important thing. Trust nobody.

Except Louisa, of course. He trusted Louisa completely.

Which didn't necessarily mean keeping her in the loop.

★

Once River had left, the house grew quiet enough for David Cartwright to replay their conversation.

Fiery damn!

ZT/53235, he'd said, and River had been sharp enough to repeat it back to him. And it wasn't a name he'd forget, because River had always been able to recite phone numbers, car registrations, Test match scores, months after reading them. It was a gift, Cartwright liked to think, the boy had inherited from him; certainly one he'd encouraged River to cultivate. So sooner or later he'd wonder how come his grandfather had got this particular name digit-perfect, when he'd been making a bit of a performance of losing details here and there.

But you didn't grow old without becoming accustomed to there being things beyond your capacity to change. So David Cartwright filed that one in a memory drawer and resolved not to let it vex him.

The fire was dying. That woodlouse: it had scuttered about in evident fear, and at the last second had thrown itself into the flames below, as if death were preferable to the moments spent waiting for it. And this was a woodlouse. That human beings in similar straits had reached the same conclusion was a matter of televised fact, and not one David Cartwright cared to dwell upon. His memory was full of drawers he kept shut.

Take Alexander Popov. If he'd never mentioned that name to his grandson, it was for the reason he'd given: that he hadn't spared the creature a thought in over a decade. And this, too, was for the stated reason: Popov was a legend, and did not exist. As for Dickie Bow, he'd clearly been a drunkard who'd seen his usefulness to the Service drawing to a close. His claim of a kidnapping had been a last-gasp attempt to score a pension. That he'd died on a bus without a valid ticket didn't strike Cartwright as an out-of-the-way ending. On the contrary, it had been on the cards from the opening credits.

But Jackson Lamb appeared to think otherwise, and the trouble with that old joe wasn't that he spent his life thinking up ways of tormenting his slow horses. It was that, like most old joes, once he got it in mind to start pulling on a thread, he wouldn't stop till the whole damn tapestry unravelled. And David Cartwright had seen so many tapestries, it was hard to know where one started and the next one stopped.

He picked up his glass again, but set it down on finding it empty. Another drink now and he'd sleep like the dead for an hour, then lie wide-eyed until morning. If there was anything he missed about being young, it was that careless ability to fall into oblivion like a bucket dropped down a well, then pulled up slowly, replenished. One of those gifts you didn't know you possessed until it was taken away.

But in addition to growing accustomed to there being things beyond your capacity to change, the old also learned that some things changed without your knowing.

Alexander Popov had been a legend, Cartwright thought. Alexander Popov hadn't existed.

He wondered if that were still the case.

He continued to stare into the dying fire for some while. But in the way of things that were dying, it didn't reveal anything he didn't already know.

5

THE WENTWORTH ACADEMY of the English Language maintained two premises. The primary site, as featured in its glossy brochure, was a handsome country house, subliminally familiar to anyone who'd watched the BBC on a Sunday evening: a four-storey, crenellated wonder boasting thirty-six rooms, sweeping lawns, a carp pond, tennis courts, a croquet lawn, and a deer park. The second, whose only advantage over the first was that it was the actual academy, was a pair of third-floor offices above a stationer's off High Holborn, and any accompanying paperwork would have had to own up to a damp-stained ceiling, cracked windows, an electric bar-heater whose highest setting scorched the surrounding plaster, and a sleeping Russian.

The fire was off when Lamb appeared in the doorway. Silently, he took the scene in: bookshelves filled with dozens of copies of that same brochure; three framed diplomas on the wall above the mantelpiece; a view of a brick wall through the cracked windows; and two telephones on the desk at which the sleeping Russian slumped, both rotary, one black, the other cream. They were only just visible under piles of what might politely be called paperwork, but more reasonably described as litter. Bills and flyers for local pizza parlours, and minicab firms, and one for someone who appeared to be new in town, and in need of a firm hand. Pushed under the desk, but not entirely hidden from view, lurked a folded camp-bed and a grubby pillow.

Once he was sure the man wasn't faking, Lamb swept a pile of brochures onto the floor.

'Ferah!'

He came out of the chair like a man who's known bad dreams. Nikolai Katinsky, his name was. Jumping, he grasped something from the desktop, but it was only a glasses case; a minor prop to anchor him to waking reality. Halfway to his feet he stopped, and slumped back. The chair creaked dangerously. He put the glasses case down and coughed for a while. Then said, 'And you are?'

'I've come about the money,' Lamb said.

It was a reasonably safe bet that Katinsky owed money, and that someone would be round to collect it soon.

Katinsky nodded thoughtfully. He was bald, or mostly bald – a crop of white stubble gilded his ears – and gave off an air of pent-up energy, of emotions kept in check; the same sense Lamb had had watching the video of him, shot eighteen years ago, through a two-way mirror in one of Regent's Park's luxury suites. Joke. These were underground, and were where the Service's more serious debriefings took place; those which it might later prove politic to deny had happened. But that man had diminished in the years since, as if he'd recently undergone a crash diet without updating his wardrobe. Flesh had tightened across his jawline, and gave the impression of sagging elsewhere. When he'd finished nodding, he said: 'Jamal's money? Or Demetrio's money?'

Tossing a mental coin, Lamb said, 'Demetrio's.'

'Figures. Tell the dirty Greek bastard to go fuck himself for his money. The first of the month, that was the arrangement.'

Lamb found his cigarettes. 'I might not mention the bit about fucking himself,' he said. Moving into the room, he hooked an ankle round a chair and tipped its burden of hat, gloves and *Guardians* onto the floor. Lowering himself into it, he undid his overcoat buttons, and foraged for his lighter. 'This school set-up fool anyone?'

'So now we're having a conversation?'

'I need to stay long enough that Demetrio's convinced we talked the ins and outs of fiscal propriety.'

'He's outside?'

'In the car. Between you and me, he might go for the first of the month.' He found his lighter, and applied it. 'You weren't on today's list. We just happened to be passing.'

He was surprising himself, how easily it came back: firing up a legend on the spot. Ten minutes from now, Katinsky's current life would be spread out between them like a takeaway. And once Lamb had picked the bones out of that, he could get to the meat of the matter.

Katinsky's debriefing hadn't actually been serious. Katinsky had been among the sweepings; the exodus of minor hoods triggered by the disintegration of the Soviet Union, all desperate to convert scraps of intelligence into a harder form of currency. They were hardly grade-A candidates. But all had to be processed, and kicked out the other side, and some even sent back, to prove there was no such thing as a free ride.

Those allowed to stay were given a small lump sum and a three-year passport they sweated over each time the renewal date came round. It was always handy, as Lamb's mentor Charles Partner once remarked, to have a supply of expendable Russians on the books. Apart from anything else, you never knew when the wheel would spin again, bringing the world back where it started. 'Where it started' was a phrase neither questioned. The Cold War was the natural state of affairs.

Katinsky, anyway, had been among the lucky. And look at him now: the once-minor hood, running his own 'school' . . . Late sixties, Lamb supposed. His arms twitched under various sleeves: charity shop tweed jacket, holey grey V-neck, scruffy white collarless shirt. And there was something off about him, even leaving aside the secondhand clothing, the stained walls, the desperate address. Something off; like that gap between the use-by date, and the moment the milk turns.

'We're busier than we look,' he said, answering Lamb's question about the school. 'We get a lot of enquiries. Web traffic. Foreign students. You'd be surprised.'

'You'd be surprised how little surprises me. Who's we?'

'It's a useful plural.' Katinsky smiled thinly, showing grey teeth. 'The school has a full complement of pupils at present, but happily we are able to offer places on our subsidiary teaching scheme. A distance-learning arrangement.'

Lamb ran a thumb down a ream of stiff paper stacked on the nearest shelf, then slid the topmost sheet off the pile. A diploma: *Advanced Studies*, it read, *specialising in*, with three rows of dotted lines underneath. Board-certified, a little rosette-shaped logo promised, without going into detail about which board, or how certified.

Katinsky said, 'We get the odd dissatisfied pupil, sure. But you consider the source, yes? The other day there's a letter, the stupid bastard can't spell bastard, that's how stupid the bastard is. I'm supposed to care what he thinks?'

'I'd have thought teaching the bastards to spell would come within your remit,' Lamb said.

'So long as they sign the cheques,' Katinsky said. 'Won't Demetrio be wondering where you are?'

'He'll be reading the paper. Picking his nose. You know Demetrio.'

'But not as well as you.'

'Probably not.'

'Which is strange, as I'm the one who made him up. Have you finished playing games yet, Jackson Lamb? And if you have, would you mind telling me what you want?'

Much earlier the pale-blue sky had been cross-hatched by contrails, and Shirley Dander was deep in unreclaimed countryside; sheep, fields, and an unignorable smell of shit. There were occasional rows of roadside cottages; one with a peacock strutting outside, for Christ's sake. Shirley stared as it swept across the road and round a hedge. Chickens, maybe, but a peacock? It was like a Richard Curtis movie.

None of which got her there faster, but at least she knew

where she was going. Mr B – Jackson Lamb's bald man – had stepped off the delayed Worcester train at Moreton-in-Marsh, which turned out larger than its name suggested. It had a reasonably substantial shopping drag, at any rate, including some outlets Shirley wouldn't have minded browsing. They weren't open, though. It wasn't long past seven. Shirley had been up all night.

The station boasted a car park and a space for taxis, currently vacant. Shirley sat under an awning while morning activity unfolded: citygoers were dropped off by tracksuited spouses, looking ever-so-harassed behind the wheels of their 4 x 4s; bolder types arrived on bikes which they locked to the nearby rack, or folded into complicated quadrilaterals. Some saddoes even turned up on foot. A taxi arrived, and disgorged a significant blonde. Shirley watched as she smiled and paid and tipped and smiled and left, then slipped into the back seat before the driver knew she was there.

'Miss your train?'

'Not even a bit,' she told him. 'Do you just do mornings, or do you take the evening shift too?'

And because a suffering look was now unfolding across his wide country features, she snapped her fingers, propelling a ten-pound note from its hiding place in her watch's wristband; a trick she pulled on waiters, when they were worth the bother.

'Last week, for instance. Were you picking up in the evenings last week?'

'Boyfriend trouble, is it?' he asked.

'Do I look like boyfriends give me trouble?'

He reached a hand out and she dropped the note into it. Then he drove them away from the neat little station just as another taxi arrived to take his place, and gave Shirley Dander a quick tour of the village while she pumped him for info on local taxi services.

A large, very large, woman lumbered past: she didn't look more than early twenties, but had amassed at least a stone for each year. She snagged Louisa's attention. Gravitational pull, probably. 'What must that be like?'

They were sitting on a stone plinth wrapped round a column, takeaway coffees in hand. Around them was a constant stream of people: heading into or out of Liverpool Street Station; disappearing round corners, or into shops and office blocks.

'Not just the effort of moving,' she went on. 'The whole shebang. How'd you get a man when you're shaped like that?'

'You know what they say,' Min said. 'Anyone with one of those can always lay their hands on one of these.'

His head movement indicated the corresponding parts of their bodies he meant.

'I wouldn't be too sure. I know some pretty lonely women.'

'Oh, well, if you're gunna have *standards* . . .'

Of the people heading by, none showed interest in them. Somebody would, sooner or later: Spider Webb had set a meeting up.

'There's two of them,' he'd said. 'Kyril and Piotr, they're called.'

'Are they Russian?' Min had asked.

'How will we know them?' Louisa said hurriedly.

'Oh, you'll know them,' Webb said. 'Pashkin doesn't get here for another couple of weeks. You can talk through the itinerary with this pair. They've been told you're from the Department of Energy, for what that's worth. Let them know to keep their feet off the furniture, but don't go putting collars on them. Never wise to stir up the gorillas.'

'Gorillas?' Min had asked.

'They're on the big side,' Webb admitted. 'They're goons, what did you think? He'd have a pair of Mini-Mes?'

'How come they're here already?' Louisa had wanted to know.

But Webb had no information. 'He's rich. Not Rolls Royce rich − moonshot rich. If he wants his cushions plumped up weeks in advance, that's his privilege.'

Gorillas, then, was already in Min's mind, but it would have popped up anyway, because they approached now like a pair of silverbacks. Both were broad-shouldered, and walked in a way that suggested their suits were chafing. One, who would turn out to be Piotr, had a tennis-ball fuzz of grey across his scalp. Kyril was darker and shaggier.

'This will be them,' Louisa said.

Really? You think? Not stupid enough to say that out loud, Min stood, sucked his gut in and waited.

The pair reached them and the one who was Piotr said, 'You're with Mr Webb, right?' His voice was low and unmistakably eastern European, but he spoke fluently. Introductions made, the pair sat. Louisa waved for more coffee from the nearby booth. It might have been pleasant; four people sitting down to business in a capital city, mid-morning; coffee on the way, and the possibility of sandwiches later. You couldn't throw a stone from here without hitting someone on their way to such a meeting; but it would have been trickier, Min hoped, to target one where half those convened were carrying guns.

'Mr Pashkin gets here week after next?' Louisa asked.

'He's flying in,' Piotr agreed. 'He's in Moscow right now.'

Kyril, it seemed, didn't talk much.

'Well, maybe we should run through some ground rules before he gets here. Just so we all know where we stand.'

Piotr gave her a serious look. 'We're professionals,' he said. 'Your turf, sure. There's no problem. You tell us the rules. We keep to them as best we can.'

After a brief moment in which he wondered whether he'd ever speak another language well enough to say *fuck you* quite so politely in it, Min said, 'Yeah, well, any rules you're not sure about, let us know. I'll have someone translate.'

Louisa flashed him the eyebrow equivalent of a kick in the shins, and said, 'It's pretty basic stuff. Like you say, our turf. And we really can't have you walking round with guns. I'm sure you understand that.'

Piotr was politeness itself. 'Guns?'

'Like those you're carrying now.'

Piotr said something to Kyril in, Min assumed, Russian. Kyril said something back. Then Piotr said, 'No, really. Why would we be carrying guns?'

'It's you I'm worried about. London's more savvy than it used to be. You're one phone call away from an armed response.'

'Ah, an armed response. Yes. London has a reputation for that.'

Oh, here we go, thought Min. You shoot one plumber.

'But I assure you,' Piotr continued, 'nobody's going to mistake us for terrorists.'

'Well, if they do,' Louisa said, 'it's Mr Harper and I who'll have to clear up the mess. It's all right for you. You'll be dead. But we'll really be in the shit.'

The look Piotr gave her was intense and blue-eyed and utterly humourless. And then the clouds cleared, and he showed big white teeth more American than Russian. 'We wouldn't want that, would we?' he boomed. He turned to Kyril and rabbited on for a bit. Min counted three thick sentences. Kyril laughed too, making a noise like a bag of marbles. When he'd finished, he produced an unbranded packet of cigarettes: stubby, filterless, lethal. A health warning would have been like subtitles on a porn film. Utterly beside the point.

Min shook his head and swallowed his last mouthful of coffee. It wasn't a warm day but was bright and clear, and had felt fresh enough when he'd cycled into work. Cycling was a new thing for Min; something to cancel out the smoking. Accepting one of Kyril's cigarettes in front of Louisa would have been tantamount to confessing he had no plans for a long-term future.

Louisa said, 'So we're agreed.'

Piotr gave an expansive shrug, taking in not only Louisa's question but the general surroundings, the sky above, the whole of goddamn London. 'No guns,' he said.

'We can get down to business, then?'

He gave a gracious nod.

Nobody took notes. They talked dates and places: when

94

Pashkin was due, what transport he'd be using ('Car,' said Kyril at this point. That was the one word of English he came up with. 'Car.'). And they talked about the Needle, where the meeting would be taking place.

'You've seen it, obviously,' Louisa said.

'Of course.'

It was over her shoulder, in fact. Its tip could be seen from where they sat.

'It's . . . cool.'

'It is.'

His eyes crinkled as he smiled.

Jesus, thought Min. He's coming on to her.

'Where are you staying?' Min asked.

Piotr turned to him politely. 'I beg your pardon?'

'Where are you staying?'

'The Ambassador. On Hyde Park.'

'Already?'

Piotr looked puzzled.

'I mean,' Min said, 'I can see your boss might want to stay there. But I'm surprised he's checked you two in a fortnight before he arrives.'

Kyril was watching him with a mildly interested expression. He understands every word I'm saying, thought Min.

Louisa said, 'Good boss to have. Can't see ours doing that.'

'He's okay,' Piotr said. 'But no, we're not actually there yet.' He nodded at Min. 'I misunderstood. I thought you meant where we'll be later. Once Mr Pashkin arrives.'

Course you did, thought Min. 'So you're . . . where?'

'Near Piccadilly. Off Shaftesbury Avenue. What's its name again?'

He rattled off some more chunky vocabulary at Kyril, who grunted back. 'The Excelsior,' he said. 'Excalibur? Something like that. Forgive me, I'm stupid with names.' His contrition was aimed exclusively at Louisa. 'Maybe I should call you later. Confirm the name.'

'Good idea,' she said. 'We'd hate you to get lost.' Fishing a card from her bag, she handed it to him.

And it seemed they were done, because the Russians were standing, offering their hands. Piotr held on to Louisa's while saying, 'This could be a good thing. An oil deal between our nations. Good for us, good for you.'

'And wonderful for the environment,' Min added.

Piotr laughed, without letting go of Louisa's hand. 'You,' he said. 'I like you. You're funny.'

Louisa freed herself. 'You'll let us know your hotel.'

'Of course. We can get a taxi from here?'

'That way.'

Kyril nodded at Min very seriously, and the pair rolled off. People heading their way, Min noted, swerved round them. Louisa said something, but he didn't catch what. 'Take this.' Slipping his jacket off, he hurled it at her.

'Min?'

'Later,' he called, but it wasn't likely she heard him; he was already twenty yards away.

It cost her a second tenner, but by 7:15 that morning Shirley Dander had had numbers for all the station's pick-up drivers, by 7:30 had deeply annoyed three of them, and by 7:40 was talking to a fourth, who'd been working the previous Tuesday evening, the night the westbound trains were late. And yes, he'd picked up a bald guy, and no he wasn't a regular. And what was this, some kind of wind-up?

It's an opportunity, Shirley told him. She'd buy him breakfast.

She was still jazzed from last night's raid on DataLok, where the train company's onboard-CCTV footage was stored. Subduing the infant on security hadn't proved taxing, and chances were the morning shift would have unwrapped him by now: the kid had thought she was going to kill him. Finding the right files had taken longer, but the system wasn't a closed book, not after four years at Regent's Park Comms, and she'd uploaded everything and more to a website she'd created yesterday and had since taken down. Then she'd gone home, woken her lover, and committed a borderline act of rape. Lover had justifiably collapsed afterwards, but Shirley had taken a twist of coke then gone piledriving through the data, decoding the filing system in minutes: date, time, train number, destination, carriage. Recording was on, she estimated, a seven-second stutter, though that might have been the coke talking. The thought inspired a second hit: if this was going to take all night, she'd need all the help she could get.

It had taken a shade over two hours.

Two hours' clock-time, anyway. Shirley was flying to her own schedule by this point. Coke, yes, but also an adrenalin high from the raid. Each seven-second onscreen jump echoed the beat of her heart. She registered plenty of bald men, baldness being as much fashion statement as male tragedy these days, but she had no doubt when she found the one and only Mr B – there he sat, oblivious of the camera at the end of the carriage, and yet so square on to its field of coverage he might as well be mouthing *cheese* . . . He sat alone, staring ahead unsmilingly. Not even blinking. Except he probably was, amended coked-up Shirley Dander, was probably blinking in the six seconds spare he had out of every seven. But it was odd, nevertheless, that all around him was a funhouse of jerky movement, as his fellow travellers conjured instant shapes from newspapers, or produced handkerchiefs out of nowhere, as if this were a magicians' convention – and Mr B alone remained stock still: a cardboard cut-out who didn't even roll with the train's movement. Or that's how he'd stayed until reaching Moreton-in-Marsh, in the Cotswolds. Which boasted, among other attractions, a nice little café, open early.

Kenny Muldoon turned out quite the breakfast fiend: sausages, bacon, egg, beans, tomatoes; buckets of tea. Enough toast to carpet a barn. Shirley, no appetite, still had raw energy pulsing through her veins. But her last twist of coke was hours ago, and she had an unbreakable rule about never leaving home while carrying, so knew she was going to crash soon, with a long drive ahead of her . . . She nibbled a piece of toast, but swallowed a whole cup of tea without pausing, then poured another. Then said:

'So you collected a bald gentleman from the station last Tuesday, yes?'

'Don't know about gentleman. Seemed a bit of a bruiser.'

'We won't argue details. Where did you take him?'

'This some sort of romantic contretemps?' Kenny Muldoon rolled *contretemps* around his mouth like it was his last piece of sausage. 'Sugar Daddy done a moonlit flit?'

Plucking the fork from Kenny's unsuspecting grip, Shirley Dander impaled his hand with it, then leaned on it heavily. Felt its tines scrape and pop through gristle; watched blood squirt like ketchup over the ruins of his full English.

'Heh, heh,' Kenny added.

Shirley blinked, and the fork remained in Kenny's hand. She said, 'Something like that. Do you remember where he went?'

Kenny Muldoon's drooping eyelid was as much response as he was prepared to give at this juncture. Taxi drivers, thought Shirley. You could squash them into the same box holding all the bankers in London, and nobody would mind if you dropped it off a cliff. Her watchstrap had long been relieved of its bounty. She produced another tenner from her pocket instead. 'I didn't realise country life was so expensive.'

'You city folk don't know you're born,' he assured her. He put his knife down, took the money, slipped it into a pocket. Picked up his knife again. 'Course I remember,' he said, as if everything that had happened between her question and this reply had been invisible business. 'Couldn't hardly not, he made such a fuss about it.'

'What sort of fuss?'

'Didn't know where he was going, did he? Starts off saying he wants to go to Bourton-on-the-Water. Got halfway there, and he shouts out like he's being kidnapped. Nearly took the car into a ditch, didn't I? That's not what you want in hard rain.'

His tone of voice made it clear that the incident still rankled.

'What was his problem?'

'Turns out he doesn't mean Bourton-on-the-Water at all, does he? Turns out he means Upshott. And tries to make out that's what he said in the first place, and I'm an idiot for not hearing properly. How long do you think I've been doing this job?'

Like she cared. 'Fifteen years?'

'Try twenty-four. And I don't mishear place names, I'll tell you that for nothing.'

In which case, wasn't she due some change? 'So what did you do?'

'What could I do? Turned round and took him to Upshott. He made me restart the clock too, on account of how he wasn't paying a fare somewhere he didn't want to be in the first place.' Kenny Muldoon shook his head at the sheer bloody injustice of a world where such outrages occur. 'You can probably guess the size of the tip, too.'

Shirley made an O-shape out of finger and thumb, and he nodded gloomily.

'So what's Upshott?'

'Upshott? It's hardly anything. It's a hundred houses and a pub.'

'Not got a railway station, then.'

Muldoon looked at her as if she'd dropped in from another planet. Fair play to him though, she was beginning to feel that way herself.

He said, 'It's not got hardly anything, but that's where I left him. Zero gratuity on a twelve-quid fare. Sometimes I wonder why I do this job.'

Spearing the last morsel of sausage, he used it to mop up

the last of the yolk, then transferred it to his mouth. From the look on his face, it was evident he found some small consolations in the role life had concocted for him.

'And that was the last you saw of him?'

'I drove away,' said Kenny Muldoon, 'and I didn't look back.'

In London, the Highway Code applies on a curve: for motorists, it's a rule book; for taxis, a guideline; for cyclists, a minor inconvenience. Min swerved into City Road without pausing, and a southbound lorry missed him by at least a yard, but blared its horn anyway. Ignoring it, he threaded through the gaggle of tourists on the crossing, scattering them for the safety of the pavement, little red rucksacks and all . . .

His bicycle had been chained to the rack on Broadgate Square, and now, helmet on and jacket off, Min was as close to being disguised as he'd ever been. Even if the Russians were looking out their taxi's back window, they wouldn't cop to him. He was just another maniac on two wheels.

Why are you doing this?

I don't trust them.

You're not supposed to trust them. That's part of the game.

It was weird the way the voice of common sense sounded like Louisa.

The taxi was heading for the Old Street roundabout. This offered a variety of directions, in any one of which it might vanish, but for now it was pausing at pedestrian lights a hundred yards ahead and in the process of changing. Min, pedalling as fast as he'd pedalled in his life, pedalled faster; pulled out to overtake a slowing bus, and banged his left elbow against it as the back-draught caught him. Briefly he was suspended in a perfect, gravity-free moment . . . The bus honked madly, and here were the traffic lights, and there they were behind him, and a taxi was kerbing twenty yards ahead, and that damned bus was gaining, and Min had no choice but to brake hard, or be smeared against the front of one or the back of the other.

He left rubber on the road's surface. His teeth clenched so hard, he didn't recognise their shape.

This is because of the way he was looking at me, isn't it?

Don't be stupid. It's because he didn't want us to know where they're staying.

So you plan to chase them home on a bicycle?

The bus passed. Min hauled his bike round the parked taxi the way he might an unruly horse, and shouted something filthy through the driver's window before starting to pedal again. His legs were cooked spaghetti, and the bike a torture device, until, with an inaudible click, they became one again, man and bike, Min and bike, and he was flowing into the Old Street round-about, which boasted yet more traffic lights at its first spoke. Beyond them, four cars ahead, was a black cab, and Min was almost positive that the two heads conferring in its back seat were Piotr and Kyril – his legs were moving faster, the ground whipping away beneath his wheels, and there was a whole long stretch of Old Street, four hundred yards of it, before the pedestrian crossing – he'd never noticed before how many obstacles to free-flowing traffic littered the city, and would have been glad of it now, had the taxi not blown through the lights on amber, and sailed away towards Clerkenwell.

Of course, if there's one thing worse than acting like a jerk, it's acting like a jerk and still coming up empty-handed . . .

Min didn't even decelerate. He clipped someone's bag as he scythed through pedestrians, and shopping scattered in his wake, a welter of apples and jars and packets of pasta. Someone screamed. The cab was way ahead of him now, might not even be the right cab, and Louisa-in-his-head was gearing up for another verbal onslaught – *Getting killed will prove what, exactly?* – when Min's heart stopped as a big white van emerged from his left, directly in his path.

The Russian opened a drawer and found cigarette papers and a packet of tobacco, embossed with rich brown curly writing.

Rolling a prisoner's pinch into a thin smoke, he asked Lamb, 'You here to kill me?'

'I hadn't given it any thought,' Lamb said. 'You deserve killing?'

Katinsky considered. 'Lately, not so much,' he said at last. Then, 'There's a shop on Brewer Street. You can get Russian tobacco there. Polish chewing gum. Lithuanian snuff.' He scratched a match, and held the flame to his tightly rolled cylinder, starting a small fire he swiftly sucked out of existence. 'At any given moment, half its customers used to be spooks. You've been described to me on many occasions.' Match extinguished, he replaced it in the box. 'So, what do you want with me, Jackson Lamb?'

'Little chat about old times, Nicky.'

'There are no old times. Don't you keep up? Memory Lane's been paved over. They built a shopping mall on it.'

'You can take the man out of Russia,' Lamb observed, 'but he'll still reckon he's some kind of tragic fucking poet.'

'You think it's amusing,' Katinsky said, 'but not so long ago a mall was what the Queen rode down on her horse, and there was only one of them. Now everywhere you look there's a mall, and they've all got *cookie* stores and *burger* joints. So I'll tell you what's really funny, what's really funny is, you still think it was Red Russia the Americans beat.' He spat into the wastepaper basket. Whether that was additional comment or a smoking-related necessity wasn't clear. 'So you want to take me down Memory Lane,' he continued, 'it'll be a forced march, you understand?'

Lamb said, 'I get the feeling making you shut up is gunna be the hard part.'

He waited while Katinsky locked up, then followed him down the stairs and onto the street. Katinsky led Lamb past six pubs before reaching one he approved of. Inside, he stopped to take bearings before heading for a corner, which either meant he was new here, or hoped Lamb would think he was. He wanted red wine. Lamb might have been surprised about this, if he was capable of surprise at another man's drinking habits.

At the bar he ordered a large scotch for himself, because he wanted to give the impression of being kind of a lush, and also because he wanted a large scotch. Memory Lane stretched in both directions. He deserved a drink. Because his scotch came first he drained it in two swallows while the wine was poured, then ordered another, and carried them back to the table.

'*Cicadas*,' he said, sliding Katinsky's wine in front of him.

Katinsky's reaction was behind the beat. He lifted his glass, swirled it as if it were something to savour and not just crappy house red, and took a sip. Then said, 'What?'

'*Cicadas*. A word you used in your debriefing. At Regent's Park.'

'Did I?'

'You did. I watched the video.'

Katinsky shrugged. 'And? You think I remember everything I said in a debriefing nearly twenty years ago? I've spent most of my life trying to forget stuff, Jackson Lamb. And this, this is ancient history. The bear is sleeping. Why poke it with a stick?'

'Good point. So, when's your passport up for renewal?'

Katinsky gave him a weary look. '*Ach*. It's not enough to suck a man dry. You have to come back and grind up the bones.' In an attempt to rehydrate himself, he gulped more wine. It was a big gulp, a drinker's gulp, requiring him to wipe his chin after. 'Ever been debriefed, Jackson Lamb?'

That was such a stupid question, Lamb didn't even bother.

'As a hostile? That's how I was treated. They want to know everything I ever heard or saw or did, and after a while I don't know if they're looking for reasons to throw me back or reasons to keep me. Like I say. They suck a man dry.'

'Are you trying to tell me you were making stuff up?'

'No, I'm trying to tell you that every scrap of information I ever had, everything I thought was useful, everything I knew wasn't, everything I didn't know what it was, I spilled it all. Every last drop. If you've watched the video, you know as much as I ever did. Maybe more, because believe me, I have forgotten more than I ever knew.'

'Including cicadas.'

Katinsky said, 'Maybe not so much cicadas, no.'

There was no way to measure the distance between Min and the end of his life in that moment. The van slammed its brakes to avoid slamming into Min instead, and the displaced air kissed Min all over, and then he was gone, leaving chaos behind him. In his wake a horn sounded, but what the hell. Near-death experiences were two-a-penny on the city roads, and it would all be forgotten in minutes.

As for now, speed had become its own point and purpose. Min's legs were pumping easily, his fists were moulded to the handlebars, and with the road disappearing beneath his wheels, the gift of being alive flowed through him like a shot of tequila. The noise he suddenly barked was halfway between a laugh and a shout, and barely human. Pedestrians stared. Few had been lucky enough to see a cyclist going this fast.

And up ahead lay the junction with Clerkenwell Road, and yet more lights, and the backed-up traffic included at least three black cabs. Min, now immortal, stopped pedalling, and free-wheeled towards the waiting cars.

So you've caught up with them. Possibly. Now what?

Kyril understood every word we were saying.

Of course he did. So?

Cruising the cycle lane he pulled level with the first cab, and risked a sideways glance. Its lone passenger was on her mobile phone. The second was its mirror image; a male, holding a phone to the opposite ear. Maybe they were talking to each other. Almost at the front of the queue now, Min stopped alongside a bus, perhaps the same one he'd had the altercation with earlier; there were now just two cars between him and the remaining black cab, which was hovering impatiently under the lights. For a moment, the world shimmied. Then his vision cleared, and he was looking at the backs of their heads: Piotr and Kyril, both facing front, lacking all interest in bedraggled cyclists.

So he had caught up with them. Now what?

He had his answer almost immediately: now the lights changed, and the taxi pulled away. Min barely had time to register the first half of its plate, *SLR6*, before it was through the junction, and heading down Clerkenwell Road. And with it went that feeling he'd had that he could cycle forever; it drifted from him like one of those Chinese lanterns you lit and let go and watched burn into nothingness. Each breath rasped through him like a match on a sanded surface – he could taste blood, never a good sign. By the time he was through the crossroads, the black cab was gone, might be miles away . . . When he registered that he was being overtaken by a pedestrian, Min pulled over, gave the finger to the car behind him out of cyclist habit, and pulled his mobile from his trouser pocket. His hands shook as he used it. His bicycle fell to the pavement.

'Yes?'

'Do you have pull at the Troc?'

'I'm fine, Min, thanks for asking. How's your morning?'

'Jesus, Catherine—'

'I don't know about pull, but I did a Comms course with one of the admin staff back in the Dark Ages. What do you want?'

'I've got a taxi heading west along Clerkenwell Road. Partial plate reads—'

'A taxi?'

'Just see if they'll run it, Cath, yeah?' He half spat the half-plate he had: *SLR6*.

'I'll do my best.'

Min slid the phone back into his pocket, then leaned to one side and very neatly threw up into the gutter.

This time, Katinsky drained his glass. Glancing at his own, Lamb found that it, too, was empty. With a grunt he headed back to the bar, where a pair of old women, dressed in what looked like their entire wardrobes, huddled in furtive conversation, while a ponytailed man in a street sweeper's jacket confided in a pint of lager. The drinks arrived. He'd barely delivered Katinsky's wine before the Russian was off again.

'At the Park, I was given to understand I was old news. As if there'd been a fire-sale, and you'd already bought everything you'd ever need. Tell us something new, I was told. Tell us something new. Or we throw you back. And I don't want to be thrown back, Jackson Lamb.' He clicked his fingers, in response to some mental trigger. 'KGB agents weren't so popular at that point in history. Actually, I'll tell you a secret. We were never popular. It's just that we were no longer in a position where that didn't matter to us.'

'Guess what?' Lamb said. 'Nobody likes you yet.'

Katinsky rolled over this. 'But low-grade information was all I had. Office gossip, interesting because the office was Moscow Centre, but nothing that hadn't been gift-wrapped a hundred times over by men who'd forgotten more than I'd ever known.' He leaned forward conspiratorially. 'I was a cipher clerk. But you already know that.'

'I've read your CV. You never set the world alight.'

The Russian shrugged. 'I comfort myself with the knowledge that I've outlived more successful colleagues.'

'Did you bore them to death?' Lamb leaned forward. 'I don't want your life story, Nikky. All I'm interested in is anything you know about cicadas that you didn't spill then. And in case you've got thoughts of stretching this out all night, that's the last drink I'm buying. We on the same page?'

A puzzled expression crossed Nikolai Katinsky's face, and he began to cough. Not the healthy, clearing out your lungs type cough, with which Lamb was familiar, but as if there were something inside him trying to force its way out. A lesser man might have offered to do something, like fetch water or call an ambulance, but Lamb contented himself with his drink until Katinsky got his shuddering under control.

When he thought he might receive a reply, Lamb said, 'Do you get that often?'

'It's worse in the damp,' Katinsky wheezed. 'Sometimes I——'

'No, I meant, if it's gunna happen again, I'll pop out for a smoke.' He waggled his lighter in illustration. 'And if I decide that display was to avoid answering questions, I'll drag you out with me and put this to use.'

Katinsky stared at him without speaking for twelve long seconds, then shifted his gaze to the tabletop. When he started speaking again his voice was steady. '*Cicadas* is a word I overheard, Jackson Lamb. Alongside a name I think you're familiar with. Alexander Popov. It meant nothing to me then, but it was spoken in a tone approaching . . . what would I say? I think I would say awe, Jackson Lamb. In a tone approaching awe.'

'Where was this?'

'It was in a lavatory. A shithouse, if you prefer. That was the use I was putting it to, certainly. It was an ordinary work day, except that it was not long before the Wall came down, so no days were ordinary. I've heard it said many times that the fall came suddenly, that nobody was prepared, but you and I know it wasn't like that. They say animals sense an earthquake before it happens, and the same holds true of spooks, yes? I don't know what life was like in Regent's Park, but in Moscow Centre it was like waiting for the results of a medical exam.'

'Jesus wept,' said Jackson Lamb. 'You were in a shithouse.'

'I had stomach cramps, so I retreated to the lavatory where I succumbed to an attack of diarrhoea. And that is where I was, in a stall, when two men came in and used the urinals. And while they did so, they exchanged words. One said, "You think it still matters?" And his companion said, "Alexander Popov thinks it does." And the first said, "Well, of course he does. The cicadas are his baby."' Katinsky paused. Then said, 'He did not actually say "his baby". But that's the closest I can come.'

'And that was that?' Lamb said.

'They finished their piss and left. I remained there some while, more concerned with my stomach than the meaning of their words.'

'Who were the men?' Lamb asked.

Katinsky shrugged. 'If I knew, I'd have said.'

'And they had this conversation without checking they weren't being overheard?'

'They must have done. Because I was there, and they had the conversation all the same.'

'Convenient.'

'If you say so. But it meant nothing to me. I gave it no thought until I was dredging things up from the back of my mind in a room under Regent's Park.' His brow furrowed. 'I didn't even know what cicadas were. I thought they were fish.'

'Instead of some kind of funny insect.'

'Funny insect, yes. With one particularly funny trait.'

Lamb said, 'For Christ's sake,' and sounded genuinely pained. 'You think I don't know?'

'They bury themselves underground for long periods,' Katinsky went on. 'Seventeen years in some cases, I believe. And then they burst out and they sing.'

'If it was a genuine codeword,' Lamb said, 'it would only mean one thing.'

'But it wasn't genuine, was it?'

'No. You were a dupe. Just another straw man feeding us a line about Alexander Popov, who didn't exist. So we'd end up chasing our tails, trying to find a sleeper network which didn't exist either.'

'So why keep me, Jackson Lamb? Why not throw me back?'

Lamb shrugged. 'They probably thought you were cheap enough to be worth a punt. Just in case.'

'In case it turned out that what I overheard was real.' Katinsky was recovering from his coughing fit. The gaps between his sentences were diminishing, and he began rolling another of his old lag's cigarettes. Placing it on the table as carefully as if it were a holy relic, he addressed his next words to it. 'Which would mean what? That your bogeyman's real too, and not only real but with an actual network. All these years after the fall. Here in dear old Blighty.'

Lamb said, 'Thanks. Now I've heard it out loud, it's clearly bollocks.'

'Of course.' Katinsky bowed his head. 'Clearly. There is no precedent for such a thing.'

'Funny.'

'Except the whole world knows there is. Is that why you turned up at my door, Jackson Lamb? You've been reading last year's papers, and got to worrying it could happen again?' He was enjoying himself now. 'It's going to look careless, isn't it? Allowing not one but two nests of Communist spies to bed down in Western comfort all these years.'

'I'm not sure anyone would care about their politics,' Lamb said. 'That dog died a while ago.'

'It certainly did. The workers' paradise is today run by gangsters and capitalists. Much like the West.'

'Missing the good old days, Nicky? We could always ship you back.'

'Not me, Jackson Lamb. I look around your green and pleasant land and I just love what you've done with the place. But you're here because you've started to think *what if*, haven't you? What if the cicadas are real after all? Who would they answer to? Not the national Soviet interest that put them here, because that no longer exists.' Raising his empty glass to the light, he tilted it so its faint red tidemark showed up like a scar. 'Imagine that. Buried underground for years and years. Waiting for the word to start their song. But whose word?'

Lamb said, 'Alexander Popov was a scarecrow. A hat and a coat and two old sticks, no more.'

'They say the greatest trick the Devil ever pulled was to make people stop believing in him,' Katinsky said. 'But all joes believe in the Devil, don't they? Deep down, during their darkest nights, all joes believe in the Devil.'

He laughed at this, which turned into another cough. Lamb watched him heave for a minute, then shook his head and dropped a fiver on the table. 'Wish I could say you'd been a help, Nicky,' he said. 'But on the whole, I think we should've thrown you back.'

When he looked back from the door, Katinsky was still heaving on the rack of his own body. But the five-pound note had disappeared.

Earlier, from his car, Kenny Muldoon had watched Shirley Dander get behind the wheel of her own, slip a pair of shades on, and go roaring out of Moreton-in-Marsh station car park. She wants to be careful, he thought. The locals didn't care for reckless drivers, and there's no one more local than a local policeman. But that wasn't his problem. He patted his breast pocket, where he'd tucked the money she'd handed him, then patted his stomach, into which he'd shovelled the breakfast she'd bought. Not a bad morning's work. And it wasn't over yet.

From his glove compartment he took a scrap of paper on which was scrawled a mobile number. Mumbling it aloud, he punched it into his phone.

A train was pulling out; one of the commuter wagons, stuffed to the gills.

The phone rang.

A woman stood on the bridge, holding a baby. She was making the child wave its hand at the departing train; holding it at the elbow, moving it left then right.

The phone rang.

A young couple in bright jackets and rucksacks examined a timetable by the platform gate. They appeared to be arguing. One gestured after the vanishing train, as if making a point.

The phone was answered.

Muldoon said, 'It's Muldoon. From the taxi. I was given this number.'

And he said, 'Yes. It was a woman, though.'

And he said, 'Yes, that's what I told her.'

And he said, 'So when do I get my money?'

Ending the call, he tossed the phone onto the passenger seat, then crumpled the scrap of paper and dropped it at his feet. And then he too left the car park.

After a while, the young couple in their bright jackets wandered onto the platform, to await the next train.

6

ODERICK HO WAS pissed off.
Roddy Ho felt *betrayed*.

Roderick Ho was wondering what it all added up to, if you couldn't trust your fellow man, your fellow woman. If your fellow woman lied to you, misrepresented herself, was not who she claimed to be . . .

A lesser man might weep.

Because you put your whole damn self into a relationship, and what did you find? You found yourself reaching out to this hot blonde chick who was into hip-hop, action movies and snowboarding, who'd reached level five of *Armageddon Posse* and was taking evening classes in twentieth-century history, and then – and he'd only discovered this because she mentioned her make of car and that she had SkyPlus, two hard facts which allowed him to trace her corporeal identity as opposed to her online character – and then it turned out that if she was into snowboarding she'd better be doing it carefully, because not many insurance companies were going to cover a *fifty-four-year-old woman* on a snowboarding holiday, because *fifty-four* was the kind of age when your bones turned brittle and you had to worry about catching a chill in case it developed into something nasty. Christ. She didn't need evening classes in twentieth-century history. She just had to cast her mind back. Roddy Ho wasn't sure his own mother was fifty-four yet. The bitch.

But anyway. Water under the bridge. The adjustments he'd made to his e-mail set-up ensured that any further communications from

Ms Geriatric Ward would be blocked. If she wondered what she'd done to upset Roderick Ho – or Roddy Hunt, rather; the DJ superstar with the Montgomery Clift profile she'd thought she was hooking up with – she needed to take a long hard look in the mirror, that was all. Truth in advertising was what she needed evening classes in. Ho wasn't easily offended – he was an easygoing guy – so it was with both sorrow and disgust that he wiped out Ms Coffin Dodger's credit rating. He only hoped she'd learn her lesson, and stick to her own side of the generation gap in future.

And as if the afternoon wasn't stressful enough, here came Catherine Standish, bearing gifts.

'Roddy,' she said, and placed a can of Red Bull on his desk.

Nodding suspiciously, Ho moved it a few inches to the left. Everything's got its place.

Catherine settled herself behind the other desk. She'd brought a cup of coffee too, and cradled it in her hands. 'Everything okay?' she asked.

He said, 'You only come in here when you want something.'

An expression he didn't recognise flickered across her face. 'That's not entirely true.'

He shrugged. 'Doesn't matter. I'm busy, anyway. And besides . . .'

'Besides?'

'Lamb says I'm not to help you any more.'

(What Lamb had actually said: 'I catch you freelancing again, I'll pimp you out to IT support. Photocopier division.')

'Lamb doesn't have to know everything,' Catherine said.

'Have you told him that?' She didn't reply. Taking this as proof of his unassailable rightness, Ho popped the tab on his Red Bull, and took a long swallow.

Watching him, Catherine sipped her coffee.

Ho thought: here we go again. Another older woman with designs. To be fair, she was after Ho's skills rather than his bod, but it all came down to exploitation in the end. Good thing he was more than a match for her. He looked at his screen. Then back at Catherine. She was still watching him. He turned back to his screen. Studied it for half a minute, which is a lot longer than it sounds. When he risked another glance, she was still watching him.

'What?'

She said, 'How's the archive going?'

The archive was an online Service resource; a 'tool for correlating current events with historical precedents', and thus of enormous strategical use, or so an interim minister had decided a few years back. As was frequently the way with the Civil Service, a notion once decreed was difficult to countermand, and the Minister's mid-morning brainwave had outlived his career by several administrations. And since Regent's Park rarely encountered a makework task that couldn't more usefully be done by a slow horse, archive maintenance and augmentation had long since ended up on Roderick Ho's desk.

'All right.'

Balancing her cup in one hand, Catherine dabbed her lips with a tissue held in the other. This was all wrong. This was his office, his space; its contents arranged according to the rightness of the places they occupied, even if, to the uninitiated, this might resemble chaos. There were spare cables and mouses, and the wispy envelopes CDs come in, and thick manuals on long superseded operating systems. And there was collateral damage in the shape of pizza boxes and energy drink cans, and that electric buzz that haunts the air around computers. It was his space. And it was wrong that Catherine Standish could just wander in and make like it was hers too.

Didn't look like she was removing herself soon, either.

'Takes up a lot of your time, I'll bet,' she said.

Working on the archive, she meant.

'Almost all of it,' said Ho. 'It's my top priority.'

'Must be handy, then, that fake task list you've rigged up,'

Catherine went on. 'You know, the one that shows anyone monitoring your logged-on activity how hard you're working.'

Ho choked on his Red Bull.

Louisa said, 'You could have been killed.'

'I was riding a bike, that's all. Thousands of people do it every day. Most of them don't get killed.'

'Most of them aren't chasing cars.'

'I think they probably are,' Min said.

'And where did it get you?'

A mile and a half, he thought, which was pretty good going in London traffic. But what he said was, 'I got the guys at the Troc to pick it up on Clerkenwell Road. They tracked—'

'*You* got the guys—'

'Yeah yeah. *Catherine* got the guys at the Troc to pick them up.' The Troc was the Trocadero, which was what the hub of the capital's CCTV network was called. 'They tracked the cab west, and the goons didn't get out at any hotel Excelsior, or Excalibur, or Expialidocious or anywhere else, but went straight on through to the Edgware Road. That's where they're staying. West End hotel? Dosshouse, more like.'

Louisa said, 'You'd think Webb would have that stuff covered. Where the goons are staying, I mean. They've been in country how long? And they're wandering round off the leash?'

Min thought he might have been given a bit more credit for slipping the leash back on them. Or at least working out where their kennel was. He said, 'Like he told us. Over at the Park, they're busy turning out their pockets for the bean counters. Haven't got time for the, ah, hands-on stuff.'

'This isn't trivial. It's security. These guys have got guns . . . I mean, Jesus, we just let them wander round the capital tooled up? How'd they get them through Customs in the first place?'

'They probably didn't,' Min said. 'I can't be certain about this, but I believe it's possible to lay your hands on illegal weaponry in some parts of London.'

'Thanks for that.'

'Not the good parts. But a lot of places out east. And north. And some parts west.'

'Are you finished?'

'And anywhere south of the river, obviously. More to the point, they were playing us, Louisa. All that time we were sitting working out the details, them saying yes ma'am, no ma'am to all your suggestions, they were basically just thinking fuck you. We can't trust them an inch. They'll say whatever we want to hear and do whatever they want to do. And Webb made it clear that if anything goes wrong, it's our fault.'

'Yes, I noticed that.'

'So . . .'

'So we make sure nothing goes wrong.'

They were sitting on the stone balustrade of one of the flower beds on the Barbican terrace overlooking Aldersgate Street. Traffic hummed below, and from somewhere behind them music played; something classical. Over the road, through one of Slough House's windows, Catherine was visible behind the spare desk in Roderick Ho's office. The back of Ho's head was a motionless black blob. They made an unlikely pair of conspirators.

Louisa put her hand on Min's, which was resting lightly on her knee. 'Okay, so they lied to us about staying in a nice hotel because they don't want us to think they're just rent-a-heavies, even though they are, and even though that's what we're gunna think anyway. Or maybe Pashkin *has* paid for a fancy hotel, and they're pocketing the difference. Either way, I don't think we should be too bothered. What worries me is the lack of back-up info. Audit or no audit, the Park should have known where they were.'

'But at least we know now.'

'At least we know now.'

'Thanks to me.'

'Yeah yeah. Thanks to you.'

'I'll take that as a pat on the head then.'

'Pat pat,' Louisa said.

'You think they'll ditch the guns?'

'I think they probably carried the guns because if they hadn't, we'd be wondering where their guns were. So yes, they'll ditch them for the time being. But they'll carry them when their boss is here. That's what goons do.'

'You're good at this.'

'I've been using my brains. While you were nearly getting yours splattered across Old Street, playing Lance Armstrong.'

'This is about the bike, isn't it?' Min said, but she didn't get it.

Over in Slough House, Catherine was still talking to Ho. In the next room, Marcus Longridge was at his computer. Min couldn't make out the expression on his face. Marcus was a cipher. Nobody was entirely sure why he'd been exiled, and nobody knew him well enough to ask. On the other hand, nobody cared, so it wasn't a big worry.

Louisa said, 'The one who was doing the talking. Piotr. You think he was coming on to me?'

'You wish. He had his arm round Kyril in the taxi. They were kissing.'

'Right.'

'Seriously. Tongues and everything.'

'Right.'

'You need your gaydar seen to.'

'You know what?' she said. 'It's not my gaydar needs seeing to.'

She gave him a sideways look he was getting to know very well indeed.

'Oh,' he said. 'Right. Got you.'

'My place tonight?'

Min stood. The music had stopped, or else got quieter. He reached out a hand, and Louisa took it.

'Bring it on,' Min said.

★

Catherine put her cup down, but kept talking. 'Don't get me wrong, Roddy, it's a neat trick, but don't you think you should have programmed it to show a few off-reservation sites? Nobody sits at their computer all day and does nothing but work.'

Ho became aware that his mouth was open, so he closed it. Then opened it again, but only to fill it with Red Bull.

'But perhaps,' said Catherine, 'you're wondering how I know about this.'

He wasn't, actually. He'd already decided it must be witchcraft.

Because Catherine Standish knew which way up a keyboard went, and probably had a certificate somewhere verifying her typing speed, but anything beyond surfing tourist sites was as far from her reach as dating . . . well, dating. Even if she'd crept in at night and logged on in his user-name, she couldn't have found the program he'd written. If Roddy hadn't been the one who'd hidden it, he'd not have been able to find it himself.

He said, 'I don't know what you're talking about.'

Catherine glanced at her wristwatch. 'That's about thirty seconds too late to be convincing. Which, in a way, proves my point.'

This time Ho really didn't know what she was talking about.

'Roddy,' she said, 'you don't get people, do you?'

'Get them?'

'Understand what makes them tick.'

He snorted. Understanding what made people tick was what he did. He tossed a mental coin, and it came up Min Harper. Take Min Harper, then. What made Min Harper tick? Hang onto your hat, lady, because Roddy Ho could tell you Harper's service record, his salary, the mortgage on his family house, the rent on his bedsit, his credit card debts, his standing order payments, the family and friends earmarked on his mobile network, how many points he's racked up on his supermarket loyalty card and what websites he's bookmarked. He can tell you Harper looks at Amazon a lot without buying much, and e-mails the *Guardian*'s over-by-over cricket blog on a regular basis. And he was about to start telling her precisely all that, but she got in first.

'Roddy.' She pointed to the computer in front of him. 'We all appreciate that you can make one of those things sit up and beg. And that the last thing you want to be doing is the kind of data processing a trainee could do after twenty minutes' instruction. And we definitely all know there's a whole suite of rooms at GCHQ keeping an eye on Five's online wanderings, in case anyone's anywhere naughty. With me so far?'

Unable to prevent himself, he nodded.

'So bearing all that in mind, I asked myself what I'd do if I had your skills and was, let's say, prone to wandering around the dark side of the web. And I decided that what I'd do is, I'd write a program that would convince anyone watching that I was doing precisely what I was supposed to be doing, which would leave me free to do whatever I wanted all day long.'

Ho felt liquid drizzling over his fingers, and looked down to find that he'd crushed the not quite empty can of Red Bull in his fist.

'And at the same time, I imagined I was the kind of, ah, compulsive personality type who it wouldn't occur to to build a little slack into the system. Something that would look convincingly like a human being was sitting at the keyboard, and not – forgive me, Roddy – a robot. Which is what I meant by not getting what makes people tick.' And now Catherine leaned back, and clasped her hands on her lap. 'So. Was I wrong about any of that?'

'Yes,' he said.

'No, I mean actually wrong. Not just that you wish I wasn't right.'

After a while, Ho said, 'You dropped a fibre-optic through the ceiling, didn't you?'

'Roddy, I wouldn't know one end of a fibre-optic from the other.'

In the face of such colossal ignorance, Roderick Ho had nothing to say.

Standing, Catherine collected her coffee cup. 'Well,' she concluded. 'I'm glad we've had this little chat.'

'Are you going to tell Lamb?'

Or the Dogs, he thought. Who would definitely have something to say about a shop-floor spook playing games on the Service network.

'Of course not,' she said. 'Lamb doesn't have to know everything, remember?'

He nodded, dumbly.

'Though I will expect you to be a little more flexible in helping out with research in future. Not just mine, either.'

'But Lamb—'

'*Mmm?*'

'Nothing.'

'That's what I thought.' Catherine paused at the door. 'Oh, and one more thing? You even think about using your online tricks to make my life difficult, and I'll feed your beating heart to a hungry dog. Understood?'

'Okay.'

'Have a good afternoon, Roddy.'

And she went.

Leaving Roderick Ho feeling pissed off, betrayed – and kind of awed.

One dark night the previous winter, Jackson Lamb had arranged a meeting with Diana Taverner by the canal up near the Angel; a meeting she'd agreed to because Lamb had her balls in his pocket. Lady Di aspired to the Park's First Desk, currently occupied by Ingrid Tearney, and the methods she'd resorted to to promote her interests had produced a situation that had threatened to become untidy. Lamb's involvement hadn't made things any tidier; but in the world of spooks – as in those of politics, commerce and sport – the fact that everything had been bollocksed up beyond belief hadn't resulted in anything changing: the desks at Regent's Park remained arranged the way they had been, and Lady Di's resentment at being barred from the top job hadn't noticeably diminished. And Lamb still had dirt on her which could get her crucified twice over: once by the media, with ink and pixels, and a second time by Ingrid Tearney, with wood and nails.

This being so, Lady Di hadn't offered much resistance when Lamb suggested a quiet natter, 'at the usual place'. She was late, but this assertion of her dominance didn't bother Lamb in the slightest, because he was even later. Approaching from the Angel end, he could see her on the bench, looking down the canal. A couple of houseboats were moored on the other side; one with a bicycle rack on its roof; the other shuttered, its door chained up. She was probably wondering if he'd rigged video surveillance from one or the other, because that's what he'd have been thinking if he were her. But he was pretty certain she hadn't rigged up anything herself, partly because he doubted she'd want their conversation on the record, but mostly because the window of time she'd had to arrange it, Lamb had been sitting on that same bench, and he'd have noticed.

Like any joe, he had his favourite spots. Like any joe, he mostly avoided them; made his visits irregular, aborting them if there were too many people around, or too few. But like any joe he needed a space in which he could think, which meant somewhere no one expected him to be. This stretch of canal fit the bill. It was overlooked by the backs of tall houses, and there were usually cyclists around, or joggers; at lunchtimes, shop and office workers wandered down and ate sandwiches. Sometimes narrowboats toiled past, heading into the long tunnel under Islington, where no towpath followed. It was so obviously a place where a spook might sit and think spook thoughts that nobody who knew the first thing about spooks would imagine any spook stupid enough to use it.

So Lamb had called Lady Di from there, and issued his

invitation and then he'd sat as the afternoon faded, looking like an office worker who'd just been made redundant, possibly for hygiene reasons. He'd chain-smoked seven cigarettes thinking through Shirley Dander's report of her trip into the Cotswolds, and as he'd lit the eighth a shudder wracked him top to toe, and he coughed like the Russian had coughed. He had to throw the still king-size fag into the canal while he concentrated on holding his body together, and by the time the fit left him, he felt he'd run a mile. Clammy sweat wrapped him, and his eyes were blurry. Somebody really ought to do something about this, he thought, before leaving the bench, so Lady Di could arrive there first.

And now she ignored his approach, barely acknowledging him as he sat. Her hair was longer than last time he'd seen her, and curled more, though that might have been art. She wore a dark raincoat which matched her tights, and when she spoke at last she said: 'If this bench marks my coat, I'm sending you the cleaning bill.'

'You can get coats cleaned?'

'Coats cleaned, teeth fixed, hair washed. I appreciate this is news to you.'

'I've been busy lately. It's possible I've let myself go.'

'A bit.' She turned to face him. 'What did you want with Nikolai Katinsky?'

'I'm not the only one's been busy, then.'

'When you go harassing former customers, they have a habit of pulling the communication cord. And I can do without the complication right now.'

'On account of your domestic difficulties.'

'On account of mind your own fucking business. What did you want with him?'

'What did he tell you?'

Diana Taverner said, 'Some story about his debriefing. That you wanted him to go over what he'd told the Dentists.'

Lamb grunted.

'What were you really after?'

Lamb said, 'I wanted him to go over what he'd told the Dentists.'

'You couldn't just watch the video?'

'Never the same, is it?' His coughing fit had entered that comfortable mental zone where it might have happened to somebody else, so he lit another cigarette. As an afterthought, he waved the packet vaguely in Taverner's direction, but she shook her head. 'And there was always the chance he'd remember it differently.'

'What are you up to, Jackson?'

He was all innocence and airy gesture: Him? He didn't even have to speak. Just wave his cigarette about a bit.

'Katinsky's strictly from the shallow end,' Taverner said. 'A cipher clerk, with no information we didn't already have from other, better-informed sources. We only hung onto him in case we needed swaps. Are you seriously telling me you're developing an interest?'

'You've looked him up, then.'

'I get word you've been rousting nobodies from the Dark Ages, of course I looked him up. This is because he mentioned Alexander Popov, isn't it? Jesus, Jackson, are you so bored you're digging up myths? Whatever operation Moscow was thinking of running way back when, it's as relevant now as a cassette tape. We won that war, and we're too busy losing the next one to have a rematch. Go back to Slough House, and give thanks you're not in the firing line any more.'

'Like you, you mean?'

'You think it's easy, Second Desk? Okay, it might not be life behind the Wall. But try doing my job with both hands tied, and you'll find out what stress feels like, I guarantee it.'

She stared at him, underlining how serious she was, but he held it easily enough, and wasn't bothered about letting her see the smile itching onto his lips. Lamb had done both field and desk, and he knew which had you gasping awake at the slightest noise in the dark. But he'd yet to meet a suit who didn't think themselves a samurai.

Taverner looked away. A pair of joggers panting down the opposite towpath broke apart for a woman pushing a pram. Only once the pair had jogged on, and the pram was approaching the incline up to the bridge, did she continue. 'Tearney's on the warpath,' she said.

Lamb said, 'Being on the warpath's Tearney's job description. If she wasn't rattling a sabre, them down the corridor would think she wasn't up to it.'

'Maybe she isn't.'

Lamb ran five fat fingers through hair that needed a rinse. 'I hope you're not about to wax political. Because, and I can't stress this enough, I don't give a flying fuck who's stabbing who in the back at the Park.'

But Taverner was venting, and not about to interrupt herself. 'Leonard Bradley wasn't just her rabbi, he was also her Westminster mole. Now she doesn't have any allies down the corridor, as you put it, and you know how jumpy she gets. So she doesn't want any boats rocked or any strings plucked. In fact, she doesn't want anything happening at all, good or bad. Bring her the next Bin Laden's head on a plate, she'd be worried where the plate came from, in case someone claimed it on expenses.'

'She's gunna love this, then.'

'Love what?'

'I'm planning an op.'

Taverner waited for the punchline.

'Is that you being quietly impressed?'

'No, this is me not believing my ears. Were you listening to a word I said?'

'Not really. I was just waiting for you to finish.' He flicked his cigarette end into the water, and a duck changed course to investigate it. 'Popov was a myth, Katinsky's a nobody, and Dickie Bow was a part-time spook long ago. But now he's a full-time corpse, and on the phone he was carrying when he died, there's an unsent text message. One word. *Cicadas.* The same word Katinsky heard in relation to a plot dreamt up by the non-existent Alexander Popov. Tell me that's not worth checking out.'

'A dying message? Are you serious?'

'Oh yes.'

Taverner shook her head. 'You know, out of your whole crew, I really didn't think you'd crack up first.'

'Keeps you on your toes, doesn't it?'

'Lamb, there's no way Tearney's going to stand for Slough House going live. Not with the Park in economic lockdown. And not any other time either.'

'Good job I've got you then, isn't it?' Lamb said. 'What with your inability to refuse me anything.'

Slough House on an April afternoon: the promise of spring on the streets occasionally broken by the farting of traffic, but still, it was there. Min could glimpse it in the sunlight glinting off the Barbican Towers' windows, and hear it in the occasional burst of song, for the students from the nearby drama school were invulnerable to embarrassment, and would happily perform while walking to the Tube.

All aches and pains from the cycle-dash, he felt good anyway. A couple of years stuck behind a do-nothing desk, but he could turn it on when he needed to. He'd proved that this morning.

For the moment, though, he was back at that do-nothing desk, completing a do-nothing task: cataloguing parking tickets issued near likely terrorist targets, in case a suicide bomber's research included checking out the facilities first, by car, without bothering to top up the meter. Min was nearly through February without a single plate coming up twice, while Louisa, immersed in an equally tedious task, hadn't spoken for a while.

Thumb-twiddling time.

There was a theory, of course, that they were given these jobs for a reason, and the reason was that they'd grow so mind-achingly bored they'd quit, saving the Service the hassle of bringing their employment to an end, with its attendant risk of being taken to tribunal. It was a good job, thought Min, that he had a morning's real work behind him, and the prospect of more to come. A dosshouse off the Edgware Road. Piotr and Kyril holed up there, waiting for their boss to show: it wouldn't hurt to know more about that pair. Their habits, their hangouts. Something to give Min an edge, if it turned out he needed an edge. You could never have too much information, unless it was about parking tickets.

It was quiet upstairs. Lamb had disappeared after listening to Shirley Dander's report on how she'd tracked down Mr B; or that's what Min assumed she'd been reporting.

He said, 'I wonder what Shirley turned up.'

'Hmm?'

'Shirley. I wonder if she found the bald guy.'

'Oh.'

Not a lot of interest there, then.

A bus trundled past the window, its top deck empty.

'Lamb seemed keen on it, that's all,' he said. 'Like it was personal.'

'Just a whim, knowing him.'

'And I doubt River was happy Shirley got to go out and play.' He couldn't help the smile that went with that. He was remembering the speed with which he'd whipped down Old Street. And of River sitting at his desk while this was happening.

Louisa was watching him.

'What?'

She shook her head and returned to her work.

Another bus went past, this one full. How did that happen, exactly?

Min tapped a pencil against his thumbnail. 'Maybe she screwed up, do you think? I mean, she didn't have a lot to go on.'

'Whatever.'

'And she was Comms, wasn't she? Shirley. You think she has much field-time?'

And now Louisa was looking at him again. Quite hard, in fact. 'What's with the mentionitis?'

'What?'

'You want to know how Shirley got on, go chat her up. Best of luck.'

'I don't want to chat her up.'

'Not what it sounds like.'

'I'm wondering if she did okay, that's all. We're supposed to be on the same team, aren't we?'

'Yeah, right. Maybe you should give her some pointers. After your morning's adventure.'

'Maybe I should. It's not like I did so badly.'

'You could show her the ropes.'

'Yes.'

'Steer her right.'

'Yes.'

'Spank her when she's naughty,' Louisa said.

'Yes. No!'

'Min? Shut up now, okay?'

He shut up.

There was still the same promise of spring outside, but the atmosphere inside the office had unaccountably reverted to winter.

'It's a good job I've got you then, isn't it?' Lamb said. 'What with your inability to refuse me anything.'

A crooked yellow smile accompanied this, in case Taverner had forgotten what good friends they were.

'Jackson—'

'I need a workable cover, Diana. I could put one together myself, but it'd take a week or two, and I need it now.'

'So you want to run an op and you want to do it in a hurry? Does any part of that sound like a good idea?'

'I also need an operating fund. Couple of K at least. And I might need to borrow a pair of shoulders. I'm under strength at the House, what with your boy Spider's recruitment drive.'

'Webb?'

'I prefer Spider. Every time I see him, I want to swat him with a newspaper.' He gave her a sly glance. 'You know about his poaching, right?'

'Webb doesn't rearrange his desk without my permission. Of course I know.' There was a sudden clatter as the duck launched itself out of the canal and headed downwater. 'And there's no way you're using anyone from the Park. We've got Roger Barrowby counting teaspoons. Trust me, he'll notice if a warm body goes missing.'

Lamb said nothing. The wheel had turned. Any moment now, Taverner would notice she'd gone from saying the door was shut to negotiating about how far it would open.

'Oh Christ,' she muttered.

There you go.

Silently, he offered his cigarettes again, and this time she took one. When she leant in to be lit he caught a wave of her perfume. Then his lighter flared and it was gone.

Taverner leaned back, past caring about any marks the bench might leave. She closed her eyes to inhale. 'Tearney doesn't like undercover,' she said. He had the feeling she was continuing a conversation she'd had in her head many times. 'Given the chance, she'd scrap Ops and double the size of GCHQ. Distance intelgathering. Just the way Health and Safety likes it.'

'There'd be fewer joes in body bags,' Lamb said.

'There'd be fewer joes full stop. And don't pretend to defend her. She'd parade your generation before a truth and reconciliation committee. Apologising for every black-ribbon adventure you ever set up, then hugging your oppo for the cameras.'

'Cameras,' Lamb repeated. Then said, 'God, you're not even joking, are you?'

'Know what her latest memo said? That those in line for

Third Desk grade should sign up for an in-house PR course. Make sure they're fully prepared for a "customer-facing" role.'

'"Customer-facing"?'

'"Customer-facing".'

Lamb shook his head. 'I know some people. We could have her whacked.'

She touched his knee briefly. 'You're kind. Let's make that Plan B.'

After that they sat in silence while she finished her cigarette. Then she ground it beneath her heel and said, 'Okay. Enough fun and games. Unless you're ready to tell me you're kidding about this?' But a quick glance told her she wasn't getting off that easy. She checked her watch. 'Lay it out.'

Lamb told her what he had in mind.

When he'd finished, she said, 'The Cotswolds?'

'I said an op. I didn't say al-Qaeda.'

'You're going to do this anyway. Why bother even telling me about it?'

Lamb looked at her solemnly. 'I know you think I'm a loose cannon. But even I'm not stupid enough to run an op on home ground without clearing it with the Park.'

'I meant really.'

'Because you'll find out about it anyway.'

'Damn right I will. You worked out which one of your newbies is reporting back to me yet?'

His expression betrayed nothing.

She said, 'This better not turn into a circus.'

'A circus? This guy planted one of ours. If we let that happen without, what would you call it, due diligence? We let that happen without checking out who, what and why, then we're not only not doing our job, we're letting down our people.'

'Bow wasn't our people any more.'

'It doesn't work that way, and you know it.'

She sighed. 'Yes, I know it. Didn't know you did speeches, though.' She thought a moment. 'Okay. We can probably rustle up a pre-used ID without ringing bells. It won't be watertight, but it's not as if you're sending anyone into Indian country. And if you fill out a 22-F, I'll pass it through Resources. We'll lay it off as some kind of archive expense. I mean, face it, you're exploring ancient history. If that's not an archive matter, I don't know what is.'

Lamb said, 'You can nick it from petty cash for all I care. No skin off my arse.'

To verify this assertion, he gave the area in question a scratch.

'Jesus wept,' said Diana Taverner. Then said, 'I do this, we're free and clear, right?'

'Sure.'

'You'd better not be pissing about on company time, Jackson.'

In a rare moment of tact, Lamb recognised when someone needed the last word, and said nothing. Instead, he watched her out of sight, then rewarded himself with a slow grin. He had Service cover. He even had an operating fund.

Neither of which he'd have got, if he'd told her the truth.

Retrieving his phone from his pocket, he called Slough House.

'You still there?'

'Yes, that's why I'm answering the—'

'Get your arse to Whitecross. And bring your wallet.'

Snapping the phone shut, he watched as the wayward duck returned, coming to a skidding halt on the canal's glassy surface, shattering the reflected sky, but only for a moment. Then it all shivered back into shape: sky, rooftops and overhead cables, all in their proper place.

Ho would have been happy about that.

7

'YOU TOOK YOUR TIME,' Lamb said.

River, who'd arrived first, knew a Lamb tactic when he heard one. 'What did I need my wallet for?'

'You can buy me a late lunch.'

Because it had been a while since his early lunch, River surmised.

The market was packing up, but there were still stalls where you could buy enough curry and rice to feed an army, then stuff it so full of cake it couldn't march. River paid for a Thai chicken with naan, and the pair walked to St Luke's and found a bench. Pigeons clustered hopefully, but soon gave up. Possibly they recognised Lamb.

'How well did you know Dickie Bow?' River asked.

Through a mouthful of chicken, Lamb said, 'Not well.'

'But enough to light a candle.'

Lamb looked at him, chewing. He kept chewing so long it became sarcastic. When he'd at last swallowed, he said, 'You're a fuck up, Cartwright. We both know that. You wouldn't be a slow horse otherwise. But—'

'I was screwed over. There's a difference.'

'Only fuck ups get screwed over,' Lamb explained. 'May I finish?'

'Please.'

'You're a fuck up, but you're still in the game. So if you turn up dead one day, and I'm not busy, I'll probably ask around. Check for suspicious circumstances.'

'I can hardly contain my emotion.'

'Yeah, I said probably.' He belched. 'But Dickie was a Berlin hand. When you've fought a war with someone, you make sure they're buried in the right grave. One that doesn't read Clapped Out when it should say Enemy Action. Grandad never teach you that?'

River remembered a moment last year when he'd had a glimpse of the Lamb who'd fought that war. So despite Lamb now being a fat lazy bastard, he was inclined to believe him.

On the other hand, he didn't like Lamb slighting his grandfather, so said, 'He might have mentioned it. When he wasn't telling me Bow was a pisshead who claimed to have been kidnapped by a non-existent spook.'

'The O.B. told you that?' Lamb cocked his head. 'That's what you call him, right? The old bastard?'

It was, but how Jackson Lamb knew passed all understanding.

Aware that River was thinking this, Lamb gave his stalker's grin. 'Alexander Popov was a scarecrow, sure,' he said. 'What else did grandpa tell you?'

'That the Park put a file together,' River said, 'to see what it revealed about Moscow Centre's thinking. It was mostly fragments. Place of birth, stuff like that.'

'Which was?'

'ZT/53235.'

'Why doesn't it surprise me you remember that?'

'There was some kind of accident there,' River said, 'and the town was destroyed. That's a detail that sticks in your mind.'

'Well, it would,' Lamb said. 'If it had been an accident.' Scraping the last of his curry from its foil container, he shovelled it into his mouth, oblivious to the look River was giving him. 'That wasn't bad,' he said. With a practised flick of the wrist, he sent his spork spinning into a nearby bin, then sponged the remaining sauce up with his last hunk of naan. 'I'd give it a seven.'

'It was deliberate?'

Lamb arched his eyebrows. 'He didn't mention that bit?'

'We didn't go into great detail.'

'He probably had his reasons.' He chewed the naan thoughtfully. 'I'm pretty sure your gramps never did anything without a reason. No, it was no accident.' He swallowed. 'You're still too young to smoke, right?'

'I'm still not stupid enough.'

'Get back to me when you've had a life.' Lamb lit up, drew in, exhaled. Nothing about his expression suggested he'd ever considered this might be harmful. 'Z whatever you called it was a research facility. Part of the nuclear race. This is before my time, you understand.'

'Didn't realise they had nuclear capability before your time.'

'Thanks. Anyway, to our best understanding, Moscow Centre decided it harboured a spy. That someone on the inside was feeding information about the Soviet nuclear programme to the enemy. Who would be us. Or friends of ours.' Lamb became still. For a few moments, the only thing moving was the thin blue trail of smoke aching wistfully upwards from his cigarette.

River said, 'And so they destroyed it?'

Lamb said, 'Did gramps never mention, all these secret history lessons he's been giving you, how fucking serious it got? Yes, they destroyed it. They burnt the place to cinders to make sure whatever was happening there stayed hidden.'

'A town of thirty thousand people?'

'There were some survivors.'

'They destroyed it with the people still—'

'More efficient. They could be reasonably sure their spy ceased his activities forthwith. The joke being, of course, that there was no spy.'

'Some joke,' River said.

Some punchline, he thought.

'That was one of Crane's favourite stories,' Lamb said.

Amos Crane, long before River's time, had been a Service legend, for all the wrong reasons. Not so much poacher turned gamekeeper as fox turned henhouse warden.

'Crane liked to say you had the whole hall of mirrors wrapped up in that episode. They build a fort, then worry we'll burn it down. So they burn it down first, to make sure we can't.'

'And Popov's supposed to be one of those survivors, yes?' River said. In his mind, he was seeing a perfect circle. 'They destroy their own town, and years later make a bogeyman from the ashes to wreak vengeance on us.'

'Yeah, well,' Lamb said. 'Like I say, it tickled Crane.'

'What happened to Crane anyway?'

'Some chick whacked him.'

Lesser talents would need a whole novel to tell you that much, River thought.

Lamb stood, gazed at the nearest tree as if in sudden awe of nature, lifted a heel from the ground and farted. 'Sign of a good curry,' he said. 'Sometimes they just bubble about inside you for ages.'

'I keep meaning to ask why you've never married,' River said.

They crossed the road. Lamb said, 'Anyway. Scarecrow he might be. Bogeyman he was. But Dickie Bow's still dead, and he's the only one who ever claimed to set eyes on him.'

'You think Mr B's connected to the Popov legend?'

'Bow left a message on his mobile, more or less saying as much.'

River said, 'Untraceable poison. Dying message.'

'Something you want to get off your chest?'

'Seems a bit . . . unlikely.'

'Tony Blair's a peace envoy,' Lamb pointed out. 'Compared to that, everything's just business as usual.'

Speaking of which, it was time for River to get his wallet out again. They stopped at a stall serving coffee. 'Flat white,' said River.

'Coffee,' said Lamb.

'Flat white?' said the stallholder.

'Pink and chubby. Since you ask.'

'He'll have what I'm having,' said River.

Cups in hand, they walked on.

'I'm still not sure why we're having this conversation.'

'I know you think I pull a lot of shit,' Lamb said. 'But I never send a joe into the field without giving him all the info to hand.'

This took five seconds to sink in.

'The *field*?'

'Can we skip the bit where you repeat what I've just said?'

River said, 'Okay. It's skipped. The field. Where?'

'Hope you've had your jabs,' said Lamb. 'You're going to Gloucestershire.'

It was late when Min left the office. Free overtime; a not unusual reward for passive-aggressive behaviour. At five he'd turned his mobile off, so when Louisa rang she'd have to leave a message, and at seven he turned it on again: nothing. He shook his head. He deserved this. Things had been going too well. He'd screwed up without noticing. But then, that's what he was famous for. He was the one who'd managed to flush his career then go home for a good night's sleep; find out about it the following morning. The one the others laughed about, secure in the knowledge that they might all have screwed up, but at least they'd known it at the time. Hadn't needed the nation's flagship news programme to point it out.

And it wasn't talking about Shirley that had done the damage. That's just what had broken the surface, like a shark's fin. No: it was about the way they were living, dividing their relationship between two lousy addresses. It was about what they could expect from the future, sharing an office and the same lack of prospects. And always, of course, it was about his other life: the children, wife and house he'd left behind when his career went up the spout. He might have separated from them, but they were still there, placing demands on his time and emotions and income that Louisa would inevitably come to resent, if she didn't already. You could see why she'd been upset. And why it was his fault, even though it wasn't.

All of which one half of Min's brain was explaining to him while the other half was guiding him over the road to a dreadful pub, where he spent ninety minutes drinking beer and morosely shredding a beermat. Another familiar feeling; a reminder of long solitary evenings endured in the aftermath of his life hitting the wall. At least he wouldn't be hearing about this one on Radio 4 in the morning. 'In a totally unsurprising development, Min Harper has screwed up his love life and can expect to be alone for the foreseeable. And now sport. Garry?'

It was here that Min decided he'd wallowed in enough self-pity.

Because Louisa was in a snit but she'd get over it, and Slough House might be a cul-de-sac, but Spider Webb had dropped a rope ladder, and Min was grabbing it with both hands. The question was, would it hold the pair of them? Min considered the pyramid of shredded cardboard he'd constructed. It was best to regard everything as a test. He'd learned that during training, and had yet to be told to stop. So: Spider Webb. On scant acquaintance Min neither liked nor trusted Webb, and could easily believe he was playing a double game. But if that game involved a prize, it would be foolish not to attempt to win it, and equally foolish not to imagine this hadn't occurred to Louisa too. Hell, it wasn't out of the question that her snit was because Min had shown he could play the big game this morning, while she was mostly showing her prowess at admin, at paper shuffling. The kind of activity Slough House was built on.

He checked his phone again. Still no message. But let's be clear about this, he told himself: he wasn't trying to pull a fast one on Louisa. In fact he'd call and apologise and head over there later. All of that. He'd do all of that, but first he called up

Google Earth on his iPhone and examined the stretch of the Edgware Road where Piotr and Kyril's taxi had stopped. Then he left the pub and collected his bike from round the back of Slough House. It was nearly nine, and growing dark.

Diana Taverner's office had a glass wall so she could keep an eye on the kids on the hub. There was nothing overbearing about this; it was a protective instinct, a form of nurturing. The old guys would tell you the field was where it counted, but Taverner knew the stresses that mounted up backstage, as sleeplessly as rust. Across all those desks on the hub beamed intel, 24/7: most of it useless, some of it deadly; all of it to be weighed in a balance that needed recalibrating daily, according to how the wind blew. There were watch-lists to monitor, snatched footage to interpret, stolen conversations to translate, and underneath all the data processing lay the knowledge that a momentary lapse of concentration, and you'd see bodies pulled from the wreckage on the evening news. It could splinter you, such pressure; it could rob you of sleep, cheat you of dreams, and surprise you into tears at your desk. So no, keeping an eye on the kids was because she had their welfare at heart, though it also allowed her to check that none of the bastards were playing funny games. Not all of Taverner's foes lay abroad.

And to make sure the surveillance was one-way, there were ceiling-to-floor blinds she could pull when needed. They were down now, and the overhead lights were dimmed, mimicking the fading daylight outside. And standing in front of her, because she hadn't invited him to sit, was James Webb, who didn't live on the hub but had an office in the bowels of the building – 'office' sounded good, but what it meant was, he was outside the circle of power.

And thus out of her line of sight.

Time to discover what he'd been up to.

'I've been hearing stories,' she said. 'Seems you've seconded a pair of slow horses.'

'Slow . . . ?'

'Don't even think about it.'

Webb said, 'It's nothing important. I didn't think you'd want to be bothered by it.'

'When there's something I don't want to be bothered by, I like to know what it is first. So I can be sure it's not something I'd rather be bothered by.'

There was a moment's silence while they both picked a path through that one. Then Webb said, 'Arkady Pashkin.'

'Pashkin . . .'

'Sole owner of Arkos.'

'Arkos.'

'Russia's fourth largest oil company.'

'Oh. That Arkady Pashkin.'

'I've been . . . having talks with him.'

Lady Di leaned back, and her chair adjusted its position with a whisper of springs. She stared at Webb, who'd been useful once. The office in the bowels had been a reward for services, and should have been enough to keep him quiet. But that was the thing about the Spider Webbs of the world: shut them out of anywhere for long, and they fog its windowpanes with their breath.

'You're having . . . *talks* with a Russian industrialist?'

'I think he prefers "oligarch".'

'I don't care if he prefers "Czar". What the hell gave you the idea you could open up diplomatic channels with a foreign national?'

Webb said, 'It occurred to me we could do with some good news round here.'

After a pause, Taverner said, 'Well if that's your notion of "diplomatic", we can no doubt expect war with Russia any day. What kind of good news did you have in mind? And do make this . . . convincing.'

'He's a potential asset,' said Webb.

And now Lady Di leaned forward. 'He's a potential asset,' she repeated slowly.

138

'He's unhappy with the way things are over there. He finds the swing towards old-era antagonism regressive, and regrets the Mafia State image. He has political ambitions, and if we could help him in any way . . . Well, that would make him quite amenable, wouldn't it?'

'Is this a joke?'

Webb said, 'I know it sounds like shooting for the moon. But think about it. The man's a player. It's not out of the question he could take the reins.' He was growing visibly more excited. Taverner carefully avoided looking at his trousers. 'And if we're with him, if we smooth his path – I mean, really. It's the Holy Grail.'

The sensible thing would be to torch him here and now, she thought. Thirty seconds of verbal creosote, and he'd leave sooty footprints all the way back to his office, and never have an idea again. That was the sensible thing, and she was mentally turning her flame up high when she heard herself say, 'Who else knows about this?'

'Nobody.'

'What about the Slough House pair?'

'They think they're running security on oil talks.'

'How did it start?'

'He made contact. Personally.'

'With you? How come?'

'There was that thing last year . . .'

That thing. Right. *That thing last year* had been one of Ingrid Tearney's brainwaves; a charm offensive to counter the recent tsunami of PR disasters: illegal wars, accidental slayings, torturing suspects; stuff like that. Tearney had made a string of public appearances, explaining how counter-terrorist measures were safeguarding the country, even if it appeared to the uninformed that they were merely creating huge delays at airports. Webb – a spiffy dresser – had carried her bags, and provided an ear into which she could whisper when she wanted to look like she was conferring. He'd been mentioned by name in the press coverage, which he'd doubtless have been insufferable about if the term 'arm-candy' hadn't been used.

She could still torch him. Bring this to a halt before its inevitable flaws came screaming into view. Instead, she said, 'And this you call unimportant? Something I wouldn't want to be bothered with?'

'Plausible deniability,' Webb said. 'If it all goes pear-shaped . . . Well, it's one of your underlings on a frolic of his own, isn't it?' He gave a short sharp chuckle. 'That happens, I'll probably end up with the slow horses myself.'

And if you give that particular answer a shake, the picture changes completely. If it all goes according to plan, Webb finds himself dropping a big juicy bone at Ingrid Tearney's feet. The first Taverner would know about it, she'd be standing outside a closed door, wondering what the briefing was about.

But bigger men than Spider Webb had made the mistake of underestimating Diana Taverner.

She said, 'And how the hell are you slipping all this past the Barrowboy?'

Meaning Roger Barrowby, who was currently running a slide-rule over every decision taken in the Park, down to and including whether you wanted fries with that.

Spider Webb blinked twice. 'By going via Slough House,' he said.

Taverner shook her head. Christ, she was losing it. That was why he was using the slow horses: they didn't fall under Barrowby's remit. Their outgoings were practically zero, if you didn't count Lamb's expenses. 'Okay,' she said. He relaxed. 'That doesn't mean you can go.' She spared her desk drawer a brief glance: her cigarettes were in there. But last time anyone had smoked in the Park, it triggered a toxin alert. 'The whole story,' she said. 'And I mean all of it. Now.'

When Kyril had heard 'hookahs', what he'd thought he'd heard was 'hookers', and nothing about the subsequent thirty seconds had shaken that conviction: there'd been a change in the law, a Pole in a pub had told him, and now all the hookers on the Edgware Road were out on the pavements, instead of behind the windows of the Turkish restaurants. 'Hubbly-jubbly!' the Pole had concluded. Kyril had nodded in agreement. For the purposes of his mission here he wasn't supposed to understand English, but he spoke it well enough, and had a firm grasp of what 'hubbly-jubbly' signified.

The joke was, there were dozens of hookers on the Edgware Road, and plenty more on the side streets, but the hookahs the Pole had meant were the *Arabian Nights* pipes that drew tobacco up through a hose. Kyril had never tried one before, and it turned out he liked it. So he'd gone back the following evening and tried it again; sitting out on the pavement under a plastic canopy; the streets dark, and traffic hissing past. He was making friends – that was okay: what The Man didn't know wouldn't hurt him – and chatting to these friends was what he was doing when the guy from this morning, Harper, cycled past.

Kyril made no sudden movements. Just kept on smoking the hookah, laughing out loud at a brand-new joke. Watching without watching, he saw Harper haul the bike off-road and disappear round the corner. That was all right. Didn't matter if a man disappeared, so long as you knew where he was going to be, which in this case was as close by Kyril as he dared get. So Kyril dallied another ten full minutes before rising and making his excuses, and walking on to the little supermarket to load up on supplies, mostly bottles and cigarettes.

When Webb finished Taverner chewed her lower lip for a moment, before realising she was doing so. 'Why the Needle?' she asked. 'This is the secret service, or didn't you get that memo? You couldn't get more high profile if you arranged a meet in the Mall.'

'He's not some lowlife I'm trying to turn. If Pashkin's spotted in a lapdancing club, it'll raise eyebrows. If he's seen going into

London's newest piece of skyline flash, nobody'll think twice. It's his natural territory.'

She couldn't argue with the logic. 'And nobody else knows about this. The real story.'

'Just you and me.'

'And you've only told me because you're on my carpet.'

He nodded along with her. 'Because of the whole—'

'Deniability thing. So you said.' Taverner directed another penetrating gaze at her subordinate. 'I sometimes worry you're going over to the enemy,' she said.

He looked shocked. 'MI6?'

'I meant Tearney.'

'Diana,' he lied. 'That would never happen.'

'And you've told me everything.'

'Yes,' he lied.

'I want regular updates. Every tiny detail. Good or bad.'

'Of course,' he lied.

Once he'd gone, Taverner wrote an e-mail to Background, requesting a CV on Arkady Pashkin, then deleted it without sending. Last thing she wanted was any flags raised, and with Roger bloody Barrowby's audit in full swing, she'd have to explain in triplicate why she was interested. So, falling back on the first-dater's method, she Googled him instead, and came up with well under a thousand hits: he flew low for a player. First up was a year-old article from the *Telegraph*, citing his achievements. It carried a photo too, revealing Pashkin to resemble a less benign Tom Conti, a conjunction which pressed a number of Taverner's buttons. With the blinds still down, she allowed herself a moment of reverie: shag, marry or push off a cliff?

Hell, the man was a billionaire. All three. In that order.

It was late. She logged off, and sat pondering. It was always possible Webb would come back with the goods, and while the chances of Pashkin ending up both in Five's debt and in the Big Seat in the Kremlin were vanishingly small, that was how the job was played. You had to back outsiders, because insiders were spoken for. Though it wasn't always clear by whom.

Damn it, she thought. Let him go ahead. If it fell apart she'd nail him to the debris, then float him out to sea for gulls to feed on. Delusions of grandeur, she'd say. That's what came of press attention.

And don't think Ingrid Tearney wouldn't grasp the import of that.

Before leaving she pulled the blinds up, so those on the hub could admire her empty office. Nothing to hide, she thought. Nothing to hide.

Nothing at all to hide.

Some days, it just comes together.

Min Harper hadn't broken records cycling west; it was a recce, that was all, just to get a taste for the area. The road was busy off Marble Arch, and he'd slowed, looking for somewhere to chain the bike, and that's when he saw him, Kyril, the one who'd pretended not to speak English. Sitting outside a restaurant under one of those plastic tent arrangements, pulling on a hookah and laughing with the locals as if he did this every night of his life. Just like that, it all came together.

He hopped off the bike, wheeled it round a corner where he locked it to a lamppost, then squashed his high-vis vest into the pannier. Back on the main road, shielded from Kyril by a wall of traffic, he went into a newsagent's whose magazine rack barricaded the front window. He browsed this intently until Kyril rose, cracked a last joke with his buddies, then ambled along to the mini-mart on the next corner. As soon as he was inside Min crossed the road and sheltered in a shop doorway, studied the cards pinned there: *Cleaning Work Offered*, *Man with a Van*, *English Lessons*. He pretended to jot down numbers. When Kyril reappeared with a carrier bag in each hand, Min waited until he was a good hundred yards away before following, cutting his way through the crowds thronging the pavement, the

Russian's bulk an easy target. Min could taste beer on his breath. Could feel pressure building on his bladder, come to that. But what he mostly felt was the thrill of the chase – it would be so easy to stop one of these people, this approaching blonde for instance, and say *I work for the security services. See that guy? I'm following him.* But the blonde walked past without a glance, and Kyril disappeared.

Min blinked, and forced himself not to break into a run. Calm regular pace, same as before. Kyril must have stepped into another shop, or a bar; maybe there was a concealed alley ahead. The danger was, Min would end up in front of him. No, the danger was, he'd lost him . . .

But there was no danger. That was what he had to remember. There was no danger because nobody knew where he was or what he was doing. Only Min would know, as he got back on his bike and slunk across the city to Louisa's, only Min would know he'd messed up a tail job, the kind a rookie could pull off without breaking a sweat.

Some days it all fell apart.

Except, except, not today, because there he was again, that beautiful bulky Russian, stepping from an alcove where he'd stopped to examine a menu . . . Min only realised his heart had been racing because it now climbed down to normal.

Keeping the same careful hundred yards behind, he followed the Russian along the Edgware Road.

Jackson Lamb was in his office, where the only light source was at knee level, a lamp that sat on a pile of telephone directories. Enough of it crept upwards to cast troll-like shadows across his face, and bigger ones across the ceiling. On the desk, next to his feet, was a bottle of Talisker, and in his hand was a glass. His chin was on his chest, but he was awake. He seemed to be studying his cork noticeboard, to which was pinned a montage of out-of-date money-off coupons, but he might have been staring straight through it:

down a long tunnel of remembered secrets, though he'd claim if questioned that he'd been wondering whose turn it was to fetch him cigarettes. A claim he'd validated in advance by recently stubbing out the last of his current pack.

He seemed oblivious to everything, but didn't so much as flicker when Catherine Standish spoke from the doorway where she'd been standing for almost a minute. 'You drink too much.'

In answer, he raised his glass and studied its contents. Then drained it in a single swallow, and said, 'You'd know.'

'Yes. That's my point.' She came into the room. 'Having blackouts yet?'

'Not that I remember.'

'If you can joke about it, you've probably not started wetting yourself. There's a treat in store.'

'You know what's good about reformed drunks?' Lamb said.

'Please tell.'

'No, I'm asking. Is there anything good about reformed drunks? Because from where I'm sitting, they're just a pain in the arse.'

Catherine said, 'You know, that would still work if you took the word *reformed* out.'

Lamb gave her a penetrating stare, then nodded thoughtfully, ruefully, as if arriving at a gentle appreciation of her wisdom. Then he farted. 'Better out than in,' he said. 'You know, that would still work if it was about you.'

Proving once and for all that she couldn't take a hint, Catherine went nowhere. Instead she said, 'I've been doing a little digging.'

'Oh god.'

'And you know what?' Moving two box files onto the floor, she claimed the chair they'd been occupying. 'The night Dickie Bow died, that mess with the trains?'

'Amaze me.'

'Someone sabotaged a fusebox outside Swindon. The network meltdown was a fix. You don't think that's suspicious?'

'I think it shows a lack of faith in First Great Western,' Lamb said. 'The idea that you need to resort to sabotage to create chaos, that's preposterous.'

'Very funny. What are you up to, Lamb?'

'It's above your pay grade. Let's just say I found a loose thread, and pulled it.' He looked at his watch. 'Are you still here?'

She said, 'Yes. And guess what? I'm not going anywhere. Because it took me a while to work it out, but I got there. I don't know why you wanted me in Slough House, but you did. And you're not going to get rid of me, are you? I don't know why, but I know it's so. You feel guilty. I don't like you and doubt I ever will, but beneath all your stupid drunken offensiveness, you're paying off some debt, and that gives me an advantage. It means you can't shut me up.'

Lamb said, 'That was cute. If this was a film you'd let your hair down now and I'd say, but Miss Standish, you're beautiful.'

'No, if this was a film I'd stake you through the heart, and you'd disappear in a cloud of dust. Dickie Bow, Lamb. He was a has-been.'

'Yep. He'd have fitted in round here like a dream.'

'He was also a drunk.'

'Further comment would be tactless.'

She ignored that. 'I pulled his records. He—'

'You what?'

'I asked Ho to pull his records.'

'I hope you're not corrupting that kid. We've already got a ringer on the premises.'

'A what?'

He said, 'Lady Di tells me one of our newbies is her snitch. Find out which, would you?'

'It's on my to-do list. Meanwhile, Bow. You know he spent the past three years on the nightshift in a Brewer Street bookshop.'

'I doubt the booktrade's what pays their rent.'

'No, he was downstairs with the dirty mags and the sex toys.'

Lamb spread his hands in a forgiving gesture. 'Really, who hasn't found themselves, one time or another, leafing through a porn mag with a dildo in their hand?'

'A fascinating glimpse into your home life. But let's not change the subject. Last time Bow was in play Roger Moore was James Bond. You really think he found a Moscow hood and tracked him halfway across the country?'

Lamb said, 'He died.'

'I know he did.'

'That's what makes me think he found a Moscow hood and tracked him halfway across the country.'

'No. Dying doesn't prove he found a Moscow hood. All it proves is he's dead. And if a Moscow hood killed him, that doesn't mean you found a thread and pulled. It means a thread was dangled, and you snapped it up.'

Lamb said nothing.

'Exactly as you were meant to.'

Lamb said nothing.

'You've gone quiet. Run out of funny comments?'

Lamb pursed his lips. He looked like he was about to blow a raspberry, which wouldn't have been the first time. But instead he unpursed them, sucked his teeth, then leaned back and combed his hair with his fingers. To the ceiling he said, 'Untraceable poison. Dying message. Give me a fucking break.'

Now it was Catherine's turn to be fazed. 'What?'

When Lamb looked at her, his eyes were clearer than they ought to have been, given the level of the bottle.

'You really think I'm stupid?' he asked.

Up ahead was the flat. It was the top floor of a dump held up by mould and damp, whose painted-over windows had trapped the air inside for decades, making it an olfactory museum of poverty and desperation, smells Kyril was familiar with. Most rooms were hot-beds: men coming home from work as others left for the nightshift. Communication was nod-of-the-head. Nobody cared about anyone else's business.

Which was how The Man liked it, but Kyril was a people person. One of his strengths. So much so it could be taken for a weakness, which was why Piotr had decided Kyril couldn't speak English this morning.

'What's the harm? They're civil servants.'

'They're spooks,' Piotr had said. 'Civil servants? They're spooks. You believe that Department of Energy crap?'

Kyril had shrugged. Yes, he'd believed that Department of Energy crap. Probably not a great thing to admit.

'So I do the talking,' Piotr said.

And Piotr had been right, because if the guy was from the Department of Energy, how come he was tailing Kyril now?

Though if he was a spook, how come he was so bad at it?

There was always the chance there were others Kyril hadn't spotted, but he figured Harper was alone, which suited him fine. Harper wouldn't present problems. Kyril could snap him in half with one hand, and throw him in opposite directions.

That made him smile. He didn't enjoy violence, and hoped the need wouldn't arise.

But if it did, he could handle it.

Shirley Dander opened her eyes. The crack running outwards from a corner of her ceiling was the shape of a continent, an unfamiliar animal, a dimly remembered birthday. For long seconds she hovered inside its reach, and then she was awake, and it was just a crack.

Her skull pulsed to someone else's beat. Whoever was playing that drum had stolen the daylight.

Risking movement, she turned her head to the window. It wasn't dark, but only because there was a city outside, pouring its electric wash over everything. So the light bleeding through her thin faded curtain was yellow and automatic, and came from a nearby lamppost.

The bedside clock blinked at her. Nine forty-two. Nine forty-two? Jesus.

At Slough House, after giving Jackson Lamb her report, Shirley had suffered a cocaine crash. These were not unfamiliar, but generally planned for, and came with a duvet, a tray of brownies and a DVD of *Friends*. When you were heading for a hard landing, an office with an inquisitive colleague was not the place to be.

'Good morning, was it?'

Marcus Longridge would not have believed the effort her grunt of reply required.

But the man would not give up. 'Enjoy your trip?'

This time she managed to shrug. 'Country. I can take it or leave it.'

'More a beach girl?'

'Less of the "girl".'

In front of her, the virtual coalface once more. One brief taste of the outside world and she was matching faces again, like trying to play snap without a twinned pair in the deck. She'd told Lamb she'd been up all night, that tracking down Mr B had been what she'd done instead of sleeping, but all that earned her was a toothy snarl. 'You'll be looking forward to home-time then, won't you?' he'd said.

Marcus was still watching. 'I need food,' he said. 'You want anything?'

A dark room, a quiet bed, the temporary absence of life.

'Shirley?'

'Maybe a Twix.'

'Be right back.'

When he'd gone, Shirley crossed to the window. After a moment, Marcus had appeared on the street below. Instinctively she'd drawn back, but he hadn't looked upwards; just crossed the road, heading for the row of shops. As he walked, he held his mobile to his ear.

Paranoia came with the territory. Every hangover she'd ever

known – beer, tequila, cocaine, sex – had left her furtive and hunted. But even allowing for that, she'd been certain she was the subject of that phone call.

Back in the here and now, she groaned softly. This did nothing to change the quality of the light, the pulsing of her skull, or the black pit that opened every time she closed her eyes.

Nine forty-five, winked her clock. She could stay where she was for another ten hours, and maybe that would make her all right again.

Maybe . . .

She gave it five minutes; then got up, dressed, and headed out into the evening.

Kyril had vanished once more. When Min turned the corner to discover this he swore under his breath, tasting beer again: but still. It wasn't the end of the world. It suggested that the target had reached his destination.

Doss house had been his first thought when he'd heard that the taxi had dropped them on the Edgware Road. He wasn't wrong. These buildings were tall and imposing-looking, but their glory days were long gone, and regeneration hadn't taken off yet: banks of doorbells showed they were multi-occupancy, and the blankets and newspapers taped across windows betrayed the low-paid status of their inhabitants.

You and me both, mate, thought Min. Then a hand like a rock gripped his shoulder, and something cold and blunt and steel pressed into his neck.

'You're following me, I think, yes?'

Min said, 'I—what? What you talking about—'

'Mr Harper. I think you're following me. Yes?' The steel thing pressed harder.

'I just—'

'You just what?'

Just need a moment to think up a story, thought Min.

The steel thing pressed harder.

'So now you know what?' Kyril said. 'Now you find out what happens to Department of Energy guys who get too nosy, know what I mean?'

Lamb opened a drawer and produced a second glass, chipped and dusty, into which he poured a careful measure of Talisker he then placed within Catherine's reach. Then he refilled his own glass, with a measure a little less careful.

'Chin chin,' he said.

Catherine didn't respond. Nor did she glance at her glass.

'The Swindon fusebox was sabotaged, yes. You really think I'd go plodding about the shires without making sure it was necessary? The trains were scuppered about the same time our friend Mr B was laying a trail for Dickie Bow.'

'Why?'

'Because you don't lay a trail down a well-kept pavement. You make the hunter work.'

'He wanted Bow to follow him.'

Lamb put his glass down to give her a slow handclap.

'And wanted you to do the same,' she said. 'You found something on his body, didn't you?'

'On the bus. His phone. With an unsent text.'

She raised an eyebrow. 'Keyed in his dying moments?'

'Keyed by Mr B, more like. There was a scrum when people realised he was dead. Mr B would have been part of it, keying the message, shoving the phone between the cushions.'

'What was the message?'

'One word,' said Lamb. '*Cicadas*.'

'Which evidently means something.'

'To me, yes. Shouldn't have meant anything to Bow, though. Another reason I know it's a fake.'

'And the untraceable poison?'

'Ten a penny. Most untraceable poisons aren't actually untraceable, but you have to find them before they fade away. A clapped-out wino has a heart attack, most post-mortems'll just read heart attack.' He made a magician's gesture with his hands. '*Pouf*. End of. But there'll have been a puncture wound some-where. Easy enough to prick someone in a crowd.'

Catherine said, 'Hardly foolproof, is it? What are the chances you'd have checked between the cushions for Bow's phone?'

'Someone would've. You don't off a spook, even a clapped-out nobody like Bow, without making waves. Didn't used to, anyway. Seems Regent's Park's got better things to do these days.' He reached for his glass. 'Someone ought to let them know. You never leave your corpses by the pool.'

'I'll circulate a memo.'

'Besides, if I hadn't found that clue, there'd have been another. All the way up to Mr B giving a taxi driver a bollocking for taking him to the wrong place. That'd not be forgotten in a hurry, would it?' Lamb curled a lip. 'The cabbie's a tripwire. He'd have been on the phone the moment Shirley left him.'

'Meaning he knows we're following his lead.'

'Like good little bloodhounds.'

'Is that wise?'

'What's wise got to do with it? We either follow his trail or forget about it. And that's not an option, because whoever's behind this is old school. Takes an old school spook to know a street rat like Bow would take his bait in the first place. Whoever's pulling the strings is playing Moscow rules. Regent's Park might be too busy to think that's worth following up, but I don't.'

'Are you going to say his name or am I?'

'Say what?'

'Alexander Popov,' said Catherine Standish.

The room was small, and the window open. It was cold, but still: a bead of sweat dislodged itself from Min's hair and trickled down his neck. The eyes of the other two men never left his. There was always the possibility he was faster than both, but deep in his gut he knew that that was slim beyond reckoning:

either one, on their own, and he might have been in with a chance, but the pair together made for formidable opposition. Once, his reflexes might have been up to this. But he was growing older every moment, and had been drinking earlier, and . . .

A fist slammed on the table.

Three shots . . .

Min was fast, but fast didn't cut it. Maybe anywhere else in London, he'd have been fine, but here and now in this room he was toast.

The third shot, he spilt most of. Piotr and Kyril were already leaning back, empty glasses lined up, roaring.

When he could speak, Kyril said, 'You lose.'

'I lose,' Min admitted. The three vodkas joined the two from the previous round, and the one from the round before that. Plus the penalty shots for having lost both. Plus the beers he'd drunk in that pub near where he worked, though finer details, such as what the pub was called, and where he worked, had grown hazy. These guys, though – these guys. These guys were kind of crazy, but it was surprising how quickly barriers broke down when you got past the job descriptions. Like his own, which was to keep an eye on these guys without them knowing he was doing so.

It was possible he'd compromised that particular part of his mission.

'So tell me,' Kyril said, 'When I did that thing with the key. When I—'

'Stuck it in the back of my neck, you bastard!'

Kyril laughed. 'You thought it was a gun, yes?'

'Of course I thought it was a gun! You bastard!'

All three were laughing now. It was a picture, for sure: Min, convinced his last moments had come. That a Russian spy had a pistol screwed into his neck, and was about to pull the trigger.

Kyril stopped laughing long enough to say, 'I couldn't resist.'

'How long did you know I was there?'

'Always. I saw you on your bicycle.'

'Jesus,' Min shook his head. But he didn't feel too low. Okay, so he'd messed up, but it hadn't had serious consequences. Though he was pretty sure it would be best if nobody else got to hear about it. Specifically Lamb, he thought. And Louisa. And everybody else. But specifically them.

Piotr said, 'Don't feel too bad. We do security. We're trained to spot faces in crowds.'

'Just like you are trained to do whatever it is you do in the . . . Department of Energy,' Kyril added. His broad smile supplied invisible quotation marks.

'Look—' Min began, but Piotr was waving a hand, as if seeing him off on a journey.

'Hey. Hey. Arkady Pashkin is an important man. You think we don't know there will be . . . interest in him? Government interest? We'd be worried if there wasn't. It would mean he was no longer important. And people who aren't important don't need people like us.'

'If my bosses found out I was here—'

'You mean,' Kyril said slyly, 'if they found out you'd botched a shadowing job.'

Min said, 'Well, I tracked you to your lair all right.'

'And now you're finding out what happens to Department of Energy guys who get too nosy.'

They all roared again. Piotr refilled the glasses.

'To successful outcomes.'

Min was happy to drink to that. '*Pravda*,' he said, because it was the only Russian word he knew.

And everyone roared with laughter again, and another round had to be poured.

They were on the topmost floor, which was a self-contained flat. This was the kitchen, and there were at least two other rooms. The kitchen was clean, though the window was smeared with the usual city grime. The fridge was full, and not just with vodka. It held cartons of juice and bundles of vegetables, plus little wrapped packets from delis. This pair were used to being away from home, Min suspected, and knew how to take care of themselves in a foreign city without resorting to takeaways. He also suspected that if he drank much more he'd forget where he lived, let alone the ability to cycle there. Last thing he wanted was to finish up under a bus.

There was a noise from elsewhere, the front door opening and closing, and someone new wandered into the room. Min turned, but whoever it had been was already vanishing back into the hallway.

Piotr said, 'One moment,' and left the kitchen.

Kyril poured more vodka.

'Who was that?' Min asked.

'Nobody. A friend.'

'Why doesn't he join us?'

'He's not that sort of friend.'

'Not a drinking man,' Min surmised. His glass flaunted itself in front of him. What had he just decided about alcohol? But it would be rude to leave a full glass, so he echoed whatever toast Kyril had proclaimed, and threw the vodka down his throat.

Piotr returned, and said something to Kyril that sounded to Min like a pile-up of consonants.

'What's up?' he asked.

'Nothing,' said Kyril. 'Nothing at all.'

Paranoia was back, if it had ever been away. Shirley Dander, all in black, fitted like a bath plug on the streets of Hoxton, but still felt out of place, as if her every step left a neon footprint.

Hardly night-time, really. Half past ten.

There was a pub she favoured, mostly because she had a contact there. She didn't like to say 'dealer': dealer implied habit; habit implied problem; and Shirley didn't have a problem, she had a lifestyle. One she had no intention of allowing to die the way her career had. That Slough House was a graveyard, she'd never been in doubt; that the earth was piled on quite so high, she'd just discovered. She'd done what Jackson Lamb had asked – done it well, without missing a beat – and all she'd earned was a back-to-your-desk. And from stories she'd heard, it was a miracle she'd been sent out at all. Slow horses came and slow horses went, and the passage between was spent tethered in their stalls. It was as if her mission had been one of calculated cruelty: give her a glimpse of the sunshine, then close the stable door.

Screw Lamb anyway, though. He wanted to make her life difficult, he'd find that was a two-way street.

The pub was crowded three deep at the bar. Didn't matter. She wasn't planning on staying. A familiar face raised a hand in greeting, but Shirley feigned abstraction and worried her way through to the toilets, which were round the far side: a sleazy corridor with a smeared mirror, and handbills pasted to the walls for open-mic poetry nights, local bands, the Stop the City rally, transgender cabarets. She didn't have to wait long. Her contact sidled through from the bar, and precisely seventeen words later Shirley was leaving, three banknotes lighter, a comfortable weight nestling in her pocket.

Black jacket. Black jeans. She should have been invisible, but felt marked out. Memories of the previous night flashed from car windscreens: that kid she'd scared half to death, raiding DataLok. That was how easy it was to terrorise. You simply had to believe your cause was just; or failing that, simply not care about the people you were doing it to . . . When she turned, Shirley was convinced there'd be someone in her wake; a face from the pub; one of the wall-huggers whose eyes were always busy, but who never dared approach. Well, stuff them. Shirley was spoken for; and besides, she didn't dance where she shopped. That's what she was thinking when she looked back, but the street was empty, or seemed to be empty. Paranoia, that's all. The comfortable weight in her pocket would take care of it.

All in black, she carried on her way.

★

'Alexander Popov,' said Catherine Standish.

Lamb regarded her thoughtfully. 'Now, where'd you come across that name?' he asked.

She let him wonder.

'I sometimes worry you're going over to the enemy.'

She looked askance. 'Regent's Park?'

'I meant GCHQ. You got me bugged, Standish?'

She said, 'You're sending River undercover—'

'Oh god, I might have guessed,' Lamb sighed.

'—into something you already know is a trap?'

'I only told him a couple of hours ago. Did he change his Facebook status already?'

'I'm serious.'

'So am I. Did gramps not teach that kid anything except how to tell stories?' Raising his glass to his mouth again, his eyes remained fixed on the one he'd poured for Catherine. It sat like a challenge, or a carefully worded insult. 'Besides, trap or not, he wouldn't care. An op's an op. He probably thinks all his Christmases just came at once.'

'I'm sure he does. But you know what Christmas is like. It always ends in tears.'

'He's going to the Cotswolds, Standish. Not Helmand Province.'

'There's something Charles Partner used to say about Ops. The friendlier the territory, the scarier the natives.'

'Was that before or after he blew his brains out?'

Catherine didn't answer.

Lamb said, 'What everyone seems to forget is that even if Alexander Popov never existed, whoever invented him did. And if the same smartarse is making a mousetrap in our backyard, we need to find out why.' He belched. 'If that means making Cartwright our designated cheese-eater, so be it. He's a trained professional, remember. Being a fuck-up is only his hobby.'

'He's your white whale, isn't he? Popov?'

'What's that mean?'

'Something else Charles once said. That it's dangerous person-alising an enemy. Because when that happens, you're chasing a white whale.' Catherine paused. 'It's a *Moby-Dick* reference. It probably works better if you don't need that explained. River doesn't know he's taking bait, does he?'

'No,' said Lamb. 'And he's not going to find out. Or your confidence about your unassailable role here might turn out to be misplaced.'

She said, 'I'll not tell him.'

'Good. You planning on drinking that?'

Catherine poured her glass's contents into Lamb's. 'Unless I decide he's in danger,' she went on. 'It's your whale, after all. No reason anyone else should die trying to stick a harpoon in it.'

'Nobody's going to die,' said Lamb. Inaccurately, as it turned out.

The phone rang.

Because the body carried a Service card, red flags went up. This meant attending police officers were demoted to traffic duty, while Nick Duffy – the Park's Head Dog – became scene boss, and his underdogs measured angles and took witness statements.

Most of the witnesses had arrived after the event, though not the car's driver, obviously. The car's driver had turned up at precisely the moment the event took place.

'Came out of nowhere,' she repeated.

She was blonde and appeared sober; an impression borne out by a breathalyser borrowed from a disgruntled cop.

'I didn't stand a chance.'

A voice tremor, but that was understandable: mash into some-one with your car, blameless or not, and you were bound to feel shaky.

It wasn't the busiest junction, this time of night, but you wouldn't want to cross it blind. Though of course, if you were drugged up or drunk, the Green Cross Code might not be top of your agenda.

'I mean, I hit the brake but—'

The shakes took her again.

Nick Duffy heard himself saying, 'Look, I'm sure it wasn't your fault.' Christ, he sounded like a special constable.

But she was blonde and reasonably fit, and the corpse had a Service card but was from Slough House, which was every bit as special as a constable; the same way some kids were special, and had special needs. When a spook died under a car, you had to poke around carefully, in case the car — metaphorically speaking — had dodgy plates, but when you found out the spook was a slow horse, you refigured the odds. Maybe they'd just been looking the wrong way. Left/right. It could be a confusing issue.

And she was blonde and reasonably fit . . .

'But I need to take a look at your licence.'

Which told him she was one Rebecca Mitchell, thirty-eight, British citizen; nothing on the face of any of that suggesting she'd just carried out a hit. Though of course, the best hits were carried out by the least likely hitters.

Nick Duffy scanned the junction again. His Dogs were checking kerbs and shop doorways: last time a car took out a spook a gun had gone missing, and Bad Sam Chapman, his immediate predecessor, had wound up on the short end of an internal inquiry. Last heard of, he was working for some private outfit. Not a fate Duffy was ready for, thanks. As he handed the licence back, a taxi arrived, and out climbed Jackson Lamb. A woman was with him, and it only took Duffy a moment to collect the name: Catherine Standish, who'd been a fixture at the Park back when Duffy was a pup, but went into exile after Charles Partner's suicide. The pair ignored him. They went straight for the body.

He said to Rebecca Mitchell, 'You'll need to make a statement. There'll be someone along shortly.'

She nodded mutely.

Leaving her, Duffy approached the new arrivals, about to tell them to back away from the body, but before he could speak Lamb turned, and the expression on his face persuaded Duffy to keep his mouth shut. Then Lamb looked down at the body again, and then up the street. Duffy couldn't tell what he was focusing on: the cross traffic at distant junctions; the lights jewelling the highway. Always, in the city, there were strings of pearls at night; sometimes fairy lights strung for a wedding; sometimes glass-and-paste baubles, hung for a funeral.

Standish spoke to Jackson Lamb.

'Who's going to tell Louisa?' she said.

Part Two

White Whales

8

To begin with what it hasn't got, Upshott has no high street, not like those in nearby villages, with their parades of mock-Tudor frontages gracefully declining riverwards, clotted with antique shops and garden-furniture showrooms; whose grocery stores offer stem-ginger biscuits and seven kinds of pesto, and whose pubs' menus wouldn't be out of place in Hampstead. It doesn't have cafés with the day's specials chalked on pavement blackboards, or independent bookshops boasting local-author events; nor are its back lanes lined with neatly coiffed hedges guarding houses of soft yellow stone. Because Upshott doesn't invite the epithet 'chocolate boxy', so often delivered through gritted teeth. If it resembles any kind of chocolate box, it's the kind found on the shelf at its only supermarket: coated with dust, its cellophane crackly and yellowing.

Take that high street, which Upshott doesn't have. What it has, instead, is a main road that curves once upon entering the village, to avoid the church, and then again three hundred yards later as it threads between the pub on its left and the semi-circular green on its right. Then it climbs past the new-build housing; past the small primary school and the village hall, a modern prefab visitors need directions to find. But then, the hall isn't Upshott's heartbeat; that would be the trinity of postbox, pub and village shop. The first of these sits on the side of the green furthest from the road, which is inconvenient, unless you live in one of the houses lining that stretch. Arranged in a curve, they are Upshott's oldest dwellings – three-storey eighteenth-century townhouses peculiarly resituated here, making strange near-neighbours for those bungalows on the rise, most of which stand empty, having once been homes for service staff on the nearby USAF base: cleaners and janitors, cooks and washers-up, mechanics and drivers. When the base pulled the plug in the mid-nineties, a lot of life drained out of Upshott. What's left mostly lives in those townhouses, or further along the main road, and sooner or later all of it turns up at the pub.

Which is called The Downside Man, and faces the green, with a small car park to its left and a tiered patio round back, overlooking the woods' curving tree line a mile distant. The Downside Man has whitewashed walls and a wooden pub sign which once flapped in the breeze, but also came loose in high winds, so has now been fixed to its post by Tommy Moult, the village's honorary odd-job man. Tommy's rumoured to have a secret life, as he's only ever seen at weekends, when he can reliably be found outside the village shop, red woollen cap pulled over his ears, selling packets of seeds from his bicycle, which he parks next to the racks of vegetables. He evidently regards this as the linchpin of his commercial enterprise, because every Saturday morning, winter or summer, there he is; networking more than selling, perhaps, because few locals pass without exchanging words.

The shop where he stands is back the way we came, on the corner facing St Johnno's. To get there from the pub is to pass, on the left, a row of stone cottages, interrupted by the old manor house, now converted into flats. On the right are larger, newer houses, yet to bed down into the landscape; they're too clean, too neatly brushed. In the gaps between them, though, views of the mile-distant tree line can still be enjoyed, and if the occasional presence of a cement mixer indicates that some of those gaps were intended to sprout houses of their own, there's little other sign of building activity. That all came to a halt years back. It might start up again once things improve, but the financial crisis remains as ill-defined as an unbuilt house; you can sketch its possible shape on the air, but there's no touching its walls to know its limits. And then the road bends again, between shop and church, St John of the Cross: thirteenth-century and pretty as a postcard, it has a lychgate and a well-tended graveyard, whose oldest occupants once inhabited the manor house, and who presumably rolled over when its conversion into flats took place. But services at St Johnno's are now on a fortnightly basis; far more reliable is the village shop, open eight till ten daily, though this bears no resemblance to the upmarket boutiques of the prettier villages, its shelves stacked high with stuff people need rather than want: tinned foods, dairy foods, frozen foods; sacks of charcoal, bags of kitty litter, breeze blocks of toilet rolls; shampoos, soaps and toothpastes; fridgefuls of lager and wine; cartons of juice and bottles of milk.

For many locals, the shop is as far as they need to go on any pedestrian expedition; the road, though, pootles on, passing a few more raggle-taggle cottages before dwindling into a minor country highway, hedged either side and badly potholed. A mile further on, it reaches the MoD range – when the American base upped sticks the Ministry of Defence stepped in, and land once leased to friendly aircraft is now home to friendly fire. When red flags fly, there's no rambling across the fields south-east of Upshott; and sometimes, after dark, great balls of light drop from the sky, illuminating the ranges for night practice. Adjoining the road, separated from it by an eight-foot wire mesh fence, lies the last remaining airstrip, at one end of which sit, like properties on a Monopoly board, a hangar and a club-house. These see civilian activity several evenings a week, and most weekend mornings during spring and summer are the launchpad for a single-engined plane, which putters over Upshott before disappearing into the open skies, though so far, it's always returned.

A quiet place, then – that gunfire notwithstanding. Sleepy, even, though in fact it wakes early by and large, as most of those who live there work elsewhere, and tend to be on the road by eight. So perhaps a better word would be *harmless* – as Jackson Lamb pointed out, it's hardly Helmand Province.

Though even harmless villages suffer screams in the afternoon.

'Jesus!' River screamed . . . too late. Full-body armour wouldn't have helped him. Prayer was all he had, and then not even that: just prayer's echo, bouncing around his thoughtless skull as his body went into spasm, and then again, and then stopped, or seemed to stop, and his eyes relaxed behind their tight-shut lids, and the darkness he was locked in became softer.

After a while, his companion said, 'Blimey,' but it didn't sound like a good blimey. Rolling off him, she pulled the sheet up to her shoulders. River lay still, heartbeat returning to normal, skin damp – he'd lasted long enough to work up a sweat.

But doubted he'd be raising that in mitigation.

It was mid-afternoon, a Tuesday, River's third week in Upshott, and he lay in the curtain-darkened bedroom of one of the new-builds on the northern rise, a house rented under his cover name, Jonathan Walker. Jonathan Walker was a writer. Why else would anyone come to Upshott out of season? Even if Upshott had a season. So Jonathan Walker wrote thrillers, and had an Amazon entry to prove it, *Critical Mass*, whose non-existence hadn't saved it from a one-star review. He was currently working on a novel set on a US military base in the eighties. Hence Upshott, out of season.

His companion said, 'I used to have a tee-shirt. *Boys wanted – no experience necessary*. Careful what you wish for, eh?'

'Sorry,' he said. 'It's been a while.'

'Yeah, I read your body language.'

Her name was Kelly Tropper, and she tended bar at The Downside Man: she was early twenties, petite, flat-chested, with crow-coloured hair; a string of adjectives River would have found dispiritingly inadequate if he really were a writer. She also had creamy, unfreckled skin, a curiously flattened nose, which gave her the appearance of pressing up against a pane of glass, and had described herself in his hearing as a cynic. She wrapped her leg round his. 'Not falling asleep now, are you?' Her hand explored him. 'Hmm. Not totally lifeless. Still need a few minutes, though.'

'Which we could fill with conversation.'

'You sure you're not a girl? No, wait. You came too fast to be a girl.'

'Let's keep that between us, shall we?'

'Depends how you make out in round two. That village noticeboard's not just for show.' She moved her leg. 'Celia Morden pinned a review of Jez Bradley there once. She said it wasn't her, but everyone knew.' She laughed. 'Don't get that in your big city London, do you?'

'No, but we have this thing called the internet. On which similar things happen, I'm told.' Which earned him a nip on the arm. She had teeth. He said, 'Were you born here?'

'Ooh, getting personal?'

'Well, not if it's classified.'

She nipped him again, a little less sharply. 'My folks moved here when I was two. Wanted to get out of London. Dad commuted for a while, then joined a practice in Burford.'

'Not farming stock, then.'

'Hardly. Mostly urban refugees round here. But we treat strangers nicely, don't you think?' She stroked him again.

'And do you get many of those?'

She tightened her grip. 'Meaning?'

'I was just wondering what kind of . . . turnover the village sees.'

'Hmm.' She resumed stroking. 'That better be all you meant. And it still makes you sound like an estate agent.'

'Background,' he improvised. 'For the book. You know, how quiet it is now the base has gone.'

'The base went years ago.'

'Still . . .'

'Well, it's pretty dead. But getting livelier.' Her eyes flashed. They were startlingly green, River thought. He was hoping she was going to come up with a sudden memory, suppressed till now: a bald man who appeared a few weeks ago; a name, an address . . . Three weeks, and he'd yet to catch a sniff of Mr B. He'd become an accepted feature at The Downside Man, and locals greeted him by name; he knew who lived where and which houses were empty. But of Mr B he'd glimpsed not hair nor hide, a silly phrase given his naked dome, but it was hard to concentrate with Kelly doing what she was doing with her fingers, and now – 'That's more like it,' she said slowly – with her lips, and then River lost his train of thought entirely, and instead of being an agent in the field he was under the covers with a lovely young woman, who deserved a better accounting than he'd managed earlier.

Happily, this time he provided it.

It was the day before the summit, and Arkady Pashkin had arrived. He was in the Ambassador on Park Lane. The traffic outside was an angry mess, a fist-fight continued by other means; in the lobby, there was only the trickling of water from a small fountain, and a polite murmur from the reception desk, whose guardians had been drawn from the pages of *Vogue*. Wealth had once fascinated Louisa Guy, the same way the flight of birds had: the attempt to comprehend something eternally out of reach could be dizzying. But three weeks since Min's death, she observed how the rich live as a series of security details. Shots fired outside would reach the lobby as corks being popped. Someone mown down by a car would be lost entirely; wouldn't be countenanced by the purified air.

Behind her, Marcus Longridge said, 'Cool.'

Marcus and Louisa had been paired. She didn't like it, but it was part of a deal she'd lately made. This deal was apparently with the Service, or more particularly Spider Webb, but in fact was one she'd made with reality. The hard part was not letting on how much she'd been prepared to give away. What she'd wanted was to stay on the job; specifically, on the assignment she and Min had been handed. What she'd been prepared to give away was everything.

Pashkin was in the penthouse. Why would anyone imagine otherwise? The lift made less noise than Marcus's breathing, and its doors opened straight into the suite, where Piotr and Kyril waited, the former smiling. He shook hands with Marcus, and said to Louisa, 'It's good to see you again. I was sorry to hear about your colleague.'

She nodded.

Kyril remained by the lift while Piotr led them across the large pale room, which was thickly carpeted and smelt of spring flowers. Louisa wondered if they pumped scent in through vents. Pashkin rose from an armchair at their approach. 'Welcome,' he said. 'You're the Energy people.'

'Louisa Guy,' Louisa said.

'Marcus Longridge,' Marcus added.

Pashkin was in his mid-fifties, and resembled a British actor she couldn't put a name to. Of average height but broad-shouldered, he had thick black hair left deliberately vague; sleepy eyes under heavy brows. There was more hair on his chest, easily visible beneath an open-necked white shirt, which was tucked into dark-blue jeans. 'Coffee? Tea?' He raised an eyebrow at Piotr, who was hovering. Had she not known him for a goon, Louisa would have assumed him a butler, or the Russian equivalent. A valet. A man's man.

'Nothing for me.'

'We're fine. Really.'

They settled on easy chairs arranged round a rug that looked a hundred years old, but in a good way.

'So,' Arkady Pashkin said. 'Everything is ready for tomorrow, yes?'

He was addressing them both, but speaking to Louisa. That was apparent.

And fine by her.

Because on that bad bad night when Min Harper had died, Louisa had felt she'd fallen through a trapdoor; had suffered that internal collapse you get when the floor disappears, and you've no idea how far away the ground is. It should have surprised her afterwards, how swiftly she'd assimilated the fact of Min's death; as if, all this time, she'd been waiting for the other shoe to drop. But nothing surprised her any more. It was all just information. The sun rose, the clock spun, and she conformed to their established pattern. It was information. A new routine.

Except, ever since, she'd had an ache at the hinge of her jaw; intermittently, too, her mouth would flood with saliva, repeatedly, for minutes at a time. It was as if she were weeping from the wrong orifice. And when she lay in the dark, she feared that if she fell asleep her body would forget to breathe, and she'd die too. Some nights she'd have welcomed this. But on most she clung to the deal instead.

It was the deal that stopped her falling further, or at least promised a survivable landing. The deal was the branch growing out of the cliffside; the open-topped truck parked below, bearing a fresh load from the pillow factory. It was in Regent's Park that it had come to life. This was four days after Min's death, and the weather had perked up, as if in consolation. There were interview suites on the Park's upper floors where they enjoyed watercooler moments rather than waterboarding incidents, and this one had comfortable seating, and framed posters from classic movies on the walls. It had been kitted out since Louisa had last been here, and even if everything else in her life had felt normal would still have rung strange. Like returning to school and finding they'd turned the sixth form into an aromatherapy centre.

James Webb did sympathy like he'd studied the textbook. 'I'm sorry for your loss.' An American textbook. 'Min was a fine colleague. We'll all miss him.'

She said, 'If he was that fine, he'd not have been at Slough House, would he?'

'Well—'

'Or gone cycling through heavy traffic pissed. In the rain.'

'You're angry with him.' He pursed his lips. 'Have you talked to anyone? That can . . . help.'

What would help more would be to plant her fist in the middle of that mouth. But she'd learned the hard way what others expect from grief, so she lied: 'Yes. I have.'

'And taken leave?'

'As much as I need.'

Which had been a day.

His gaze turned towards the windows. These overlooked the park across the road, and because it was mid-morning there was a lot of pre-school traffic out there: women, prams, toddlers exploring grass verges. A car backfired and a flock of pigeons erupted, swam a figure eight through the air, and resettled on the lawn.

'I don't mean to sound insensitive,' he said, 'but I have to ask. Are you okay to continue the assignment?'

He had lowered his voice. This was theoretically a grief meeting, but they were alone, and she'd known he'd bring up the Needle job.

'Yes,' she said.

'Because I can—'

'I'm fine. Angry, okay, I'm angry with him. It was a stupid thing to do, and he ended up – well, he died. So yes. Angry. But I can still do my job. I need to do my job.'

She thought she'd pitched that right – with the right amount of emotion. If he thought her a zombie, that would be as bad as thinking her hysterical.

'You're sure?'

'Yes.'

He looked relieved. 'Well. Okay then. That's good. It would be, ah, awkward to have to rejig—'

'I'd hate to be an inconvenience.'

Spider Webb blinked, and moved on. 'Keep me abreast of developments, then.' A phrase from another textbook; one with a chapter on how to let subordinates know the meeting was over.

He walked her to the door. There'd be someone outside to take her downstairs, repossess her visitor's badge, and see her off the premises, but these signs of exile, which once would have loosed bees in her mind, were irrelevant. She was still assigned to the Needle job. It was a done deal. That was all that mattered.

As he held the door, Webb said, 'You're right, though.'

'I'm sorry?'

'Harper shouldn't have been on the road after drinking. It was an accident, that's all. We looked into it very carefully.'

'I know.'

She left.

Perhaps, she thought, as she was guided downstairs; perhaps, once this was over, and she'd found out why Min had died, and killed those responsible, she'd come back and throw Spider Webb through that window he enjoyed looking out of.

It depended on her mood.

While Kelly showered River pulled boxers and a shirt on, then roamed the bedroom, collecting clothes. Some, it turned out, were still downstairs. Well, she'd only come round for coffee. In the sitting room he found her shirt; also her shoulder bag, a bulky thing which had shed its load across the floor. He uprighted it, returning to its recesses her mobile, her purse, a paperback and her sketchpad, but he leafed through the sketchpad first: the nearby tree line, the road as it left the village, a group gathered on the patio behind the pub. She wasn't good at faces. But there was a nice study of St Johnno's, and another of its graveyard, each headstone a pencil-shaded stubbiness around which long grass wilted; and several aerial studies of the village – Kelly Tropper flew. The last page was strange, not so much a sketch as a design: a stylised city landscape, its tallest skyscraper struck by jagged lightning. Scribbled-over words had been scrawled along the bottom edge.

'Jonny?'

'Coming.'

He carried her shirt up to the bedroom, where she stood draped in a towel.

'You look . . .'

'Gorgeous?'

'I was going to say damp,' he said. 'But gorgeous works.'

She stuck her tongue out. 'Someone's pleased with himself.'

He lay on the bed, enjoying the view while she dressed. 'Didn't know you drew,' he said.

'A bit. Saw my book, did you?'

'It fell open,' he confessed.

'Don't tell me. I can't do faces. But you need a hobby round here.'

'And flying is . . .'

'Not a hobby.' Her green eyes were serious now. 'It's the most alive you can ever be. You should try it.'

'Maybe I will. When are you next going up?'

'Tomorrow.' A smile came and went. A special secret flashed. 'But no, you can't come with.' She kissed him. 'Gotta go. Need to do stock before we open doors.'

'I'll be along later.'

'Good.' She paused. 'That was nice, Mr Walker.'

'I thought so too, Ms Tropper.'

'But that doesn't mean you can look at my stuff without permission,' she said, and bit his earlobe.

When he heard the front door close, he rang Lamb.

'If it isn't 007. Got anywhere yet?'

'Nothing but dead ends and blank looks,' River said. He was staring at his bare toes. 'If Mr B was ever here, he dropped out of sight immediately afterwards.'

'Blimey. So he might be, what, *hiding*? Or something?'

'If he was ever here. Maybe his feet didn't touch the ground. Maybe he was heading somewhere else before the taxi driver flipped his for-hire sign.'

'Or maybe you're useless. How big's that place anyway? Three cottages and a duck pond? Have you checked the cowshed?'

'Why come all the way from London to hide in a cowshed? If there was one. Which there isn't.' River noticed a sock hanging from the curtain rail. 'He doesn't live here. Not as Mr B or under any other name. I guarantee it.'

'You've infiltrated the community, then?'

'I've, er, made some progress, yes.'

'Oh Christ,' said Lamb. 'You're shagging a local.'

'Most of the population's either retired, or commutes, or tele-works, but a lot of the houses are empty. There's talk of the local school closing, always a sign of a dying community . . .'

'If I want a bleeding heart editorial I'll read the *Guardian*. What about the MoD place?'

'Well, they don't like you to wander about, but they don't test secret weapons there, do they? It's a target range.'

'Which used to belong to the Yanks. Who knows what toys they kept in their cupboards?'

'Whatever they were, I doubt they're there now.'

'But if there's evidence of them ever being there, it could still cause embarrassment,' said Lamb.

Like you're an expert on that, thought River. 'Yeah.' He retrieved his sock. 'Which is what I was calling about. I'm going in tonight, take a look around.'

'About time.' Lamb paused. 'Are you dressed? You don't sound dressed.'

'I'm dressed,' River said. 'How's Louisa?'

'Doing her job.'

'Good. Yes. Obviously. But how is she?'

Lamb said, 'Her boyfriend got smeared by a car. I don't suppose she wakes up whistling happy tunes.'

'You checked out the accident?'

'Did we change places when I wasn't looking?'

'Simple question.'

'A pissed cyclist. Which part doesn't spell organ donor?'

'Fuck off, Jackson,' River said bravely. 'Harper was one of yours. If he was struck by lightning, you'd be questioning the weather. I'm just asking what came up.'

There was a pause, during which River heard the click of a lighter. Then Lamb said, 'He was drunk. He'd been over the road, had several beers there. Stopped elsewhere and loaded up on vodka. They'd had a row.'

River squeezed his eyes shut. Course they had. You have a row; you get pissed. How it works. 'Where'd he drink the vodka?'

'We don't know. You want to guess how many bars there are west of City Road?'

'Does he show up on—'

'Why didn't we think of that?' Down the line, Lamb sucked up smoke. 'He flashes past cameras on Oxford Street, or we think he does. Black and white footage, and all cyclists look the same. And there was nothing at the scene. Camera was buggered up when a car sideswiped its pole.'

'Now there's a coincidence.'

'Yeah. One which says it's a junction where accidents happen. The Dogs okayed it.'

'Huh.' Even River didn't know what he meant by that. The Dogs were the Dogs. 'Okay then. I'll call later.'

'Do that. And Cartwright? Next time you tell me to fuck off, make sure you're a long way away.'

'I am a long way away,' River explained.

'Apology accepted.'

He dropped the phone and went to shower.

'So,' Pashkin said, addressing them both, but speaking to Louisa. 'Everything is ready for tomorrow, yes?'

'It's all under control.'

'And not wanting to throw any spanners around, but you're not from the Department of Energy.'

Longridge opened his mouth, but Louisa beat him. 'No.'

'MI5, yes?'

'A branch of it.'

Marcus said, 'The details aren't important.'

Pashkin nodded. 'Of course. I'm not trying to compromise you. I'm just establishing . . . parameters. I have my men here to protect me—'

He had Kyril by the door, and Piotr hovering nearby; an entirely different pair today to the brusque, almost jolly couple they'd seemed three weeks ago, the day Min . . .

'—and you, I presume, have been assigned to make sure all other arrangements run smoothly.'

'They will,' Marcus said.

'I'm pleased to hear it. Department of Energy or not, you'll be aware your government is keen to, ah, reach a mutually beneficial understanding regarding certain fuel demands my company can meet.' His features adopted a self-deprecating expression. 'Not enough to drive your entire country, of course. But a reserve. In the event of difficulties arising elsewhere.'

He spoke fluently, with a medium-thick accent Louisa suspected was cultivated. A deep and sexy growl never hurt when you were opening negotiations, whatever they happened to be.

'And given the obvious delicacy of the situation, it's in all our interests that the meeting goes smoothly. And with that in mind, I have a request.'

Watching his mouth form words, Louisa had the impression they were little clockwork toys he was winding up and setting free, to waddle across this wide expanse of carpet. 'All right,' she said.

'I would like to go there. This afternoon.'

'There . . . ?'

'The Needle,' he said. 'That's what the building's called, yes?'

'Yes, the Needle.'

'On account of its mast,' Marcus said.

Pashkin looked at him politely, but Marcus had nothing to add. He returned his gaze to Louisa. 'I want to see the room. To walk the floor.' He touched the top button of his shirt with his right index finger. 'Before we get down to business. I want to feel comfortable there.'

Louisa said. 'Give me five minutes. I need to make a phone call.'

When he'd finished speaking to River, Lamb sat for a while wearing what Catherine Standish called his dangerous expression: the one where he was considering something other than what to eat or drink next. Then he checked his watch, sighed, and with a heavy grunt rose and picked up a shirt from the floor. Scrunching it in a fist, he crossed the landing to Catherine's room.

'Got a carrier bag?'

Looking up from her desk, she blinked.

He waggled the shirt. 'Anyone home?'

'In there,' she said, pointing at a canvas bag slung from her coatstand.

Thrusting a hand into it, Lamb withdrew half-a-dozen plastic carriers. He shovelled his shirt into one. The others fell to the floor. He turned to go.

'Leaving early?' she asked.

Lamb hoisted the bag above his head without turning round. 'Laundry day,' he said, and disappeared down the stairs.

She stared for a while, then shook her head and returned to work.

In front of her were fragments of lives, fillets of biography, snatched from online sources and official records: HMRC, DMLV, the ONS; the usual crowd. It was like eating alphabet soup with a fork.

Raymond Hadley, sixty-two, had been a BA pilot for eighteen

years, and now busied himself with local politics and environmental issues, his commitment to which didn't prevent him owning a small aeroplane.

Duncan Tropper, sixty-three, was a solicitor; formerly with a high-powered West End interest, he currently put in a couple of days a week at a firm in Burford.

Anne Salmon, sixty, was an economics don at the University of Warwick.

Stephen Butterfield, sixty-seven, had been sole owner of Lighthouse Publishing, a small concern specialising in left-leaning history, until one of the industry monoliths had gobbled it up, leaving a smoking pile of money in its place.

His wife Meg, fifty-nine, part-owned a clothes store.

Andrew Barnett, sixty-six, was Civil Service (retired); something in the Ministry of Transport, which – a first in Catherine's experience – actually meant he'd been something in the Ministry of Transport.

And the rest, and the rest, and the rest. Someone from the Financial Services Authority; two TV producers (one Beeb; one independent); a chemist who'd worked at Porton Down; graphic designers; teachers; doctors; a journalist; business refugees (construction, tobacco, advertising, soft drinks): it added up to a bunch of successful professionals who'd managed to combine busy careers with a quiet life in the Cotswold village of Upshott; the kind of quiet life, Catherine guessed, you'd need a busy career to fund. Many had taken early retirement. Most had children. All drove.

And, Catherine reminded herself, none of it was her business, let alone her job; and in her job, minding her business was paramount. But she was missing River Cartwright, sort of. And hoped he'd return safely, not dead.

The Cotswolds, Standish. Not bleeding Helmand Province.

Which was true, as was the fact that Lamb had staked River out like a sacrificial, well, lamb, to see what would happen next. And given that what had happened first was a murder, there were no guarantees River's country exile would prove idyllic.

She looked at Stephen Butterfield's brief profile again. A left-leaning publishing house. Too obvious? Or just the right amount?

Without more background it was impossible to say, and while Upshott had a small population, running a solo check on every villager was an uphill task. But of this, Catherine was convinced: that if every current inhabitant lined up in front of her, Mr B would not be among them. Because if Lamb was right, and poor Dickie Bow had been killed in a drag hunt, then Mr B's role had come to an end once he'd finished laying his trail. The question was, why did that trail lead to Upshott?

The clue was that word, *cicadas*. Part of the Popov legend, intended to have the Service tying itself in knots, looking for a network that didn't exist. But in the spooks' hall of mirrors, that didn't mean it couldn't be real . . . The Cold War was history, but its shrapnel was everywhere. Maybe, all these years later, Upshott harboured a cicada, who was getting ready to sing.

Though the biggest damn mystery of all, Catherine thought, was why had their attention been brought to it in the first place?

In sudden irritation, she dropped her pen and stood. There were always displacement tasks; tiny mindless things to distract her from the larger, equally mindless tasks Lamb imposed. A smear on her window, for example. Attempting to wipe it clean, she found it was on the outside, but as she stood there Catherine saw a curl of smoke above distant rooftops. Fingers poked her heart, but before they could take a grip she remembered that a crematorium lay that way, and that the smoke funnelling from its chimney marked a private tragedy, not a public cataclysm. But still. You couldn't see smoke on the city skyline without a shiver of fear that it, or something like it, was happening again. This was so much a reflex that *it* could remain undefined.

Then she yelped in sudden shock when someone spoke.

'Oh, sorry, I didn't—'

'No. I was miles away, that's all.'

'Okay. Sorry,' Shirley Dander said again. And then, 'You might want to see this.'

'You found him?'

'Yes,' Shirley said.

Webb said, 'Sure. Give him the tour.'

'He's calling the shots?'

'He's a rich man. They like to take control.'

Because Webb was oh-so-used to rich men's foibles. The corridors of power were where he left his shoes out overnight.

Louisa said, 'Okay. Just thought I'd check.'

'No, that's good. That was a good thing.' He hung up.

Her vision blurred then cleared. She'd been patted on the head by Spider Webb. But that, too, was part of the deal: to take whatever shit came her way. Just so long as she remained on the job.

Through the lobby's glass doors, she watched three buses trundle past; the third an open-topped double-decker, from which tourists peered raptly, admiring buildings, the park, other traffic. There was always a temptation to imagine tourists had no life other than the one you saw them leading; that they were constantly wowing at landmarks and wearing inappropriate shirts. Which was something Min had said, that she would remember every time she saw a tour bus.

She turned to Marcus. 'It's not a problem.'

Marcus rang upstairs. 'We'll see you outside.' He disconnected. 'They're coming now.'

Waiting on the pavement was a lesson in rich man's time-keeping: *now* meant when Pashkin got round to it. Louisa dulled her mind counting black cars: seven, eight, nine. Twenty-one.

Marcus said, 'Oil deal. Right.'

'What?'

He said, 'Come on.'

Cars passed uncounted.

'He's negotiating an energy deal with the British government? Off his own bat?'

'He owns an oil company.'

'And Securicor own armoured vehicles, but you don't see them parading down the Mall on Remembrance Day.'

'I assume you're making a point.'

'That there's a world of difference between private ownership and national interest. You think the Kremlin's enthusiasm for private enterprise extends this far? Dream on.'

Louisa hadn't wanted Marcus Longridge, but that too was part of the deal. But she'd hoped he'd glide through it silently: keep his mouth shut; carry bags. Not feel the need to speculate, or not do so out loud.

'Did you read that profile? This isn't someone who's gunna buy a football team and marry some pop stars. He's got an eye on the big chair.'

To carry on not answering would look deliberate. She said: 'So why's he want to meet with Spider Webb?'

'Other way round. Why wouldn't Webb want to meet with him? Guy with a shot at the Kremlin, Spider's got to be creaming his pants at the thought of being in the same room.'

Now Louisa couldn't help herself. 'Webb wants to *recruit* him?'

'Be my guess.'

She said, 'Because that's the first step to political office, isn't it? Sell yourself to another country's intelligence service.'

'It's not about state secrets,' Marcus said. 'Agent of influence, that'd be his role. And what's in it for him is Western support when he makes his move.'

'Right. A profile in the *Telegraph*'s just the start. Wait till Webb gets his picture in *OK*.'

'Twenty-first century, Louisa. You want to strut on the world stage, you've got to be taken seriously.' He scratched the tip of his nose with his little finger. 'Webb can get Pashkin in the room with people. The PM. A royal. Peter Judd. Trust me, that'd count with Pashkin. He'll need all the international coverage he can get if he wants to make waves back home.'

'Twenty-first century, Marcus,' Louisa agreed. 'But still the Middle Ages here and there. Pashkin starts bigging himself up at Putin the Great's expense, he'll find his head on a stick.'

'You get nowhere if you don't take risks.'

The lift doors opened, and Pashkin appeared, Piotr and Kyril at his heels like wolfhounds.

'End of,' she said, and Marcus shut up.

The first-floor office was noisier than Catherine's. You noticed the traffic more; could see faces on the buses that trundled past in an unbroken stream for minutes at a time, before vanishing for half-hours at a stretch. But those weren't the faces the two women were studying now.

'It's him all right.'

It was him. Catherine had no doubt about that.

Shirley's monitor was frozen on a split screen. One half showed a still from the CCTV coverage she'd stolen from DataLok: Mr B on his westbound train, his posture indicating a freakish stasis even allowing for it being a photograph. Behind him, a young woman was caught in the act of movement; an incomplete thought working across her features. But Mr B sat docile and concentrated, like a shop dummy on a day trip.

The other picture showed the same clothes, same expression, same bald head. And Mr B was once again the still centre of his world, though this world was blurrier, more active. He was standing in line, while all around him people were caught in a motionless bustle, hauling luggage across shiny floors.

'Gatwick,' Shirley said.

'How very low profile,' Catherine murmured.

But it gave weight to Lamb's hypothesis. If you were laying a trail, you wanted it followed to the end. Mr B, or whoever gave him his orders, had wanted his departure registered, and would doubtless be surprised it had taken this long. But then, they couldn't have known it would be Slough House doing the fieldwork. Regent's Park had access to surveillance from all national airports, and could run it through state-of-the-art recognition software. On Aldersgate Street, they had Shirley Dander running stolen tape through an out-of-date program.

'A morning flight,' Shirley said. 'To Prague.'

'When?'

'Seven hours after he was dropped off in Upshott. Why go all the way there if he was catching a plane next morning?'

'Good question,' said Catherine, as a way of not answering it. 'Okay, we know where he went. Let's find out who he was.'

That was a good thing.

Webb laid his phone neatly on his desk: he liked things aligned. Then he smoothed his hair. That too.

That was a good thing he'd said to Louisa Guy, and had meant it. Anything that happened before tomorrow he wanted run past him first. If he had one skill − and he had bags of the damn things − but if he had one skill above all, it was averting disaster.

On that bad bad night when Min Harper had died, for example, Spider Webb got the news early. So he'd been on the scene before Jackson Lamb. Averting disaster was about good timing. Then he'd walked to the Embankment and sat facing the dark galleries on the far bank and thought hard for as short a time as possible. Strategy was nine-tenths reaction. Study any situation too long, you can think yourself into paralysis.

He'd called Diana Taverner. 'We've got a problem.'

'Harper,' she said.

'You've heard.'

She suppressed a sigh. 'Webb? I'm Second Desk. On your best day, you're a gopher. So yes, I heard about Min Harper getting killed before you did.'

'*Getting* killed?'

'Being knocked over. It's a verb.'

'I've been monitoring the situation.'

She said, 'Excellent. If his condition changes—'

'I meant—'

'—do let me know, because we can put a positive spin on it. "MI5 agent comes back to life." That would boost recruitment, don't you think?'

When he was sure she'd finished Webb said, 'I meant I've talked to Nick Duffy. He's been on the scene since first thing.'

'That's his job.'

'And he reckons it's clean. That it's what it appears to be. An accident.'

Silence. Then: 'His exact words?'

Duffy's exact words had been, *No way of telling until we've run all the angles. But he smells like a brewery, and it's not like it was hit and run. The driver remained on the scene.*

Webb said, 'Pretty much, yes.'

'So that's what his report will say.'

'It's the timing I'm worried about. With the Needle thing coming up . . .'

'Jesus Christ,' Di Taverner said. 'He was a colleague, Webb. You worked with him. Remember?'

'Well, not closely.'

'And don't you think, before you start worrying what impact his death'll have on your career prospects, you should consider what impact it might have on mine?'

'I have been. I'm thinking about both of us. Once Duffy's report pegs this as a traffic thing, we can mourn Harper, obviously, but we can also get on with the job in hand. But if his death comes under scrutiny, his last days will be under the microscope. And if Roger Barrowby gets wind we were running Harper off the books while this audit's in full swing—'

'"We"?'

Webb said, 'I logged our conversation, of course I did. I had to. When it comes off, and we have Arkady Pashkin as an asset, our asset, then everyone between Regent's Park and Whitehall will want a slice of the credit. Especially—well, you know.'

Ingrid Tearney, his silence spelt.

'Best to have it clear from the get-go who's done all the work.'

What he was hearing now was Diana Taverner thinking.

Mobile pressed to his ear, Webb looked up. No stars, but there rarely were in London: you had the weather, you had the light pollution, you had all the heavy artillery a city threw at the sky, and these things generally won. Except that didn't mean the stars weren't there.

At last she said, 'What are you asking?'

'Nothing. Not much. A quick call.'

'To?'

'Nick Duffy.'

'I thought you said he was happy?'

'He is. He is. All we need is for him to put that in a report, even an interim one. To make sure everyone stays calm until the Needle job's done and dusted.'

More silence.

'And we've pulled off the intelligence coup of the—'

'Don't push it.' She thought more. 'There's no chance Harper's death has anything to do with this op?'

'It was an accident.'

'But what if it turns out to have been a *very good* accident that has something to do with this op?'

'It won't. Pashkin's not even in the country yet. And if anyone had wind he's planning to join our team, well, it wouldn't be Min Harper bearing the brunt. He was only a minor cog.'

'A slow horse, you mean.'

'It's not like he even knew what's going on. As far as he was concerned, he was babysitting an oil deal.'

She said, 'You realise that if this gets out, Roger Barrowby's the least of your worries? Harper might only have been a slow horse, but let's not forget who's in charge of that stable.'

'Don't worry. I'll tread carefully round any bruisable toes.'

She laughed. 'Jackson Lamb bruises like an elephant.' She made a small noise: changed hands on her phone or something. 'I'll speak to Duffy.' She hung up.

And what Webb had thought then, and had seen no cause to change his mind about since, was that the thing about elephants was, they grew old and died. There'd been a documentary: an elephant carcass left by a watering hole. Hours it lasted, before the flies moved in, and the birds, and the hyenas. After that, it was parts. Jackson Lamb had been a legend in his day, they said, but they said that about Robert De Niro.

That was a good thing.

Louisa Guy was handling her end, and no one at the Park, barring Lady Di, had wind of the Pashkin op. After tomorrow, he, James Webb, could be pulling the strings on the most important asset Five had reeled in since, well, ever.

All that mattered was that things kept moving smoothly.

9

ARKADY PASHKIN said, 'WHY aren't we moving?'

Middle of the city, traffic in front, traffic behind, a big sign saying roadworks ahead, and a stop light clearly visible through the windscreen. So why aren't we moving? Louisa wondered. You had to be rich to ask.

Pashkin said, 'Piotr?'

'Traffic's heavy, boss.'

'Traffic's always heavy.' To Louisa he said, 'We should have outriders. Tomorrow, I mean.'

'I think they're reserved for royals,' she said. 'And government ministers. VIPs.'

'They should be available to those who can afford them.' He glanced at Marcus briefly, as if estimating his net worth, then his gaze returned to Louisa. 'You'd think, with all the practice you've had, you'd be better at capitalism than us.'

'I don't think anyone's surprised what quick studies you turned out to be.'

'Is that a clever remark? This is not my first language.' Without turning his head, he spoke to Piotr and Kyril in that one. Kyril replied: Louisa couldn't read the intonation. Possibly deferential. But it was like being in New York, where someone could ask you the time in a way that suggested you'd just punched their mother.

Their car had a separate driver's compartment, though the dividing window was rolled down. Louisa and Marcus sat facing Pashkin, who was facing front. Immediately behind the car, a red bus loomed. It was full of less-rich people moving through London very slowly, and probably no less aggrieved by it than Pashkin, who shook his head in irritation, and began to study the *Financial Times*.

The car shunted forward and rolled over something bumpy, which probably wasn't a cyclist.

Louisa blinked as pain stabbed her eyeballs, but it soon went. If you carried on looking like you were holding it all together, pretty soon you were holding it all together.

Pashkin tutted, and turned a page.

He looked like a politician, spoke like one too; he had charisma, probably. Maybe Marcus was right, and he also had front-line ambitions, and this mini-summit had less to do with oil deals than under-the-table promises about future conduct, future favours. That could only be a good thing, unless it turned out a bad one. Political alliances often turned unhappy: some hands got shook, some arms got sold, but it never looked great for HMG when the torturing bastards were strung up by their own people.

Beside her, Marcus shifted, and his leg brushed hers. And now a bicycle whizzed past, and this time instead of a pain in her eyes Louisa felt her heart lurch, and the tired old logic unreeled again in her mind: that Min had got drunk after a row was possible, even after a row so trivial Louisa couldn't remember what it had been about. And that Min had been knocked off his bicycle and killed – yes, that could happen too. But not one after the other. Not those two things in a row. To believe that would mean accepting some kind of cosmic continuity, an organised randomness of events. So no, there'd been something deeper at work, some human agency. And that could only mean this job she was working on now, and these people in this car. Or others, who knew about the summit, and wanted to stop it happening, or turn it into something else.

She started drawing up a mental list of everyone she didn't trust, and had to stop immediately. She didn't have all day.

And then, with the suddenness of a tooth freeing itself from its socket, the car was through the snarl-up and moving smoothly. Above them glass and steel buildings did their best to pierce the sky, and on the pavements sharply dressed men and women threaded between each other, hardly ever bumping. Min Harper had been dead three weeks. And here was Louisa, doing her job.

By the time Lamb's taxi reached the laundrette, near Swiss Cottage, it would have been cheaper to bin the shirt and buy several new ones. While it swam away in the never-ceasing stream of traffic, Lamb lit a cigarette and perused posters in the laundrette's window: a local quiz night, stand-up gigs, tomorrow's Stop the City rally, an animal-free circus. Nobody paid him attention. When his cigarette was done he ground it out and entered.

Machines lined both walls, most of them sloshing rhythmically, making sounds Lamb's stomach made when he woke at three, having drunk too much. A familiar noise. Dividing the room was a series of benches on which four people sat: a young couple wrapped round each other like an interlocking puzzle; an old woman rocking back and forth; and, up the far end, a short dark middle-aged man in a raincoat, engrossed in the *Evening Standard*.

Lamb sat next to him. 'Any idea how these things work?'

The man didn't look up. 'Do I have any idea how washing machines work?'

'I assume they take money.'

'And washing powder,' the man said. Now he did look up. 'Jesus, Lamb. You never been in a laundrette before? Short of tearing a postcard in half, I thought this couldn't have got more old school.'

Lamb dropped the bag to the floor. 'I was your other kind of undercover,' he said. 'Casinos, five-star hotels. World-class hookers. Laundry was mostly room service.'

'Yeah, and I jet-packed to work, before they fired me.'

Lamb extended his hand, and Sam Chapman shook it.

Bad Sam Chapman had been Head Dog once, Nick Duffy's role now, until a high-profile mess involving an industrial amount of money meant he'd had his arse handed back on a plate: no job, no pension, no reference, unless you counted 'Lucky to be leaving upright'. He now worked for a detective agency which specialised in finding runaway teenagers, or at least in taking credit card details from the agonised parents of runaway teenagers. Since Chapman's arrival their success rate had tripled, but that still left a lot of missing kids.

'So how's life in the secrets business?' he asked.

'Well, I could answer that . . .'

'But then you'd have to kill me,' Chapman finished.

'But it'd bore your tits off. Got anything?'

Bad Sam passed him an envelope. By its thickness, it contained maybe two folded sheets of paper.

'This took you three weeks?'

'Not like I have your resources, Jackson.'

'The agency not got pull?'

'The agency charges. Any special reason you couldn't do this in-house?'

'Yeah, I don't trust the bastards.' He paused. 'Well, maybe a couple of the bastards. But not to actually do a proper job.'

'Oh, that's right. Your crew's special needs.' With his index finger, Chapman flicked the envelope in Lamb's hand. 'Someone was ahead of me on this.'

'I'd hope so. The cow killed a spook.'

'But not all the way,' Sam continued.

Down the bench one of the youngsters abruptly stood, and Sam paused. It was the boy, or possibly the girl – or possibly they were both boys, or both girls – but whatever, they fed the nearest drier with a clatter of coins so it came grunting back to life, then sat and wrapped themselves round their other half again.

Lamb waited.

Chapman said, 'Someone ran the numbers on her, and I expect they gave her a clean bill of health.'

'Because she's clean?'

'Because they did a half-arsed job. She looks clean now, but go far enough back and it's a whole other story.'

'Which you did.'

'But my successor didn't. Or whichever minion he assigned.' Chapman slapped the newspaper on the bench without warning. The *thwock* stopped the old woman rocking for a moment, though the kids didn't react. 'Christ,' he said. 'Me, they sack just to balance the books. If I'd been incompetent, I'd still have a job.'

'Yeah, but it'd probably be round my gaff.' Lamb tucked the envelope into a pocket. 'Owe you one.'

'There's another possibility,' Bad Sam said. 'Maybe they didn't do a proper job on her because they already knew what they'd find.'

Jackson Lamb said, 'Like I say, I don't trust the bastards.' He rose. 'Don't be a stranger.'

'You've forgotten your shirt,' Sam called.

Lamb looked at the canoodling couple as he passed. 'I'll never forget that shirt,' he told them kindly.

On the whirling metal circus of the road, it took him five minutes to find a taxi.

Ambling down the road to The Downside Man, River pondered the task in hand. A contact – Mr B had come to Upshott to make contact: with his handler or his joe. And who that might be, River still had no idea.

It hadn't taken long to embed himself into the village. He'd been half-expecting a Wicker Man scenario, with locals in sinister masks, but turning up at the pub every night and attending evensong at St Johnno's was all he'd had to do. Everyone was friendly, and nobody had tried to set fire to him yet.

His cover as a writer helped. On the outside, Upshott had less going for it than other Cotswold villages; it wasn't as picturesque; it had no galleries, no cafés, no bookshop; nowhere the culturally minded could gather to discuss their artistic leanings. But it remained as much a middle-class haven as its neighbours: a poster for a recent county-wide Arts Week indicated four local venues, and one of the fake barns along the main road housed a pottery, whose prices were comfortably ridiculous. An author fitted in hand-in-glove.

As for the locals he'd met, they were largely retired, or teleworkers, their livelihood independent of the village itself. Those who'd been employed at the USAF base had moved on long ago, but there remained a smattering of agricultural workers, and a handful who ran trades from vans or garages – carpenter, electrician; two plumbers – but even among the artisans, there was an air of quality craftsmanship, and bills to match.

And few of them were Upshott born and bred. The twenty-somethings in evidence were the offspring of incomers, Kelly among them; her father, a solicitor, practised nearby. Kelly had a politics degree, and her job in the pub wasn't a life choice; more a treading of water while she decided what to do next. It appeared that a politics degree was about as useful as it sounded. But she seemed happy enough: was the centre of a group of friends who worked as estate agents or graphic designers or architects as far afield as Worcester, but returned to Upshott each evening and colonised the pub, when they weren't in their clubhouse by the MoD range, piloting and taking care of Ray Hadley's little aeroplane. Which, River thought, was the real umbilical cord: if they wanted the freedom of the skies, they had to keep returning to the village. River, not much older, reckoned they were still young enough to find that a price worth paying.

On the other hand, it didn't explain what had attracted Mr B. Maybe Lamb was right, and the old American base was at the heart of it. That was what had put Upshott on the map, even if the base itself hadn't appeared on maps at the time. It was why he'd placed it at the heart of his cover; the setting for his supposed novel. And now it was gone, and in its place was the Ministry of Defence artillery range, which rendered even more unlikely the chances of anything secreted there having survived fifteen years . . . But still, it needed looking at, if only because River was running out of ideas. And he needed to see it the way Mr B had, if that's what Mr B had done: after dark and over the fence. Which was what he planned to do later.

And because he was a stranger here, and had no desire to end up in a ditch or under arrest, he wasn't going alone.

Like Marcus had said, the Needle was called the Needle on account of its mast, but everything about it looked sharp. All 320 metres of it burst into daylight out of a shallow crater, which was paved in red brick, laid in tiers and studded with huge bronze pots, each boasting a tree as yet too spindly to cast shade, though the size of the pots suggested they'd grow tall and leafy. Stone benches were set here and there, around which small graveyards of cigarette stubs had been flattened, and spotlights were trained at intervals on the Needle's sides. At night, it was lit like a carnival. In daylight, from this angle, it looked dark, vaguely monstrous, and out of place – like it was asking for trouble.

Of its eighty storeys, the first thirty-two belonged to a hotel which hadn't opened yet, or Pashkin would doubtless have booked a suite there. The rest were privately leased, and not yet fully occupied. But security was tight, and had lately risen several notches with the arrival of Rumble, the out-of-nowhere Apple rivals who were preparing to launch a new version of their world-conquering e-reader; plus the diamond merchants de Koenig, and BiffordJenningsWhale, the Chinese-owned market traders. Here, along with all the other banks, insurers, inter-dealer brokers and risk management consultants, were the wealthy embassies of offshore havens, drawn by the bright lights and big views. Quite the little United Nations, though without the avowed intent of doing any good except unto themselves.

On her first visit, Min in tow, Louisa had taken the stairs to the next landing down, but had been unable to access the floor. The stairwell doors were one-way, unlocking only in the event of fire or other emergency, while the business lifts – separate from the hotel's – were restricted access. Cameras monitored every lobby. As for the suite Spider Webb had finagled, she didn't know who owned that. A deliberate omission from the paper-work. Whoever it was, they were evidently open to persuasion, but then, Webb was a collector of other people's secrets. Min had found him laughable, but Spider Webb was the kind of joke you laughed at then looked behind you, in case he'd heard.

She shook her head abruptly. Don't think about this. Don't think about Min. Do the job. Collect secrets of your own.

'A problem?'

'No. Nothing.'

Arkady Pashkin nodded.

And keep your thoughts inside your head, she added. She didn't like the way Pashkin looked at her, as if reading a script from her features.

They were in the lift, heading swiftly skyward. Their names had been recorded on entry, security protocols demanding a register be kept of who was in the building at all times. For the meeting with Webb, they'd be sidestepping this: Webb had supplied a keycard for the service lift which could be accessed from the underground car park. They planned to be above the City but under the radar. No one would know they were there.

Today, though, they'd been shepherded through the atrium, where a small rainforest now flourished. This, the eco-flash of the new hotel, had taken root in the last three weeks. Guests would be able to take walks in the undergrowth when they tired of the big city, and emerge for a drink and a sauna when they tired of nature. All around the greenery, ever-diminishing people pursued a variety of tasks integral to the grand opening of a world-class hotel, which was still a month off.

'In China,' Pashkin remarked, 'buildings this size, even with all these fancy, these fancy—'

Losing his way, he snapped a word at Piotr, who replied, 'Trappings.'

'All these fancy trappings, they go up inside a month.'

Marcus said, 'I gather they're not overburdened with health and safety.'

In the suite, Pashkin strode round the table as if measuring it. He spoke several times in Russian: short blunt sentences Louisa guessed were questions, because to each Piotr or Kyril made an even shorter response. Meanwhile, Marcus stationed himself by the door, arms folded. He'd been Ops, she reminded herself; would have worked on bigger jobs than this before losing his nerve, if that's what had happened. For now, he seemed unfazed by the views, and was mostly watching Piotr and Kyril.

Pashkin stood with thumbs hooked into his jacket pockets, lips pursed. He might have been a prospective tenant, looking for an angle to hang a price reduction on. Nodding at the cameras affixed above the doors, he said, 'I assume they are off.'

'Yes.'

'And there are no recording devices of any sort here.'

'None.'

As if following a mental checklist, he then said, 'What happens in an emergency?'

'There are stairwells,' Louisa said. 'North and south walls.' She pointed, to be clear. 'The lifts freeze, and won't take passengers. The wells are reinforced, and all the doors are fireproof, obviously. They unlock automatically.'

He nodded. What kind of emergency was he expecting, she wondered? But then, the whole point about emergencies was you didn't expect them.

It was difficult, once you'd embarked on such a chain of thought, not to become entangled in its linked banalities.

Pashkin said, 'That's a lot of stairs.'

'It could be worse,' she said. 'You could be coming up them.'

He laughed at that; a deep laugh from the heart of his burly frame. 'That's a good point. What kind of emergency might that be, that would have you running up seventy-seven flights of stairs?'

Whatever kind it was, she thought, if it wasn't serious to start with, it certainly would be before you reached the top.

The pair of them, and the other two Russians, crossed to the window. Last time she'd been here, she'd been overwhelmed by the space on offer; all that sky overlooking all that city. It was beautiful, but stank of wealth, which was what had been weighing on her that day: her need for money, her need for a better place for herself and Min; a bigger slice of all that space. And Min had been there, of course, in touching distance. They didn't have much money, and didn't have enough space, but they'd had a hell of a lot more than she had now.

An air ambulance swam into view, carving up the distance between east and west. She watched its silent progress; an orange dragonfly, oblivious to its own ridiculous shape.

'Maybe,' Pashkin said, 'we should try going down the stairs, yes? To see how well we'd cope with an emergency.'

She turned. Marcus had moved to the table, was leaning over it, his palms resting on its surface. She had the sense of interrupted movement, but his expression was unreadable.

'I've a better idea,' she said. 'Let's use the lift.'

In the back of the cab Jackson Lamb opened the envelope Chapman had given him to find just two sheets of paper. He read them, then spent the rest of the journey so distracted he almost forgot to demand a receipt.

When he reached his office Standish was there, her cheeks tinted, as if she were the one who'd just climbed four flights of stairs. 'Mr B has a name,' she said.

'Oh god. You've been investigating.'

He shrugged off his coat and threw it. She caught it and

folded it over one arm. 'Andrei Chernitsky.' The words rolled off her tongue darkly. 'He used a passport in that name when he flew out. It's on the Park's books.'

'Don't tell me. Second-rate hood.' Running a hand through greasy thinning hair, Lamb parked himself behind his desk. 'Not ranking KGB, but showed up in a supporting role when heavy lifting was needed.'

'You already knew?'

'I know the type. When did he leave?'

'The morning after he killed Dickie Bow.'

'I note the absence of "allegedly". You starting to believe me, Standish?'

'I never didn't believe you. I'm just not sure sending River out on his own is the right way to find out what's going on.'

Lamb said, 'Yeah, I could have prepared a report. Presented it to Roger Barrowby, who's evidently running things these days. He'd have had three other people read it and make recommendations, and if they came up positive, he'd have formed an interim committee to investigate possible avenues of reaction. After which—'

'I get the point.'

'I'm so glad. I was beginning to bore myself. Do I take it you've recruited Ho to do your research? Or is he still playing computer games on the firm's time?'

'I'm sure he's hard at work on the archive,' Catherine said.

'And I'm sure he's hard at work on my arse.' Lamb paused. 'That didn't work. Pretend I didn't say it.'

'Andrei Chernitsky,' Catherine persisted. 'Did you recognise him?'

'If I had, don't you think I'd have mentioned it?'

'Depends on your mood,' she said. 'But the reason I ask is, Dickie Bow obviously did. Which suggests Chernitsky did time in Berlin.'

'They didn't call it the Spooks' Zoo for nothing,' Lamb said. 'Every tuppenny lowlife turned up there one time or another.'

He found his cigarettes, and put one in his mouth. 'You've got a theory, haven't you?'

'Yes. I—'

'I didn't say I wanted to hear it.' He lit up. The smell of fresh tobacco filled the room, displacing the smell of stale tobacco. 'How's the day job? Shouldn't there be reports on my desk?'

She said, 'When Dickie Bow was kidnapped—'

'We used to call it "bagging".'

'When Dickie Bow was *bagged*—'

'I really have no choice but to hear this, do I?'

'—he said there were two of them. One called himself Alexander Popov.' Catherine batted away smoke with her hand. 'I think Chernitsky was the other. Popov's muscle. That's why Bow dropped everything to follow him. This wasn't some stray spook from the old days. It was someone Bow had a very specific memory of, someone he might even have wanted revenge on.'

Cigarette notwithstanding, Lamb appeared to be chewing. Maybe it was his tongue. He said, 'You realise what that would mean?'

'Uh-huh.'

'Uh-huh you do, or uh-huh, you're making a noise so I'll spell out what it means and you'll pretend you knew all along?'

'They bagged him. They force-fed him alcohol. They let him go,' Catherine said. 'There was no point to it at all, except that he get a look at them. So that one day they could swish a coat in his path, and he'd trot after it like a trained poodle.'

'Jesus.' Lamb breathed out grey air. 'I'm not sure what disturbs me more. The thought that someone's got a twenty-year plan, or the fact that you'd already worked that out.'

'Popov took a British spy off the streets twenty years ago with no motive except to use him as an alarm bell when the time was right.'

'Popov never existed,' Lamb reminded her.

'But whoever made him up did. And apparently this was part of his plan. Along with the cicadas. A sleeper cell.'

Lamb said, 'Any plan a Soviet spook came up with two decades back is long past its sell-by date.'

'So maybe it's not the same plan. Maybe it's been adapted. But either way, it's in play. This isn't you chasing ghosts from your past any more. It's a ghost from your past jumping up and down, shouting "look at me!".'

'And why's that?'

'I haven't a clue. But it demands a more coherent response than just letting River Cartwright off the leash. Chernitsky went to Upshott for a reason, and the only logical reason is that that's where this network's ringleader is. And whoever that is, you can bet your life they already know River's not who he's pretending to be.'

Lamb said thoughtfully, 'Or I could bet River's life. Which would be safer for me and more convenient.'

'It's not a joke. I've been checking up on the names in River's reports. None of them scream "Soviet agent". But then, if any of them did, they'd not have successfully buried themselves all this time.'

'Are you still talking to me, or just thinking aloud?' Lamb took a final drag on his cigarette and dropped the stub into a coffee cup. 'Bow was killed, yes. Sad, but shit happens. And the point of killing him was to lay a trail. Whatever that's about, it's not to set up River Cartwright. Someone wants one of us there for a reason. Sooner or later, probably sooner, we'll find out who and why.'

'So we do nothing? That's your plan?'

'Oh, don't worry. There's plenty to chew on in the meantime. The name Rebecca Mitchell ring a bell?'

'She's the driver who ran down Min.'

'Yeah. Well, him being drunk and her a woman, it's no surprise the Dogs signed off on it. But they shouldn't have.' Pulling Bad Sam's envelope from his pocket, he tossed it onto the desk. 'They looked at her last ten years, during which she's been a squeaky clean lady, if you leave aside her killing one of my team.

Which they shouldn't have done. What they should have done was to take her entire life and shake it in a high wind.'

'And find what?'

'And find she used to be a different kind of squeaky altogether. Back in the nineties she was bumping uglies with all sorts, and had a particular yen for your romantic Slav. Spent six months sharing a flat with a pair of charmers from Vladivostok, who set her up in her catering business before they buggered off. Though of course,' he added, 'that's just circumstantial, and she might be Snow White. What do you think?'

Catherine, who rarely stooped to profanity, swore.

'Indeed. Me also.' Lamb picked up the coffee cup, raised it to his lips, then noticed it was an ashtray. 'As if I didn't have enough to be getting on with, it turns out whatever these shady Russian bastards of Spider Webb's are up to, it's dodgy enough to get Harper killed.' He put the cup back down. 'Just one thing after another, isn't it?'

They returned the Russians to the hotel, then headed for the Tube. Marcus suggested cabbing it; Louisa gestured at the traffic, which was sclerotic. She had a hidden agenda: in a taxi, she'd have little choice but to suffer Marcus's conversation. On the Tube, he'd be more likely to give it a rest. That was the theory. But as they headed into the underground he said, 'What do you make of him?'

'Pashkin?'

'Who else?'

She said, 'He's the job,' and slapped her Oyster card on the platen. The gates opened and she slipped through.

One step behind her, Marcus said, 'He's a gangster.'

Webb had said as much. One-time Mafia. But these days he was establishment, or rich enough to pass, and she didn't know how it worked in Russia, but in London, once you were rich, being a gangster was a minor offence, on a par with wearing a tie for a club you didn't belong to.

'Nice suit, nice manners, and his English is better than mine. And he owns an oil company. But he's a gangster.'

At the top of the escalators a poster warned of disruption to services during tomorrow's rally. Being anti-bank, chances were the rally would be well attended and turn ugly.

She said, 'Maybe. But Webb says we treat him like royalty, so that's what we do.'

'Meaning what, we pimp him an under-age masseuse? Or suck his dick for a wrap of coke?'

'Those probably weren't the royals Webb was thinking of,' she said.

On the train Louisa closed her eyes. Part of her brain was juggling logistics: the rally would be a factor. You couldn't dump a quarter-million pissed-off citizens into the mix without complicating things. But these thoughts were an alibi, parading through her consciousness just in case anyone had developed a mind-reading machine. By tomorrow, details like their route to the Needle were going to be as useful as Christmas crackers.

Marcus Longridge was talking again. 'Louisa?'

She opened her eyes.

'Our stop.'

'I know,' she told him, but he was giving her a quizzical look anyway. All the way up from platform to street, he was a step or two behind her. His attention took the form of a heat spot on the back of her neck.

Forget about that. Forget about tomorrow. Tomorrow wasn't going to happen.

Tonight was.

10

When River stepped into the pub, it was to greetings from two separate tables. He thought: you could spend years propping up the bar at your London local, and they wouldn't know what name to put on the wreath. But maybe that was just him. Maybe the River who made friends easily was the one pretending to be someone else. He returned all greetings, and stopped at the Butterfields' table: Stephen and Meg. Neither needed a drink. Kelly was at the bar, polishing a glass on a tea towel.

'How nice to see you,' she said.

Playing with him, definitely, but that was okay.

He ordered a mineral water, and she raised a mild eyebrow. 'Celebrating?' While she fetched it, he felt a twinge he hoped wasn't his conscience. If he'd met Kelly anywhere, he'd have done his best to end up exactly where he'd been that afternoon. So why was he certain that if she discovered he wasn't who he claimed to be, she'd chop off his—

'Pickled eggs?'

'Sorry?'

'Would you like a pickled egg with that? They're a popular local delicacy.'

Carefully enunciated, as if inviting comparison with other local delicacies he might have recently enjoyed.

'Tempting, but I'll give it a miss,' he said. 'Flying club not in tonight?'

'Greg popped in earlier. Were you hoping to grab anyone in particular?'

'No one I haven't already grabbed,' he said quietly.

'Walls have ears.'

'My lips are sealed.'

'That's good,' she said. 'We'll make a spy of you yet.'

With that ringing in his ears, he made his way back to the Butterfields.

Stephen and Meg Butterfield. Parents of Damien, another member of the flying club. He was retired from publishing; she part-owned a boutique in Moreton-in-Marsh. In the country but not of the country, as Stephen put it; in the country, but happy to pop up to London twice a month to eat, visit friends, catch a play, 'remember what civilisation feels like'. But happy too to wear a tweed cap, a green V-neck, and carry a silver-topped stick. In the country and blending in nicely, more like. He asked River:

'How goes the writing business?'

'Oh, you know. Early days.'

'Still researching?' said Meg. Though her eyes were on River, her long, nervous fingers toyed with the smoking equipment in front of her: packet of tobacco, Rizla papers, throwaway lighter. Her greying blonde hair was under wraps tonight, coiled beneath a black silk headscarf; and this too, and the wrinkles at her eyes, and even her clothes marked her out a smoker – the ankle-length skirt glittering with silver threads, and the black cardigan with deep pockets, and the red-fringed shawl she wore like a displaced Bedouin. In London, he'd have dismissed her as a superannuated hippy; here, she seemed more like an off-duty witch. He could see her knocking up a remedy for lovesick swains, if that was still a word. Probably was round here. Not much call for it in the city.

The couple sat next to each other on the bench, which River thought sweet. 'Ninety per cent of the job,' he said. Funny how simple it was to be an expert on writing. 'Getting it down on paper's the easy part.'

'We were talking about you with Ray. You met Ray yet?'

River hadn't, though the name was all too familiar. Ray Hadley was the maypole around which the village danced: he was on the parish council, on the school's board of governors; on everything that required a name on a dotted line. He was the éminence grise of the flying club, too: a retired pilot, and the owner of the small plane housed near the MoD land. And yet he remained elusive.

'I haven't, no.'

Because Hadley always seemed to have just left, or was expected any moment but didn't turn up. There weren't many places in Upshott that weren't the pub, but Hadley had contrived to find most of them these past few weeks.

'Ray was great mates with the brass at the base,' Meg went on. 'Always in and out of there. Wasn't he, darling?'

'Give him half a chance, he'd have joined up. Still would. The chance to fly one of those Yank jets? He'd have given his right bollock.'

'I can't believe your paths haven't crossed yet,' Meg said. 'He must be hiding from you.'

'Actually, I might have seen him this morning, heading for the shop. Tall bald man, yes?'

Meg's phone rang: *Ave Satani*. 'Son and heir,' she said. 'Excuse me. Damien, darling. Yes. No. I don't know. Ask your father.' She handed the phone to Stephen, then said to River, 'Sorry, dear. Busting for a fag,' and collected her paraphernalia and headed for the door.

Stephen Butterfield began a lengthy explanation of what it sounded like was wrong with Damien's car, waggling an apologetic eyebrow at River, who made a no-matter gesture and returned to the bar.

The pub had oak rafters onto which paper currency had been pasted, and whitewashed walls on which farm implements hung. In a corner were photographs of Upshott through the years. Most had been taken on the green, and showed groups of people metamorphosing through black-and-white austerity to the Hair Bear Bunch fashions of the seventies. The most recent was of nine young adults, more at ease with their youth and good looks than earlier generations had been. They stood on a strip of tarmac, three of them women; Kelly Tropper at their centre. In the background was a small aeroplane.

He'd been looking at this photo on his first evening there, and had recognised the woman who'd just served him a pint, when a man approached. He was about River's age though broader, and with a head like a bowling ball: hair trimmed to the skull, an equally sparse fuzz prickling chin and upper lip, and eyes sharp with cunning or suspicion. River had seen similar eyes in other pubs. They didn't always spell trouble, but when trouble broke out anyway, they were usually right near the middle.

'And who might you be?'

Let's be polite, thought River. 'The name's Walker.'

'Is it now.'

'Jonathan Walker.'

'Jonathan Walker,' the man repeated in a sing-song voice, to underline the effeminate nature of anyone limp-wristed enough to be called Jonathan Walker.

'And you are?'

'What makes that your business?'

And now a third voice chimed in, and here was the bartender, offering a brisk 'Behave, you.' To River she said, 'His name's Griff Yates.'

'Griff Yates,' River said. 'Should I repeat that in a stupid voice? I'm not sure I've grasped the local customs yet.'

'Oh, we've got a clever one,' Yates had said. He put his pint down, and River had a sudden glimpse of what his grandfather would have made of this. *You've been under cover five minutes, and you're about the same distance away from a public brawl. Which part of* covert *is giving you trouble?* 'Last clever one we had in here would have been that city twerp who took the James' place for a summer. And you know what happened to him?'

River had little option. 'No,' he said. 'What happened to him?'

'He fucked off back where he came from, didn't he?' Griff Yates paused a beat, then roared with laughter. 'Fucked off back where he came from,' he repeated, and kept laughing until River joined in, then bought him a pint.

Which had been River's first Upshott encounter, and a little bumpier than those that followed, but then Griff Yates was the odd one out; Griff Yates was local stock. A little older than the crew known as the flying club, he existed at a tangent to them: part envy, part blunt antagonism.

He wasn't here now, though. Andy Barnett – who was known as Red Andy, having voted Labour in ninety-seven – was at the bar instead, or technically was, his unfinished pint and Sudoku puzzle claiming the area for the duration. Andy himself was temporarily elsewhere.

With no immediate audience, Kelly smiled a welcome. 'Hello again, you.'

He could still taste her. 'I haven't bought you a drink yet.'

'Next time I'm your side of the bar.' She nodded at his glass. 'And it won't be mineral water, I can tell you.'

'You working tomorrow?'

'And the night after.'

'What about tomorrow afternoon?'

'Habit-forming, is it?' There was a look women could give you once you'd slept with them, and Kelly bestowed this upon him now. 'I told you. I'm flying tomorrow.'

'Of course. Going anywhere nice?'

The question seemed to amuse her. 'It's all nice, up there.'

'So it's a secret.'

'Oh, you'll find out.' She leaned forward. 'But I'm finished here at eleven thirty. If you want to pick up where we left off?'

'Ah. Wish I could. Kind of busy.'

She raised an eyebrow. 'Kind of busy? What kind of busy can you be after closing time round here?'

'Not the kind you're thinking of. It's—'

'Hello, young man. Chatting up our lovely bar staff?'

And this was Red Andy, back from having a smoke, if the fumes clinging to his jacket were any guide.

'Andy,' said River.

'Just been chatting with Meg Butterfield out there.' He paused to drain his pint. 'Another one of these, Kelly dear. And one for our visitor. Meg tells me you're well on with your book.'

'Nothing for me, thanks. I'm about to leave.'

'Pity. I was hoping to hear about your progress.' Andy Barnett was everybody's nightmare: a genuine local author, whose self-published memoir had been quite the succès d'estime, don't you know. Which anyone who'd met Andy Barnett did two minutes later. 'Be more than happy to look at anything you're ready to show.'

'You'll be first in line.'

A draught at River's back indicated someone new had just come in, and Barnett said, 'Here comes trouble.'

River didn't have to turn to know who this was.

It was growing dark when Louisa emerged at Marble Arch among crowds of young foreign tourists. She threaded past giant rucksacks and breathed the evening air, tasting traffic exhaust, perfume, tobacco, and a hint of foliage from the park. At the top of the steps she unfolded a pocket map, an excuse for pausing. After inspecting it for two minutes, she put it away. If she was being followed, they were good.

Not that there was reason for anyone to be following. She was just another girl on a night out, and the streets were heavy with them: whole migrating herds of fresh young things, and some less fresh, and some less young. Tonight Louisa was a different woman to the one she'd lately been. She wore a black dress which stopped above the knee and showed off her shoulders, or would do once she removed her jacket, which was four – no, five – years old, and starting to look it, but not so much a man would notice. Sheer black tights; her hair pulled back by a red band. She looked good. It helped that men were easy.

She carried a bag on a strap, just big enough for a few feminine essentials, the definition of which varied from woman to woman. In her own case, alongside mobile phone, purse, lipstick, credit card, it included a can of pepper spray and a pair of plastic handcuffs, bought off the internet. Like many internet-related activities, these purchases were amateurish and ill-thought out, and part of her wondered what Min would have said, but that was arse-backward. If Min had been in any position to know, she'd not have been carrying this stuff.

The Ambassador looked different at night. Earlier, it had been another imposing urban monolith, all steel and glass and carefully maintained kerb-flash. Now, it glittered. Seventeen storeys of windows, all catching reflections of the whirlwind traffic. She used her phone as she approached, and he answered on the second ring. 'I'll be straight down,' he said.

She'd hoped he'd ask her up. Still: if not now, later. She'd make sure of that.

In the mirrored lobby, it was impossible not to catch sight of herself. Again: What would Min have thought? He'd have liked the dress, and the way her tights showed off her calves. But the thought that she'd scrubbed up for someone else would have struck ice through his heart.

And here came the lift, and out of it stepped Arkady Pashkin. Alone, she was relieved to note.

Crossing the lobby, he was careful not to show teeth, but there was a wolfish gleam in his eyes as he took her hand and – yes – raised it to his lips. 'Ms Guy,' he said. 'How charming you look.'

'Thank you.'

He wore a dark suit, with a collarless white shirt, its top button undone. Knotted round his neck was a blood-red scarf.

'I thought we might walk, if that's all right,' he said. 'It's warm enough, yes?'

'Perfectly warm,' she said.

'And I have so few chances to see the city as it should be

seen,' he said, nodding at the young woman on reception as he guided Louisa out onto Park Lane. 'All the great cities – Moscow, London, Paris, New York – they're best enjoyed on foot.'

'I wish more people thought so,' she said, raising her voice to be heard above the traffic. She looked round, but no one was following. 'It's just us, then.'

'It's just us.'

'You've given Piotr and—sorry, I've forgotten—'

'Kyril.'

'And Kyril the night off? Very good of you.'

'It's the modern way,' he said. 'Treat your workers well. Or they look for pastures new.'

'Even when they're goons.'

He had taken her arm as they crossed the road, and she felt no increase in pressure. On the contrary, his voice was amused as he replied: 'Even when, as you say, they are goons.'

'I'm teasing.'

'And I like to be teased. Up to a point. No, I gave them the evening off because I took the liberty of assuming that tonight is not business. Though I was surprised to get your call.'

'Really?'

'Really.' He smiled. 'I won't play games with you, I get calls from women. Even from English women, who can be a little . . . is *reticent* the word?'

'It's a word,' Louisa allowed.

'And this afternoon, you seemed so businesslike. I don't mean that as a criticism. On the contrary. Though in this particular case, it means I have to ask, was my assumption correct?'

'That tonight's not business?'

They were safely across the road, but he had not released her arm.

She said, 'Nobody knows I'm here, Mr Pashkin. This is entirely personal.'

'Arkady.'

'Louisa.'

They were in the park, on one of its lamplit paths. It was warm, as Louisa had promised, and the traffic's hum receded. Last winter, she'd walked this path with Min, heading for the Christmas fair – there'd been a Ferris wheel and skating, mulled wine, mince pies. At an air-rifle booth, Min had missed the target five times in a row. *Cover*, he'd said. *Don't want everyone knowing I'm a trained sharpshooter.* Bury that, she thought. Bury that moment. She said, 'We seem to be heading somewhere. Do you have a plan, or are we just seeing where the moment takes us?'

'Oh,' he told her, 'I always have a plan.'

That makes two of us, Louisa thought, and her grip tightened on the strap of her bag.

Two hundred yards behind them, out of reach of the lamplight, a figure followed silently, hands in pockets.

There was damp in the air, and overhanging clouds; a grey mass, hiding the stars. Griff Yates set off at a lick, but River kept up. They met nobody on the village's main road, and few houses were lit. Not for the first time, River wondered if the place existed in a time warp.

Perhaps Yates read his mind. 'Missing London much?'

'Peace and quiet. Makes a nice change.'

'So'll being dead.'

'If you don't like it, why do you stay?'

'Who says I don't like it?'

They passed the shop and the few remaining cottages. St John of the Cross became a black shape and vanished into bigger darkness. Upshott disappeared quickly at night. The road curved once, and that was it.

'Some of the people, mind. I'd happily be shot of them.'

'Incomers,' River said.

'They're all incomers. Andy Barnett? Talks like he's farming stock, but he doesn't know the business end of a bull.'

Which probably depended on whether you were a cow or a rambler, River thought. 'What about the flying crew?'

'What about them?'

'They're a young crowd. Weren't any of them born here?'

'Nah. Mummy and daddy moved here when they were small, so the kiddies could grow up *in the country*. You think real locals have aeroplanes to play with?'

'It's still their home.'

'No, it's just where they live.' Yates stopped abruptly, and pointed. River turned, but saw nothing: only the dark lane, hedgerowed either side. Larger outgrowths were trees, waving at the sky. 'See that elm?'

River said, 'Yes,' though had no idea.

'My grandad hanged himself from that. When he lost his farm. See? History, that is. Means your family's blood's been spilt there. Somewhere doesn't belong to you just because your parents bought a chunk of it.'

'It kind of does, though,' River said. 'You know. In the strictly legal sense.'

They walked on.

'That's bullshit about your grandad, isn't it?'

'Yeah.'

They reached a crossroads, one fork of which was a farm track: two ruts in a narrow passage. Griff marched down it without altering speed. The surface was slick underfoot, with random outcroppings of rock. River had a pencil-torch he couldn't use, partly because they were approaching the MoD land, but mostly so Griff wouldn't think him a wuss. It was very dark. There must be a moon, but River had no idea where, or what shape it would be if it showed itself. Meanwhile Griff marched without stumbling or slowing, proving a point: this was his territory, and he could navigate it eyes shut. River gritted his teeth and picked his knees up. Less chance of stumbling.

Griff halted. 'Know where we are?'

Of course I bloody don't. 'Tell me.'

Griff pointed left, and River squinted. 'Not seeing it.'

'Start at the ground and move your gaze upwards.' River did

as told, and about eight feet from the ground became aware of a change in texture. This wasn't hedgerow any more. Catching light from somewhere it winked at River briefly, and he understood: this was the MoD range, bordered on all sides by wire-mesh fence, along the top of which razor wire curled.

'We're going over that?' He was whispering.

'Can if you like. But I'm not.'

They trudged on.

'Common land, this used to be,' Griff said. 'Before the war. Till the government invoked some whatyecallit, emergency provision, and used it for training. Then the war ended, but they never gave it back, did they? Leased it to the Yanks, then when they buggered off, it went back to the M of bloody D.' He hawked noisily, and spat. 'For more training. So they say.'

'Artillery range, isn't it?'

'Oh aye. But that might just be cover.'

'For what?'

'Weapons research, maybe. Chemical weapons, you get? Or other stuff they don't want us knowing about.'

River made a non-committal noise.

'You think I'm joking?'

'Truthfully,' River said, 'I haven't the faintest idea.'

'Well here's your chance to find out.'

It took River a moment to realise Yates was pointing at a section of dark overgrowth. It looked no different than any other stretch they'd passed this last half hour, but that's what Griff was here for: to show him a way in he wouldn't find for himself.

'After you,' he said.

'So how long have you been with the, ah, Department of Energy?'

'I thought we agreed. No business.'

'Forgive me. One of my vices, I find it difficult to relax.' He glanced at her chest, a fair proportion of which was on display. 'Not impossible. Just difficult.'

'We must see what we can do about that,' she said.

'Something worth drinking to.' He raised his glass. She had already forgotten the name of the wine he'd ordered, and its label was obscured now as it wallowed in its bucket, but he'd specified the year, and that was a first for Louisa. Her dining experiences mostly involved sell-by dates, not vintages.

'I was sorry to hear about your colleague,' he said. 'Mr Harding?'

'Harper,' she said.

'My apologies, Harper. And my condolences. Were you close?'

'We worked together.'

'Some of my closest friendships have been born of work,' he said. 'I'm sure you miss him. We should drink to his memory.'

He raised his glass. After a moment, Louisa raised hers to meet it.

'Mr Harper,' he said.

'Min.'

'I'm sure he was a good man.' He drank.

After another moment, so did she.

The waiter arrived and began unloading food, the sight and smell of which made her want to gag. She'd just drunk a toast to Min's memory with the man she was sure was the force behind his death. But now would not be a good time to retch: she had the whole evening to get through. Keep him sweet and keep him happy; keep him eager until they were back in his suite. Then business could begin.

She wanted to know who, and she wanted to know why. All the questions Min himself would seek answers to, if he were here.

'So,' she said, her voice far away. She cleared her throat. 'So. You're happy with tomorrow's arrangements?'

He waved a finger like a disappointed priest. 'Louisa. What were we just saying?'

'I was thinking about the building. Impressive, isn't it?'

'Please. You must try this.' He was arranging bits of starter on her plate. She still had no hunger; she had an ache inside, but it wasn't food she needed. She forced a smile and thought she must look grotesque, as if her mouth had fish-hooks at the corners. But despite his enormous wealth, he was too much the gentleman to shudder or point.

'Impressive, yes,' he said, and she had to change mental gear: he was talking about the Needle. 'Capitalism at its most naked, rearing high above the city. You don't need me to mention Freud, I'm sure.'

'Perhaps not this early in the evening,' she heard herself say.

'And yet it's impossible to avoid. Where there is money, there is also sex. Please.' He gestured with his fork. 'Eat.'

It was as if he'd prepared it himself, and she wondered if that were a symptom of wealth; that you assume yourself the source of all your company's needs and pleasures.

She ate. It was a scallop, over which had been drizzled a nutty-looking sauce which tasted of too many things for her tongue to process. And yet that ache inside, which food could not pacify, rolled over on its back and quietened. Eat. Eat some more. It wasn't wrong to be hungry after all.

He was saying, 'And where there's sex, trouble follows. I've been seeing posters everywhere, hearing news reports. This Stop the City rally. Are your masters at the Department of Energy worried about it?'

That joke could wear thin. 'It's not ideal timing. But our route avoids it.'

'I'm surprised your authorities allow it on a weekday.'

'I suppose the organisers felt there was little point in bringing the City to its knees at the weekend, when the City's out of town.' Her bag buzzed. That was her phone receiving a text, but there was nobody she wanted to hear from. She ignored it, and speared another scallop.

He said, 'And it won't get out of hand?'

Similar demonstrations had seen burning cars and shattered windows. But the violence tended to be contained. 'These things are strenuously policed. The timing's a pain, but it's just one of those things. We'll work round it.'

Arkady Pashkin nodded thoughtfully. 'I'll trust you and your colleague to get me there and back safely.'

She smiled again. It felt more natural this time. Maybe because she was thinking that there was no chance Pashkin would be trusting her to do anything, once this evening was over.

Always supposing he was still alive.

For some reason River had expected it to be different, this side of the fence; lighter, perhaps; easier underfoot. But having followed Griff through not much of a gap in the spiky under-growth, to a sheared-through section of the wire fence that peeled back, he found everything much the same, except that there was no defined track, and he was muddier.

'Where now?' he asked, breathing hard.

'The main complex's two miles that way.' River couldn't tell which direction Griff was pointing. 'We pass some abandoned buildings first, half a mile or so. Ruined. Leave buildings untend-ed, that's gunna happen.'

'How often do you come here?'

'When I feel like it. It's a good place for rabbiting.'

'How many other ways in are there?'

'That one's easiest. Used to be another towards Upshott, where you could lift a post clean out of the ground and just walk in over the fence. But it was cemented back in place.'

They began to walk. The ground was slick, and inclined downwards; he slipped and would have hit the ground if Griff hadn't steadied him. 'Careful.' Then the clouds thinned, and a sliver of light gleamed from behind a gauzy curtain. River saw Griff's face clearly for the first time since leaving the pub. He was grinning, showing teeth as grey as his pitted skin, his mottled scalp. He seemed to be reflecting that scrap of moon.

Darker shadows waited at the foot of the incline. River couldn't make out whether they were trees or buildings, then understood they were both. There were four buildings, mostly roofless, and jutting out from their broken walls were long spectral branches, which caught a shiver of wind as he watched, and beckoned him onwards. Then the heavens shifted again, and the moonlight faded.

'So,' River said. 'If someone just turned up looking for a way in, he'd not be likely to find it?'

Griff said, 'Might, if he was smart or lucky. Or both.'

'You ever run across anyone in here?'

Griff made a snickering noise. 'Scared?'

'I'm wondering how secure it is.'

'There's patrols, and some places are wired. You want to avoid them.'

'Wired?'

'Tripwires. Lights and sirens. Mostly near the base, though.'

'Any round here?'

'You'll know soon enough, won't you? If you tread on one.'

That would be a laugh, thought River.

Holding an arm out for balance, he followed Griff towards the smashed-up buildings.

Pashkin said, 'I ought to ask, you're not married?'

'Only to the job.'

'And these, ah, messages you're getting. They're not from an irate lover?'

Louisa said, 'I have no lover. Irate or otherwise.'

She'd received three further texts, but hadn't read them.

They had eaten their starters, and their main courses; had drunk the first bottle, and most of the second. It was the first proper meal she'd eaten since Min's death. Pricey, too. Not a detail that would bother Arkady Pashkin, who owned an oil company. Louisa wondered if condemned men reviewed their final meals; sent compliments to the chef en route to the scaffold. Probably not. Though they had the excuse of knowing they were condemned.

She would blind him with the pepper spray. Plasti-cuff him hand and foot. Then all she'd need was a towel and a shower hose. In the Service they trained you in interrogation resistance, which was a covert way of teaching you interrogation methods. Pashkin was a big man, seemed in good health, but she imagined he'd last five minutes. Once she'd learned how Min had met his death, and which of Pashkin's goons had killed him, she'd put him out of his misery. There'd be something around she could use: a letter opener. Picture wire. They taught you to be resourceful, in the Service.

'So,' he said. 'You don't want to know the same of me?'

'Arkady Pashkin,' she quoted, 'is twice married, twice divorced, and never in want of attractive female company.'

He threw back his head and roared. All around the restaurant, heads turned, and Louisa noticed that while the men scowled, the women looked amused, and some of their gazes lingered.

When he'd finished, he dabbed his lips with his napkin and said, 'It seems I've been Googled.'

'The penalties of fame.'

He said, 'And it doesn't, ah, put you off? This so-called play-boy image?'

'Attractive female company,' she said. 'I'll take that as a compliment.'

'So you should. And as for "never in want", journalists exag-gerate. For headline value.'

A waiter arrived, and asked if madam, sir, would like to view the dessert menu? He went off to fetch it, and Pashkin said, 'Or we could walk back across the park now.'

She said, 'I think so, yes. But would you excuse me?'

The cloakroom was down a flight of stairs. When they called them cloakrooms, you'd moved up a notch on the restaurant scale. This one had old-fashioned pewter sinks in a wooden unit, lighting dim enough to flatter, and proper cotton towels, not air-blowers. She was alone. From elsewhere came the muffled percussion of cutlery; the conspiratorial hum of conversation; the throaty drone of an air purifier. She locked herself in a cubicle, peed, then checked her bag. The plasti-cuffs seemed weedy and impractical until you tugged them, whereupon their tensile strength became apparent. Once you'd wrapped them round someone, they had to be cut free. As for the spray, the label warned of serious damage if applied directly to eyes. A nod was as good as a wink.

She left the cubicle. Washed her hands. Dried them on a proper cotton towel. Then stepped out of the door and into the lobby where she was seized and pulled through another door into a small dark space. An arm was round her throat; her mouth clamped shut. A voice whispered into her ear: 'Let's have the bag.'

Where the slope bottomed out the ground was stony, and clumped with grass. River heard trickling water. His night vision was picking up, or maybe there was more to see. The first house was right in front of them, broken like a tooth, one side collapsed to reveal the cavity within. Wooden beams straddled its upper half, supporting an upper storey that was no longer there, and the floor was a litter of brick, tile, glass and broken stonework. The other buildings, the furthest no more than a hundred yards away, seemed in similar fettle. From inside the next River heard a rustling as its tree stirred, and branches scraped against what remained of its walls.

'Was this a farm?' he asked.

Griff didn't answer. He glanced at his wrist, then moved off towards the further building.

Instead of following, River walked round the first house. The tree inside was big enough that its upper branches poked above the highest remaining wall. He wondered how long a tree took to grow so big, and figured the house had been a ruin for decades. He saw no sign that anyone had been here recently. He was standing in cold ashes, the remains of a fire. But that was long dead.

If Mr B's purpose had involved the MoD base, he might have met his contact here, in this hollow; among these victorious trees and smashed houses. River wondered whether this area was patrolled, or if it was only the perimeter the guards took notice of. Griff would know. Where was Griff?

He walked back round the front. He couldn't see more than a dozen yards ahead, and didn't want to shout. Plucking a chunk of rock, he hurled it at the house. It hit with a *thock* loud enough to alert Griff, but no figure appeared. He waited a minute, then did it again. Then checked his watch. It was seconds off midnight.

The dark dispersed, as if a switch had been thrown. A shining ball burst into being overhead with a noise like tearing paper. It hovered in the sky, casting unearthly light, and instantly made the landscape strange – the battered houses with their intruder trees, the pocked and hillocked ground; all became alien, another planet. The light was orange, edged with green. The noise faded. What the hell? River spun round as another noise ripped the world apart, a banshee scream so loud he had to slap hands to his ears. It ended in a crash he couldn't tell how far away, and before its echoes died another erupted into the night, and this time he saw in its wake a red-hot scar that burnt its shape into his eyes. And then another. And another. The first explosion shook the ground, and warm wind blasted past him; the second, third, fourth turned him on his heels. The blasted ruins were no shelter, but they were all there was.

River leapt a ruined fragment of wall and landed on a strew of broken tiles. And then he was sprawling on the ground as furious noises crashed nearby, and he had to crawl for the shelter of the tree – the nearest thing to safety he could currently imagine. He closed his eyes, made himself small as possible. Way over his head, the night sky fizzed and boiled with angry lights.

Jesus wept, he thought, with that part of his mind not screaming in terror. Of all the nights to pick, he'd chosen one when the range was in use . . .

Another explosion took his breath away, and he thought no more.

I I

TONIGHT, HE'D BE breaking hearts.

This was new territory. Roderick Ho wasn't without experience in the gentle art of trashing stuff: he'd wrecked credit ratings, disassembled CVs, altered Facebook statuses and cancelled standing orders. He had systematically dismantled the offshore tax arrangements of a couple of old school chums – who's the dweeb now, dickheads? – and once had broken an arm – she'd been six; he'd been eight; it was almost certainly an accident. But hearts, no, he'd broken no hearts yet. Tonight would put that right.

Roddy had first met Shana – let's be precise; first *encountered* Shana – on Aldersgate Street: they were heading for their respective offices, and she'd barely noticed him. Well *barely* might not be the word. *Not* might be the word. But he'd noticed her, enough that the second time they passed he was half-looking out for her, and on the third was actually waiting for her, though nowhere she'd see him. He'd tailed her to her office, which turned out to be a temping agency near Smithfield. Back at Slough House, it hadn't proved much of a stretch to take a peek at its intranet, check out staff listings, and there she was: beaming photo and all. Shana Bellman. After that, it was a hop and a skip to Facebook where, among other things, Roddy found Shana to be a workout addict, so next up was a wander round the membership files of the local gyms. The third one he tried, he found her address. Couple of hours later they were best friends, which is to say that Roddy Ho now knew everything there was to know about Shana, up to and including the name of her boyfriend.

Which is where the heartbreak came in. The boyfriend had to go.

He smiled at her image, a wistful smile acknowledging the pain that precedes happiness, and downsized her photo into the tab at the foot of his screen. Then flexed his fingers, making a satisfying crack. Down to business.

And it's going to work like this. Shana's boyfriend is going to strike up a friendship with a couple of skanks on an internet chatsite, a conversation which is going to move from inappropriate to downright graphic within the space of half-a-dozen exchanges, at which point, with the kind of fat-finger error it's almost impossible not to see as willed, as if the cheating bastard actually wants to be caught, he's going to accidentally copy Shana in on the entire thread. And *sayonara*, boyfriend.

After that, it was gravy. Tomorrow morning – make it the day after; let the dust settle – all Roddy would have to do, passing Shana on her way to Smithfield, would be to make some friendly observation: *Hey beautiful, why so sad?* And then, *Hey, men are jerks. Tell me about it.* And then, after she'd gratefully been taken to dinner or a movie or whatever, *Hey baby, you want to take this in your—*

'Roddy?'

'Crawk!'

Catherine Standish made less noise than a draught. 'I hate to bother you when you've got your hands full,' she said. 'But there's something I need you to do.'

If he stood dead centre of his sitting room, Spider Webb was exactly three paces from the nearest piece of furniture, which itself sat in open space – this was his sofa, which was long enough to lie full-length on, with wiggle room on either end. After another couple of paces, you reached the wall, against which you could lean back and spread your arms wide without meeting obstruction. And while you were doing this you could feast your eyes on the view, which Spider kept behind big glass doors giving onto his balcony: treetops and sky; the trees organised in a neat row because they lined a canal, along which quiet narrowboats glided, decked out in royal reds and greens. Beat that, he thought. This was a catch-all phrase, applicable to whoever happened to be handy, but in Spider Webb's personal lexicon, it had a specific target.

Beat that, River Cartwright.

River Cartwright occupied a one-bedroom flat in the East End. His view was a row of lock-up garages, and there were three pubs and two clubs within chucking-up distance, which meant that even once River had negotiated his way through chavs, tarts, drunks and meth-heads, he'd still get no sleep for the racket they'd make till it was time to roll home for their giros. Which neatly underlined the way things were: River Cartwright was a fucking loser, while James Webb was scaling heights like Spider-Man's smarter brother.

It might have been different. Time was they'd been friendly. They'd undergone training together, were going to be the next bright lights of the Service, but this was what happened: Spider had been compelled to become instrumental in River's downgrading to slow horse; and subsequently, many long months later, River had demonstrated his poor-fucking-loser status by smashing Webb in the face with a loaded gun.

Still, that had only hurt for a while. A long while, true, but the facts remained: Spider lived in this apartment, worked in Regent's Park, and was on Diana Taverner's daily contact list, while River sweated out interminable days in Slough House, followed by noisy nights in the arse-end of the city. The best man had won.

Now the best man was meeting Arkady Pashkin in London's smartest new building in the morning, and if all went as planned, he'd be recruiting the most important asset the Service had seen in twenty years. A possible future leader of Russia in Regent's Park's pocket, and all it would cost Webb was promises.

After that, Lady Di's daily contact list would look like small beer. Besides, anyone forming a long-term alliance with Taverner was going to end up being Nick Clegged. Snuggling up to Ingrid Tearney was the better bet. Side by side with Tearney, he'd be seen as first-anointed. And for all the modernising policies the Service tipped its hat at, that counted for a lot.

Everything to play for, then, and he'd done everything right too – from the moment Pashkin had made contact Webb had played it like the high stakes game it was. And luck had been with him. Roger Barrowby's security audit had played into his hands, giving him the perfect alibi to outsource security details to Slough House, whose drones would follow orders without their activities registering on the Park's books. Even the location had been swiftly arranged: Pashkin had asked for the Needle, and it had taken Webb just three days to secure it. The suite's leaseholder was a high-end trading consultancy, currently brokering an arms deal between a UK firm and an African republic, and only too happy to cooperate with an MI5 agent. The date, chosen to fit with Pashkin's commitments, had been manageable too. Webb ran his tongue round mostly new teeth, a tangible reminder of River Cartwright's assault. All the details had fallen into place. If it weren't for Min Harper's death, it would have been textbook.

But Harper had died because he'd been drunk, and that was an end of it. There was nothing to suggest any last-minute snags, so all Webb had to do was get his head down and sleep the sleep of the just, full of the easy dreams and anticipations of success that would seem to River Cartwright like memories from another life.

So that's what he'd do now. Soon. In a bit.

Meanwhile, Spider Webb stood gazing round his bright well-appointed apartment, congratulating himself on his charmed existence, and hoping nothing would fuck it up for him now.

★

From her office, Shirley watched Catherine Standish enter Ho's room and close the door behind her. Something going on. And this was the pattern: when Shirley could be useful, some crap job was dumped on her. The rest of the time she was out in the cold.

Even Marcus Longridge was more wired in than her. Longridge had stepped into Min Harper's shoes, at least as far as the job went. Where Louisa Guy was concerned, Shirley doubted he'd be taking up Harper's slack any time soon. Louisa had turned into a wraith since Harper's death, as if actively prolonging some symbiotic relationship: he was dead, so she was a ghost. But still, she was out there, on a live job, while Shirley was stuck peeping over her monitor at someone else's closed door.

She'd found Mr B – found him twice. Tracked him to Upshott and nailed him at Gatwick too, which was like following a minnow through a shoal. But she didn't know what those triumphs amounted to, because no one was telling her squat.

It was late, and she should have been on her way hours ago, but she didn't want to go home. She wanted to know what was going on.

Shirley knew enough about stealthy movement not to fart about trying to move quietly. She strode into the hall and put her ear to Ho's door. And now she could make out a murmur. How it translated into English, she wasn't sure: Catherine was speaking softly, and Ho filled the gaps by remaining silent. The only distinct sound was a creak. A very slight creak. Trouble was, it came from behind her.

Slowly, she turned.

Jackson Lamb, on the next landing up, gazed down at her like a wolf who'd just separated a sheep from its flock.

Back across the park they walked. The traffic maintained an insectile buzz, and up above airliners circled, stacked on the Heathrow approach. Arkady Pashkin held her by the arm. Louisa's bag was lighter now. When it banged her hip, she felt only the usual baggage: mobile, lipstick, purse. But her heart was thumping wildly.

Pashkin pointed out the shapes of trees; how streetlights dancing behind quivering leaves made it seem a ghost was passing. He sounded very Russian saying this. When a motorbike fired up his grip tightened briefly, though he made no comment; and a short while later he tightened it again, as if to underline that he had been unperturbed by the sudden explosion, that it had coincided with his decision to squeeze her arm.

She said, 'It must be late,' and her voice sounded as if she were at the far end of a hall of mirrors.

They rejoined the pavement. Black cabs thundered past, their flow interrupted by the occasional bus. Through tinted windows, faces gazed at London's brilliant parade.

Pashkin said, or maybe repeated, 'Are you quite well, Louisa?'

Was she? She felt like she'd been doped.

'You're cold.' And he draped his jacket over her shoulders like a gentleman in a story, the kind you didn't encounter any more, unless they were trying to impress you because they planned to get you naked.

They arrived at his hotel's territory; a broad sweep of pavement lined with terracotta pots, and she stopped, feeling the tug of his arm for a moment before he too halted.

His face was polite puzzlement.

'I ought to go,' she said. 'There's a lot to do tomorrow.'

'A swift nightcap?'

She wondered in how many languages he could say that.

'Not the best time.' She shrugged his jacket off, and as he reached for it his eyes grew colder, as if he were re-evaluating the night's conversation and concluding that he'd made no basic errors; that this unsatisfactory conclusion was due to her having supplied incorrect data. 'I'm sorry.'

He made a slight bow. 'Of course.'

I had planned to come upstairs. He wouldn't have been

surprised to hear that, this man with more money than the Queen. I had planned to come upstairs, have a nightcap, fuck you if necessary. Anything to get you into a state where I could truss you like a Sunday goose and force answers from you. Like: what did Min find out that meant he had to die?

'I'll get you a taxi.'

She kissed him on the cheek. 'This is not over,' she promised, but luckily he had no notion as to what she meant.

In the taxi, she told the driver to let her out round the corner. He sighed theatrically, but stopped when he caught her expression. Only a minute after she'd left it, the evening air struck her like a new thing, tasting dark and bitter. The taxi pulled away. Footsteps approached. Louisa didn't turn.

'You saw sense.'

'I had no choice, did I? Not once you'd taken my gear.'

Christ: she sounded like a petulant schoolgirl.

Maybe Marcus agreed. 'Yeah, well, you wouldn't answer your phone,' he said. 'I could have let you give it your best shot. But it would have been a good way to get seriously damaged. Or dead.'

Louisa didn't reply. She felt used up. Ready to crawl under the covers, and hope daylight never came.

Nearby traffic thundered along Park Lane, while up in the dark skies aircraft ploughed through clouds, their tail lights bright as rubies.

'Tube's this way,' said Marcus.

Shana was a memory. Her boyfriend was reprieved. The pair could spend another night in their fools' paradise, because Roddy Ho had other fish to fry.

. . . One day he was going to sit Catherine Standish down and explain to her exactly why he didn't have to do everything she said. It would be a short conversation which would doubt-less end with her in tears, and he was already looking forward to it as he loaded the names she'd given him onto his computer and started doing everything she'd said.

And because he was who he was, the digital tasks in front of Roderick Ho bloomed, and eclipsed the resentment boiling inside him. Catherine slipped into his rearview then vanished, and the list of names became the next level of the online game he was constantly playing.

As ever, he played to win.

Lamb said, 'She was listening outside when you were talking to Ho.'

'And I was inside when you caught her doing that,' Catherine said. 'So how come I didn't hear you disembowelling her?'

'Oh, she had an excuse.'

Catherine waited.

Lamb said, 'She wanted to hear what you were talking about.'

'That would cover it,' Catherine agreed. 'You think she's Lady Di's plant?'

'Don't you?'

'She's not the only possibility.'

'So you assume it's Longridge. What are you, Standish, racist?'

'No, I—'

'That's even worse than thinking it's the dyke,' Lamb said.

'I'm so glad we've got you to grade our discrimination issues.'

'Ho's looking at the Upshott menagerie?'

She was used to him switching topics. 'I've got as far as I can on my own. There are plenty of candidates, no obvious suspects.'

'Would've been quicker to use him in the first place.'

'I wasn't supposed to be doing this in the first place,' she pointed out. 'Has River checked in?'

'Earlier today.'

'He okay?'

'Why wouldn't he be? Whatever's going on, it's not a big plot to assassinate Cartwright.'

'This summit happens in the morning. The Pashkin thing.'

'And you think there's a connection,' he said flatly.

227

'Arkady Pashkin,' she said. 'Alexander Popov. That doesn't worry you?'

'Give me a break. I've got the same initials as . . . Jesus Christ, but I don't go on about it. This isn't an Agatha Christie.'

'I don't care if it's a Dan Brown. If the two are connected, then something'll happen in Upshott. Soon. We should let the Park know.'

'If Dander's Taverner's mole, they already do. Unless you want to take a punt on this initials thing.' Lamb scratched his chin thoughtfully. 'Think they'll call a COBRA session?'

'You're the one who put all this in motion. And you're just going to wait and see what happens?'

'No, I'm just going to wait for Cartwright's call. Which he'll make when he's back from the MoD place. You think I'm still here this time of night because I've nothing better to do?'

'Pretty much,' Catherine said. 'What's happening at the MoD place?'

'Probably nothing. But whoever laid a trail didn't do it to keep what's going to happen a secret. So I'm assuming Cartwright'll find a clue somewhere. Now bugger off and leave me in peace.'

She rose but paused at the doorway. 'I hope you're right,' she said.

'About what?'

'That whatever's going on isn't a plan to assassinate River. We've already lost Min.'

'They staff us with screw-ups,' Lamb reminded her. 'We'll be back up to strength in no time.'

She left.

Lamb tilted his chair back and gazed at the ceiling for a while, then closed his eyes, and became very still.

Ho sucked his teeth as he worked. What Standish had done with her data was old school: she'd processed it looking for common threads. You could do the job faster if you just printed it out and read it, biro in hand.

Going Amish, they called that. Applied to Catherine Standish too. The woman wore a hat.

Ho's method didn't have a name, or not one he could think of. What he did came naturally, like water to a fish. He took the names, plus their DOBs, ignored everything else Standish had supplied, and ran them blind through engines both backdoor and legal. Legal was anything in the public domain, plus various government databases his Service clearance gave him access to: tax and National Insurance, health, driving licence; what he thought of as data fodder.

The backdoor stuff was more potent. For starters, he had a SOCA trapdoor. Ho limited himself to brief forays, because its security was improving, but it gave near-instant rundowns on even peripheral involvement with criminal investigations. It wasn't likely a deep-cover spook would have form, but it wasn't impossible, and Ho liked to keep in practice. After that came the premier division. Back when he'd been a junior analyst at the Park Ho had been given one-off access to the GCHQ network, and had made a clone from his temporary password. He'd subsequently upgraded himself to administrator status, and could pull up all existing background on any name he chose. This covered not only subversive activity – which included relationships with foreign nationals from any country on the suspect list; travels to unfriendly nations, which for historical reasons included France; and any contact whatsoever, up to vague geographical proximity, with anyone on the watch-lists, which were updated daily – but also digital footprint, phone use, credit rating, litigation record, pet ownership: everything. If GCHQ sold user lists to direct mail advertising companies, it could fund the war on terror by itself. In fact, an enterprising freelancer might take advantage of this, Ho thought; a topic worth researching, though maybe not right this moment.

He let himself in, entered the target names, created a destination folder for the results, and exited. No point hanging around while the Matrix did its stuff, which was to accumulate, assess and regurgitate data, with crossover points neatly highlighted so even an Amish could assimilate the bullet points. Kind of like playing Tetris. All the little blocks of info, settling into place. No gaps.

Like that, only much more cool . . . If Shana could see him now, that boyfriend of hers would be dust. And Roderick Ho lapsed into happy daydream, while the machine-world did his work.

'Why'd you stop me?'

The Tube was quiet: a few homegoers down the far end; a lone woman plugged into her own little iWorld; a drunk man by the doors. But Louisa kept it low, because you never could tell.

Marcus said, 'Like I told you. Trying to take down Pashkin on your own's a good way of getting hurt.'

'And what's that to you?'

'I was Ops. We had this thing about watching each others' backs.' He didn't appear offended. 'You think he killed Harper, don't you?'

'Or had him killed. You think I'm wrong?'

'Not necessarily. But don't you think he's been looked at?'

'By Spider Webb.'

'Who's not been straight with us.'

'He's a suit, he's the Park. He wouldn't be straight if you rammed a telegraph pole up his arse.' She stood. 'I change here.'

'You're going home?'

'Now you're my dad?'

'Just tell me you're not heading back for another crack at him.'

'You took my cuffs, Longridge. And my spray. I'm not going back for another crack, no, not with just my bare hands.'

'And you'll be there in the morning.'

She stared.

He spread his hands wide: look at me; nothing to hide. 'Maybe he had Min whacked, maybe not. But we've still got a job to do.'

'I'll be there,' she said through gritted teeth.

'That's good. But one other thing, yeah?'

The train pulled into the station, and suddenly there were white tiles and lurid posters visible through the windows.

'Tomorrow, I'm working security. And my job's to neutralise any threat to the principal. Understand what I'm saying?'

'Good night, Marcus,' she said, stepping onto the platform. By the time the train moved off, she'd disappeared down an exit tunnel.

Marcus remained in his seat. Two other people had left at Louisa's stop, three more had got on, and he knew exactly which were which. But as none represented a threat, he closed his eyes as the train picked up speed, and for all the world looked like he'd fallen asleep.

Ho woke, straightened his neck, and the thread of drool bridging the corner of his mouth and his shoulder broke and pooled on his shirt front. He wiped his mouth blearily, dabbed at his shirt with his fingers, and wiped his fingers dry on his shirt. Then he turned to his computer.

It was making a contented humming sound; the friendly noise it made when it had finished a task he'd set it.

He rose. This was a sticky business – his clothing clung to his chair. In the hallway, he paused. Slough House was quiet, but didn't feel empty. Lamb, he guessed, and probably Standish also. He yawned and padded to the toilet, peed mostly into it, then padded back to his office and slumped back into his chair. Wiped his fingers on his shirt again, and drank some energy drink. Then tilted his flatscreen to see the results of his searches.

As he scrolled down, he leant forward. Information interested

Ho to the precise degree that it might prove advantageous, and the data he was looking at had no relevance to himself. But it was of interest to Catherine Standish. Among the names he'd processed, she hoped, was that of Mr B's contact; a Soviet sleeper from the old days. Finding out who it was would impress her. On the other hand, she already knew he was shit-hot at this, and while it was true she was nicer to him than anyone else in this dump, the fact remained that she'd blackmailed him into—

Something caught his attention. He stopped scrolling, scrolled back up again, checked a date he'd just registered. Then re-scrolled down to where he'd been.

'Hmph.'

Ho pushed his glasses up his nose with a finger, then sniffed the finger and made a face. He wiped it on his shirt and returned his attention to the screen. A moment later, he again stopped scrolling.

'You're kidding,' he muttered.

He scrolled down further, then stopped.

'You have got to be kidding.'

He paused and thought. Then he keyed a phrase into the search box, hit return, and stared at the results.

'You have got to be fucking kidding,' he said.

This time, he didn't stick to the chair at all.

12

H E HEARD A VOICE.
'Walker.'

The booming noises remained, but only inside his head: a pulse like a dull metal drumbeat, caroming round his skull. With every contact a starburst was born, died, and rose again. His body was one big fist, its knuckles raw.

'Jonathan Walker.'

River opened his eyes to find he'd been captured by a dwarf.

He was where he'd always been; curled at the foot of an indestructible tree, the only thing fixing the earth to the sky. The ruined building had shrunk – or everything else had grown – and his heart was trying to burst free from its cage.

How long had he been here? Two minutes? Two hours?

And who was the dwarf?

He unclenched himself. The dwarf wore a red cap, and twinkled in an evil way. 'Enjoy the show?'

River spoke, and his words swelled up as they left his mouth. His head had been swallowed by a balloon.

'Griff? He's long gone.' River could have sworn the dwarf rolled back on his heels, like a toy you couldn't push over. Then he loomed back into River's face. 'Not likely to stick around during artillery practice, is he?'

He hauled River to his feet, and it turned out he wasn't a dwarf at all, but a medium-sized man. Unless River had shrunk. Terror could do that. He shook his head, and when he stopped the world carried on shaking. He looked up, which was another mistake, but at least the sky had calmed down. No new scars ripped it apart. He looked back at the no-longer dwarf.

'I know you,' he said, and this time his voice more or less behaved itself.

'Maybe we should move.'

River pressed his hands to his temples. This suppressed all movement for a while. 'We in danger here?'

'The night's young.'

The man in the red cap – not a dwarf, but that cap remained real – turned and plodded out of the shell of the building. River stumbled after him.

Lamb wiped his face with a meaty hand. 'This better be good.' He'd been asleep in his chair, and looked barely awake in it now. But when Roderick Ho had appeared in the doorway, printout in hand, his eyes had snapped open, and for a moment Ho had felt like a rabbit who'd wandered into a lion's cage.

'I found something,' he said.

Catherine appeared. If she'd been sleeping, too, she'd been less messy about it than Lamb, who was smeared with big red blotches. 'What kind of something, Roddy?'

She was the only person who called him that. Ho couldn't decide whether he liked it that way, or wished more people did.

He said, 'Don't know. But it's *some*thing.'

'That wasn't the best sleep I've ever had,' Lamb said. 'But if you woke me to play twenty questions, you'll be sharing a room with Cartwright when he gets back.'

'It's the village. Upshott. The population spread.'

'It's pretty tiny,' Catherine said.

Lamb said, 'It's bloody Toytown. With fewer amenities. You have any information we don't already know?'

'Fewer amenities, exactly.' Ho was starting to feel confident again. Remembered he was a cyber-warrior. 'There's nothing there. And even when there was, it was the Yank airbase, and none of the names on the list had anything to do with that.'

Lamb lit a cigarette. 'First of the day,' he said, when Catherine flashed him a look. It was ten past midnight. 'Look, Roddy.' This was said kindly. 'All that crap I lay on you? The name-calling? The threats?'

'It's okay,' Ho said. 'I know you don't mean it.'

'I mean every bloody word, my son. But it will all seem trivial compared to what'll happen if you don't start making sense sharpish. *Capisce?*'

The cyber-warrior leaked away. 'None of them were connected with the airbase. Something else must have attracted them to Upshott, but there's nothing else there. So—'

'Urban flight?' Lamb asked. 'It's what happens in cities when too many undesirables turn up.' He paused. 'No offence.'

'Except that's a gradual thing,' Ho said. 'And this wasn't.'

The smoke from Lamb's cigarette hung motionless in the air.

Catherine said, 'What do you mean, Roddy?'

And here was his night's triumph, though it involved fewer blondes than he'd wanted. 'They moved into the village in the space of a few months. A whole bunch of them.'

'How many?' Lamb asked.

Handing his printout to Catherine, Ho said, 'Seventeen of them. Seventeen families. And they all arrived in Upshott between March and June, nineteen ninety-one.'

And he had the satisfaction of seeing, for once, Lamb lost for an instant reply.

Stomping up the slope Griff Yates had led him down earlier, River had to rest halfway. But the pounding in his head was fainter, and he was starting to notice he was alive, when he could easily have been sprayed across this landscape as a fine red mist.

The thought of encountering Griff again was starting to energise him too.

Redcap waited at the top. He was little more than a dark outline, but River's brain was firing again, and a name popped into it. He said, 'You're Tommy Moult.' Outside the village shop, selling packets of seeds from his bike basket. That was where River knew him from, though they'd never spoken beyond a hello. 'What are you doing here this time of night?'

'Picking up strays.' Tufts of white hair sprigged out from Moult's cap. He must have been seventy: he had a well-lined face, and dressed like he lived under a hedge with an ancient tweed jacket that smelled of outdoors, and trousers that were knotted round his ankles. Makeshift bike clips, River supposed, though less sanitary possibilities occurred. His voice was a rough gargle: the local accent poured over pebbles. An unlikely saviour, but a saviour all the same.

'Well, thanks.'

Moult nodded, turned and walked. River followed. He had no idea which direction they were headed. His inner compass was spinning crazily.

Over his shoulder, Moult said, 'You'd have been all right. They don't target the buildings. If they did they'd be rubble, and those trees would be matchsticks. See the humps in the land back there?'

'No.'

'Well, they're Bronze Age barrows. The military don't plant ordnance on them. Draws criticism.'

'I suppose Griff knows that too.'

'He didn't plan on you being blown to bits, if that's what you're asking.'

'I'll bear that in mind next time I see him.'

'He just wanted to scare you shitless.' Moult halted so suddenly River nearly bumped into him. 'What you probably ought to know is that Griff's been in love with young Kelly Tropper since she took the stabilisers off her bike. So what with you and her being so friendly – and in the middle of the day – well, you can see he might take that amiss.'

'Jesus wept,' said River. 'That was like – that was *this afternoon*.'

Tommy Moult glanced skywards.

'Yesterday afternoon. And he knows about it? *You* know about it?'

'You're familiar with the phrase global village?'

River stared.

'Well, Upshott's the village version of that. Everyone knows everything.'

'Bastard could have killed me.'

'I suppose, to his way of thinking, it wouldn't have been him doing the killing.'

Moult tramped off. River followed. 'It seems further than it did before,' he said after a while.

'Same distance it's always been.'

A penny dropped. 'We're not heading back to the road, are we?'

'Be a shame,' Moult said, 'to go to all this effort, not to mention having the poop scared out of you, and then just scoot home with your tail between your legs.'

'So where are we going?'

'To find the only thing round here worth finding,' Moult said. 'Oh, and by the way? It's top secret.'

River nodded, and they walked on into the dark.

'Okay,' Lamb said at last. 'That must be why I keep you round. Now back to your toys, button-boy. If they're all sleepers then they're long-term fakes, fakes being the operative word. Their paperwork must be good, but there'll be a chink of light somewhere. Find it.'

'It's after midnight.'

'Thanks,' Lamb said. 'My watch is fast. And when you've done that, do a background on Arkady Pashkin, which is spelt exactly like I've just said it.' He paused. 'Is there a reason you're still here?'

Catherine said, 'That's good work. Well done, Roddy.'

Ho left.

She said, 'Would it kill you to tell him well done?'

'If he doesn't do his job, he's just taking up space.'

'He found this.' Catherine waved the printout. 'And another thing – "chink of light"?'

There was a moment's silence.

'Christ, I'm getting old,' said Lamb. 'Don't ever tell him, but that was unintentional.'

She went out to the tiny kitchen, and put the kettle on. When she returned, he'd pushed his chair back and was staring at the ceiling, an unlit cigarette in his mouth. Catherine waited. At length, he spoke.

'What do you make of it?'

It appeared to be a genuine question.

She said, 'I presume we're ruling out coincidence.'

'Well, it's not like Upshott had a sale on. And like Ho said, there's no other reason to move there.'

'So an entire sleeper network just descended on a Cotswold village and, what, took it over?'

'Sounds like *The Twilight Zone*, doesn't it?'

'To what end? It's basically a retirement village.'

He didn't reply.

The kettle boiled, and she went back out and made tea. Came back with two mugs, and put Lamb's on his desk. He made no response.

She said, 'It's not even a dormitory town. No direct rail link to London, or anywhere else. It's got a church, a shop and a few mail-order outlets. There's a pottery. A pub. Stop me when it starts sounding like a target.'

'The base was still there when they moved in.'

'Which suggests that if their presence had anything to do with the base they'd have left by now. Or done whatever they meant to do while it was still operational. And who buys a house to carry out a covert op, for heaven's sake? Half of them took out mortgages. That's how Ho found them.'

Lamb said, 'No, please, keep talking. I find silence oppressive.'

Without shifting his gaze from the ceiling, he began fumbling for his lighter.

She said, 'If you light that, I'm opening a window. It already stinks in here.'

Lamb removed the cigarette from his mouth and held it above his head. He rolled it between his fingers. She could hear him thinking.

He said, 'Seventeen of them.'

'Seventeen families. Or some of them are families. Do you think the kids know?'

'How many we talking about?'

Catherine checked the printout. 'About a dozen. Most of them well into their twenties, but at least five still have strong ties to the village. River says—' Lamb jerked upright and she paused, her thread broken. 'What?'

'Why are we assuming they know about each other?'

She said, 'Ah . . . Because they've all been there twenty years?'

'Yeah. It must come up at dinner parties all the time.' His voice rose a key. 'Did I ever mention that Sebastian and I spy for the Kremlin? More Chablis?' He resumed his search for his lighter. 'Sleepers operate solo. They don't have handlers, just a call-code. Do this. Over and out. Years can go by in-between, and they have no contact with anyone else.'

His face had assumed its bullfrog expression. He found the lighter and lit his cigarette but did so on autopilot. He didn't even comment when Catherine crossed the room, raised the blind, and opened the window. Dark night air rushed in, eager to explore this brand new space.

He said, 'Think about it. The Wall comes down. The USSR breaks up. Whatever the network was for, at this point it's tits up. So maybe the mastermind running it, who we're assuming's the same guy who dreamed up Alexander Popov, decided to mothball it. But instead of calling them home, he sends them out to the sticks instead. Why not?'

Catherine jumped onto his train of thought. 'They've spent

years burrowing into English society. They've all got jobs, all successful in their own fields, and then they're instructed to move out into the countryside, like countless other middle-class successes. Maybe they're not sleeping any more. Maybe they've become who they've been pretending to be.'

'Living normal lives,' said Lamb.

'So I was right. It is a retirement village.'

'Though it seems someone plans to wake them up.'

'Either way,' said Catherine, 'it might be an idea to let River know.'

Moult opened the fridge and from its freezer compartment produced a bottle so frosted River couldn't read its label. Finding glasses on a shelf, he set them on the workbench. Then he uncapped the bottle, filled each glass, and handed one to River.

'That's it?' River said.

'You expected a slice of lemon?'

'We've walked seven miles across pitch-black moorland, and your top secret is, you know where there's free booze?'

'It was barely two miles,' Moult pointed out. 'And there's a quarter moon.'

On the moor, they'd had to drop to the ground when a jeep passed, carving out chunks of the night, small parts of which glittered – insects, darting about like aerial shards of glass, and reflecting the security patrol's headlights. Not long afterwards, they'd come through the fence, but not the same way Griff Yates had led River in; instead, they'd emerged onto a stretch of tarmac along which they'd been trekking for over a minute before River registered what it was: not a road but a landing strip. And then the building up ahead took shape, and it was the hangar where the flying club kept their aeroplane. Next to it was a smaller construction, the clubhouse itself, which turned out to be not much more than a garage with added amenities – the fridge Moult was raiding; a few chairs; an old desk cluttered with paperwork; a stack of cardboard boxes, half-covered by a plastic sheet. Light came from a bare overhead bulb. The key to all this treasure had been on a ledge above the door, which would have been the first place River looked, had Tommy Moult not already known it was there.

Tommy Moult, who was now looking at his empty glass as if trying to puzzle out how it had got that way.

River said, 'I'm guessing you're not actually a full member of the club?'

'It's not a club as such,' Tommy said. 'Not with rules and membership lists.'

'So that would be a no.'

He shrugged. 'If they wanted their door locked, they'd keep the key where it couldn't be found.'

There were photos magneted to the fridge. One was of Kelly in flying gear: jumpsuit, helmet, broad smile. Others, alongside bills and newspaper clippings, showed Kelly's friends: Damien Butterfield, Jez Bradley, Celia and Dave Morden; others River couldn't put names to. An older man standing by the neat aircraft that was the flying club's pride and joy looked very much the pilot in pressed trousers and silver-buttoned blazer. His white hair was immaculately tended; his shoes shined to perfection.

'That's Ray Hadley, is it?'

'Aye,' Tommy said.

'How'd he afford his own plane?'

'Maybe he won the Lottery.'

Hadley was the club's founder, if a club that wasn't a club could have a founder. Through his encouragement Kelly and Co. had taken flying lessons; because of him, their lives had come to centre around this garage and the hangar next door.

In one of their first conversations River had asked Kelly how they managed to afford it all, and slight puzzlement had flitted across her face as she'd explained that their parents had paid. 'It's not much more expensive than riding lessons,' she'd said.

Above the desk was a calendar, the month's days marked off in small square boxes. Several had been X'ed out with thick red marker pen. Last Saturday, River noted, and the Tuesday before that. And tomorrow. Underneath it, holiday postcards had been Blu-Tacked to the wall: beaches and sunsets. All a long way away.

His mobile vibrated in his pocket.

'I'll be outside,' he told Tommy, which was where he checked the incoming number before answering.

It was Catherine Standish, not Lamb.

'This is going to sound odd,' she promised.

Catherine gone, Lamb closed his window, pulled down his blind and poured a glass from the Talisker kept, true to cliché, in his desk drawer. As he drank, his gaze slipped out of focus. Anyone watching might have thought he was slipping into a booze-fuelled nap, but Lamb asleep was more restless than this – Lamb asleep made sudden panicky movements, and sometimes swore in tongues. This Lamb was still and silent, though his lips shone. This Lamb was impersonating a boulder.

At length, this Lamb spoke aloud: 'Why Upshott?'

If Catherine had been there, she'd have said, Why not? It had to be somewhere.

'And if it was anywhere else, I'd be asking why there?' Lamb replied. But it wasn't anywhere else. It was Upshott.

And whoever had decided that that's where it should be had Kremlin brains in a Kremlin head. Which meant they didn't choose breakfast without weighing up the consequences. Which meant there was a reason for it being Upshott which didn't involve a map and a pin.

Eyes closed, Lamb summoned up the Ordnance Survey map he'd studied once a day since River Cartwright had become an agent in place. Upshott was a small village among larger towns, none of which had any strategic significance; they simply nestled in the heart of the British countryside, attracting tourists and photographers. They were towns where you bought antiques and expensive sweaters. Places to go to when you were sick of cities. And if you wanted an image of England, they were the places you thought of, once you'd used up Buck House and Big Ben and the Mother of Parliaments.

Or at least, he amended, they were the places a Kremlin brain in a Kremlin head might think of when thinking of England.

Now Lamb stirred, and sat up. He poured another scotch and drank it; the two actions twin halves of a single seamless gesture. Then he pawed at his collar with a meaty hand, to confirm he already wore his coat.

It was late, but he was still up. And in Lamb's world, if he was still up, there was small reason why any other bugger should be sleeping.

Needing a Russian brain to pick, he left Slough House and headed west.

River said, 'You *what*?'

Catherine repeated herself. 'Half the names you've mentioned, Butterfield, Hadley, Tropper, Mor—'

'*Tropper?*'

Catherine paused. 'Any special reason for singling him out?'

'. . . No. Who else?'

She read them out; Butterfield, Hadley, Tropper, Morden, Barnett, Salmon, Wingfield, James: the rest . . . seventeen names, most of which River had encountered. Wingfield – he'd met a Wingfield at St Johnno's. She was in her eighties; one of those old ladies who seem half bird: bright of eye and sharp of beak. Used to be something at the Beeb.

'River?'

'Still here.'

'We thought Mr B was in Upshott to meet a contact. It could have been any one of them, River. It looks like the cicada network exists, all right. And is right there, right now.'

'There a Tommy Moult on that list? M – O – U – L – T.'

He could hear the printout shimmy in her hands. 'No,' she said. 'No Moult.'

'No, I didn't think there would be,' River said. 'Okay. How's Louisa?'

'The same. It's this summit thing tomorrow. Your old friend Spider Webb and his Russians. Except . . .'

'Except what?'

'Lamb came up with background on the woman who ran Min over. It looks like the Dogs might have been hasty, writing it up as an accident.'

'Jesus,' he said. 'Louisa know?'

'No.'

'Keep an eye on her, Catherine. She already thinks Min was murdered. If she gets proof . . .'

'I will. How do you know she thinks that?'

'Because I would,' he said. 'Okay. I'll watch my step. But so far, I've got to tell you, Upshott appears to be what it looks like on the map. A small piece of nowhere in some pretty country-side.'

'Roddy's still digging. I'll get back to you.'

River stood a while longer in the dark. Kelly, he thought. Kelly Tropper — maybe her father, yes, former big-shot lawyer in the capital; maybe he was the kind of long-term burrower the old-style Kremlin might have put in play. But his daughter had barely been born when the Wall came down. There was no reason to suspect she might be part of the network. What were the chances that this little nowhere was nurturing a new generation of Cold War warriors, and what would they be fighting for if it did? The resurrection of the Soviet Union?

Through the window he watched Tommy Moult pour more vodka, then take something from his pocket and put it in his mouth. He used the alcohol to wash it down. He still wore his red cap, and the hair that poked from it seemed comical. His skin was tight across his jaw, and bristled with white stubble. The gleam in his eyes was lively enough, but there was an air of weariness about him. The cap struck a jaunty note at odds with everything else.

Turning, River faced the hangar. The big doors giving onto the landing strip were padlocked, but there was an unsecured side entrance. He stepped inside, listening hard, but the only sounds were those of an empty structure, and when he swept the interior with his pocket torch's beam, nothing scuttled from its reach. The plane loomed in the shadows. A Cessna Skyhawk – he'd not been this close to it before, but had seen it ploughing the skies above Upshott, where it seemed a child's toy. It wasn't that much more substantial now: about half as tall as River himself, and maybe three times that long. It was single-engined, with space for four passengers; white with blue piping. When he laid a hand on its wing it was cold to the touch, but promised warmth; the warmth of coiled potential. He hadn't really registered until now that Kelly flew. Had known it as a fact, but not felt it. Now he did.

The rest of the structure was mostly clear floor space, everything else being stacked against the walls. A flatbed trolley's handle reared up like a hobbyhorse. Whatever it held was draped in canvas. This was secured to the trolley with clothesline, and River had to fiddle with a knot, torch in mouth, before he could peel it free. Having done that, it took him a moment to work out what it was that was stacked there, three sacks deep. He put a hand to it. Like the plane it was cold, but warm with the same coiled potential.

What felt like a pair of darts struck him on the neck.

A flash of light ignited River's brain, and the world turned to smoke.

The Wentworth Academy of the English Language was quiet, no lights showing from its third-floor offices above the stationer's off High Holborn. This suited Lamb. He'd prefer to find Nikolai Katinsky asleep. Being woken at this hour would stir memories, and render him amenable to questioning.

The door, like Slough House's, was black and heavy and weathered, but where the latter hadn't been opened in years, this saw daily use. No groaning from the tumblers as Lamb slipped a pick into its keyhole; no squealing from the hinges as he eased it open. Once inside he waited a full minute, accustoming himself to the dark and the building's breathing before tackling the staircase.

It was often observed of Lamb that he could move quietly when he wanted. Min Harper had suggested that this was only true on his home ground, because Lamb knew every creak and wobble of Slough House, having doctored the noisier stairs himself. But Harper was dead, so what did he know? Lamb went up without a sound, and paused at the Academy's door barely long enough to squint through its frosted window, or so it appeared, though the pause proved long enough for him to gain entry. He closed the door behind him as silently as he'd opened it.

Again, he stood a moment, waiting for the atmospheric disturbance his entrance had made to settle, but it was wasted caution. There was nobody there. The door to the next office hung ajar, and there'd be nobody in there either. The only living thing was Lamb himself. Slivers of streetlight broke through blinds, and as his eyes adjusted he could make out the shape, under the desk, of the still-folded camp bed; its thin mattress folded round its metal frame like a diagram of an unlikely yoga position.

Lamb carried no torch. Torchlight in a darkened building screams burglary. Instead, he switched the anglepoise on, flooding the desk with cold yellow lamplight and puddling the rest of the room. Everything looked as it had on his previous visit. Same bookshelves holding the same thick catalogues; same paperwork littering the desk. He opened drawers and scuffled through papers. Most were bills, but a letter lay among them, handwritten, peeping from a coyly curling flap. A love letter, of all things; not even an explicit one, but expressing regret at parting. It seemed that Nikolai had seen fit to end an affair. Neither the fact that he had done so, nor that he had embarked upon an affair in the first place, surprised Lamb. What he did find curious was that Katinsky had left the letter in what amounted to plain view. All it took was for someone to break in and rifle his desk. Katinsky had never been a player – a cipher clerk, one among many; barely known to Regent's Park before his defection – but still, Service life should have taught him Moscow rules, and Moscow rules should never be forgotten.

He replaced the letter. Examined a desk diary. No appointments had been noted for today. The remainder of the year was empty too: a string of blank days stretching ahead. Lamb flipped back and found annotations: brief reminders, initials, times and places. He put it down. In the small adjoining office was a filing cabinet which held clothing; in a mug on a shelf, a razor and toothbrush. A shirt hung on the back of the door. In a corner, a blue coolbox held tubs of olives and houmous, slices of ham and a chunk of mouldy bread. In a cupboard he found a stash of empty pill bottles, none with prescription labels. 'Xemoflavin', one read. He dropped it in a pocket, then surveyed the tiny room once more. Katinsky lived here all right. He just wasn't here now.

Lamb switched off the anglepoise and left, locking the door behind him.

13

L ONDON SLEPT, BUT FITFULLY, its every other eye wide open. The ribbon of light atop the Telecom Tower unfurled again and again, traffic lights blinked through unvarying sequence, and electronic posters affixed to bus stops rotated and paused, rotated and paused, drawing an absent public's attention to unbeatable mortgage deals. There were fewer cars, playing louder music, and the bass pulse that trailed in their wake pounded the road long after they'd gone. From the zoo leaked muffled shrieks and strangled growls. And on a pavement obscured by trees, leaning on a railing, a man smoked a cigarette, the light at its tip glowing brighter then dying, brighter then dying, as if he too were part of the city's heartbeat, performing the same small actions over and over, all through the watches of the night.

Unseen eyes observed him. This stretch of pavement was never unregarded. What was curious was that he'd been allowed to stand there so long without interference. A half-hour crawled by before a car turned up at last and purred to a halt. Its driver spoke through its rolled-down window. His tone was weary, though this might have had less to do with the time of night than with the man he was forced to address.

'Jackson Lamb,' he said.

Lamb tossed his cigarette over the railings. 'Took your time,' he replied.

When River came round he was staring at the sky, and the ground was rolling beneath him. He was on a trolley. Doubtless the one he'd seen in the hangar. Was bound to it, in fact; with the same clothesline – was strapped like Gulliver: wrists, ankles, across the chest, across the throat. In his mouth a wadded-up handkerchief, secured in place by tape.

Pushing the trolley was Tommy Moult.

'Taser,' he said. 'If you're interested.'

River arched his back and flexed his wrists, but the line held firm. The only give came from his flesh.

'Or you could lie still,' Moult suggested. 'Want to be Tasered again? I'm out of cartridges, but I can give you a contact blast. It'll hurt.'

River lay still.

'Up to you.'

The one name not on Catherine's list was Tommy Moult. It hadn't occurred to him to wonder why Moult was here on a Tuesday night, when he was usually only seen at weekends.

A wheel hit a rock, and if River hadn't been tied in place he'd have been thrown clear. The clothesline bit into his throat and he made an indecipherable noise: pain, fury, frustration, all muffled by the gag in his mouth.

'Whoops.' Moult stopped pushing and wiped his hands on his trousers. He said something else, but the wind dragged it away.

River twisted his head to ease the pressure on his throat. He was less than a foot from the ground. All he could see was black grass.

And he thought again of what he'd found in the hangar, packed onto the trolley he was tied to now. Which meant it wasn't on the trolley any more.

He assumed it was on the aeroplane instead.

They sat in the car. Nick Duffy's cheek wore a crease-mark stamped by a pillow. 'So what did you think was going to happen?' he asked. 'It's gone two in the morning, and you're out-side the Park's front door, smoking like a madman and doing sod all. You're lucky they didn't unleash the Achievers.'

The Achievers were the guys in black, who turned up slightly before things turned violent.

'I do have clearance,' Lamb pointed out.

'Only on the understanding you never attempt to use it,' Duffy said. 'So I'm dragged out of bed because the duty staff are worried you're about to storm the place. They all remember last year's bomb scare.'

Lamb nodded complacently. 'Good to know I'm not forgotten.'

'Oh, your memory lingers on. Like herpes.' Duffy nodded towards the nearby building. 'No way are you getting inside, so whatever you were after, put it in a memo. Lady Di'll be thrilled. And now, as I'm one of the good guys, I'll give you a lift to the nearest taxi rank. But only if it's on my way home.'

Lamb clapped his hands, once, twice, three times. Then again, and then some more. He kept this up until any humour in it was long since gasping for breath, and only then said, 'Oh, sorry. You were finished?'

'Fuck off, Jackson.'

'Maybe later. After you've taken me into the Park.'

'Were you listening?'

'Every word. See, we could do this your way, but then I'd have to walk back from the taxi rank and do things less subtly. Which means making a fuss, and, oh yeah, fucking up your career.' He produced his cigarette packet, examined its empty recess, then tossed it onto the back seat. 'Up to you, Nick. I haven't fucked up anyone's career in months. It's fun, but the paperwork's shocking.'

Duffy was facing the road, as if the car were moving, and the way ahead had grown complicated.

'If you didn't already know you'd screwed up, we'd be on the move.' Lamb reached across and patted Duffy's hand, which had grown whiter since his grip on the steering wheel had tightened. 'We all make mistakes, son. Your latest was signing off on Rebecca Mitchell without doing the full-court press.'

'She was clean.'

'Yeah, you established she was a virgin. Which maybe she is, but she didn't use to be. Not back when she was playing spin-the-bottle with a pair of likely lads from, where was it? Oh yeah, Russia. And she just happens to mow down Min Harper, who's babysitting some visiting goon from, oooh, where was it again? You really want me to fill in the gaps?'

'Taverner was happy with the report.'

'And I'm sure she'll continue to be. Until somebody holds it to the light and points out the cracks.'

'Don't you get it, Lamb? She was happy. With. It.' He tapped the words out on the steering wheel. 'Told me to wrap it in ribbons and file it away. So it's not me you're screwing with, it's her. Good luck with that.'

'Grow up, Nick. Whatever order she gave, you're the one carried it out. So if anyone gets thrown to the wolves, guess who it'll be?'

For a moment they sat in silence, Duffy still tapping out unspoken words on the wheel. Then the tapping grew disjointed, faltered, stopped, as if the words were trailing away even in his mind. 'Christ,' he said at last. 'My mistake was answering the phone after midnight.'

'No,' Lamb said. 'Your mistake was forgetting Min Harper was one of mine.'

They got out of the car, and headed for the Park.

Long before the journey was over every nerve in River's body was screaming for release. He felt like a tambourine, rattled to someone else's rhythm.

Moult, too, looked like he'd been fed through a wringer. Every five minutes he had to pause and rest. Earlier, approaching the clubhouse, they'd had to drop from sight when a patrol passed. That didn't happen now. Moult knew the patrol's routine, that was clear. Whoever he was, he knew what he was doing.

As to where they were going, he was keeping that to himself.

Pausing, he scratched his scalp through his hat and everything shifted, as if his head had slipped off its axis. He caught River watching, and grinned an evil grin.

'Nearly there.'

'Records.'

Duffy had grown paler now they were inside; wore a tight expression suggesting he might soon spring a leak and deflate into an empty, angry bag. 'Records,' he repeated.

'That's still downstairs, right?'

Duffy jabbed the lift button as if it were Lamb's throat. 'I thought your boy Ho was working on an archive.'

'Yeah, well, he might not have done as much as he likes to pretend.'

Some floors down – but some floors above the lowest – they stepped into a blue-lit corridor. A door hung open at its far end, and the light streaming through it was warmer, library-like. Some of it was blocked by a squat, suspicious shape: a woman in a wheelchair; quite round, with a messy cap of grey hair, and a face powdered to clownish white. As they approached, her expression changed from suspicion to pleasure, and by the time the two men reached her, she had opened her arms.

Lamb bent down for her hug, while Nick Duffy looked on as if witnessing an alien landing.

'Molly Doran,' Lamb said, when the woman released him. 'And not looking a day older.'

'One of us has to keep in shape,' she said. 'You've got fatter, Jackson. And that coat makes you look like a vagrant.'

'It's a new coat.'

'New when?'

'Since I last saw you.'

'That's fifteen years.' She released him and looked at Duffy.

'Nicholas,' she said pleasantly. 'Fuck off. I won't have the Dogs on my floor.'

'We go wherever we—'

'Ah-ah.' She waggled a short fat finger. 'I won't. Have. The Dogs. On. My. Floor.'

'He's just going, Molly,' Lamb assured her. He turned to Duffy. 'I'll be here.'

'It's the middle of the—'

'Waiting.'

Duffy stared, then shook his head. 'He used to warn me about you. Sam Chapman did.'

'He had a few things to say about you too,' Lamb said. 'Once he'd run the numbers on Rebecca Mitchell. Here.' He produced the pill bottle he'd taken from Katinsky's office. 'Get this checked out while you're at it.'

Whatever Duffy had to say in reply was lost as the lift doors closed.

Lamb turned to Molly Doran. 'How come they've got you on the nightshift?'

'So I don't frighten the youngsters. They take one look at me, see their future, and piss off to the City instead.'

'Yeah, I thought it would be something like that.'

Her wheelchair, which was cherry-red with thick velvet armrests, had the turning-circle of a doughnut. She spun it on the spot and led Lamb into a long room lined with upright cabinets which were set on tracks like tramlines, so they could be pushed together when not in use: one huge accordion structure, each row containing file after file of dusty information, some of it so ancient that the last to consult it had long since faded to dust himself. Here were Regent's Park's older secrets. Which could all be stored on the head of a pin, of course, if the budget were there to squeeze it into shape.

Upstairs, the Queens of the Database ruled their digital universe. Down here, Molly Doran was the keeper of overlooked history.

In a cubby-hole was Molly's desk. A three-legged stool sat to one side, but the space in front was left free for Molly's wheelchair. 'So. This is where you've ended up.'

'As if you didn't know.'

'Social calls. Never really been a people person.'

'I don't think either of us were cut from that cloth, Jackson.' She wheeled herself into her customary place. 'It's okay. It'll take your weight.'

He lowered himself onto the stool, glaring at her upholstered chariot. 'All right for some.'

She laughed a surprisingly bell-like laugh. 'You haven't changed, Jackson.'

'Never seen the need to.'

'All those years undercover, pretending to be someone you're not. I think they drained you of pretence.' She shook her head, as if remembering something. 'Fifteen years, and here you are. What do you need?'

'Nikolai Katinsky.'

'Minnow,' Molly said.

'Yes.'

'Cipher clerk. One of a shoal of the damn things, we couldn't give them away in the nineties.'

'He came with a piece from a jigsaw,' Lamb said. 'But it didn't fit anywhere.'

'Not a side piece. Not a corner. Just a bit of the sky.' Molly's face had altered now they'd reached the meat. Her grossly over-painted cheeks shone pinker, their natural colour showing through. 'He claimed to have heard of the cicadas, that phantom network that other phantom set up.'

'Alexander Popov.'

'Alexander Popov. But it was all just one of those games Moscow Centre liked to play, before the board was tipped over.'

Lamb nodded. It was warm down here, and he was starting to feel clammy. 'So what paper do we have on him?'

'It's not on the Beast?'

The Beast was Molly Doran's collective name for the Service's assorted databases: she refused to differentiate between them on the grounds that when they crashed – which they were bound to, sooner or later – there'd be no telling them apart anyway. Just one dark screen after another. And she'd be the one holding the candle.

'Bare details,' Lamb said. 'And the tapes of his debriefing. You know what it's like, Molly. The young guns think a twenty-minute video's worth a thousand words. But we know better, don't we?'

'Are you trying to sweet-talk me, Jackson Lamb?'

'If that's what it takes.'

She laughed again, and the sound went fluttering into the stacks like a butterfly. 'I used to wonder about you, you know. Whether you'd go over to the enemy.'

Lamb looked affronted. 'CIA?'

'I meant the private sector.'

'Huh.' He glanced down briefly, taking in his stained, untucked-in shirt, scuffed shoes and undone fly, and seemed to enjoy a moment's self-awareness. 'Can't see me being welcomed with open arms.' Not that he bothered zipping up.

'Yes. Now I see you, there was nothing to worry about, was there?' Molly pulled away from the table. 'I'll see what we've got. Make yourself useful, and put the kettle on.'

As she rolled off, her voice floated back: 'And you dare light up, and I'll feed you to the birds.'

And here they were again.

Had River slept? Was that possible? He must have drifted off on some naturally produced anaesthetic; his body refusing to submit to more punishment. Through his mind, various nightmare pictures had flitted. Among them, a retrieved image; the page from Kelly Tropper's sketchbook showing a stylised city landscape, its tallest building struck by jagged lightning.

And now they were here again, and every bone in his body

groaned. Unless that was the noise the tree made as the wind shook its branches, scraping them against the ruined walls of the battered house.

'Home sweet home,' said Tommy Moult.

Lamb sucked a biro he'd found, and leafed through Katinsky's file. This didn't take long. 'Not a hell of a lot,' he said.

'If it hadn't been for his mentioning the cicadas,' Molly said, 'he'd have been thrown back. As it was, he got the low-grade treatment. Background established he was who he said he was, then got onto frying bigger fish.'

'Born in Minsk. Worked in transport administration there before being recruited by a KGB talent spotter, subsequently spent twenty-two years at Moscow Centre.'

'His existence was first noted in December seventy-four, when we got hold of a staff rota.'

'And we never made a pass,' Lamb said.

'The file would be thicker if we had.'

'Odd. You'd think we'd at least have taken a look.'

Placing the file on Molly's desk, he stared into the darkness of the stacks. The pen in his mouth rose slowly, slumped, and rose again. Lamb seemed unaware of this; unaware of anything, as his hand slipped inside his still open fly and he began to scratch.

Molly Doran sipped her tea.

'Okay,' Lamb said at last. It was quiet in Records, but grew quieter still now, as Molly held her breath. 'What if he's not a minnow? What if he's a big fish pretending to be a minnow? How would that have worked, Molly?'

'A strange thing to do. Why would anyone hide their light? Run the risk of being chucked back with the rubbish?'

'Strange,' Lamb agreed. 'But could he have done it?'

'Faked a cipher clerk? Yes. He could have done it. If he was a big fish, he could have done it.'

They shared a look.

'You think he was one of the missing, don't you?' Molly said. 'One of those we lost sight of when the USSR collapsed.'

Of whom there'd been more than a few. Some had probably found their way into shallow graves; others, they suspected, had reinvented themselves and flourished even now in different guises.

'He might have been. He might have been one of those Kremlin brains who gave us so much trouble. Who wanted out when the war was lost, but not to spend the rest of his life being poked at by the winners.'

Molly said, 'It would have meant placing that name on the rota years in advance. He couldn't have been sure we'd even see it.' And then checked herself. 'Oh—'

'Yeah,' Lamb agreed. 'Oh. Any idea how it came our way?'

'I could run it down,' Molly said doubtfully. 'Possibly.'

He shook his head. 'Not a top priority. Not right now.'

'My point stands though. He'd have had to do it years before he could know he needed it. December seventy-four? Nobody saw the end coming. Not that far in advance.'

'You didn't have to see it coming,' Lamb said. 'You just had to know it might.' He looked at the biro in his hand, as if wondering how it got there. 'There's nothing a joe likes more than knowing he's got his exits covered.'

'There's something else, isn't there? You've got the look.'

'Oh, yes,' he said. 'There's more.'

Tommy Moult's breathing had slowed to normal. He'd wheeled the trolley over the rubble that had once been the house's floor, a bone-wrecking distance for River, who was starting to feel his teeth loosen. He continued to tremble even now they'd come to a halt. Where his bonds cut into him he burned, and his ears throbbed in time to pounding blood. What was holding him together was rage; rage at himself for being so stupid twice in one night. And because he'd had a glimmer of what Moult was planning, and couldn't believe it, but couldn't disbelieve it either.

The tape was ripped from his mouth. The handkerchief was pulled free. Suddenly River was gulping mouthfuls of night air, making up for the night's thin rations, breathing so deeply he almost gagged. Moult said, 'You needed that.'

River could almost talk. 'What the. Fuck. Are you doing?'

'I think you already know, Walker. Jonathan Walker, by the way? Bit of a tired old name.'

'It's mine.'

'No. It'll be the one Jackson Lamb gave you. Still, won't be needing it much longer, will you?'

He knew Lamb; knew River was a spook. There was little point feigning innocence. River said, 'I'm supposed to check in. An hour ago. They'll come looking.'

'Really? Miss one call and they send out the coastguards?' Moult pulled his red cap off. His hair disappeared with it; those white tufts that had sprigged from underneath. He was bald, or nearly bald, with only a fringe stubbling his ears. 'Miss tomorrow's, and maybe they'll get worried. Though by then they'll have other things on their minds.'

'I saw what you had on the trolley, Moult.'

'Good. Give you something to think about.'

'Moult?'

But Moult had stepped out of River's line of vision, and all he could hear was feet tracking over rough ground.

'Moult!'

Then not even that.

As carefully as he could, River moved his head to face the sky again. He took a deep breath and bellowed and at the same time arched his back, as though the same rage was trying to burst through his stomach. The trolley rattled, but the clothesline bit deeper, and River's bellow became a scream that soared into the branches above, then howled around the broken walls surrounding him. And when it was done he was still secured in place, flat on his back on a trolley in the dark.

He was nowhere near escape, and there was no one near to hear him.

And time, he'd come to realise, was running out.

Behind its powder, laid thickly as butter on bread, Molly Doran's face was immobile. Even once Lamb had finished she remained silent for upwards of a minute. Then: 'And you think it was him. Katinsky. All those years ago, you think he was the one took Dickie Bow.'

'Yes.'

'And he's waited all these years to make his second move.'

'No. Whatever the plan was then, it was rendered obsolete by the end of the Cold War. No, he's up to something else now. But Dickie Bow came in handy.'

'And the cicadas? They're real too?'

'The best disguise for any network is if the opposition think they're ghosts. Nobody went looking for Alexander Popov's cell, because we thought it was a legend. Like Popov himself.'

'Who Katinsky invented.'

'Yes. Which to all intents and purposes,' Lamb said, 'means that's who he is. Nikolai Katinsky is Alexander Popov.'

'Oh Christ, Jackson. You've raised the bogeyman, haven't you?'

Lamb leaned back. In the soft light, he looked younger, possibly because he was reliving ancient history.

Molly let him think. The shadows over the stacks had grown longer, here in this sunless cellar, and experience told her this was her mind playing tricks; adjusting her surroundings to the rhythms of a normal day. Outside, morning was coming. Regent's Park, never entirely asleep, would soon be shaking off its night-creeps, those spidery sensations that occupy buildings when they're dark. The day shift would have been alarmed to learn of their existence.

When Lamb stirred, she prodded him with a question. 'So what's he up to, then? Popov?'

'I don't know. Don't know what and don't know why now.'

'Or why he grouped his network in Upshott.'

'That either.'

'Dead lions,' Molly said.

'What about them?'

'It's a kids' party game. You have to pretend to be dead. Lie still. Do nothing.'

'What happens when the game's over?' Lamb asked.

'Oh,' she said. 'I expect all hell breaks loose.'

His mobile phone was in his pocket.

As information went, this was on a par with a knowledge of penguins' mating habits: partly a comfort, partly a puzzle, but of no real practical value. The puzzle part was wondering why Moult hadn't taken it. But either way, it might as well have been lodged in a branch of the tree above him.

He'd stopped struggling, because this only brought pain. Instead, he was sorting through everything he knew, or thought he knew, about what Moult was up to, and however far and wide his speculation ranged, it always returned to the same point: the sacks of fertiliser he'd found stacked on the trolley in the hangar.

Why had Moult even taken him there, if it housed secrets he wanted to keep? And if Catherine's information was accurate, and the village was packed with Soviet sleepers, where did Moult fit in anyway? Though as light seeped into the sky, these questions faded into the background, and the image of those sacks of chemical fertiliser took their place.

Fertiliser, which, under the right conditions, acted exactly like a bomb.

And which River had last seen stacked next to an aeroplane like so much luggage.

Lamb went out for a smoke, but on the pavement remembered he'd finished his last cigarette earlier, so walked to the Tube station and bought a packet at the all-night convenience store. Back near Regent's Park's front door he lit a second from the stub of his first, and gazed up at a sky that was lightening by the minute. Traffic was now a constant hum. Days began like that now; a gradual accrual of detail. When he'd been younger, they'd started like a bell.

Nick Duffy appeared again, as he had earlier. He emerged from a parked car, and joined Lamb on the pavement.

'You smoke too much,' he said.

'Remind me what the right amount is?'

Across the way, trees stirred as if troubled by bad dreams. Duffy rubbed his chin. His knuckles were scraped red.

He said, 'Every month she gets a cheque. Once in a while, a little job to do. Providing bed and board to someone passing through under the radar. Or being a post office, or an answering service. All low-key shit, the way she tells it.'

'Until Min Harper.'

'She got the call late. Whoever it is used the code she responds to. Bring your car, underground garage round back of Edgware Road.' Duffy had slipped into telegraphese, to spare himself unnecessary words. 'Two of them plus, her words, a drunk bloke they're carrying.'

'She ever see them before?'

'Says not.'

He paused again. Then told Lamb what Rebecca Mitchell had told him, eventually: that one of the pair had smashed Min Harper's head against the concrete floor of the garage, while the other had backed Rebecca Mitchell's car up. The next part had been like a kids' game: balance the man on the bicycle, smack the car into him. Once they'd made sure his neck was broken, they'd loaded bike and body into their own car, and moved the scene somewhere else.

When he'd finished, Duffy stood staring at the trees, as if he suspected their rustling was a secret conversation, and what they were talking about was him.

Lamb said, 'It should have been picked up.'

'They took photos. Laid the body and bike out the way they fell in the garage.'

'Still should've been picked up.' Lamb threw his cigarette away, and sparks burst. 'You did a half-arsed job.'

'No excuses.'

'Damn right.' He wiped his face with a hand smelling of tobacco. 'Was she keen to talk?'

'Not so much.'

Lamb grunted.

After a while, Duffy said, 'He must have seen something he wasn't supposed to see.'

Or someone, thought Lamb. He grunted again, then went back through the big door.

This time, stepping out of the lift, he was met by an over-grown boy in a sweatshirt with Property of Alcatraz stamped on it, and glasses with heavy black frames. 'You're Jackson Lamb?' he asked.

'What gave it away?'

'The coat, mostly.' He shook the pill bottle Lamb had given Duffy earlier. 'You wanted to know what this is.'

'And?'

'It's called Xemoflavin.'

'Right. Wish I'd thought of reading the label.'

'Basic research tool,' the kid said. 'Name aside, it's a whole lot of not much. Aspirin, mostly, in a sugarshell coating. Orange, if it matters.'

'Don't tell me,' said Lamb. 'They sell it on the internet.'

'Bingo.'

'As a cure for?'

'Liver cancer,' said the kid. 'Doesn't work, though.'

'There's a surprise.'

The kid dropped the bottle into Lamb's waiting hand, pushed his glasses up his nose, and stepped into the lift Lamb had vacated.

Lips pursed, Lamb wandered back into Molly Doran's space.

She'd made herself more tea, and sat nursing it in her alcove. Steam rose in thin spirals and disappeared in the upper dark.

Lamb said, 'I checked his diary, did I tell you? He has no plans for the future.'

Molly took a sip of tea.

'And he's broken things off with the woman he was seeing.'

Molly placed her cup on the table.

'And he's taking some quack cancer remedy.'

Molly said, 'Oh dear.'

'Yeah,' said Lamb. He dropped the pill bottle into the waste-paper bin. 'Whatever he's up to, at least we know why. He's dying. And this is his last hurrah.'

14

MORNING. LIGHT. SURPRISINGLY strong, breaking through the curtains, but then it had been sunny lately; unseasonably warm. Summer in April, full of unreliable promise. If you turned your back on it too long, the temperature would drop.

Louisa didn't so much wake as realise she'd been awake for some time. Eyes open, brain humming. Nothing especially coherent; just little mental Post-its of the day's tasks, beginning with get up, shower, drink coffee. Then bigger things: leave the flat, meet Marcus, collect Pashkin. Everything else – like last night – was just a black mass boiling in the background, to be ignored as long as possible, like clouds on an unreliably sunny day.

She rose, showered, dressed, drank coffee. Then went out to meet Marcus.

Catherine was back in Slough House so early it felt like she'd never left, but even so, she travelled there through a city whose fuse had been lit. The underground was full of people talking to each other. Some held placards – STOP THE CITY was a favourite. Another read BANKERS: NO. At Barbican station, someone lit a cigarette. Anarchy was in the air. There'd be glass broken today.

But early as she was, Roderick Ho had beaten her. This wasn't unusual – Ho often seemed to live here: she suspected he preferred his online activities to emanate from a Service address – but what was different was, he'd been working. As she passed his open door, he looked up. 'Found some stuff,' he said.

'That list I gave you?'

'The Upshott people.' He brandished a printout. 'Three of them, anyway. I've tracked them back as far as they go. And there's paperwork, sure, they've paperwork coming out their ears, but the early stuff is all shoe and no footprint.'

'Which would be one of those internet expressions, yes?'

Ho flashed a sudden smile. This was even weirder than people chatting on the Tube. 'It is now.'

'And it means . . . ?'

'Well, take Andrew Barnett. His CV's got him attending St Leonard's Grammar School in Chester in the early sixties. It's a comp now, with a good IT department, and one of its projects is putting the school records online.'

'And there's no match-up,' Catherine finished.

Ho shook his head. 'Must have seemed a fair bet at the time. These guys have papered over their early lives all you want. But it was pre-web, and they'd no way of knowing the paper would start to peel.'

She glanced at the printout. As well as Barnett, he'd run down Butterfield and Salmon and found similar gaps in their histories. And there'd be more, there'd be flaws in the others' lives too. It was all true, then. A Soviet sleeper cell had taken root in a tiny English village. Perhaps because it no longer had a purpose. Or perhaps for some other reason they had yet to fathom.

'This is good, Roddy.'

'Yeah.'

And maybe she'd been hanging round Lamb too much, because she added: 'Makes a change from just surfing the net.'

'Yeah, well.' He looked away, colour rising. 'All that archive crap, I could pull an all-nighter, get it finished in a sitting. This is different.'

She waited until his gaze met hers again. 'Good point,' she said. 'Thanks.' She glanced at her watch. It was nine. Louisa and Marcus would be on their way to pick up Arkady Pashkin, which reminded her: 'Did you do the background on Pashkin?'

And now his expression became the more familiar put-upon scowl. Spending a life among computers had a way of prolonging adolescence. There was probably a study on it. It was probably online. 'Been kind of busy?'

'Yes. But do it now.'

Shame to leave him on a sour note, but Roddy Ho had a way of sticking to his own script.

They met near the hotel a little after nine. The Tube had been full, the streets crowded; there was a huge police presence, not to mention camera crews, news trucks, rubberneckers. Crowds were gathering in Hyde Park, from where the smells of a hundred variations on breakfast drifted. Instructions booming from a loudhailer, *This is a CO11-notified event, which means that the police will be marshalling the route*, were drowned by music and chatter. The atmosphere was one of burgeoning excitement, as if the world's biggest party was waiting for its DJ.

'Looks like someone's out for trouble,' was Marcus's greeting. He gestured at a group of twentysomethings heading for the park, a banner reading *Fuck the Banks* lofted above their heads.

'They're pissed off citizens,' Louisa said. 'That's all. You ready?'

'Of course.' Today he wore a grey suit, a salmon-pink tie, neat shades: he looked good, she noticed, the same way she might notice any other irrelevant detail. 'You?'

'I'm fine.'

'Sure?'

'Just said so, didn't I?'

They turned the corner.

He said, 'Look, Louisa, what I said last night—'

His mobile rang.

You couldn't call it sleep. Call it overload: pain, stress; all of it tumbling over and over like an argument trapped in a washing machine; over and over until its rhythm rocked River out of

266

consciousness and dropped him down a well of his own making. In that circular darkness the same half-chewed facts nipped at him like vermin: the fertiliser loaded on the plane, which Kelly would be soaring away in this morning; the sketch she'd drawn of the cityscape, with that lightning bolt smiting that tall building. An aeroplane was already a bomb, but that wasn't the first thing you thought of when you looked at one. It was only when you loaded it with bags of nitrogen-rich fertiliser that you underlined its essential explosiveness.

And over and over in his tumbling mind, the image repeated itself; of Kelly Tropper – why? – steering her pride and joy into London's tallest building; searing a new Ground Zero into the eyeballs of the world.

Over and over, until at last River lost his grip on the here and now, and – having long since bellowed himself dry – slipped out of his mind.

While Marcus was on the phone Louisa watched the rally assembling. It was like seeing a hive mind being born; all these different particles coming together, out of which one conscious-ness would arise. Marcus was probably right. There'd be trouble later. But that was a sideshow, another part of the ignorable background. She wondered if last night would turn out to be her only chance of getting Pashkin on his own. If he'd jet away as soon as the talks were done, leaving her forever ignorant of the reason Min had died.

Marcus said, 'Sorry about that.'

'Finished? We're on a job, not an outing.'

'It won't ring again,' he said. 'And you're not throwing Pashkin out of any high windows, right?'

She didn't answer.

'Right?'

'Lamb put you up to this?'

'I don't know Lamb as well as you. But it doesn't strike me his team's welfare is his top priority.'

'Oh, you're looking out for my welfare, are you?'

'Those gorillas Pashkin has? They're not for show. Make a move on their boss and they'll take you apart.'

'Like they did Min.'

'Whatever happened to Min, we'll sort it. But there's no point in revenge if it costs you everything, and believe me, what you'd planned last night would have cost just that. Anything Pashkin's goons didn't do to you, the Service would have done instead.'

A sudden outburst of chanting from across the road splintered into gales of laughter.

'Louisa?'

'Why are you with us?' She hadn't known she was going to ask until she heard herself speak. 'At Slough House?'

'That's important?'

'You're appointing yourself my handler, yes, it's important. Because what I heard is, you lost your nerve. Couldn't take the pressure. So maybe this concern for my well-being is just you making sure your life stays quiet, and I don't rock your boat.'

Marcus stared for a moment over the top of his shades. Then he pushed the glasses into place. When he spoke, his tone was milder than his look had promised. 'Well, that sounds plausible. Bullshit, but plausible.'

'So you didn't lose your nerve.'

'Shit, no. I gamble, that's all.'

Someone called his name.

It sounded like his name. It wasn't, but it sounded like it – it hauled River out of the darkness, and when he opened his eyes daylight spackled through the branches overhead. The sky was wide open, and he had to close his eyes again, scrunch them shut, as protection against its bright blueness.

'Walker? Jonny?'

Hands were on him and suddenly the tightness loosened and

he could move properly, which brought fresh pain coursing through his limbs.

'Fuck, man. You're a mess.'

His saviour was a blurry creature, fuzzy patches held together like a walking Rorschach test.

'Get you out of this shit.'

Arms pulled River upright and his body screamed, but felt good at the same time – aching its way out of cramp.

'Here.'

A bottle was pressed to his lips, and water poured into his mouth. River coughed and bent forward; spat; threw up almost. Then blindly reached for the bottle, grabbed it, and greedily gulped down the rest of its contents.

'Shit, man,' Griff Yates said. 'You really are a fucking mess.'

'I gamble, that's all,' Marcus Longridge said.

'You what?'

'Gamble. Cards. Horses. You name it.'

Louisa stared. 'That's it?'

'Quite a big it, actually. Incompatible with efficient operational mode, apparently. Which is a joke. Ops can be the biggest gamble of all.'

'So why didn't they just boot you out?'

'Tactical error. See, one of the HR bods decided I was suffering a form of addiction, and sat me down with a counsellor.'

'And?'

'He counselled.'

'And?'

Marcus said, 'Well, I wouldn't say it took, exactly. Not a hundred per cent. That was a bookie just now, for instance.' He paused for a barrage of car horns; an impromptu symphony likely to become the day's soundtrack, as traffic found itself relegated to second-class status on the city's streets. 'But anyway, it turned out that once they'd given me a shrink, they couldn't fire me. In case of legal hassle. So instead . . .'

So instead, he'd joined the slow horses.

Louisa glanced at the hotel, through whose big glass doors they'd be walking any moment. 'Are you Taverner's line into Slough House?'

'Nope. Why would she want one?'

'Catherine says she does.'

'Can't see why,' Marcus said. 'We're basically the Park's outside lav. If she wants to know anything, can't she just ask Lamb?'

'Maybe she'd rather not.'

'Fair enough. But I'm nobody's snitch, Louisa.'

'Okay.'

'That mean you believe me?'

'It means okay. And the gambling's not a problem?'

'We had a fortnight in Rome last year, me and Cassie and the kids. Paid for by my, ah, *addiction*.' He pushed his shades up again. 'So fuck 'em.'

It was the first time he'd mentioned his family in her hearing. She wondered if that was intended to win her confidence.

He looked at his watch.

'Okay,' Louisa said again, which this time meant he had a point: time was getting on. She led the way into the hotel lobby.

Since they were partnered, it was probably as well he was in full possession of his nerve, she thought.

But today was a babysit. It wasn't like his Ops experience would be needed.

Catherine called River, got Number Unavailable; then Lamb, with the same result. Then studied paperwork. 'All shoe and no footprint.' The more weight you carried, the deeper marks you made. But the early lives of these Upshott folk wouldn't have left tracks in icing sugar.

Stephen Butterfield had owned a publishing company, and a quick dip online showed him numbered among the chattering class's great and good: always ready to weigh in on the issues of the day, on Radio 4, in the *Observer*. He'd served on a parliamentary commission on illiteracy; was a trustee of a charity supplying schoolbooks to developing countries. But go back, and his early life dissolved into mist. The same went for the others Roddy had backgrounded: light- to middle-weight persons of substance; embedded in an establishment that invited them to its high tables, to sup with captains of industry and cabinet ministers. Control was about influence . . .

With a start, she realised Ho was in her doorway. She had no idea how long he'd been standing there.

He said, 'You're kidding me, right?'

'Kidding you? What do you mean?'

He looked puzzled. 'That you're having a joke.'

Catherine had the ability to make it clear she was taking a deep breath without actually taking one. She did this now. 'What am I kidding you about, Roddy?'

He told her.

'It was meant to be a joke.'

Some joke.

'They never target the old houses. Once you know that, it's kind of cool, actually.'

Once you know that was the key phrase here.

'And I can't believe Tommy would've . . .'

River ached all over, and couldn't move as fast as he wanted – they were heading uphill. There was no signal in the dip.

He said, 'And this was because of Kelly?'

Christ. He had the voice of a ninety-year-old.

Yates stopped. 'You don't get it, do you?'

'I get it,' River said. 'I just don't care.'

'She's all I ever—'

'Grow up.' She makes her own choices, he nearly said, but the thought of Kelly's choices killed the words. He tried his mobile again, his hands taking fat-finger to a new level. No signal yet. An engine drifted into earshot and he looked up, half-expecting to see Kelly zipping through the blue in her flying bomb – but if that's what she was in, she wouldn't be buzzing over Upshott.

She'd be in the air by now. He had to raise the alarm.

There's a plane going to fly into the Needle – our very own 9/11.

On the same day a Russian oligarch with political ambitions would be on the seventy-seventh floor.

Of course, if he was wrong, it would make crashing King's Cross look like the pinnacle of his career.

And if he was right, and didn't sound the warning in time, he'd spend the rest of his life grieving for innumerable dead.

'Come on.'

'That's the wrong way,' Griff told him.

'No it isn't.'

The hangar. He had to get to the hangar; see if he was right about the fertiliser.

Two steps more, and his phone buzzed in his hand. The signal was back.

A jeep crested a hillock in front of them.

When Pashkin emerged from the lift, he gave no indication that last night had ever happened; or at least not to him, not to her. He wore a different suit today. Gleaming white shirt, open at the neck. A flash of a silver cufflink. A hint of cologne. He carried a briefcase.

'Ms Guy,' he said. 'Mr Longridge.'

The lobby echoed like a church.

'The car should be outside.'

And so it was. They sat in the same formation as the previous day, in similar slow-moving traffic. But what difference, Louisa wondered, would it make if they were ten minutes late? There was only Webb waiting. For a supposedly high-level summit, it was low key. She texted him anyway, to let him know they weren't far off.

At a junction on the edge of the City, the car rolled past

three police vans: black, with shaded windows. Figures lurked inside; human shapes distorted by uniform and helmet, like American football players, absurdly padded up for a kick-about.

Pashkin said, 'Trouble is expected, then.'

Louisa didn't trust her voice in his presence.

He said, 'Your liberal values, they take a back seat when your banks and buildings are threatened.'

Marcus said, 'I'm not sure I have liberal values.'

Pashkin looked at him, interested.

'And besides. A few troublemakers get their heads broken, or thrown in a cell overnight. We're hardly talking Tiananmen.'

'Isn't there a phrase for that? The thin end of the wedge?'

The police vans were behind them now, but a hefty cop presence remained on the pavements. Most were wearing high-visibility jackets, not battle armour. Officer Friendly was the first face shown. Sergeant Rock stayed indoors until things got hairy.

But these rallies had a habit of turning nasty, thought Louisa. It wasn't just the banks the marchers were targeting. It was corporate greed in all its manifestations; all the visible symbols of the rich getting richer, while others had their salaries cut, their debt increased, their jobs rationalised, their benefits slashed.

Not her problem, though. Not today. She had her own battles to fight.

Piotr spoke, and Pashkin replied, in a language thick as treacle. Maybe her face asked the question. Either way, Pashkin chose now to address her directly. 'He says it is nearly over.'

'Over?'

'We're nearly there.'

She'd lost track. But here they were indeed, at the foot of the Needle; the car pulling into the root of its enormous shadow, then disappearing underneath it, to the car park below.

Their plate was registered as belonging to a contractor;

officially, their party was meeting with the one of the hotel's kitchen supervisors in a utilities room below the building's lobby.

Their entry into the Needle itself would go unrecorded.

James Webb had entered in the same way earlier. Up on the seventy-seventh now, he was considering placement. The tricky thing was, it wasn't immediately clear which side of an oval table was the head. He tried the chair facing the window. All he could see was a lone plane scarring the blue. Some days you could sit here and be at the heart of a cloud. Right now, he was higher than parts of the sky.

Though hadn't yet flown as high as he intended to.

'So, Mr Pashkin. How can we make things easier for you?'

That was the line he'd be taking. That Pashkin had nothing Webb wanted; all that mattered was that Pashkin's path be made smooth. Later, debts would be called in; suggestions made as to how Pashkin might repay the kindness of foreigners. Even if no tangible favours were bestowed, simply meeting Webb rendered Pashkin compromised. But that was the lure of power. Ambition tended to the reckless, a seam Webb planned to mine.

'I'm here to help. Officially, I don't speak for HMG.' Modest cough. 'But any requests you make will find a sympathetic hearing where it will do most good.'

Cosmetic aid was what Pashkin would want. To be seen in the company of movers and shakers, and reckoned a force in the world. A photo op with the PM, drinks at Number 10, a little attention from the press. Once you were taken seriously, you were taken seriously. If Pashkin's star rose in the west, it would cast light in the east.

His phone buzzed. Marcus Longridge. They were in the garage. Webb listened, said, 'Oh for Christ's sake, he's an honoured guest, not a security risk. Use your common sense.'

After hanging up he rose, walked round the table, and tried the other side, so he was facing into the room, with the big view behind him.

Yes, he decided. That was it. Leave the windows for Pashkin to gaze out of. Show him the sky was the limit, and wait for him to bite.

He went to the lobby to wait for the lift.

Behind him, in the far distance, the sun glinted off the wing of a tiny aeroplane, making it seem, for a moment, far larger than it was.

'This Arkady Pashkin character?' said Ho.

Catherine didn't want to ask. 'What about him?'

'You read that feature? Supposed to be from the *Telegraph*?'

'Supposed to be,' she repeated flatly.

Ho said, 'You look at it closely?'

'I read it, Roddy. We all did.' She shuffled papers, moved a folder, found it. Not the actual newspaper, but a printout from the web. She waved it at him. '*Telegraph*. July seventh, last year. What's your problem?'

'It's not my problem.' Ho plucked it from her hand. It ran to three pages, complete with photograph. 'Here.' He stabbed the address box at the top of the page. 'See that?'

'Roddy. What are you on about?'

'It looks like the *Telegraph*, sounds like the *Telegraph*, and you want to scrumple it up and eat it, it probably tastes like the *Telegraph*. But it's not.' He held it in front of her. 'You took it from the man's own website. Did you even check the newspaper's archive?'

'It's all over the web,' she said numbly.

'Course it is. Because some dude's posted it all over the web. But you know where it's not? In the newspaper's own archive.'

'Roddy—'

'I'm telling you, that thing's fake. And you take it away, you know how much evidence there is for Arkady Pashkin even existing, let alone being some big-shot Russian oligarch?'

He made a zero sign with finger and thumb.

'Oh,' Catherine said.

Ho said, 'There's references, true. He's got Facebook presence, and a Wiki page, and he's on lots of sites where you drop your marker in and everyone assumes you're someone. But chase the mentions down, and they're all referring to each other. The web's stuffed full of straw men.' He coloured slightly: must have been excitement. 'Pashkin's one of them.'

'But how . . . ?' But she already knew how. The research on Pashkin had been done by Spider Webb: Regent's Park's Background section had been out of the picture, because of that damned audit. Odds on it had been Pashkin who'd approached Webb in the first place . . .

She said, 'This Needle summit. Whatever Pashkin's up to, that's what it's about. I'll pull the plug. Roddy – get over there.'

'Me?'

'Take Shirley.' He stared as if she'd slipped into another language. 'Just do it, okay?' She reached for her phone, and even as she did so it rang. To Ho's departing back she said, 'And Roddy? Don't ever say dude again,' and answered her call.

'Catherine?' said River. 'Call the Park. Possible Code September.'

Miles away, somewhere between the two ends of this phone call, Kelly Tropper guided the blue and white Cessna Skyhawk through a clear blue sky. Ahead of her lay swathes of nothingness – that was how it felt; that she was cleaving an absence, which healed itself the moment she'd passed. And if a painful truth sometimes threatened to intrude, that the scars in her wake were as enduring as they were invisible, she generally managed to tamp this knowledge down, and smother it under the conviction that nothing so central to the core of her being could be evil.

She glanced at her companion, who'd agreed to accompany her mostly because he fancied her, and wondered if he knew she'd slept with Upshott's newest resident the previous afternoon. It was possible he did. A village was porous when it came to private life. Either way, telling him would add to the frisson she already felt. Tomorrow, people would read about her in their newspapers. Read about her, picture her, and know she'd done something they were incapable of. Some, indeed, would remember watching her pass overhead.

Another frisson. Her companion turned to her, curious.

The ground was a memory, and Kelly Tropper was where she belonged: up in the brighter element, with a comrade-in-arms.

Just the two of them, and their inflammatory cargo.

15

As MID-MORNING BLOOMED, and only a few stray clouds, like the mildest twinges of conscience, ruffled central London's skies, it became apparent that today would fulfil the forecasters' promise, and be the warmest day of the year so far. A fact that few of the evening's news reports would fail to mention.

The mob was heading east, *mob* being what others declared it. But it was moving, was mobilised, so that's what it was, a mob, if for the most part a highly organised one; marshalled by policemen, but arranged according to its own lights, and eager to indicate to gathering camera crews that it represented a spontaneous outburst of public anger rather than a cynical manipulation of public concern. A vociferous and placard-wielding contingent headed it up, marching in time to a troupe of drummers; their stencilled placards read STOP THE CITY and SMASH THE BANKS and HALT THE CUTS, or showed cartoons of top-hatted fat cats lighting cigars with fifty-pound notes. Bobbing above head-height here and there were rag-and-plaster effigies, like out-of-season guys looking for bonfires; they wore bowler hats and pinstripes and expressions of unsatiated greed. Stewards with loudhailers chirped at random intervals, and flitting about on the flanks were diehards in donkey-jackets, peddling *Socialist Worker*. But for every dreadlocked, safety-pinned crusty in view there were half-a-dozen fresh-faced youths in summer casuals. It was a rainbow coalition of the pissed-off, and their chanting grew in volume as the march progressed.

The middle group was more placid, their placards handcrafted, and replete with knowing cultural references: DOWN WITH THIS SORT OF THING, AND BANK BALL-OUTS? NO THANKS! Dancing in and out among the throng were children who'd been face-painted in Hyde Park, and now were cats or witches, dogs or wizards, their pink and green faces alive with astonishment. They ran about in giggling bunches, begging the mounted policemen for rides, while their parents enjoyed the nostalgic frisson of public dissent, the occasional self-mocking call and response of *Maggie! Maggie! Maggie! – Out! Out! Out!* underlining the degree to which this was a rally down memory lane. There was even communal, if self-conscious, singing; Bob Marley songs mostly: 'One Love' and 'Exodus' and even a ragged 'Redemption Song'. When a helicopter hovered overhead, this section burst into cheers, though no one knew why.

And finally, dragging up the rear, came the seemingly less committed, viewing the occasion not so much as an outlet for airing social outrage as an opportunity to stroll through a London cleared of traffic. They waved for the cameras, posed for tourists, chatted with police officers assigned to shepherding duties, and generally blew kisses to a watching world, but among this contingent – as among the others – marched some with masks in their pockets and larceny in their hearts, for banks are evil, and bankers self-serving bastards, and not a single soul-sucking money-magnet among them would mend their ways for the sake of a well-behaved procession. No: reformation required broken glass, and today would see plenty of it.

Though even the anarchists didn't yet know how much.

The rally processed along Oxford Street, and up towards High Holborn.

'Mr Pashkin.'

'Mr Webb.'

'Jim, please. Welcome to the Needle.' Fatuous, on both counts; nobody called Spider Jim and Pashkin had been here before. But the moment had passed, Pashkin putting his case on the

279

floor to take Webb's right hand in both of his: not the bear-hug he'd been expecting, but a solid citizen's grasp all the same. 'Can I get you anything? Coffee? A pastry?' The smell of both wafted from the kitchen.

'Nothing. Thank you.' Then, as if in retrospective validation of Webb's comment, Pashkin looked round as if he'd never been here before. 'Magnificent,' he said. 'Truly.'

Webb glanced towards the rest of the party: Louisa Guy, Marcus Longridge, the two Russians. He gestured towards the kitchen. 'If you want coffee or anything.'

Nobody did.

Downstairs, in the underground garage, Marcus and Louisa had frisked Kyril and Piotr for weapons, and allowed themselves to be patted down in return. Marcus had then examined Arkady Pashkin, after which he'd gestured at his case. 'Do you mind?'

'I'm afraid I do,' Pashkin had said smoothly. 'There are documents in there – well, I don't need to spell it out.'

Marcus had glanced at Louisa.

'Call Webb,' she'd said.

Who'd told him, 'Oh for Christ's sake, he's an honoured guest, not a security risk. Use your common sense.'

So now Pashkin was laying his unchecked case on the table. He snapped at his men in their shared language. Piotr and Kyril peeled away from the group, and Marcus instinctively grabbed the nearest by the arm: this was Kyril, who spun back, fist raised, and just like that the pair were a heartbeat off knocking seven bells out of each other until a shout from Pashkin froze them: *'Please!'*

Kyril dropped his fist. Marcus released Kyril's arm.

Piotr laughed. 'You, you're fast.'

'Forgive me,' said Pashkin. 'I simply asked them to check the cameras.'

'They're off,' said Webb. 'Aren't they?'

Louisa looked at Pashkin. 'They're off. As I told you.'

He gave her a formal nod. 'Of course. But all the same . . .'

Marcus raised an eyebrow, but Webb, seeing an opportunity to regain the initiative, said, 'As you wish.'

They watched as Piotr and Kyril dealt with the cameras above the door and in the corner, twisting wires free of their casing in a way that didn't look temporary.

Pashkin said, 'You understand my position.'

Webb looked like he was trying to, while wondering whether this destruction of security equipment was going to come bouncing back at him. Pashkin, meanwhile, opened his case and removed what looked like a microphone. When he placed it on the table, it hummed into life.

Marcus Longridge said, 'I thought everything had been made clear.' He was cradling one hand in the other, as if a blow had actually been landed. Nodding at the device, he said, 'This isn't being recorded.'

'No,' Pashkin agreed. 'And now we can all be certain of that.'

The device pulsed gently; invisibly converting into white noise anything picked up by eavesdropping equipment.

Kyril stood with his big hands clasped in front of him, studying Marcus with what might have been amusement.

Louisa said, 'Anything else in that case we should know about?'

'Nothing to cause alarm,' Pashkin said. 'But please.' He made a sudden expansive gesture, as if releasing a dove. 'Let's sit. Let's start.' He glanced at his wristwatch. 'Do you know,' he added, 'maybe I will have that coffee after all.'

River had the phone to his ear when the jeep reached them and a soldier jumped out: a young guy, fit-looking, wide across the shoulders.

'Catherine?'

'Would you put the phone down, sir?'

'Is there a problem?' This was Griff Yates. 'We're out walking, got a bit lost, like.'

'Call the Park. Possible Code September.'

'Sir? The phone?'

The soldier approached.

'Today. This morning.'

'The phone. Now.'

When the soldier laid hands on him, a night's worth of stress and fear found brief release. River knocked his arms aside, opening the guy up; he kicked his knee, then jabbed him in the throat with his phone-free hand as the soldier slipped off-balance.

'Jesus, man!' Griff shouted, as the other soldier leaped from the jeep, drawing a sidearm.

'River.' Catherine's voice was very calm. 'I need to hear the protocols.'

'Phone down! Hands up! Now!' Screamed, not spoken; either this was the way they were taught, or Soldier Number Two was going off on one.

'Manda—'

The word was cut off by a gunshot.

'So,' Ho said, 'you got a car?'

'Are you kidding?'

He hadn't been. He looked up Aldersgate for a taxi; looked down it too; and when he turned back to Shirley Dander, she was on the other side of the road, moving fast.

Oh, shit.

He waited another second, hoping this was a joke, but when she disappeared round the corner, he accepted the dismal truth: they were heading for the Needle on foot.

Cursing Shirley Dander, cursing Catherine Standish, Roderick Ho began to run.

Manda—

Mandarin was the first of River Cartwright's protocols, the others being *dentist* and *tiger*. But when Catherine had called back, her only reward was the Number Unavailable mantra.

Code September. That part he had completed. *Possible Code September. Today. This morning.*

Catherine was alone in Slough House. Lamb hadn't turned up yet; Ho and Shirley Dander had just left at a lick.

Code September . . . It wasn't an official designation, but was frequently used; its reference point the obvious. Code September didn't simply signify a terrorist event. It meant someone was planning on flying an aeroplane into a building.

With the thought, new currents fizzed in her veins. Two courses of action were open. She could assume River had lost his mind. Or she could trigger a major response to an alert for which she had no concrete evidence.

She called the Park.

The rally was a long and winding worm now, the gap between its head and the waggly remnants of its tail wriggling through the heart of London. The front had crossed the viaduct at Holborn; some of the stragglers were still on Oxford Street. There seemed no hurry. The warmer it got, the truer this became.

At Centre Point, where building-site barriers blocked Charing Cross Road, the noise of excavation drowned the chanting. As the rally squeezed past the narrowed junction, a small boy pulled his hand from his father's and pointed at the sky. Squinting upwards, the man caught a flash of something; sunlight reflecting off a window of the distant Needle. He scooped the boy onto his shoulders, making him laugh, and they continued on their way.

When Soldier Two fired, River dropped his phone. The shot went overhead, but it was anyone's guess where he'd been aiming. Soldier One scrambled upright and threw a punch in River's direction; sidestepping it, River slipped and fell to his knees. A heavy foot stamped on his phone. Griff Yates shouted in anger or innocence, and River reached for his Service card—

Hands in the air!

Drop it!

Flat on the ground! Now!

River flung himself onto the dirt.

Empty your hands! Empty your hands!

His hands were empty.

Soldier Two, with terrifying casualness, swung the butt of his handgun into Griff Yates's face, and Yates dropped to his knees, blood spinning all around.

'I'm with British Intelligence,' River shouted. 'MI5. There's a national emergency about to—'

'Shut it!' Soldier One screamed. 'Shut it now!

'—break and you're not helping—'

'Shut it!'

River placed his hands on his head.

Yates, half-sobbing, was still audible. 'You *cunt!* What you bloody do that for, you bloody—'

'Shut it!'

'—*cunt?*'

Before River could speak, Soldier Two swung at Griff Yates again.

In Regent's Park one of any number of chic, sleek and drop-dead efficient women answered a phone, listened, placed the speaker on hold and buzzed the glass-walled office on the hub, where Diana Taverner was two hours into a morning she wasn't enjoying, because she wasn't alone. Roger Barrowby, currently overseeing the daily outgoings and incomings of the Service's operational nexus, was sharing her personal space as if bestowing a favour – lately he'd taken to turning up at the Park as early as Lady Di herself, his thinning sandy hair teased into an attitude that lent it body; his prominent chin pinkly shaved and dabbed with cologne; his middle-aged body parcelled into the subtlest of pin stripes; all of this intended, apparently, to convey the impression that she and he *were in the same boat; were shoring up the ruins.* Taverner was starting to worry that it was a courtship ritual. Barrowby wasn't bothered about the Service's financial competence. He simply wanted to demonstrate that he was pulling the strings that made everyone jump, and making it obvious that hers were the strings he enjoyed tugging most. Perhaps because she tugged back.

Today, he was studying, rather than occupying, the black leather and chrome visitors' chair Taverner had inherited from her office's previous incumbent. 'Is this actually a Mies van der Rohe?'

'What do you think?'

'Because they're awfully expensive. I'd hate to think that in these straitened times, the Service budget was being stretched to coddle posteriors.'

Coddled posteriors was very Barrowby. He had moments so arch, he made Stephen Fry look level.

'Roger, it's a chainstore knock-off. The only reason it's not in a skip is that in these "straitened times", the Service budget doesn't "stretch" to replacing it.'

Her phone buzzed.

'Now, would you mind?'

He settled himself on the object under discussion.

Suppressing a sigh, she answered the phone. After a moment, she said: 'Put her through.'

The pavement pounded beneath Shirley Dander in time with the thudding of her heart – she'd have to slow down soon; run a bit, walk a bit, wasn't that how you were supposed to do it?

In the jogging books, maybe. Not in the Service manual.

She risked a look. Ho was several hundred yards behind, running like a drunk with a sprain, in no state to observe her. So she stopped, nursed her ribs with her left hand, steadied herself against a wall with her right. She was in a small park: trees, bushes, a playground, grass. A clutch of mothers, their offspring strapped in buggies or loaded onto swings, were drinking coffee from a breakfast stall this side of the alley onto Whitecross Street. Shirley passed through it, and at the far end looked up. There it was, the tip of the Needle; visible even here, in this built-up canyon.

Something was going on over there, and Shirley had no idea what, but at last she was involved.

A gulp of air. Another spurt of speed. No sign of Ho, but that was okay. If you couldn't get Windows to start, Ho was your man. The rest of the time, he took up space.

Her head buzzing like her haircut, on she ran.

At the entrance to the same park, Roderick Ho gripped the railings and prayed for something. He wasn't sure what. Just something that would make his lungs forgive him. They felt like he'd been gargling fire.

Behind him, a car rumbled to a halt. 'You all right, mate?'

He turned, and here was his miracle. A black cab. A great big beautiful black cab, open for business.

Falling onto the back seat, he managed to gasp, 'The Needle.'

'Right you are.'

Away he went.

River blinked.

Soldier Two swung at Griff Yates again, and in a moment so smooth it looked choreographed, Yates seized his arm, twisted his wrist, relieved him of his gun and put him on the ground. The blood masking Yates's face painted him a demon. For a moment, River thought he was going to shoot, but instead he turned it on Soldier One. 'Drop it!' he screamed. 'Now.'

The soldier was just a boy – they were both boys. The gun trembled in his hands. River plucked it free.

Then said to Yates, 'You too.'

'This bastard smashed my face in!'

'Griff? Give me the gun.'

Griff gave him the gun.

River said, 'I'm with MI5.'

This time they listened.

★

The building had come to life over the past few hours, but on Molly Doran's floor there was only the gurgling of plumbing, as hot water negotiated clumsy bends in monkey-puzzled piping. The sleek and glossy surfaces of Regent's Park masked the elderly exoskeleton on which it had been hoisted, and like a spanking new estate erected on a burial ground, it sometimes felt the tremblings of unlaid ghosts.

Or so Molly put it.

'You're on your own a lot, aren't you?' said Lamb.

They had worn out the possibilities of new discovery. Everything they knew about Nikolai Katinsky, about Alexander Popov, could fit on a sheet of paper. A set of interconnecting lies, thought Lamb, like one of those visual puzzles; the outline of a vase, or two people talking. The truth lay in the line itself: it was neither. It was pencil marks on a page, designed to fool.

'What now?' Molly asked.

'I need to think,' he said. 'I'm going home.'

'Home?'

'I mean Slough House.'

She raised an eyebrow. Cracks had appeared in her make-up. 'If it's quiet you want, I can find you a corner.'

'Not a corner I'm after. It's a fresh pair of ears,' Lamb said distractedly.

'As you wish.' She smiled, but it was a bitter thing. 'Someone special waiting over there?'

Lamb stood. The stool creaked its thanks. He looked down at Molly: her overpainted face, her round body; the absences below her knees. 'So,' he said. 'You been all right then?'

'What, these past fifteen years?'

'Yeah.' He tapped a foot against her nearest wheel. 'Since ending up in that gizmo.'

'This gizmo,' she said, 'has outlasted most other relationships I've had.'

'It's got a vibrate setting?'

She laughed. 'God, Jackson. Use that line upstairs, they'll prosecute.' And she put her head to one side. 'I don't blame you, you know.'

'Good,' he said.

'For my legs.'

'I don't blame me either.'

'But you stayed away.'

'Yeah, well. New set of wheels, I figured you'd want some private time.'

She said, 'Go away now, Jackson. And do me one favour?'

He waited.

'Only come back when you need something. Even if it's another fifteen years.'

'You take care, Molly.'

In the lift, he tucked cigarette in mouth in readiness for the great outdoors. He was already counting the moments.

River said to Griff, 'Why'd you come looking for me?'

They sat in the back of the jeep; the soldiers up front. He'd returned both their guns. This was borderline risky – there was a chance the kids would shoot them and bury them somewhere quiet – but once they'd clocked his Service card, they'd slipped into cooperative mode. One was on his radio now. The hangar would soon be crawling with military.

Yates's face was grim. His handkerchief was a butcher's mess, but he'd only succeeded in smearing blood across his features. 'I said, man, I'm sorry I—'

'Not what I'm asking. Why, specifically, did you come looking for me?'

Yates said, 'Tommy Moult . . .'

'What about him?'

'I saw him up the village. He asked if you'd got back all right. Made me worried you'd been, you know. Hurt.'

Blown up, he meant.

'Shit,' River said. 'It was his idea, wasn't it? Leading me onto the range? And leaving me there?'

'Jonny—'

'Wasn't it?'

'He might have suggested it.'

The jeep had no doors. It wouldn't have been a second's work to tip the bastard out.

'Tommy Moult, man,' Yates said. 'He knows everything happens in Upshott. You think he just sells apples from his bike, but he knows everyone. Everything.'

River had worked that out already. He said, 'He made sure I was there. And saw what I saw. Made sure I'd be freed in time to do something about it.'

'What you on about?'

'Where was he? This morning?'

'Church end.' Yates rubbed his cheek. 'You really a secret agent?'

'Yes.'

'Is that why Kelly—'

'No,' said River. 'She did that because she wanted to. Deal with it.'

The jeep cornered, braked sharply, and they were at the flying club, with its toytown airstrip, and empty hangar.

River hit the ground running.

Roger Barrowby had gone white, which gladdened Diana Taverner's heart. Her morning was new-made. Ingrid Tearney was out of the country; as Chair of Limitations, Barrowby could claim First Desk, but it looked like the only snap decision he'd be making was which direction to throw up in. The arch comments were history. He should have stayed in bed.

She said, 'Roger, you've got four seconds.'

'The Home Secretary—'

'Has final say, but she'll base that on our best info. Which you now have. Three seconds.'

'An agent in the field? That's all it comes down to?'

'Yes, Roger. Like in wartime.'

'Jesus, Diana, if we make the wrong call—'

'Two seconds.'

'—what's left of our careers will be spent sorting the post.'

'That's what keeps life interesting on the hub, Roger. One second.'

He threw his hands up. Taverner had never seen this cliché happen before. 'I don't know, Diana – you've got half a message on a mobile from a slow horse out in the sticks. He didn't even cite his protocols.'

'Roger – you do know what Code September means?'

'I know it's not an official designation,' he said peevishly.

'I've run out of numbers. Whether this is real or not, keep it from the Home Sec any longer, and you're in serious dereliction of duty.'

You're: she enjoyed that syllable.

'Diana . . .'

'Roger.'

'What do I do?'

'Only one thing you can do,' she said, and told him what that was.

They'd been talking for ten minutes, but nothing meaningful had been said. Arkady Pashkin was sticking to Big Picture topics: what was going on with the euro, which way Germany would lean next time one of the partners needed bailing out, how much money Russia's World Cup bid cost. Spider Webb had the air of a dinner party host waiting for a guest to shut up about their children.

Marcus seemed more serene but was watchful, his attention divided evenly between Kyril and Piotr. Louisa remembered Min – she barely ever stopped remembering Min – and how he'd distrusted this pair on sight. Partly because that was his job, but partly because he was Min, and yearning for action. Her mouth filled, and she swallowed. Pashkin dragged the topic onto fuel prices, the ostensible reason for the meeting, but Webb still didn't look happy. It wasn't going the way he'd intended, Louisa thought. All he's managed is *I see* and *Oh yes*. He planned this as a recruitment exercise, but he's got no idea what he's doing. And Arkady Pashkin had his own agenda, which seemed to consist of wasting time until . . .

Until a high-pitched looping wail came from everywhere at once; above, below, from outside the doors. It didn't pierce so much as throb, and its message was immediate and unmistakable. Leave now.

Marcus turned to the huge windows as if to spot approaching danger. Webb got to his feet so suddenly his chair hit the floor. He said, 'What's that?' which Louisa decided was the stupidest question ever. Which didn't stop her echoing it: 'What's happening?'

Pashkin, still seated, said, 'It sounds like the emergency we discussed yesterday.'

'You knew about this.'

Reaching into his briefcase, Pashkin produced a gun that he handed to Piotr. 'Yes,' he said. 'I'm afraid I did.'

The hangar looked bigger in the Skyhawk's absence. The doors hung wide, and sunlight fleshed out its corners, drawing attention to everything that wasn't there. Those bags of fertiliser headed this list. There was a faint spillage where they'd been, as if one of the bags had a rip in it, but that was all.

Behind him, Yates said, 'She went up earlier. I saw her go.'
'I know.'
'There's something wrong, isn't there? With the plane?'

Except it wasn't only in that one place: sinking to his knees, River scanned the floor from as low an angle as his battered frame would allow.

Another jeep pulled up outside, and he could hear the clenched barking of an officer. New arseholes were being torn.

Across the concrete, a faint trail of crumbly brown dust snaked away to the side door.

He had the feeling he was on the end of a long piece of string. And the bastard at the other end kept tugging.

Yates said, 'If Kelly's in danger . . .'

He didn't finish. But judging by his blood-streaked face, it would involve punching something until it turned to jelly.

'What's going on?'

And here was the officer, in an officer's uniform, a detail he seemed to think outweighed his being on civilian turf.

River said to Yates, 'You tell him,' and headed for the side door.

'You! Stop right there!'

But River was already outside, on the east wall of the hangar with a view of the mesh fence bordering the MoD range; of the range itself, which was a bland expanse of overlapping greens of a brimful wheelie-bin chained to one of the fence posts and of a stack of bags of fertiliser, the topmost of which was split down one side. A gentle trickle had spilled onto the ground River kicked the stack, but it remained solid and real.

And then he had company.

'You attacked my men,' he was told. 'And they say you claim you're with the secret service. Exactly what's going on?'

'I need a phone,' River said.

16

U P IN THE SKIES AND miles south and east, over London's outer settlements – massed clusters of red and grey rooftops, connected by winding stripes of tree-bordered tarmac and interspersed with golf courses – Kelly Tropper could feel excitement building. This was no ordinary flight. It would have a different ending.

As if to underline this, the radio was babbling. They should identify themselves immediately. If they were experiencing difficulties, they should state them now; failing which they should return to their filed route, or face severe consequences.

'What do you think that means? Severe consequences?'

'Don't worry about it.'

Damien Butterfield said, 'I thought we'd be closer before they noticed us.'

'It's okay. Tommy said this would happen.'

'But he's not here, is he?'

This wasn't worth replying to.

Like the other flying club members, she and Damien had grown up together; the children of incomers, whose parents had moved from bigger, brasher places to pretty, vacant Upshott. An unfathomable decision, the children had agreed, and yet they too had all remained rooted there. For Kelly, it was the only way she could have access to the aeroplane, owned by Ray Hadley, but for which she and the others paid maintenance and rental fees. Sometimes she had wondered if there weren't more to it than that; if it weren't cowardice that had anchored her in her childhood village; a fear of failing in the big world. Though Tommy had told her—

It was funny about Tommy; everyone thought he just sold apples from his bike, but he knew everyone in Upshott, and everything that happened there, as if he received reports from everyone; as if he were the centre of a web. You could always talk to Tommy, and he always knew what was going on in your life. This was true for her; true for her friends; true for her parents too. Her father never failed to chat with Tommy on the mornings he was outside the shop, or doing his rounds of the village, picking up the odd jobs that sustained him, though he disappeared mid-week, and nobody had ever found out where. Perhaps he had another village somewhere, where he lived a similar existence with a different cast, but Kelly had never discussed the idea with anyone, because you never did discuss Tommy Moult – he was everybody's secret. So yes, it was funny about Tommy, but a kind of funny she'd long ceased to question; he was simply part of life in Upshott, and that was that.

What Tommy had told her was, there were ways of proving your bravery to yourself, and making your mark on the big world. Many ways.

It was hard, now, to remember whose idea this had been; her own, or Tommy Moult's.

Beside her, Damien Butterfield said, 'Are we nearly there yet?' and laughed at his own joke.

The radio squawked again, and Kelly Tropper laughed too, and turned it off.

Somewhere to the north-west two more planes took to the air: sleek, dark, dangerous and on the hunt.

The taxi driver had kept up a relentless stream of invective about bloody marchers, who were achieving nothing except mucking hard-working cabbies about, and if anyone *really* wanted to know what to do about the banks—

'Here's fine,' said Ho.

He threw a note at the driver, and jumped out into the path of Shirley Dander.

'Sh-sh-i-i-i-it,' she managed, in a kind of elongated hiccup. Ho was pleased to observe she looked like crap.

They were right by the forecourt of the Needle, through whose huge glass walls Ho could see a living breathing forest – but before he could comment on this, a barrage of sirens erupted, as if every car alarm in the City had been triggered at once.

'What?'

For a moment, Ho thought the rally had arrived – he could hear it not far off, a rumbling mobile chant like a rootless football match. But the types pouring into view from doorways all around were wearing suits and smart outfits: more marched against than marching. Through the Needle's revolving doors they came too, appearing unsure as to their next move; pausing, most of them, to look back at the building they'd emerged from, and then staring round as it became clear that whatever was happening was happening everywhere.

Shirley was upright again. ''Kay. In we go.'

Ho said, 'But everyone's coming out.'

'Jesus wept – you're aware you're MI5, right?'

'I'm mostly research,' he explained, but she was already shoving her way through the emerging crowds.

The gun looked natural in Piotr's fist, no more surprising than a coffee cup or beer bottle. He pointed it at Marcus. 'Hands on the table.'

Marcus laid his hands on the tabletop, palms down.

'All of you.'

Louisa complied.

After a moment, Webb did the same. 'Shit,' he said. Then, 'Shit,' he said again.

Pashkin snapped his briefcase shut. The alarm was still looping, so he raised his voice. 'You'll be locked in. Those doors, they're pretty good. You'll be best off waiting for help.'

Webb said, 'I thought we were—'

'Shut up.'

'—doing something here—'

Kyril said, 'You were. You were helping us out.'

'Thought you couldn't speak English,' Louisa said.

Marcus said, 'They're not just going to lock us in.'

'I know.'

Kyril said something that made Piotr laugh.

The alarm wailed on, swelling then diminishing. Other floors would be being evacuated; the lifts would have frozen, and the doors into the stairwells automatically unlocked, allowing access either way. Crowds would assemble at designated points outside, and names be checked off against lists held by security, or matched against the keycards currently in use. But no one on the seventy-seventh floor would appear on either of those lists. Their presence was off-grid.

Webb said, 'Look, I don't know what the alarm's for, but I promise—'

Piotr shot him.

Seventy-seven storeys below, people trooped onto the streets; some wearing that fed-up look that comes with unwelcome interruption; others happily lighting unscheduled cigarettes; and all – once they realised that not only their own but every building in sight was evacuating – changing mood: standing still, looking skyward. All were used to drills and false alarms, but these happened one at a time. Now, everything was happening at once, and the grim possibilities took root and flowered. The City broke into a run. Its directions were various, but its intentions clear: to be somewhere else, immediately. And still people kept appearing, because the buildings were ten, fifteen, twenty storeys high, and each floor was packed with workers. Whether at desks, in meeting rooms, huddled round water coolers or chatting in corridors, all were hearing the same thing: their building's alarm, instructing them to leave. Those who paused to look from their windows saw scattering crowds below. This was not conducive to orderly evacuation. Jostling gave way to shoving. Ripples of panic became waves, and the voices of reason drowned in the swell.

This didn't happen everywhere, but it happened often. As the City warned its worker bees of a possible terrorist event, some of those bees turned on each other, and stung.

Most of the resulting injuries, it was later calculated, happened in those buildings containing bankers. Well, bankers and lawyers. It was too close to call.

Smoking again, Jackson Lamb slouched across a highwalk in the Barbican complex, heading for Slough House. Above him rose Shakespeare or Thomas More, he could never remember which tower was which, and ahead was a familiar bench. He'd fallen asleep on it once, clutching a cardboard coffee cup. When he'd woken, it held forty-two pence in small change.

He sat on the bench now to finish his cigarette. Above and behind him loured the 1970s, wrought in glass and concrete; below him the Middle Ages, in the shape of St Giles Cripplegate, and to the east, the up-to-the-minute sound of sirens, which had been building for some while, but only now crashed through his absorbed state. A pair of fire engines blared along London Wall, followed by a police car. Lamb paused, fingers halfway to his lips. Another fire engine. Dropping the cigarette, he reached for his phone instead.

Taverner, he thought. What have you done?

Webb was thrown to the floor as a thin pink spray fritzed the air, then laid a pattern across the carpet. Marcus and Louisa dropped at the same moment, and a second shot carved a chunk from the tabletop, coughing up splinters. But there was no other shelter. They had a second, maybe less, before Piotr crouched and fired directly into their heads: panic blooming, Louisa looked to Marcus, who was ripping something from the underside of the table, something which fitted his hand as naturally as a coffee cup or beer bottle. He fired and someone screamed and a body hit the floor. Raised voices swore in Russian. Marcus scrambled up and fired again. The bullet hit closing doors.

On the far side of the table, Kyril lay clutching his left leg, which was all messed up below the knee.

Louisa pulled out her phone. Marcus ran for the doors, gun in hand. When he pulled them they gave just enough to reveal the U-lock threaded through the outer handles – another gift from Pashkin's damned briefcase. He tugged again then leaped back as a bullet slammed into the doors from the other side.

In the lobby, the alarm swirled. Beneath its noise, Marcus could make out the sound of the two men entering the stairwell at the end of the corridor.

As the rally neared the City – its head winding round St Paul's; its tail back beyond the viaduct – a new awareness rippled through it, a morphic resonance fuelled by Twitter, allowing its entire length to hear the rumours at once: that the City was collapsing, its buildings emptying. That the palaces of finance were crumbling at the mob's approach. With this news came a change of mood, spilling over into aggressive triumphalism; the kind that wants to see its enemy spread on the pavement with its head split open. Fresh chanting broke out, louder than ever. The pace picked up. Though already, in counterpoint to the hints of victory, another tremor was wavering west: that the rug had been pulled, and danger lay ahead.

At first sight, this took the form of official resistance.

'Due to unforeseen circumstances, this rally has now been cancelled. You're to turn and calmly make your way back towards Holborn where you'll be able to disperse.'

The black armoured units that until now had been discreet shadows had disgorged bulked-up shapes in shields and helmets, and barriers were blocking Cheapside. Somewhere behind them was a man with a loudhailer.

'*The streets ahead are closed. I repeat, the route is closed, and this rally is now cancelled.*'

The sound of sirens wafting from a distance underlined his words.

For two minutes that stretched into four the head of the mob went no further, but swelled in size, filling the junction on the cathedral's eastern side. And still, up and down its length, messages were relayed, the way a worm communicates to itself the news of its own dicing. At intervals behind them, more tactical units were breaking the march up, rerouting groups into narrow streets and squares, and sealing their exits. Singing died and curdled into anger; tempers frayed and broke. Cats and dogs, witches and wizards, clung to their parents' legs, while once-mild protestors sprayed spittle in the faces of unmoving policemen. Overhead, the *whump-whump* of helicopter blades throbbed in and out of hearing, sometimes drowning the shrill alarms from the City, sometimes becoming its rhythm section, while from the City itself a less organised procession fled the rumours of destruction, arriving in a rabble behind the police rows blocking Cheapside.

'The streets ahead are closed, and this rally is cancelled.'

The first bottle appeared in a low arc from the middle of the crowd. It spun neck over base, spraying liquid which might have been water, might have been piss, onto the heads of the policemen below, before shattering on the road. It was followed by others.

And up and down the route of the march, tucked away inside what had been a mob, and was now a collection of smaller mobs, those who'd come with masks in their pockets recognised their cue and slipped them on. The time for breaking glass had arrived, and for torching cars, and throwing rocks.

The first flames burst into being like early blossoms of spring: easily caught on the wind, and scattered for miles.

★

'It's a credible threat, Lamb.'

'Credible? Some Sunday aeroplane's going to crash into a City building – you sure about that?'

'Sure enough not to take the risk.'

'You're gunna shoot it down?'

'There are Harriers in the air. They'll do what's necessary.'

'Over central London?'

'If that's what it takes.'

'Are you mad?'

'Jackson, look. This—this is what we've worried about for years. This or something like it.'

'What, a cut-price 9/11? You think a clapped-out Soviet spook would do this? Katinsky's a Cold War survivor, not a New World Order barbarian, for Christ's sake!'

'And you think it's a coincidence that Arkady Pashkin's meeting—'

'This is not about Pashkin, Taverner. If Moscow knew you and Webb had cooked up some scheme to recruit him, they wouldn't do this. They'd wait till he got home and run him through a compactor.'

'Lamb—'

'We've been led here, every step. Killing Dickie Bow, laying a trail to Upshott, they've lit a damn flare path. Murdering Min Harper's the only thing they've tried to keep wrapped. Whatever's really going on, it's not what we think. What's happening at the Needle?'

Taverner said, 'We've alerted security. There are fire teams on the way.'

Lamb said, 'What happens when that building goes into lockdown?'

In the flying club's office, things had changed: the fridge remained, and the chairs; the old desk was still cluttered with paperwork, but the stack of cardboard boxes was a tumbled pyramid, and its plastic sheet lay crumpled on the floor. River dropped to one knee and foraged through the boxes. They'd contained paper, stacks of A4-sized sheets, several copies of which were stuck to the bottom of one. Both showed the same design.

Griff Yates burst in, panting. His face was still streaked with blood, but in his hand he had a phone. 'I borrowed this.'

River grabbed it, his thumb pressing numbers before his brain could process them. 'Catherine? It's not a bomb.'

For a moment, she didn't reply.

'Catherine? I said—'

'So what is it, then?'

'Did you sound an alert?'

'River . . . You called a Code September.'

'That's not even a—'

'I know what it's not. But I know what it means. So I told the Park. What's going on, River?'

'What did the Park do?'

'Put the City on terror alert. Imminent danger.'

'Oh Jesus!'

'High buildings are being evacuated, especially the Needle, because of the Russian thing. River, talk to me.'

'There's no bomb. The plane's not—it's not a terror attack.' He looked at the papers in his hand. They were reproductions of the same image: a stylised city landscape, its tallest skyscraper struck by jagged lightning. Along the foot of each page ran the words STOP THE CITY. 'They're leafleting the demo.'

'They're bloody *what*?'

'Leaflets, Catherine. They're dropping leaflets on the rally. But somebody, somebody wanted us to think there was a bomb. The terror alert, that's the whole point. The evacuation.'

'The Needle,' she said.

Louisa had no signal. Nor did Marcus. The microphone-shaped device on the table was gone; taken by Pashkin and Piotr, but still nearby, and blocking their phones.

She checked Webb. The bullet had hit him in the chest, but he was alive, for now. Shallow breaths bubbled out of him, and whistled back in. She did what she could, which wasn't much, then turned to Marcus, who was standing over Kyril.

'You put that there yesterday?'

The gun, she meant. But how else could it have got there? Taped to the table's underside.

'Fixing the odds,' Marcus said. 'I don't wander into situations blind. Not with hostiles.'

Kyril was conscious and moaning; a dull counterpoint to the alarm's shrill wail. Louisa put her hand on his wounded leg. 'This hurt?'

He swore in Russian.

'Yeah yeah. You don't speak English. This hurt?' She pressed harder.

'Jesus bitch you fuck!'

'That'll be a yes. What's going on?'

Marcus left her for the kitchen.

'They've left you behind. You think they're coming back?'

'Bastards,' he said. He might have been talking about his absent comrades.

'Where've they gone?'

'Downstairs . . .'

From the kitchen, she heard breaking glass. Marcus reappeared with the fire-axe in his hand.

Louisa turned back to Kyril. 'Downstairs,' she said, and understanding dawned. 'Rumble? Their new iPhone? That's what this is about? You're stealing a fucking prototype?'

Marcus swung the axe, and the doors shuddered.

She put her hand on the fallen man's wound once more. 'Before he gets through that,' she said, 'you're going to tell me why Min died.'

Outside was warm spring air and a drift of pollen. The irritated officer had heard enough to know that whatever was happening

302

was bigger than a trespass on MoD land, and was currently on his phone, establishing the level of national alert. Griff Yates was washing his face somewhere. And nearby, at forlorn attention by the jeep, stood one of the two soldiers they'd had their altercation with.

River showed his Service card again. 'I need to be somewhere.'

'Yeah, right.'

'And you'll need a friend once this morning's done,' River added, thinking *So will I*. 'Get me back to the village in the next two minutes, and you'll have one.'

'You're James Bond, are you?'

'We use the same gym.'

'Huh . . .'

A bird of prey wheeled overhead, loudly mewing.

'What the hell. Get in. Quick.'

River used the two-minute journey to speak to Catherine again. 'Have they called the Harriers off?'

'I don't know, River.' There was an unaccustomed tremor to her voice. 'I've called the Park, but – are you anywhere near a TV?'

'Not exactly.'

'All hell's breaking loose in the City. Half the world's trying to get out, and the rally's trying to get in: Jesus, River . . . That was us.'

Me, he thought.

He said, 'And they told me I'd never top King's Cross,' but a tight knot of dread had formed in his stomach.

'And you're sure now, are you? The plane's not heading for the Needle?'

'We've been played, Catherine. Me, Lamb, everyone. You don't need to send a plane into a building to cause chaos. You just have to make us think it's going to happen.'

'There's more to it. That Russian, Pashkin? He's not real.'

'So who?'

'Don't know yet. Louisa's phone's dead. So's Marcus's. But Ho's on his way there now. With Shirley.'

'It's all part of the same thing,' said River. 'Must be. Don't let them shoot that plane down. Catherine. The pilot's been played, just like us.'

'I'll do what I can.'

River slapped the jeep's roof in frustration. 'Here,' he said. 'Here.'

Church end, Yates had said. That's where Tommy Moult had been. The church end of the high street.

The jeep crunched to a halt by St John of the Cross's lych-gate, and River left it at a run.

As Marcus swung the axe a crunch shook the floor, and Louisa shrieked: '*Jesus*, was that you?'

He paused, the axe inch-deep in the door. 'Plastic,' he said, and pulled the axe-head free.

Plastic. She looked at Kyril. 'That's the plan? The building goes into terror mode, and you bust into Rumble with plastic explosives?'

'Millions,' he said, through gritted teeth.

'It'd have to be. No one goes to this effort for petty cash.'

Another dull crunch from below. They were blowing open doors down there, and it wouldn't take them long. Then all they'd have to do was head for ground level and slip away with the crowds. No one would check off their exit, because no one had signed them in. There'd be a car waiting, and one less to share the proceeds with.

Thwack! went the axe, and splinters flew.

She kicked Kyril. 'Min saw him, didn't he?'

The Russian groaned. 'My leg. I need doctor.'

'Min saw Pashkin, or whoever he really is. When he was supposed to be in Moscow being a fucking oil baron. Except he wasn't, he was in a dosshouse on the Edgware Road, because the Ambassador's a little pricey when you don't need to be there, isn't it? When you're not really a fucking oil baron, just a fucking thief. And that's why Min died.'

'Didn't mean it to happen. We were having a drink, that's all—*gah!* My leg—'

Thwack!

'Tell you what, Kyril. Once I've put your scumbag friends in a box, I'll come back and see what I can do about your leg, yeah?' She leaned in close. 'We've got a fucking axe, after all.'

Nothing about her expression suggested she was joking.

The next *thwack* was followed by a *thunk*.

'Through,' said Marcus.

Louisa patted Kyril's shattered leg again, and made for the door.

She'd never flown in radio silence before, and it added an odd dimension to the morning, as if all this were taking place inside a dream, in which the bluntly familiar – the panel of instruments before her; the view of empty skies; Damien by her side – rubbed surfaces with the strange. London was gathering shape; coagulating into an uninterrupted mass of rooftop and road, its districts strung together by buses and cars.

Stacked behind them were masses of the leaflet she'd designed; the one that would tell the marchers what they were doing – stopping the city; smashing the banks. The details remained vague, but it was enough to be a part of the crusade. There was greed and avarice and corruption in the world, and probably always would be, but that was no excuse for not attempting to make a change.

'We should put the radio on,' Damien said. 'It's dangerous. It's illegal.'

She said, 'Don't worry. We're too low to be on anyone's flight path.'

'I didn't think we'd be so . . .'

'What do you think they'll do, for Christ's sake? Shoot us down? You think they'll shoot us down?'

'Well no, but—'

'A few more minutes, we'll be over the centre. They'll see what we're planning on doing, and yeah, they'll escort us home and we'll be arrested and fined and all that. We knew that before setting off. Grow some balls.'

But she could hear, beneath the hum of the Skyhawk's engine, a bass note, a growl, a pair of growls, and in that instant a different future occurred to Kelly Tropper; one in which, instead of proving herself a radical daredevil, scattering her self-designed leaflets on the marching crowds below, she became an object lesson in the lengths to which a once-bitten nation might go to protect itself. But that seemed so far-fetched, so at odds with the scenario she'd planned, that she was able to dismiss it, even as Damien began to babble louder, and with audible fear, that this wasn't the good idea it had sounded back in The Downside Man; that maybe they weren't invulnerable after all.

That last part, though, surely couldn't be true, thought Kelly. And on they flew towards the heart of London, its buildings growing closer together now; its spaces further apart; even as the noises she could hear beneath her own plane's hum grew louder, and took up more room, and swallowed everything else.

Tommy Moult, or the man who used to be Tommy Moult, was in St Johnno's graveyard, on the wooden bench dedicated to the recent memory of *Joe Morden, who loved this church*. This faced the church's western wall; the side on which its bell tower stood, and through whose rose window the setting sun would warm the church's interior with soft pink light. At the moment, it remained in shadow. Moult had lost his red cap, along with the sprigs of hair that had tufted from under it, and which had been as familiar a sight in the village as the hawthorn trees flanking the lychgate. Bald, older-looking, he did not rise at River's approach. He seemed lost in contemplation of the medieval church, around which earlier versions of Upshott had risen and fallen. In one hand he nursed an iPhone. The other, dangling over the arm of the bench, hid from view.

River said, 'Busy morning.'

'Not round here.'

'You're Nikolai Katinsky, aren't you? Lamb told me about you.'

'Some of the time.'

'I guess that makes you Alexander Popov, too,' River said. 'Or the man who invented him.'

Now Katinsky seemed interested. 'You worked that out yourself?'

'Seems kind of obvious at this point,' River said. He sat on the bench, leaving a foot of space between them. 'I mean, all these hoops you've had us jumping through. That's not the work of a language school scam artist. Or even a cipher clerk.'

'Don't knock cipher clerks,' Katinsky told him. 'Like any other branch of the Civil Service, all the work's done low on the food chain. Everyone else just has meetings.'

In the shadow of the tower he looked grey, and though his head was mostly smooth, bristle stubbled his chin and cheeks. This was grey too, as were his eyes, which looked like the covers placed on wells to prevent accidents: things falling in. Things climbing out.

'On 7/7,' River said, 'London kept a stiff upper lip. It's how we knew we'd won, no matter how many bodies we buried. But this morning, the whole damn City looks like day one of the Harvey Nicks' sale.'

Katinsky waved his phone. 'Yes. I've been watching.'

'That's what all this was about?'

'Only incidentally. Your Mr Pashkin – not his real name either, I'm afraid – he's taking advantage of the chaos to relieve the Needle's tenants of some of their assets.' Moult glanced at his phone again. 'He hasn't rung, though. It's possible not everything's gone according to plan.'

'His plan. Not yours.'

'We have different aims.'

'But you're working together.'

'He has access to various things I needed. Andrei Chernitsky, for a start. Some years ago, Andrei and I abducted your friend Dickie Bow. I was building the Popov legend, and wanted one of your people to get a glimpse of him, though nobody so reliable their words would be trusted. When you're making a scarecrow, you don't do it in plain sight, you understand.'

'I get the picture.'

'Well, since then, like a regrettable number of former colleagues, Andrei has turned to private enterprise to earn his crust. In short, he was in the employ of one it'll be simpler to keep calling Arkady Pashkin.'

'And you needed him to lay a trail Dickie Bow would follow.'

'Precisely. So Pashkin and I came to a mutually beneficial arrangement, which even now he's reaping the benefit of. Or trying to. Like I say, he hasn't rung.'

River shook his head. He ached all over, but underneath that a sense of wonderment pulsed. For the first time in his life, he was facing the enemy. Not his enemy, exactly, but his grandfather's, and Jackson Lamb's; he was putting a face to the history that previous spooks had battled with, and it was happening here, in a country churchyard, witnessed by the uninvolved dead.

He said, 'And that's it? You bring the City to a grinding halt for a morning, and that's it? Christ, what a waste of effort. A few hand-wringing editorials and it'll be forgotten.'

Katinsky laughed. 'What's your name? Your real name?'

River shook his head.

'No, I suppose not. You don't have a cigarette, do you?'

'They're bad for you.'

'Is that a sense of humour poking through? There's hope for us yet.'

'That's what this is to you? One big joke?'

'If you like,' Katinsky said. 'So tell me. Do you want to hear the punchline?'

★

308

He must be on the twentieth floor, Roderick Ho thought, chest heaving, breath thick with the taste of blood. At least the twentieth. He'd crashed through the lobby in Shirley Dander's wake; had waved his ID at the lone security guard, who was sticking to his post though the City crumbled; had followed his pointing finger to stairs that led forever up. And now he must be at least on the twentieth floor, and Shirley was out of sight. All he could hear was the crashing boom of the alarm, louder in the stairwell as it bounced off walls and skittered off the staircase, while he panted like a dog, on all fours, his forehead resting on the stair above. Drool unspooled from his lip. Everything was a blur. What was he doing this for?

Louisa and Marcus in trouble – didn't care.

Pashkin not who he said he was – didn't care.

Shirley Dander thinking him a wuss – didn't care.

He should be back in his office, deep-sea diving on the web. *You're aware you're MI5, right?*

Yeah: he didn't care.

It occurred to him that the program he'd written to fake his work pattern would have kicked in by now, and anyone checking up on him remotely would find him hard at work on the archive: sorting and saving, sorting and saving. If he'd had breath to spare, he'd have laughed. It was a shame he had no one to share the joke with because it was, after all, pretty funny.

What was her name: Shona? Shana? The chick from the gym he'd planned to meet, once he'd trashed her relationship. Except, he thought, he'd never do that, would he? Trash her relationship, yes; or at any rate, throw a virtual spanner into its works – he could handle that, no problem. But actually going up and talking to her? Never going to happen. And even if it did, how would he explain to her about the program he'd written to fake his work pattern?

Catherine Standish, on the other hand. She knew about it. And you know, Roddy had the feeling she actually found it pretty amusing.

And that's what he was doing this for, come to think of it. He was here because she'd told him to be here. To help Louisa Guy and Marcus whatshisname.

Sighing, he hauled himself to his feet, and staggered up towards what must be the twenty-first floor.

Though was in fact the twelfth.

Marcus went through the fire doors low, arms outstretched, gun pointing ahead, then left, then right, then up. Nothing. He said, 'Clear,' and Louisa followed him out of the stairwell. They were on the sixty-eighth, and the logo on the glass doors read *Rumble* in a streamlined font. There were lights on inside, but no one visible. The reception desk, in front of a huge repro of *A Bigger Splash*, was uncrewed. Marcus tried the door. It wouldn't open.

'Maybe they locked it behind them.'

'They're using plastic,' Marcus pointed out. He took a step back, braced himself, and kicked, to no effect. The noise this made was swallowed by the alarm. No one appeared inside the Rumble suite.

'Ideas?'

'Maybe they went through a wall.'

'Or maybe . . .'

Marcus raised an eyebrow.

Louisa said, 'Maybe he was lying. What floor are the diamond people on?'

One breath, two breath. One breath, two.

There was a City challenge, Shirley had seen a poster for it: you ran to the top flight of a 'scraper, then down, then ran to another one and did it again. It must be for charity, because it couldn't be for fun. She wondered how many folk died halfway through.

Her legs were soup. A label on a fire door read *32*. She'd seen nobody since the twentieth, when a dishevelled couple had burst into the well, asking, 'Are we too late?' as if they'd missed the emergency. Shirley had pointed the way down, and carried on climbing.

And now she must be getting used to the constant wail of the damned alarm, fishtailing round the stairwell, because she was hearing other sounds too – some kind of explosion some minutes back: nothing you wanted to hear this high up.

She'd not been able to raise Louisa or Marcus, but had talked to Catherine, who'd told her the alarms were false; no terrorist bombs were expected . . . It had sounded like a bomb to her though, if a small one.

One breath after another, at least one of which was a sigh. Arkady Pashkin wasn't who he said he was, and had two thugs in tow. Shirley had no weapon, but she'd put people on the floor with her bare hands before now. Come to think of it, that's why she was in Slough House in the first place.

It didn't matter that her legs were soup, or that she was less than halfway up. The City was coming apart, and that seemed to be Pashkin's plan. So she wasn't going to lie here panting while Guy and Longridge stopped it by themselves. Not if a ticket back to Regent's Park was involved.

Grinding her teeth, she took the next flight.

From way above her, more noise. It might have been a gunshot.

The sixty-fifth. De Koenig. The diamond merchant's. Its outer room was kitted out on a desert theme, with silks hanging off the walls and a clutch of palms forming a centrepiece, though these had been bent and torn by the blast that had shaken the floor twelve storeys up. Smoke still hugged the ceiling, and any furniture not fixed into place was scattered against the right-hand side of the room. Midway along the facing wall a metal door hung off its hinges.

'They're gone,' she said.

'Never assume.' Marcus went through the metal door the same way he'd entered the suite: every direction covered. Louisa followed.

It had been a secure room, lined with narrow deposit boxes, a good dozen of which had been blown open. From the floor glinted a shard of broken glass, which wasn't broken glass, Louisa realised – Jesus, it was a diamond, the size of a fingernail.

And Piotr too, a chunk of his head removed by a bullet, and smeared on the nearest wall.

'Pashkin's travelling light,' Marcus said.

'He must be on the stairs.'

'So let's go.'

They ran for the stairwell again, but at the fire door Louisa paused. 'He could be on any floor.'

'He wants out. Once the scare's over, it won't be so easy.'

He had to bend into her ear to speak. The scare wasn't over yet, though the alarm seemed to be winding down, as if running on a tired battery.

Louisa checked her phone. 'Still no good,' she said. 'And Webb's bleeding out for all we know. I've got to find an outside line.'

He said, 'Okay. I'll keep going.'

'Shoot straight,' Louisa said.

Marcus continued down the never-ending stairs, and Louisa went back into de Koenig's.

'You were a Kremlin brain.'

'Yes. Until I became, instead, a Moscow cipher clerk. With just enough of the right sort of information to be granted entry into your Jerusalem.'

'You invented Popov, who we knew was a legend. So we thought the cicadas were a legend too, but they were real. Why'd you bring them to Upshott?'

'They had to be somewhere,' Katinsky said. 'Once Moscow fell apart. Besides, they were sleepers, and where better to sleep?'

'They were agents of influence.'

'They were bright talented people, with access to people with access, and they reached right into the heart of the establishment.

312

It would have made for an interesting game, if it hadn't come to a premature end.'

'You mean if you hadn't lost, you might have won,' River said. 'Do they even know? About each other, I mean?'

Katinsky laughed. He laughed so hard he started to wheeze and had to put a hand up as if instructing River to stop right there, put everything on hold. It was the hand that held his iPhone. The other remained out of River's view.

At length he said, 'On the whole, I think not. Though they may have suspicions.'

River said, 'All these years, and you decided to come back to life. There's got to be a reason for that. You're dying, aren't you?'

'Liver cancer.'

'That's one of the painful ones. Too bad.'

'Thank you. You liked the girl, didn't you? Young Kelly Tropper. I mean, I know you screwed her, but it went beyond business, didn't it? Spies screw girls when they're called upon to do so, and young men screw girls when the opportunity presents. Which were you when you bedded her, Walker?'

'Did it bother you, sending her out to die?'

'Sending her? She'd say it was her own idea.'

'I'm sure she thought so. Are you really waiting for a call?'

'I might be. Or I might be waiting to make one.'

'It's over, you know.'

'It was over a long time ago,' Katinsky said. 'But that's the thing about dying. It encourages you to tidy up.'

'To settle scores,' River said.

'I prefer to think of it as redressing a balance. You don't think this is about ideology, do you?'

'Well, I don't think it's about a heist. Why Upshott?'

'You already asked.'

'You didn't answer. Nothing you've done's been accidental. You came here for a reason.'

The sun was trying to clear the bell tower, and given time

313

and patience, would succeed. It always had done before. Behind them, gravestones were soaking in warmth, but the bench remained in shadow. Katinsky gave the impression that this was where he belonged. For all his solidity, River half-expected him to evaporate once the sun's rays touched him.

'Why do you think?'

No, River thought; it wasn't his grandfather the man reminded him of. It was Jackson Lamb.

He said, 'It's England.'

'Oh come on. So is Birmingham. So is Crewe.'

'Picture postcard England. Medieval church, village pub, village green. You wanted to park your network at the heart of a vision of rural England.'

Like a grudging tutor, Katinsky nodded. 'Maybe. What else?'

River said, 'When you chose it, it had a military base. Most of the town existed just to serve it. There was nothing else here.'

'A small place with no proper existence . . . Why would the man who invented Alexander Popov choose such a place, I wonder?'

A passing wind crawled through the neatly trimmed grass, shaking the spray of daffodils in a tin vase by a headstone. For no reason he could think of, River remembered the O.B., his grandfather, reaching with a twig to rescue a beetle from a burning log in his grate. And then the memory fizzed and vanished, the way the beetle itself had popped when the fire swallowed it. But the connection had been made. Here in the quiet churchyard, River recalled a distant conflagration.

'ZT/53235,' he said.

Katinsky said nothing. But his eyes answered yes.

'That's where you're from,' River said, and even as he spoke, Katinsky's words, *I prefer to think of it as redressing a balance*, swam into his mind, and despite the encroaching sunshine it grew colder on their bench.

Louisa found a phone; called emergency services, but couldn't get through – what the hell was going on? Through the window, traces of black smoke spread inkily across the sky. Way down below, London was burning.

She called Slough House and filled Catherine in.

'He was still alive when you left him?'

'He was breathing. I'm not a doctor.'

She was having second thoughts about having left Webb on his own. Or not even on his own: the other Russian was there too. Also in pain, though that was of less consequence to her.

'Where's Pashkin now?'

'On his way down, I imagine. With Marcus in hot pursuit.'

'I hope he's careful.'

'I hope he kills the bastard.'

'I hope the bastard doesn't kill him first. Or the others.'

Roderick Ho and Shirley Dander were on the scene too.

'It's chaos out there, Louisa. God knows when you'll see reinforcements.'

'We need medics first.'

'I'll get a chopper sent.'

'Oh, shit,' said Louisa.

The roof.

'ZT/53235,' said River. 'That's where you're from.'

'No legend worth the name springs from virgin soil. I gave Popov my own past, yes.'

'So you . . . you must have been a child.'

'Hard to believe, isn't it? But apparently I carry the memory within.' He grimaced. 'It wasn't a healthy town to be born in. Even before you burned it to the ground.'

'Your own government destroyed it,' River said. 'Because they thought there was a spy there. But there wasn't. There never was. The town was destroyed for no reason.'

'There are always reasons,' the Russian said. 'The spy wasn't real, but the evidence was. That's how the mirror world works, Walker. Your service wasn't able to plant a spy there because security was too tight. So it did the next best thing, and planted evidence to suggest a spy. So the government did what governments do, and destroyed the town. What your Service would now call a result. Back then, they called it a victory.'

'It was all a long time ago,' said River, as if that meant anything now, or ever had.

'I came from a place that epitomised the Soviet world in English eyes,' said Katinsky. 'And it was destroyed by fire. So here I am, in a place that epitomises England to the rest of the world. Tell me. What happens next?'

River moved at exactly the moment Katinsky revealed what his right hand held, and River pulled back but not fast enough. Katinsky caught his elbow with the Taser, and the force of the voltage threw him onto the path.

Katinsky stood. 'I told you Pashkin had various things I needed. Where do you think I got this from?' Bending, he zapped River again. Sparks burst and the world swam red and black. 'A source of plastic explosives was another. Being a career criminal opens all sorts of doors. Knows no borders, you might say.'

'There was no bomb,' River managed to squeak.

'No. The plane was a decoy, for Pashkin's benefit. The plastic's still here. All around us.'

He meant the gravestones, River thought dizzily.

Then: No.

He meant the whole village.

Katinsky said, 'Each of the cicadas has enough to create one large bomb. And each has been told where to plant it. It's the instruction they've been waiting for for years. Now they know why they were dispatched to Upshott. It was to be in place to destroy an enemy.'

'You're mad. They won't have done it.'

'I gave them everything,' he said. 'Their identities, their start in life. And for more than twenty years they've been waiting, Walker. Waiting for the call that will activate them. That's what cicadas do. They wake up and sing.'

'Even if they've planted these bombs. What good will it do?'

'I told you. It will redress a balance. And demonstrate that history never forgives.'

'You're absolutely fucking insane.'

'You're not so confident, then? That they won't do it?'

River had been hoarding strength. All that energy that fizzed through his body, all of it that hadn't been dissipated by the longest night of his life, was being summoned, and in a second he'd leap to his feet. Strange that he still felt fluid and helpless. 'They're not who you think. Not any more. They've been here too long.'

'We'll see.' He held up the iPhone. 'I'll do a ring-round.'

'You're going to ask them?'

Katinsky laughed and took a step back. 'No, boy,' he said. 'I'll talk to the bombs. What, you think they're attached to a fuse? They detonate remotely. Like this.'

He pressed numbers.

Webb was breathing, and his eyelids fluttered as Louisa bent over him. 'Don't die,' she said. He didn't react. 'Prick,' she added. He didn't react to that, either.

Kyril wasn't there. He'd handily left a trail of blood, though.

Still panting, she followed it. He'd made for the stairwell, but had gone up, not down. It must have been slow progress, judging by the blood. And came to an end two landings up, where he lay slumped against the wall, his face twisted into an agonised scribble.

'Making a run for it?'

'Bitch.'

It was a scratchy whisper. It didn't seem likely he'd be shouting any warnings.

'He's on the roof, isn't he? You've got a chopper coming.'

But Kyril rolled his eyes and said no more.

He carried no weapon. If Pashkin was up there, she'd be a sitting duck. So she went through the last door carefully, or tried to. But the wind caught it and slammed it open.

Three hundred metres above London's streets, there was a fair lick of breeze.

The mast was on the opposite side of the roof: a graceful thin blade reaching up into the blue. Between here and there was a shanty-like collection of air-con vents, aerial casings, lightning rods and what looked like concrete stylings of garden sheds, housing lift machinery or other staircases. Oddly seedy for a high-pomp building, but most slick operations had their grimy underside: this is what was going through her mind when a bullet chipped the door behind her.

She rolled behind a ship's funnel-shaped vent and scrambled to a sitting position.

'Louisa?'

Pashkin. He had to shout to be heard up here, higher than the birds.

'Nowhere to go, Pashkin,' she shouted back. 'The cavalry are coming.'

He was behind one of the shed structures lining the building's west side, it sounded like. The east side dropped a level to a flatter expanse, where a helicopter could land, but hadn't yet. To left and right she saw no city, only sky, faintly smudged by oily smoke. A ludicrously thin railing marked the edge of the roof. If that was all there was to keep her from pitching into the void, she hoped the wind didn't pick up.

'Yes,' he shouted back. 'I've booked a ride. Have you got a gun, Louisa?'

'Of course I bloody have.'

'Perhaps I'll come and take it from you.'

It seemed she was out of range of his signal blocker out here, because her phone rang.

'Kind of busy.'

'I sent for an air ambulance. They say there's already one on the way. Louisa—'

'Way ahead of you.'

Why arrange for your own pilot when you could hijack an air ambulance?

He was behind one of those shed structures, unless he wasn't. Might even be right behind this vent, crawling round to her. Part of her hoped so.

Louisa wasn't stupid. She'd brought the fire-axe with her.

'Louisa? Go back inside. Close the door. I'll be gone in a few minutes. No harm, no foul, isn't that what they say?'

'Not in this country they don't.'

She hoped her voice sounded steady. A thin wisp of cloud above was scudding so fast it was making her dizzy. If she closed her eyes, she might roll to that railing, and beyond.

'Because otherwise, I'll have to kill you.'

'Like you had to kill Min?'

'Well, you I'll shoot. But the outcome will be the same, yes.'

Oh Christ, she thought. Crouching with her back to an air-con vent atop the City's tallest building while a well-dressed gangster cracked wise. I'm in *Die Hard*.

'Louisa?'

He sounded nearer, but it was hard to tell. Last night, she'd have taken him with pepper spray and plasti-cuffs, and all this would have been over. But bloody Marcus had interfered so here she was instead, way above London, and Pashkin had a gun.

And what did I think I was doing, racing up here unarmed?

Though the answer was no further away than her memories of Min, whom this bastard had murdered for an armful of diamonds.

She thought she could hear a helicopter.

Choices, choices. She could do as he'd said, and head back to safety. Which didn't mean he wouldn't shoot her in the back before hijacking the helicopter. On the streets below, all was chaos. He'd force it down in Hyde Park, disappear among the crowds. *Think!* she thought. Or rather, didn't think: she stood instead, and launched herself across the gap between where she'd been crouching and the next place of shelter, a sturdy chunk of concrete inside which lift machinery silently waited.

She landed flat, expecting gunfire which didn't come. The fire-axe skittered from her grasp, and came to rest a few feet away.

'Louisa?'

'Still here.'

'That was your last chance.'

'Toss the gun over here. That'll knock a few years off your sentence.'

There was definitely a helicopter, and it was definitely getting nearer.

'You aren't armed, Louisa. This won't end well.'

The fire-axe had given that away. Nobody with a gun would have come hefting a heavy blade.

Which lay outside the range of her shelter. She stretched for it, and this time he did shoot: missing her hand but hitting the axe handle, making it spin wildly. She yelped.

'Louisa? Are you hurt?'

She didn't reply.

The steady *whump-whump* of the helicopter blades grew louder. If the pilot saw an armed man, he wouldn't land; he'd go *whumping* away . . . She had to show him Pashkin had a gun. If Min were here, he'd tell her what a stupid plan that was, but Min wasn't here because he was dead, and if she didn't do something now, the man who'd killed him would be whisked off. The axe might come in useful. She reached for it again, and a black brogue crunched onto her hand.

She looked up into Pashkin's eyes. He glared back, genuinely irritated that she was putting him to this trouble. In one hand he held a cloth bag, swollen to the size of a football. Lot of diamonds.

In the other he held the gun, aimed straight at her head.

'I'm sorry, Louisa,' he said. 'Really I am.'

Then Marcus shot him, and Pashkin, gun and bag of diamonds all dropped, though only the diamonds went scattering this way and that, like small bright marbles in a children's game; some of them tumbling to the edge of the roof, and over.

Louisa could only imagine what that must have been like – tiny glass raindrops falling onto distant streets, while the *whump-whump* of the helicopter blades beat the air into slender nothings.

In the moment after Katinsky dialled the number to detonate the bombs, silence hung around the churchyard, around the whole village, like a plastic dome around a cake. Sunshine stopped, the wind paused, a blackbird choked off mid-note, and even River's aches and pains were suspended as he waited for the series of cracks that would split the sky like lightning, and bring Upshott tumbling down. The weeks he'd spent here kaleidoscoped through his mind, and he thought of the pub and the village shop, of the graceful curve of eighteenth-century townhouses lining the green, of the one-time manor house, all turned into a series of craters to satisfy some dying spook's vision of vengeance. It would be a rustic Ground Zero, memorial to a long-forgotten town that died in a long-forgotten fire; ZT/53235, an ancient casualty in the mirror-game played by spies.

It would be futile and useless, but would scorch the earth behind it.

And then the sun shone, and the breeze stirred again, and the blackbird caught its breath and resumed its song.

Nikolai Katinsky was just an old man, staring at the phone in his hand as if its technology were beyond him.

River said, 'See?' and his voice was close to normal.

Katinsky's lips moved, but River couldn't make out what he said.

He struggled to get up, and this time made it. Then he leant against the bench, his limbs still wobbly. 'They've been here years,' he said. 'They're not yours any more. They don't care what brought them here. This is their life. It's where they live.'

There were cars arriving. He recognised the sound of jeeps' engines, and felt a brief surge of hysteria as he wondered how this would play out; a village community revealed as a sleeper cell, one sleeping so hard, it had no desire to wake.

'Still,' he said, 'nice try,' and released his grip on the bench. There you go, River thought, you can stand; and thinking so, he set off along the path to the lychgate, through which military types would soon be swarming.

'Walker?'

He looked back. Katinsky was draped in sunlight, which this past minute had crested the bell tower.

'Not all of the bombs were theirs. One was mine.'

He hit another number on his phone.

The blast, which took out the west wall of St Johnno's, killed Katinsky instantly, standing as he was right in its path. In later nightmares, River saw a chunk of ancient stonework cleave the old spook in two, but in reality he was bowled over by the shock wave, and by the time rocks were raining to earth was curled inside the lychgate itself, head between his knees. So he heard and felt, rather than saw, the slower death that followed Katinsky's, as the belltower swayed and hovered and lost its grip on the vertical. When it dropped, it fell away from River's shelter, or he'd have joined the old man in whatever afterlife was waiting. As it was, the tower's descent onto the graveyard and the foot-path beyond seemed to last for whole minutes, for acres of time, as befitted its brute removal from a skyline it had kissed for hundreds of years; and for hours afterwards it seemed to continue happening, as the shock reverberated through the suddenly emp-tier landscape, making new shapes out of silence and dust.

Marcus made sure Pashkin was dead, then helped Louisa to her feet.

He said, 'I met Shirley on the stairs. He hadn't passed her. So I figured maybe he'd come to the roof.'

'Thanks,' she said.

'Like I told you. They made me a slow horse cos I gamble. Not cos I'm a fuck-up.'

The helicopter landed, and he went to meet it.

17

Throughout the day of the aborted rally, parts of London burned.

Cars were torched, a bus was set alight, and a Jankel – one of the police armoured units – was baptised by a petrol bomb on Newgate Street. A photo of St Paul's obscured by oily smoke duly graced the front pages next morning. But before nightfall the rally that had become a riot became a rout: mindful of criticisms of too softly-softly an approach to recent disturbances, the police went in hard, and broke heads, and made arrests. Free-ranging mobs were dispersed, ringleaders bundled into vans, and those who'd spent the day kettled up in backstreets were allowed to make their way home. It had been, the day's Gold Commander announced at the inevitable press conference, an effective demonstration of firm, no-nonsense policing. Which did not alter the fact that the City had been well and truly stopped.

Rumour had fanned the flames. It turned out that through the course of that morning, a whisper on Twitter – that a bomb-laden aeroplane had been shot down by the RAF – had cajoled its way into fact; the less incendiary truth, that a Cessna Skyhawk had been intercepted and escorted to an RAF base, where it was found to be bearing a load of amateurish leaflets, did not become general knowledge until the following day. At about the same time, responsibility for the headlong evacuation of the Square Mile was being laid firmly at the door of the security services, or more precisely, at the shoes of Five's Chair of Limitations, who had effectively been First Desk at the time, and upon whose advice the Home Secretary had sounded the City's alarm. Roger Barrowby impressed many with his ready acceptance of blame; he had the air, it was remarked, of a man who knew when he'd been castled. His resignation was discreetly handled, and he was reported to have been touched by his leaving gift, an imitation Mies van der Rohe chair.

In the immediate aftermath, many shops and businesses in central London remained shut, and roads witnessed less traffic than usual. There was a communal holding of breath, and the general intention of having an early night. Even on some of the busiest streets, barely a mouse stirred.

But if a mouse wanted to, it could enter Slough House with ease. No mouse worth its whiskers would have problems threading under that long-shut door, nor up the uncarpeted staircase, whereupon – pausing on an office threshold – it might weigh up the attractions of a wobbling tower of pizza boxes and an array of still-sticky cans, and set them against the deterrent of a snoozing Roderick Ho, who, worn out by unaccustomed exertion, lies with his cheek on his desk, his glasses askew. It's even possible that the dribble puddling from his open mouth might present a third lunch option for our mouse, but a sudden blart, halfway between a snore and a raspberry, decides the matter. A tail is turned . . .

. . . and into the adjoining office our wee friend scurries, where its incursion is regarded not, as would once have been the case, as a possible test, but simply as enemy action, for an air of paranoia now taints this room, and it seeps off the walls and soaks into the carpet. Both Shirley Dander and Marcus Longridge know that one of them is thought to be Diana Taverner's stooge, and as each knows it isn't them, both believe it to be the other. The only words they have exchanged today have been 'Shut the door,' and their post-Needle debriefings remain undiscussed. Had they pooled what each had gleaned, they might have reached certain conclusions regarding the likely official verdict: that inasmuch as James Webb had laid a trap for the gangster masquerading as one Arkady Pashkin, the operation had been worthwhile, but — its outcome having been badly compromised by the involvement of the slow horses — few citations for valour and even fewer recalls to Regent's Park would be offered. This wouldn't have lightened the atmosphere much, though, were he minded to do so Jackson Lamb could have improved matters, being aware that, in telling him one of the newbies was reporting to her, Diana Taverner was merely trying to mess with his head. Taverner is something of an expert in this field, as Roger Barrowby might attest, but any time she thinks she's put one over on Jackson Lamb, thinks Jackson Lamb, she ought to count her pocket change. If she had an ear in Slough House, she'd have known of Webb's having seconded two slow horses before Lamb told her. And besides, Lady Di already has a black mark against her name in Lamb's book, since it was on her instructions that Nick Duffy did such a half-arsed job of investigating Min Harper's death. For this there will be retribution. Meanwhile, in this office, a sense of betrayal hangs heavy, something no good-natured mouse can support for long, so off it goes again, up the stairs, seeking out new horizons.

Which it finds in the shape of River Cartwright. River is also quiet, having just ended a call to St Mary's Hospital, which is where Spider Webb was taken, a little longer after being shot than accident and emergency rooms recommend. The news of his former friend's current status might be what he contemplates now, and our mouse cannot tell whether it brings pain or pleasure; though River might equally be occupied by other emotions; by the suspicion, for example, that the reason the name ZT/53235 came tripping so lightly from his grandfather's memory was that it had long resided there, the O.B. himself having been responsible for convincing the Soviet authorities that the closed town nurtured a traitor. It was in 1951 that ZT/53235 burned, with the loss of thousands of lives, and David Cartwright would then have been much the age his grandson is now, prompting River to wonder whether he has it in him to play the mirror game as if the stakes were spent matches instead of human lives. And to wonder, too, if such thoughts will intrude the next time he visits the old man, or whether he will bury them like any spy's secrets, and greet his grandfather as fondly as ever.

As this is not a problem our mouse can help with, it retreats, to find in Louisa Guy's room a different kind of silence, the kind used to smother a soft noise. This finds no echo, as there is nobody to offer one, the spare desk here being just that: spare, untenanted, redundant. Given time, a fresh body will turn up to commandeer it – as Lamb has pointed out, Slough House is staffed by screw-ups, of which there's never any shortage – and perhaps it's that future occupation that causes Louisa to gently sob now, or perhaps it's the current emptiness awaiting her at her flat, which once seemed too small for two, and is now too large for one; a situation unassuaged by her recent acquisition, currently nestled among her newer, less practical, now uncalled-for underwear, of a fingernail-sized diamond; its weight less than that of a doughnut, and its value a mystery to her. Ascertaining this would be another step over a line she never intended to cross in the first place, so for now it remains wrapped and hidden; its only promise that of an escape from one empty place into another, which is all the future seems to offer to Louisa; one empty space after another, like an infinity of mirrors reaching all the way to nowhere.

Small wonder she sobs; even less that our mouse tiptoes discreetly away from a grief it can't comfort. Further up, on the final floor, it pays a brief visit to Catherine Standish, for whom a mouse holds no horrors, provided it's real. Catherine has seen her share of phantom mice, small shapes that scurried from sight when she turned to look, but those days are long past, and the only day that matters is the one that lies ahead. Which she will deal with in the same calm manner she has come to deal with most things; a talent honed by daily exposure to the irritating

Jackson Lamb, who is currently in his own room, door firmly closed, which presents as much an obstacle to our murine explorer as the inelegantly heaped pile of telephone directories, atop which it pauses at last, whiskers quivering, snout a-tremble. Jackson Lamb has his feet on his desk and his eyes closed. On his lap is a newspaper, folded at a bizarre little story about a localised earth tremor in the Cotswolds, for heaven's sake; a seismic shrug which caused a much-loved church to collapse, thankfully with only a single fatality. And so, thinks Lamb, the ghost of one Alexander Popov, as embodied by one Nikolai Katinsky, fades into nothingness in the heart of a village which in no way resembled the town he'd emerged from, except in the manner of the destruction he'd hoped to wreak upon it. As for the cicadas – that collection of long-buried sleepers, who'd slept so deeply their false existences had displaced the real – for them there'd be no awakening, cruel or otherwise, the school of thought from Them Down The Corridor being to let sleeping spooks lie. Lying, after all, is what spooks do best.

Thinking such thoughts Jackson Lamb reaches blindly out for something, probably his cigarettes, and when his questing hands come up empty, resorts to opening his eyes. And there in front of him – snout quivering, whiskers a-tremble – sits a mouse. For a moment Lamb has the uncomfortable sensation that this mouse is staring into a past he has tried to bury, or peering into a future he'd sooner forget. And then he blinks, and the mouse is nowhere, if it was ever there at all.

'What this place needs is a cat,' grumbles Lamb, but there's no one there to hear him.

For the further misadventures of Jackson Lamb
and his crew of no-hopers,
pick up a copy of

REAL
TIGERS